BOYS COME FIRST

AARON F

Belt Publishi

ADVANCE PRAISE FOR
BOYS COME FIRST

"Uproarious, sharp, bruising, hip, and real. Aaron Foley's *Boys Come First* moves along with a graceful self-assurance, spot-on characterizations, and a genuine assessment of the extraordinary yet mundane plight of Black queer men—how we must navigate the world, protect ourselves from violence and cruelties, construct our own safe spaces, and stitch together community from the strands of chosen family. This book is so brutally honest that it's hard to believe it's fiction."

—Robert Jones Jr., author of *The Prophets*,
New York Times bestseller and 2021 National
Book Award finalist

"Imagine the thirtysomething angst of *Insecure* meeting the queer Black friendships of *Noah's Arc*, intersecting with the dating dilemmas of *Waiting to Exhale*, all rolled up into the dynamics of a gentrified Detroit, and you've got *Boys Come First*. It's a fun novel that will have you eager to turn every page to find out what's coming next for Dominick, Troy, and Remy."

—Frederick Smith, author of *Down for Whatever*

"It's all fun and games with friends Remy, Dominick, and Troy until they hit their thirties. As their fraught situationships and sexy entanglements start to reveal hard truths about themselves, the friends must deal with life's hard questions. Foley has written a delicious romp about the game of love. But at its core, *Boys Come First* is a laugh out loud story about Foley's first love—the city of Detroit."

—Desiree Cooper, Pulitzer Prize-nominated
journalist and author of *Know the Mother*

WINTER

WINTER

CHAPTER ONE

I better not get my Black ass pulled over in hoe-ass, bitch-ass Pennsylvania,
Dominick Gibson thought to himself for what must have been the
fortieth time, speeding westward through the Keystone State in a rented
Kia Soul that could barely maintain the eighty-fiveish miles-per-hour he'd
been doing since he'd first merged onto I-80 coming out of Manhattan.

Although, getting pulled over in one of these dreary towns filled
with Trump voters in whistle-stop diners and letting the officer, inevitably
white and male, humiliate, beat, or haul Dominick off to jail—or maybe
some combination of all of the above—would fit right in with the total
shitstorm of events he'd endured over the last week and a half.

Just eleven days ago, Dominick had been enjoying monogamy and
gainful employment in New York City. Now, in the darkest hours of this
Pennsylvania night, neither existed. He'd had goals before everything had
fallen apart: marriage by thirty-five, a kid one year after that, a vacation
home by forty, and his own advertising firm by forty-five. But here he was
now, thirty-three years old and with eight years with his ex, Justin, having
led absolutely nowhere. Time was running out. Though when you're
Black, gay, and thirtysomething, time *always* feels like it's running out.

The thirtysomething years are critical for gay men like Dominick
because they have to have everything figured out by then if they don't want

to become walking stereotypes later. While Dominick was busy getting older, everyone else around him just kept getting younger. Whenever he took a lingering look in the mirror, it seemed his hairline had receded another millimeter. Meanwhile, a new crop of boys, all with healthy hair and more-elaborate-than-ever skincare routines, kept rolling off the assembly line.

Is everybody at the club twenty-two now? he thought. *They google how to douche; we had to learn the hard way.*

Those younger men were forbidden fruit, and they would chase guys like Dominick once he got to a certain age—that age when, if he reached it while he was still single, he would turn into the full-blown stereotype. Leering. Predatory. Old. The last thing Dominick wanted was to be someone's *daddy*, a sixtysomething single man with a wrinkled chitterling dick and a hog maw butthole who thinks he's forty years younger and creeps on anybody and everybody.

That's the thing. If Black gay men don't have their shit together in their thirties—the job, the apartment with more than one bedroom, and the boyfriend who's about to become a fiancée and then a husband—then they're still going to be figuring it all out in their forties and fifties when the crow's feet start showing. And Dominick certainly did not want to be in the dating pool at forty when everyone else was twenty-two. He didn't want to be struggling with his career at the same time either, so as he had worked hard to hold onto Justin, he had also made sure to keep climbing in the advertising world. Before it all fell apart, the two of them were planning to settle down with each other and their peak incomes and leave all the broken and broke fortysomethings behind.

Plans gone awry consumed Dominick's thoughts as he sped through the rest of Pennsylvania and Ohio. He barely had enough gas to make it to his mother's front door in Detroit. But despite his infrequent visits of late, he still remembered one thing about his hometown: do not stop for gas in the middle of the night. The low-fuel light gleamed in the dashboard as he pulled into his mother's driveway, and he muttered a little prayer of thanks that he'd made it there without any issues. Though after almost ten hours in the car, intermittently talking to God, his best friend Troy, Siri, and an annoying woman from a collection agency, Dominick knew he would now have to talk to his mother, Tonya Gibson, who was standing in the doorway at 3:38 a.m., wondering why her son had decided to drive all the way to Detroit from his apartment in Hell's Kitchen on a Thursday.

A half-hour later, after a quick, evasive chat and an excuse that he had a headache and just needed to sleep, Dominick lay on the full-size bed in his teenage room, his back already aching from the lumpy Art Van mattress his mother hadn't replaced in fifteen years.

He was a gay man, a *Black* gay man, with a setback and without explanation.

White gay men are afforded things Black gay men aren't. No judgment for dating a decade-plus younger, no slut-shaming, and above all, no worrying about what their families might say when something like this happened. The *this*, in Dominick's case, was losing his job in a profession his parents had never wanted for him in the first place.

Working in advertising was rebellious. In Detroit, Dominick's parents were, until their divorce, one of the city's power couples—his father was an oncologist and his mother an anesthesiologist. They had met in very Detroit fashion, as high school students on the dance floor of *The Scene*, a televised dance program broadcast by the city's only Black-owned station. Back then, Tonya had plans to go to Wayne State, but instead, she had followed Craig to Howard on the condition that they would stay together and come back to Detroit to start a family. They did. And after thousands of dollars for private school for their little one—Waldorf for elementary and middle, then University of Detroit Jesuit after that—they expected Dom would find his way along a similar path. He'd go to Howard and pledge Kappa Alpha Psi just like his father, and he'd marry a Delta Sigma Theta who was just like his mom. Nobody seemed to notice that while all these plans were taking shape, Dominick was actually making short movies and fake commercials with his friends. Nobody noticed that instead of spending nights reading a gifted copy—Christmas, 1998—of *Gray's Anatomy*, Dom was devouring Nick at Nite reruns, old movies on AMC, and, if he tuned his antenna just right, British soaps on the CBC affiliate across the river in Windsor. And almost certainly no one noticed that marriage to a woman wasn't in the cards, but that was only because his mother and father were so preoccupied with Dominick choosing advertising as his major instead of premed.

Turns out, coming out as a doctor's son who's uninterested in medicine and more interested in pop culture was harder than coming out as gay. (Although, to be fair, Dom's interest in pop culture was practically forced on him in utero. Probably a third of Black kids born in the mid-1980s were named after *Dynasty* characters like Krystle, Fallon, Alexis, or, especially, Dominique, the name Tonya had had her heart set on until she found out she was having a boy.) Dominick made his big announcement during winter break of his freshman year—this was when he for sure, for sure knew he was gay after his first maybe, maybe not boyfriend in Detroit and five and a half intense lovemaking sessions with a would-be Alpha at Howard who dropped line out of fear of being outed. Both Tonya and Craig were unfazed, telling Dom it was about time he told them. They did wonder, though: *Were you ever going to think about switching your major?*

He didn't. He kept with advertising, getting a copywriting job immediately after graduation. He became quite good at it, too, starting in DC and moving to Manhattan three years after that. He felt as long as he was on track to be married by thirty-five and have a kid shortly after, he'd never have to explain himself to his parents again.

But everything was not on track. And if he had taken the time to explain everything to Tonya as it had really happened, it only would have solidified all her long-held worries about the instability of an artistic career.

It had gone something like this:

On December 11, Atomic Ranch, a chic, millennial-targeting marketing agency where Dominick had been working after being plucked away from Tandy and Simms, the multinational giant that had made him an *Ad Age*-certified rising star on the East Coast, folded. Atomic Ranch had been founded on the idea of creating snappy video content that would connect stodgy brands with young readers who were now flocking to Vice, Vox, and BuzzFeed. When Tom Boyle, T&S's global creative director, cobbled together nearly $10 million in investor funds to fly the coop and put down Atomic Ranch's roots in a $5,000-a-month coworking space in Cobble Hill, Dominick was his first hire. He became creative director—no small feat for a Black man in advertising, since there were so few to begin with.

It turns out that in the startup world, $10 million dissipates pretty quickly. So too do the tastes of young readers. And when the digital media darlings all announced dips in readerships and a pivot back to original content *after* pivoting to video, Atomic Ranch crumbled. Fast.

In the dark of his mother's house, Dominick tried to remember if he'd packed the USB drive that had his most current resume and his best writing clips on it. He'd certainly need them for his job search in . . . wherever his job search was going to be.

Do I pick up where I left off here in Detroit? Do I keep going west? LA? San Francisco? Maybe Singapore needs copywriters? Literally anywhere but New York, he thought. But restarting in Detroit seemed like the likeliest outcome, even if Dominick was hesitant about it. *Here, I could at least maybe still get my career back on track by thirty-five.*

He couldn't stop thinking about how Tom had pulled him aside to tell him Atomic Ranch was over.

"Vox isn't renewing. BuzzFeed isn't renewing. Bustle is done. All of Gizmodo is done. And Slate, oh my God, goddamn Slate—they fill you up with promises and lead you on to absolutely fucking nowhere and then just piss the bed in the end. Unless a fucking miracle happens, we're finished."

Dominick had been talking almost all his life, starting with his first word, "apricots," at eight months old in his highchair. But now, he was speechless.

"Do you understand what's going on, Dom?" Tom asked. "We have to shut it all down."

"Are you fucking kidding me?"

"I'm sorry, but don't . . ."

"Don't what? After all the shit I've put up with in this motherfucker, this is how it's going to go down? For real? I'm the one that has to go?"

"We all have to go!"

"Muhfucka, I put my entire career on the line for you!"

Despite Atomic Ranch's be-your-best-true-self ethos, Dominick had hardly ever cursed in the office before, and he realized he had just said two different versions of the word "motherfucker" directly to his boss. And that second "motherfucker" was a "muhfucka." Living in a hip Manhattan enclave with fellow NYC transplants and working in a mile-a-minute Brooklyn office had softened him. But now, with that "muhfucka," his Detroit was showing.

By the time Dom could gather his thoughts, he was walking out the office's front door with a box of his belongings. The HR rep, some permalancer temp, had asked Dom to sign some paperwork; Dom did it without reading a word. The quicker he could escape, the better. *I probably should have saved my emails*, he thought, but that concern had disappeared completely by the time he was halfway to the Jay Street/ MetroTech subway stop.

Tom, red-faced and out of breath, followed him the whole way, stopping Dominick just as he was about to swipe his phone over the OMNY reader.

"I'm sorry, Dom. I'm so sorry," he said.

Dominick briefly thought about dragging Tom through the turnstile and pushing him over the platform. He imagined the train wheels grinding over his boss's flesh, blood splattering across the walls, crimson trails dripping toward the garbage on the tracks. Then he thought about what he would tell the transit officer—there were so many of them now compared to when he had first moved to the city—when they arrested him, and then later the judge and jury who would no doubt send him away for life.

He backed away from the turnstile to allow other passengers to pass, leaned against a MetroCard machine, and looked up at his now-former boss. He exhaled, making sure his words were as pointed and clear as any piece of copy he'd ever written.

"I'm sorry, too, Tom. I didn't mean to say what I said. I just need to go."

"Let's talk about this later, OK? When you're not so upset."

"I've just been fired, Tom. What did you expect?"

"You weren't fired. You've done amazing work for us. It's not going to be the same without you."

"Then why . . ."

Dominick caught himself and looked around the station. His face was hot, but even though his eyes were misty, no tears came. He looked at Tom and tried not to blink. Too much blinking would cause the tears to flow, and he didn't want anyone to see him cry right now.

"I just need to go. If there's anything I need from you, I'll let you know."

"OK," Tom said. He slowly backed away from Dominick, turned, and headed up the stairs, disappearing back out to the streets of downtown Brooklyn.

That had been the first setback.

The second one happened thirty minutes later, when Dom trudged up four tedious flights to his and Justin's well-decorated apartment in

Hell's Kitchen, inserted his key in the lock, and found the door was already open. Detroit had taught him to lock his doors everywhere he went, no matter if he was in the pockmarked hood or the picket-fenced suburbs. Justin had always been more lax about this, having grown up in suburban Columbus, and it was something Dom could never count on him to do. But lately, he hadn't counted on Justin to do much of anything.

Dominick didn't expect Justin to be home. Although he hadn't expected to be laid off either, so perhaps he should have tempered his expectations. The unlocked door was a curiosity. So was the TV being on and the thick odor of marijuana in the air. But when Dom walked into the bedroom to find Justin butt naked, legs spread in the air, with a mysterious man balls deep inside him, it all started to make sense—that is, once Dom had another one of what he called his "little out-of-body experiences," in which he temporarily dissociated and lost himself.

When he came to, the two men were rushing to clean themselves up and put on some semblance of clothing. In the moment, Dom found the only thing he could muster was a whispered prayer in his head.

Dear God, please don't let me go crazy. Please don't let me die, but please don't let me kill both of them where they stand, either.

Nobody died. And as badly as Dominick wanted to grab the big Japanese chef's knife from the Williams Sonoma block that Justin had insisted they buy (even though neither of them ever *used* that many knives), he resisted. Justin and the mysterious man didn't bother explaining themselves. They just hurried out of the apartment half-naked while Dominick stood silently, trying not to hyperventilate.

In retrospect, nobody had ever asked him why he loved Justin. In heterosexual relationships, it's undeniable when a man and a woman are in love. They say things at weddings about completion—"You *complete* me." It suggests there's something incomplete about both parties, doesn't it? And it suggests love, the love that enables a person to strive and do better for the recipient of that love, can't catalyze until the two are brought together.

When two gay Black men are in a relationship, though, the question isn't about love. It's about work. As in, "How do you make it *work*?" or "What *works* for you?" Two Black men together isn't a relationship. It's a strategic partnership.

Work is what drives the gay Black relationship because both parties are expected to already be complete upon meeting. It is not "How do you complete me?" It is "How do you advance me?" It is about work, because gay men do not have time to fill each other's holes—the metaphorical holes that is. The Black gay man's trajectory is always upward. There is never time to slow down. There is no room to fail. And they need partners who can more quickly take them to where they ultimately need to be.

And where was that exactly? For Dominick, he knew where he and Justin were trying to get to, and all the *stuff* they had accumulated along the way: the designer wardrobes, the Sur-La-Table-and-Williams-Sonoma-everything kitchen, the Provincetown trips, and the curated Instagram accounts. But did they ever have true love? Was that ever going to come, or was it just another thing they would order from some catalog along the way?

Dominick and Justin sometimes said "love you" to each other. An "*I* love you" was rare, though. And "love you" really worked more like an obligatory conversation ender: "Don't forget to get bread. See you when you get here. Love you." It was just something they had started saying to each other, maybe a year and a half into the relationship. There was no big discussion among separate groups of friends about who had used the L-word first, nor was there a period where Dom and Justin separately contemplated what it meant to finally have the word—just the word—"love" in their regular conversation. And if he had to pinpoint the exact time when the "love-yous" began . . .

Dominick lay in his teenage bed, staring at the ceiling in his mother's house, and exhaled deeply. He knew exactly when they had started saying it, and there was a reason he didn't want to think too much about it.

They had met on Black Gay Chat, a forerunner to Grindr, Tinder, and all the rest. At that point, they had only lived for a few years in New York; they both lived in Harlem, not too far away from each other. Justin was fresh out of law school at Columbia and wanted someone to ride his own trajectory—a trajectory that included moving out of Harlem and into Hell's Kitchen, which had more of the "fun" (read: "desirable") gays he wanted to be around. There was a plethora of Black gay men to choose from there, but Dom and Justin were drawn to each other because they actually had conversations—long ones—online before meeting in person.

They didn't do it after their first date, when they met for drinks and Jamaican takeout at one of the twenty-four-hour places in Harlem before going their separate ways. A day later, though, when Dominick's roommate was gone, they had sex for the first time. It lasted an embarrassing thirteen minutes. The next day, it was fifteen. It was the same the day after that.

Justin, then coming into his own as a power bottom, had had enough. "Take it slow with me," he told Dom, "Don't just put it in and ram it. Slow down."

Their sex-having—no one could quite call it "lovemaking" at that point—became more nuanced. Justin showed Dominick how to stroke longer and endure without coming so quickly. And Dominick learned the power of his dick—how to control it, how it moved inside Justin, and how each of their bodies would respond.

They went from fifteen-minute hoedowns to hour-long sweat competitions to see who could last longest. The sex got better when they stopped using condoms, too—Dominick loved coming inside Justin, and Justin was eager to receive. Sometimes, Justin would have to tap out and ask Dominick to come on his chest, or sometimes Dominick would wear out and ask Justin to lay on his stomach so he could finish.

But then there was that one Sunday afternoon. They hadn't had sex in four, maybe five, days. Neither of them had plans. They lay in bed watching home-repair shows, which turned into making out—it always did—and then Justin got up to shower and clean himself out. They moved into a now-usual routine for them: Justin going down on Dom, then sixty-nining for a little bit before Justin straddled Dom and rode him to get reaccustomed to his dick. But rather than do the usual, Dom wanted to fuck Justin missionary for as long as he could. Justin lay on his back and put his legs up, and the two of them stared into each other's eyes the whole time. Justin started to convulse. He lost breath. He reached for his own dick, but Dominick stopped him. He grabbed Justin's wrist, squeezing it like a lemon while he used his other arm to keep Justin's legs in the air. Dom's lower half was on autopilot, his thrusting moving in rhythm like a steam train. Justin wanted to scream, but no voice would come. What did come: Justin's orgasm, achieved hands free. Dom had figured Justin out. He'd hit the right spot. And twenty seconds later, Dom exploded inside him after skillfully holding it all in.

In their postcoital exultation, drunk off each other's energy, Justin lay with his ear on Dom's chest, listening to his heartbeat.

"So how was that?" Dom asked. The words reverberated through Justin's eardrums.

"I love you, and I love what you do to me," Justin said, moving his hand up and down Dom's torso.

That was the first time, on the Lord's Day, when someone who wasn't blood-related to Dominick had told him they loved him.

And now, as he tried futilely to fall asleep alone in his teenage bedroom, he wondered if anyone else ever would.

CHAPTER TWO

When you're little, they should really make it extra clear you should be careful what you wish for. When I was eight, I asked for what I wanted, and now that I'm in my thirties, I'm not even sure I still want the shit anymore. Oh, don't get me wrong. I work real fucking hard, and I appreciate every little thing I've got. But they never tell you that working hard is relative. Everybody's pushing boulders up a hill. It's just mine's the size of Pluto. I'm a gay man, too. Just call me Sissy-phus, I guess.

Hi, hello, whatupdoe, or whatever. My name is Remy Patton, and, first things first, ever since I can remember, I've had a thing for Detroit houses. I'm from Promenade and Gunston—here in Detroit, you identify yourself by which intersection you grew up on—and all the houses there look identical. But when I was growing up, my dad and I used to ride around the east side, where things were different. We'd ride to Grosse Pointe or ride over to Belle Isle or just ride. Shit, it's all Detroiters know how to do: *Drive*.

He'd pick me up from the house and that would be our time together, seeing as he only had shared custody—shout-out to all my Friend-of-the-Court babies. He wasn't all that creative, so I was the one who'd ask him to take me everywhere my mother wouldn't or couldn't because we didn't have the money. *Take me roller skating. Take me to the arcade. Can we go to the Giant Slide?* But my dad didn't have a whole lot of money in those days either, so a lot of times we'd just ride, him driving and talking and me sitting next to him, absorbing the city around us.

Indian Village was his favorite place to ride, and soon enough it became my favorite too. We'd ride up and down Seminole, Iroquois, and Burns, the prettiest streets in all of Detroit. The further down you went to Jefferson, the bigger the houses got. And I could never pick a favorite.

My father always said I was smart, and the smartest thing he ever did was talk my mom into putting me into private school. I went to a raggedy little Catholic school way over near Virginia Park all the way up until eighth grade. Then, the summer before ninth grade, my father got locked up on some dumb shit. Like, how are you legit all your life and suddenly decide you want to sell dope? He was selling crack and robbed a muhfucka at gunpoint. The cops found him hiding at my grandmother's house, and he's still locked up today, seventeen years after the fact. That's exactly when the extra money for private school stopped. And rather than take a DDOT bus all the way to Cass—I did take the test and got in, thank you—I just went to Denby with everyone else.

Denby was some real hood shit, but I knew as long as I kept my head down, I'd be OK. And that's exactly what the fuck I did. I always made the honor roll, and I ended up graduating as co-valedictorian. (Would've been just me, but Taneisha Stout was just too damn smart. Oh well, she's pregnant with baby number three anyway and moved out to Clinton Township just like everybody else from the east side these days.) You should've seen my yearbook picture. Courtesy of Motown Photography, of course. They've gotten better about taking pictures of dark-skinned people since then, but I was still glistening. I had a fake diamond stud in one ear, an S-curl, and a pair of fake buffies that I had to go all the way to Greenfield Plaza to get.

After high school, I went to Oakland University on a full scholarship. They needed more Black folks from Detroit to balance out the quotas, so I affirmative-actioned my way to a free ride. I had a ball at OU, not gonna lie. It was fun. Well, most of the time it was. And anyway, it was where I met my best friend, Troy.

I knew I wanted to work in real estate, so after graduation, I got my first car—an old 1994 Mercedes with 190,000 miles on it—and I started driving around the city by myself. I went to open houses and watched how agents worked. I studied their branding; I loved the big, tall signs for Higbie Maxon Agney, the high-end Grosse Pointe realtor. I called and asked to shadow Magda Bogosyan, Lafayette Park's queen of selling condos. I got my license, and with my experience with Magda, plus the sales skills I learned at my first, and only, college job slanging Nextels at Sprint (remember those?), I got a desk at Real Estate One in Southfield.

This was right when the recession hit. But the thing was, none of the agents in my office were touching Detroit properties back then. They were all over the suburbs because the old people there were the ones refinancing and dealing with ballooning payments. When people wanted to sell in Detroit, they were having a hard time finding somebody to help them. So I started building up my client base in the city. All the other agents thought I was crazy.

I didn't make a ton of money at first. Housing prices in the city hit rock bottom. But I got to know the market. I got to know the houses. And soon, I started to notice a brand-new crop of buyers coming into your Indian Village, Boston-Edison, and Palmer Woods-type neighborhoods.

White folks with money.

Because no other agents wanted to touch Detroit proper, I did exactly what Magda had done in Lafayette Park: I honed in on one area and made it mine. I made it my mission to take over all the Villages: Indian Village, West Village, Islandview, the Gold Coast, and all those condos up and down the river.

That's my turf now.

It's also my home. I'm not in my big Indian Village mansion yet, not like the one Troy grew up in with his dad. But I bought a cute townhouse on St. Paul smack-dab in the middle of West Village for pennies, and with all the work I've put into restoring it and all the white folks who have suddenly decided they want to live here—shit, I'm not taking anything less than $700,000 for it.

The commissions eventually started going up. *My* price started going up. I started to treat myself because I had come too far from layaway at the old Kmart on Sherwood and Outer Drive not to. I saw a Romare Bearden print in the window of DuMouchelle's downtown and bought it at auction. I got myself some of that good Le Creuset cookware at Sur La Table in Somerset. Hell, I *live* at Somerset. I got three pairs of buffies—real ones, in the Cartier box and everything—though I don't wear them in front of my white clients, of course. I tailored my suits and started serving Veuve Cliquot at my open houses to loosen up potential buyers. I also got a Dodge Charger, all-wheel-drive for the winter, purple with blacked-out wheels, and named her Betsy.

I knew I had to get my mama out of our old house on Promenade. Even though it was paid for, it wasn't worth shit. So while prices were still low, I bought an apartment on the twelfth floor of 1300 Lafayette for eight grand—that shit would go for at least 100K now—and moved her in. She deeded the Promenade house over to me, and now I rent it out to my cousin Annesha and her little boy, Paris. Annesha's trying to move up in the world, and I at least want to help her have a stable house while doing so. Besides, Promenade really isn't *that* bad if you mind your business. I mean, you could say that about all of Detroit.

Once things started falling into a comfortable place, I started my own agency, and now I'm founder, agent, CEO, president, and HNIC of the 2501 Agency. It was a gift to myself on my thirtieth birthday, a storefront space right on Kercheval. And just like my house, I got my office just in time because soon enough, they built all this new shit on Van Dyke and Kercheval and now it doesn't even look like Detroit. To advertise, I put my face on three billboards around town—one on the east side, right on Jefferson and Van Dyke a few blocks from the agency, one on the west side on Grand River near Rosedale Park, and one in Southwest on Springwells—and called myself Mr. Detroit. That's probably when my real problems started.

In the two years since those billboards have gone up, I've had no privacy. My Twitter followers went from like two hundred people to more than 10,000. I got a weekly, half-hour show on the Black AM radio station to discuss real estate tips, and broke boys who probably don't even have a Footaction Star Card to their name have messaged me on Facebook just to tell me my voice is sexy. It's like everyone in the city knows who I am. I hardly ever wear my buffies anymore because Lord knows I don't want a viral video of me on CrimeInTheD talking about how they got snatched at the Woodward or some shit. Then there are the panel discussions, the Black male mentorship programs, the two boards I sit on, the keynote speeches, and the fact that I can't tweet a goddamn thing without *Detroit Hotline* turning it into a headline and a headache. There aren't that many celebrities in Detroit, but if this is what it's like to be one, now I understand why all those muhfuckas left as soon as they had the chance. Detroit's a small town, and my business is all the way out there.

And right now, that business may be on the cusp of being out there even more if this new deal I'm working goes through. You see, this father and son, the McQuerrys—they're new to this scene. They own a bunch of commercial property all the way out in Novi, but they've decided to invest here in Detroit because, like every suburban white man with a little bit of money, they wanna cash in. They've reached out to me because they've acquired a plot of land on Grandy Street and are looking to break ground on a sixteen-unit townhouse complex—four units on a side, and I can guarantee you each will look as personality-less as the others. I also know exactly who's going to be paying top price to move in once they're done.

I can't be mad at it, though. Suburban white men and Arabs own this city now. I wish we could do more. "We" meaning Black folks, of course. We have restaurants but not the buildings where we lease the space. I'm trying to get there, though. I'd like to own a building and lease to minority-owned businesses—Troy says I shouldn't call them "minority-owned," but shit, that's what I grew up calling them and it never hurt anyone all this time. And if I have to get there through the McQuerry family, I guess that's how it's going to be.

Anyway, I digress. Once I became Mr. Detroit, I had to take all my face pics off the dating—heh, "dating"—apps because people would be like, "Hey, the guy from the billboards!" in the first message. But I don't mind not being able to rely on the apps to get laid because I've built a roster of regulars. Dudes I can call when I need a fix. And I do need my fix. Often. Janet Jackson once said, "Sex is a gift from God." Well, God is *good*, OK? What a mighty God we serve! Can I get an amen?

But recently, I'm definitely starting to feel . . . something . . . weird. I don't know the right term for it, but something's not right. I'm talking about the fact that all these men will fuck but won't stay.

Two on the roster have stayed longer than one night. There's Roland, this British Jamaican dude, my number-one friend with benefits, if people even still use that term. Dark skin, beautiful white smile, that British accent . . . *oof.* I don't know what to call us. Wait . . . *us.* Let me stop. Ain't no *us.* He's a flight attendant based in London working at Virgin Airlines, we met on Scruff, and we're both vers with each other although he's usually more top. I can ride dick like the penny horse at Meijers, but vice the fuck versa when need be, OK? His route brings him into Detroit twice a month—sometimes more than that.

I can't even lie. Roland and I been sleeping together for a little over a year and a half, but it's gotten better in the last few months. It was never bad, don't get me wrong. But something's happening, and I can't quite explain it. I couldn't get Roland to go out with me in public in Detroit at first. We'd spend all our time in my bed or his hotel room at the Marriott in the RenCen. But now we've started having brunch downstairs at Andiamo. And that's turned into walks along the Riverwalk. And you know for Detroit standards, a romantic walk on the Riverwalk is damn near a marriage proposal.

He's my secret, make-believe boyfriend, I guess. A real estate agent and a flight attendant—could it be any more gay? He once referred to me as his Motown Man (apparently, they *love* Motown in the UK, but I'd be good never hearing another Temptations song in my life to be perfectly fucking honest), and OK, maybe it's got me a little twisted. Men in general seem to be allergic to monogamy, and I haven't had anyone call me their man in a minute. But now I'm Roland's Motown Man and have been for, well, a while. But we're not official. No confirmation on Facebook, and come to think of it, I don't even think we have any selfies together.

Two months ago, though, just as summer was ending, he got me a buddy pass and I flew to visit him in London for two weeks. Troy was the only one who knew about it; he always knows the whole situation cause that's the homie. All of the things I'd ever wanted to do with a man in Detroit, Roland and I did in London. He said "we." He said "us." He said "if we" and "when we." You know what else he said? "When you finally move to London, I'll show you what you've really been missing." And then he said, "I should get a Scorpio tattoo to match yours, love," because the week we were there was the week before our respective birthdays. Then, as we walked through Brixton, he said, "This is where we could settle if you lived here."

Back home, I can't get a nigga to drive me past Southfield.

Troy calls Roland my weekend boyfriend. With a weekend boyfriend, you do all the things a real couple does: hold hands in public, buy groceries together, have petty, meaningless arguments, and—the thing Roland and I have been doing a lot—talk about the future. But still, it's hard to ignore the empty condom wrapper on his windowsill that he clearly forgot to throw away, or the two empty wine glasses on his nightstand, or the fact that he always keeps his phone turned over no matter what city we're in. Are we exclusive and monogamous? Certainly not. I know he's fucking other people. So am I. But . . . shit, it'd still be nice to be his endgame. But whatever. Blasé-blasé.

So rather than lay in bed and watch some sad little white gay boy shit on Netflix, I've got other irons in the fire. If Roland is my number one, Terrell is my number two. Now, Terrell is a little complicated. He grew up around the way from me and was a year above me at Denby. One day, a few months ago, as I was walking downtown, he pulled over to say wassup. One minute, we were sitting in his car in a parking space, catching up over everything that had happened in the last fifteen years, and the next, he took my hand and put it on his crotch, where I felt his erection through his Trues. And even though I tried to ignore the fact that someone was still wearing True Religion in this day and age, I couldn't ignore the fact that, through the denim, I could feel exactly how thick his dick was.

"We should get together sometime," he said.

"Sometime" ended up being six hours later in my bed. If you think these thirtysomething limbs can handle sex in a Jeep Renegade, think again.

Troy once told me Terrell could be "sexually fluid." I don't know what that means exactly, but the way Troy said it made sense at the time. Basically, Terrell is not DL, and maybe not exactly bisexual either. But first of all, I'd never fuck a DL dude. Oprah fucked everything up for a whole generation of young Black gays when she had that lame J. L. King on her show, telling the whole world that any Black man who even so much as bent his wrist a little too much was going to give you AIDS. Women had to get the message about men who sleep with other men, but goddamn, that one little episode pushed so many Black men back into the closet because suddenly, every Black woman had something negative to say about us. It was hell for us younger gays coming up then. No matter how masculine I tried to present myself, I still occasionally got called "DL" and "suspect" and "fag." But now we have "sexually fluid," I guess. Troy said Terrell could be attracted to both men and women without putting one over the other. I said that made him bisexual, but Troy said it went deeper than that. Whatever. I can't keep up with all these new terms these girls are using. I just think you're either this or that with nothing in between.

After sleeping with Terrell for the past five months, though, here's what I do know. He really only wants to be my man when he's inside me. When we make love—no, when we fuck, because making love is only for real couples—he's more attentive than any lover I've ever had. He's taken time to get to know all my spots: behind my ears, the sides of my neck, the insides of my thighs. When he's in me, he's slow, calculating, tender, and smooth. I've never had a bad experience with him. Never. With him I come hard, and he loves to suck the head of my dick each time, making my legs shake and my eyes roll back. The few times he's let me top him, he's been patient and understanding, and although he thinks it's a little weird when we do it, he's appreciative, especially during those times when I know he likes it. He'll say my name over and over, groaning in between when I go in and out. I'm the only one who's done him like this. At least I assume.

But it's always over so quickly. I mean, the sex lasts long, but as soon as we're done, he cleans up with one of my good Hotel Collection towels, puts his clothes back on, and leaves. No kiss goodbye and barely a hug. My high comes down immediately. I feel cheap. Used. For once, I'd like to cuddle and bask in the afterglow. I'd like to feel wanted, something more than his temporary escape. I'd like to make love. I spend so much time in this bed, whether it's with Terrell or anyone else, that I've forgotten what it's like to go out and have dinner with a man who's not my best friend, or go to a concert with someone other than a bunch of girls needing a plus one, or get a morning text that isn't from the doctor's office reminding me of my quarterly blood draw to re-up on these Descovy pills. Like I said, Roland will at least get brunch with me or walk around the city. The rest of these muhfuckas, though, it's like, *damn*.

In my mind, I'm only Terrell's gay fantasy. He'd never do all the things he does with me with any woman. But because he and I only do what we do in the dark of his bedroom or mine, I wonder more and more.

Maybe Troy's right and Terrell is "fluid" or whatever. I'm starting to think he may just be DL.

Not too long ago, I tried to confirm it at my place. I had my good, sexy-time playlist going, and Calvin Brooks and Hari Paris's "My Favorite Thing" had just come over the Bluetooth speaker. That's my shit—one of those quiet storm, 107.5-type classics that sounds like riding in the back of my auntie's Oldsmobile Ninety-Eight Regency.

"You must really like this song," Terrell said.

"Why you say that?"

"I only hear it at your house."

"It's not that well-known, but my mom used to play it to death when I was little. Did I ever tell you about her?"

"You talk about her, but . . ."

"She was a receptionist at WJLB for a few years, and she used to come home with all the CDs the record companies sent. She's had a few different jobs. Now she works at Greektown Casino."

"I remember you telling me that."

"But this song has always stayed with me. It's one of her favorites and now it's one of mine."

"It's all right."

I leaned closer to Terrell. He's dark like I am, and when I caught a glimpse of us in the mirror across the room, the two of us looked smooth as mousse. How could I tell this muhfucka that I didn't just want to fuck? I took his arm and put it around me.

He asked me, "What you thinking of?"

"Nothing," I lied. I was thinking that he should ask me out on a real date. I was thinking that we were at a point where we should think more about our relationship instead of just being fuck buddies. I was thinking he should have said something before I did.

But I just tried to bring my heart rate down. I lay my head against his chest, took a deep breath, and closed my eyes. My stomach started to calm, and my muscles relaxed. I felt the warmth between my face and his torso, and he started to rub his hand up and down my side. He works at the Chrysler plant—he's worked there ever since high school and he's dedicated to both the job and the union—but he still keeps his hands soft. Just like a gay man. Or sexually fluid, or whatever.

He reached for my shirt to take it off, but I stopped him.

"Let me just lay here for a minute. Slow down."

"All right."

"Are you doing anything Tuesday night?" I asked him. "I've got two tickets to this show at the Michigan Opera Theatre."

"Did you buy them just for me?"

"Nope, I got them as a complimentary gift. They're trying to boost memberships with millennials, so they gave them to me. I was going to ask Troy, but I know he's busy."

I was not, in fact, going to ask Troy.

"I've never been to an opera," Terrell said.

"You probably did in elementary school. I know I did."

Say what you want about Detroit schools now, but back in the day, they made sure our little Black asses were cultured.

"Tuesday night? Yeah, I'm free."

"You really want to go?" I said, propping myself up.

He smiled and laughed.

"Yeah. Let's go."

"With me?"

"Who else?"

I was in disbelief. Temporarily insane. Maybe Terrell wasn't DL after all.

"Bet," I said. "You'll have to dress up. Do you have a nice suit?"

"I can pull something together."

"You can't have me out here looking stupid. Let's go shopping this weekend."

Lord, what was I doing? I knew I shouldn't have pushed it. I should just have felt lucky that I had gotten this far.

"And buy a suit?" he asked.

"I'll take care of it for you."

"What?"

"I'm really good at finding things on sale."

Lies. I buy all my shit full price, and if happens to be on sale, so be it.

"Bet. I mean, if you say so," Terrell said. "I'll pay you back."

"Don't worry about it."

"Nah, nah, you not about to be no sugar daddy. I'll pay you half now, half later."

"That's fine. We'll go to Somerset."

"Uh, can't we go to Cannon's? Or K&G? Somewhere a little more in my budget?"

I'd planned on taking him to Nordstrom or, at the very least, Macy's. And I was going to pay for it anyway. I wanted a quality suit for him, something he could wear over and over and still look good in. I knew he didn't have one. I suppose I was looking ahead—as long as he had one good suit, he'd be ready to go anywhere with me. But then I thought that if we went to K&G, they might have one of those two-for-one deals, and I could get him something decent and get a little something for myself.

"K&G. I almost forgot about them. Yeah, let's go there."

"Bet," he said, fingering my chest. He leaned in to kiss me. I felt butterflies in my stomach because the whole conversation had been dangerous. But as I lay on my back and let Terrell undress me, I started to calm. He kissed all over my body, fondled my thighs with those massive hands of his, and nibbled at my waist as I tried not to cry out too loud. I had a feeling I was in for one hell of a night.

CHAPTER THREE

Troy Clements was horny. He was laying in his queen-sized bed—a hand-me-down from his father's much larger house in Indian Village—in his two-bedroom apartment on East Grand Boulevard. There was low lighting indoors, but a brand-new LED streetlight outside was shining directly into his bedroom window. For years, his block had sat in near darkness until the city installed new light poles. In the past, Troy hadn't minded not having curtains. But now, with the bright light streaming in, he not only had to put up room-darkening shades so he could sleep at night, but the room was so lit up that anyone could see exactly what he was doing: gently fingering the rim of his asshole, contemplating whether to go full dildo.

A man was supposed to be in bed with him. His name was Roderick, and he was Troy's boyfriend of six months. The two had met at the Woodward, a gay bar further east up the boulevard where it hit Woodward Avenue. Troy had gone there with his best friend, Remy, who actually despised going there but always agreed to if the two boys needed to dance and unwind. And with Remy's constant aggravations with title agencies, mortgage brokers, and any of the other cast of characters real estate agents in a gentrifying city have to deal with, and with Troy's need to be around adults after working full days at the Mahaffey School, where he'd taught sixth grade for the last nine years, the two of them, in fact, found they regularly needed a little unwinding.

Mahaffey was a charter school, which meant its staff reported to a five-member board, which itself reported to the school's operator, the University of Detroit Mercy. Almost every charter school in the city was operated by a university or corporation, some entity with more money than Detroit's always flailing public school district. They seized upon half-enrolled or completely empty schools and enacted their own curriculums—ideologies, really—essentially teaching the kids of desperate Detroit parents whatever they saw fit. UDM's School of Social Justice operated Mahaffey, which was fine in the eyes of most people who were on staff or who sent their children there. But three years ago, the socialist-minded old board had been voted out, and an opportunist new board had been brought in. With charter schools, that was a threat. To make things worse, UDM had been facing a slew of financial setbacks. Troy tried to keep his hand out of gossip at work—he focused on the kids and how he could help them—but even he couldn't help but overhear the whispers in the teachers' lounge that UDM was starting to think twice about whether it could continue to invest money in a school on the city's east side.

Troy taught what he was supposed to teach, but he eschewed the school policy concerning how a teacher should dress for the job. Rather than ties and button-downs, Troy instead wore a different color hoodie each day. It was his way of signaling that no one should be viewed as a threat based on how he dressed, especially a Black man. It was his subtle fuck-you to the norm, and Troy, who had a master's in education, wanted his kids to see that you could be successful wearing whatever you felt comfortable in. He was old enough to remember when his father had lectured him about how Black boys in the nineties shouldn't wear hooded clothing, and that if they did, the hood should be turned down at all times. Troy was over Black respectability and the fear of white dominance that it stemmed from. And if the school wanted to incorporate social justice into the curriculum—it had been named for the late Detroit

City Councilwoman Maryann Mahaffey, a champion of Detroit's poor who believed in social justice before the term was in vogue with Tumblr millennials—Troy figured he should look the part.

When Troy locked eyes with Roderick for the first time at the Woodward, social justice certainly wasn't on his mind. But when they exchanged numbers and met up after the club let out at Detroit One Coney Island down the street, social justice did in fact find its way to the top of their conversation. And later that night, Troy let Roderick hit, in the same queen bed where he was waiting for him now.

It turned out Roderick, who worked at the new Amazon warehouse in Romulus, was passionate about Black liberation, something Troy found incredibly important—and sexy—because he himself was working to discover his own identity as a Black man. Bill, Troy's father, had married Suhas, his second wife, while he was building his million-dollar printing company, and Troy had spent a lot of years being other. There aren't many Black-Bangladeshis in Detroit after all, or in America for that matter. Throughout his teens and early twenties, Troy had spent time being half-Black, half-South Asian, Blasian, or even being Brown. But he abided by the one-drop-of-blood rule now. To anyone who looked at him, who saw that his skin tone was light enough to pass the paper-bag test but still a unique shade of light brown most Black-Black folks didn't have, they knew he was a little different somehow. But on paper, he was Black, African American.

When Troy was old enough to realize that in a city where anyone not white, Latino, or Arab was simply Black—not half-this or half-that—he made it his mission to be, well, just Black. That meant aligning with Black causes—Black Lives Matter on the national level and By Any Means Necessary on the local one. Somehow, he thought, it was essential for the just-Blacks, the half-Blacks, the kinda-Blacks, and the Black-Blacks to realize their status in a white world. And in Detroit, that meant understanding that even though 80 percent of the city was made up of just-Blacks and Black-Blacks, white people were now arriving at a steady enough rate to become a threat. Unity was needed as soon as humanly possible, but liberation—freedom from white supremacy—had to come first.

Troy could talk about all this with Roderick, who talked the same shit by bringing up his own experiences growing up poor on the east side even though his mother had a college degree, and about how he could have made it further if she hadn't been denied opportunities in the corporate world and instead been forced to take suburban buses out to places that didn't respect her abilities. Roderick had whole theories about how the white powers that be in Michigan had systematically destroyed Detroit's public school system, thus laying the groundwork for the neighborhoods around crumbling schools to fall apart even faster. Hearing Roderick talk about that turned Troy on even more than the fact that for the first three months of their relationship, they were fucking raw at least four times a week.

When Roderick eventually moved into Troy's apartment, he brought two garbage bags of clothes, a box of Black nationalist books, and a toothbrush.

"Minimalism," Roderick said, "is the way forward."

Six weeks earlier, in lockstep with every property owner across Detroit, Troy's landlord had raised his rent by $200. The Mahaffey School already didn't pay that well, though Troy had always been comfortable. But with the rent hike, and with the recent rumors that the school might move to a different part of the city or, worse, go under, minimalism didn't seem like such a bad idea. Troy also thought it might be another way to piss off his father, who reveled in luxury and finer things.

But whereas Roderick was a staunch anti-capitalist, when Troy thought about the kids he taught at Mahaffey, he sometimes wondered whether their families could benefit from even the slightest taste of gentrification. Was it fair that the only places where neighborhood families could shop for school uniforms were far-flung discount stores? Or that liquor stores were the only places where some of them could buy groceries? Was it fair that apartments in Detroit were crumbling with broken furnaces and death-trap elevators, and that the landlords didn't seem to give a shit? If the city could undergo some new, thoughtful development, would, as economists always liked to theorize, the rising tide lift all Detroit's boats? These were the kinds of nuances that got lost when Troy couldn't speak—due to the fact that his mouth was full physically and his mind gone figuratively—because of Roderick's newfound influence.

"This shit is going to be all gentrified in a few years. Watch," Roderick once told him as they waited for a table at Union Street in Midtown.

"You're always so pessimistic," Troy said. "Detroit could use some nicer grocery stores."

"Anyway. Is this restaurant ever going to seat us?"

The two were having one of their usual talks about the changing demographics of the clientele at the bar, which had been there for as long as either of these born-and-raised Detroiters could remember. A few blocks down from Union Street, where the couple regularly challenged each other to finish "dragon eggs"—a blisteringly spicy appetizer of chicken breast meat soaked in habanero sauce—construction crews were putting the finishing touches on a brand-new condo complex behind a Whole Foods.

"We should have gone to They Say," Roderick said, doing a half-turn away from Troy. "Do any of you white people mind hurrying up and finishing your meals so that two Black people who are actually from the city of Detroit can enjoy this fine restaurant as well?"

A few patrons looked at them and then awkwardly went back to their meals.

"*Don't,*" Troy said, pulling his arm. "This is Midtown. We can't do that shit here anymore without them calling the police."

"Cass Corridor."

"I guess I've gotten used to calling it Midtown."

"And that's how it starts. They want us to call it that shit. It's the Cass Corridor."

Cass Corridor was what the neighborhood north of downtown Detroit used to be called, and there were plenty of sticklers who still called it that instead of the more user-friendly "Midtown." The new name was bland and generic. It helped erase what most Detroiters associated with the neighborhood's original name: drugs, vacant buildings, homeless vagrants, and prostitutes.

Troy knew that past scene well. After his mother's death, Bill would wake Troy up early, drive him out to the bus stop on the corner of Cass and Henry, and drop him off just in time to catch the Dexter bus across town to Renaissance High School. That year, each day before the sun had its chance to rise, Troy waited for the bus, trying to ignore the scantily dressed women who asked if he wanted a blow job or if he knew where they could get a fix.

When Troy was born, his father was already forty-three. At that age, Bill wasn't sure if he wanted to be chasing a toddler around the 5,800-square-foot Indian Village home he and Suhas had worked so hard to acquire. Their home was not meant for children. It was meant for business meetings and grand dinners, a peaceful escape from the loud printing presses Bill and Suhas endured all week. To this day, it was likely Bill's dining room was the quietest place in Detroit.

At the dining room table, Troy's father would often recount stories about his childhood in Palestine, Arkansas, to remind his family of how far he'd come. He'd tell Troy how people in Black Bottom, the Detroit neighborhood he lived in when his family first came north, were always sick because everyone lived so close together. How they'd ride through rich neighborhoods in December to see how the wealthy decorated their homes because Bill's own family couldn't afford Christmas lights. How there were always knife fights in the streets; a scar on Bill's shoulder corroborated those violent encounters. If William Cordell Clements had stayed in that environment, he told his son, he would have ended up dead, a teenage father to a child he didn't want, or just walking the streets drunk.

Children had never been a part of Bill's imagined future. He had always just been working toward a life of luxury and leisure, gallivanting across a champagne-soaked world without having to stop to change diapers. Troy could still remember the evening a few months ago when he'd gone over there for dinner. He sat across from Bill, with only the ticking of the grandfather clock as their background noise.

"Why'd you invite me to dinner?" Troy asked.

He always asked this.

"I'd like to know what my son has been up to."

"I wasn't sure you had interest."

Bill sighed.

"I do. So tell me what's been going on with you."

"I've been seeing someone."

"His name?"

"Roderick."

"You must like him. You never tell me about your flings."

"This is more than a fling, Dad."

"Sure then."

"It's been a few months. I let him move in."

"Do you need anything from me?"

"I'm paying the rent just fine."

"Should be, as cheap and run-down as that rat trap is you live in. I don't understand why you can't just live closer over here."

"I'm sorry I don't have $700,000 to spare for a house in Indian Village."

"West Village. It's right there. No more than $1,400 a month."

"I'm not paying that much for an apartment and you know that."

"Doesn't your friend? What's his name? Randy?"

"Remy. Yes, he's a lot like you. Extravagant."

"Hold on there, boy."

"I'm sorry."

"I can be extravagant because I earned all this. I've tried to give the same to you. And you came out good, but . . . .." Bill sighed again. "I don't know what I did that made you want to be a teacher and not make any money out here. Have you thought about what you might want to do in the future? You planning on teaching at that school five years from now? Ten?"

"I made my own choices. I paid my way through college, and I'm making my way through life now. You never had to rely on your father, right?"

"I didn't have a father to rely on. You did."

"I did?"

"Don't start this bullshit, boy."

Troy looked down at his food, barely eaten. He knew dinner would end the same way it always did. He'd leave his father with a half-eaten plate and a half-hearted goodbye, go pig out alone at Grandy's Coney Island, get fucked by whatever dick dealer he was with at the moment, and then go get drunk off wine and high on weed with Remy.

That had been months ago, and at least now there was some disruption to these old routines. Troy's other best friend, Dominick Gibson, was coming back to Detroit after living for years out East. They'd first met as high school students at a weeklong summer journalism camp at Michigan State University—there had only been a few Black kids there, so they naturally gravitated toward each other— and they'd kept in touch through AOL Instant Messenger, their first Nextel phones, Facebook, the occasional Skype call, and postcards from all the places Dom had traveled for work.

In recent months, the correspondence had turned sour on Dom's end. Though they had only seen each other in person a handful of times over the years, they never stopped talking about the intimate details of their life. Troy was the first person Dom came out to after he told his parents. Soon after that, Troy came out, too, though it was another year before he told his father or anyone else. ("You know I low-key knew you were gay when we first met at State lol," Dom texted him.) They trusted each other.

First, Troy had noticed the sporadic complaints about Justin, Dom's boyfriend. But soon enough, Dom was straight up asking for relationship advice, telling Troy he was ready to dump Justin and leave. Troy listened and helpfully took it all in. But as a novice to relationships himself, he didn't quite know how to respond. He always told Dom to know his worth, to keep his cool, and to not let anyone diminish his shine. And if that meant leaving Justin, he'd better have a plan in place that wouldn't fuck up any of the former.

• • •

Dominick Gibson
I left his ass. Driving back to Detroit now.
Can I crash on your couch lol
Just kidding, going to stay with my mom until I figure things out

Troy Clements
You know you're welcome here anytime.
I'm glad you came to your senses

Dominick Gibson
Almost hit a pothole
Wasn't ole girl supposed to fix these roads?
We have so much to talk about. I can't wait to hang out

Troy Clements
Don't text and drive
Text me as soon as you get to the big tire

• • •

How do you take a friendship that's largely digital and turn it into something tangible and real? Troy had been thinking about this a lot ever since Dom had started dropping hints that he might be coming home. He fretted that Dominick would find his Detroit life dull. To be frank, it was. Dealing with kids all day, barely speaking with his father, and being in a relationship that, lately, seemed more about fucking than anything else made little for a lively existence—though Troy did have one new hobby that kept things interesting.

It was at Motor City Wine where Troy had his first snort of coke. Late Sunday afternoons were always busy at the bar because that was when service industry workers and educators joined together to drink away their fear and frustration of the upcoming workweek. Troy was there on the patio with Marlie and Noelle, two fellow Mahaffey teachers, and all three were lubricating their troubles with the house-made sangria.

White millennials moving to Detroit were thorns in the side of residents who were annoyed by their mere presence, but for aspiring dope boys looking for a new hustle, they hit a lick, and there was a usual dealer at Motor City Wine who had the place covered. Like clockwork every Sunday, he'd go from table to table, asking if anyone wanted to buy. Troy knew Marlie and Noelle casually used. As he put it, white girls loved white girl. But Troy had never done anything harder than weed, and he'd always been the one telling the girls they better quit the coke if they knew what was good for them. So imagine their surprise when he copped his first baggie of blow and asked if they wanted to share.

Deep down, Troy just wanted a vice. For too long, he'd played everything straight. (Figuratively.) But he also didn't want to embarrass himself, so after Marlie and Noelle said they would get their own, he excused himself, went to the men's room, sat on the toilet, and blew his first rail off a tapas plate. His nostrils burned. He coughed and cleared his throat a bit. And then he returned to the girls, who'd each done their respective lines already. Forty-five minutes later, long enough for him to get used to the bitter nasal drip running down the back of his throat, Troy was the life of the party. The next day, he called in sick.

When Roderick finally came home, Troy had popped a Xanax and was sipping an Australian merlot with the shades drawn.

"Who were you texting?" Roderick asked.

"Nobody, just Dominick. See?" Troy turned the screen of his phone toward Roderick. Troy never had anything to hide, but he found he was offering this courtesy to Roderick a lot more lately.

"Oh. What's he up to?"

"We're making plans to hang out. He broke up with his boyfriend in New York."

"That's too bad."

"You could say a little more," Troy said. "Where have you been?"

"I'm home now."

"Yeah, but before now."

Roderick sat next to Troy and cupped his chin and stroked his cheek.

"I was at Marcus's house. We were smoking and watching movies."

"You don't smell like weed."

"What are you trying to say?"

"I hadn't heard from you."

"Don't be like that. You think I'm cheating?"

Troy was silent.

"If I'm cheating," Roderick said, "then explain this."

Roderick stood up, unzipped his pants, and slid them down to his knees. His erect penis poked out from the fly in his boxers. He and Troy looked at each other, and Roderick moved in for a sloppy kiss. Troy, feeling the Xanax begin to wash through him, tasted the marijuana on Roderick's tongue and kissed him back. Maybe Roderick wasn't lying after all.

CHAPTER FOUR

Four days after his return to Detroit, Dominick still wasn't sure how to verbalize what had happened between him and Justin. He knew his mother was still waiting on a full explanation. Knowing Tonya Gibson—she still carried her married name, even though she'd been divorced since Dom's sophomore year at Howard—she hadn't slept properly in those same four days either, wondering why her baby had been driving halfway across the country in the middle of the night. Dom knew what she thought of Justin—too uppity and saddidy. Funnily enough, Justin hadn't liked Tonya for the same reasons.

But what kind of explanation could Dominick offer her now? *I'm going broke, I'm horny as hell because I haven't fucked in nearly a month, the person I was regularly fucking is a cheating piece of shit, and I'm trying not to get fucked over professionally from sudden unemployment?*

Until clarity arrived, Dominick figured he'd break the awkward silence between him and his mother by asking to borrow his grandfather's Mercury Marauder, which Tonya had stored in her garage for over a decade.

"I have a job interview," he said.

"You still haven't told me what happened with the old agency."

"It shut down. Things . . . just didn't work out and . . . let me just say, nothing happened with me. I did everything I was supposed to, but this is just the risk you take with startups. But now I just want to move forward. Does the Marauder still work? I should've asked beforehand if I could use it."

"It still runs. Your father showed me how to keep it running."

"You still talk to him?"

"I never stopped."

"*Mom.*"

"Mom *what?* He and I divorced—we're not enemies. No matter what you go through with an ex, it's OK to still be cordial with them. Remember that. And anyway, he still gave me you."

Dominick sensed his mother's attempt to further break the ice about what had happened. He still didn't know what to say, so he countered with a response that had worked since childhood whenever he wanted to avoid parental conflict.

"It's fine, whatever. Can I lie down?"

"You don't have to ask. Go upstairs to your room, and I'll bring you some warm tea."

Dominick began to climb the stairs when he heard a robotic voice call out from the phone in the kitchen.

"*Oliver Lewandowski calling. Oliver Lewandowski calling.*"

"Who is that?" Dominick asked.

"Oh, it's the neighbors."

"We have neighbors named Oliver Lewandowski? That's a white-ass name, Mom."

"Oliver and Michelle moved in six months ago. They call to check in occasionally. I'll call them back later. And watch your language."

"Mom, you tell me so much. The church people, the nurses at the hospital—I can't keep up. But you definitely could've told me white people were moving into the neighborhood."

"I did. You probably forgot. But they're here."

"Since when?"

"Like I said, since six months ago," she laughed.

"It's not funny, Mom. We live off Joy Road! There are white people off Joy Road now?"

"The nice part of Joy Road! It's Detroit! This is how it is now."

———————————

Dominick had agreed to meet Troy downtown for dinner, and when he first got there, he was surprised by the lights. Winters in downtown Detroit used to be stock-still. The buildings stood tall and still as redwoods, a concrete forest where it was easy to camouflage yourself. Nights were longer and darker and allowed for mischief.

But the lights downtown now were new. *Downtown Detroit is lit the fuck up, OK?* Dominick thought. The buildings had movement. The lights on every floor were on well after dark. String lights hung everywhere. There were headlights from the cars passing around Campus Martius and on a new, seemingly very slow streetcar running up and down Woodward. *Where did that streetcar come from, anyway?* Smartphones glowed as tourists took selfies in front of the fountains. There was even a bright red glow coming from the sign of a new H&M. *Wait, there's an H&M?*

There were also people. People on foot. People on pedal pubs. People on Spin scooters—in the winter! Where, exactly, had all these people come from? There had always been people in Detroit, and there had always been people downtown. But not this many, not that Dominick could remember.

And my God, Dominick thought, *a shit-ton of these folks are white. Are they jogging through here, too? For real, though?*

Troy came up behind him, dressed for Michigan winter in a heavy coat, a knit cap with DETROIT printed across the front, and thick gloves.

"It is so fucking cold!" he said.

"Boy, come here and give me a hug," Dominick said. "It's been too long."

They reached out toward each other, their embrace nearly driving them to tears.

"I missed you," Troy said.

They stopped to look at each other, then Troy suggested they walk around before dinner so he could show Dom downtown.

"Bitch, we coulda did this when it was warm!" Dominick said.

"We'll warm up soon enough! I'll take you to the tent over there and we'll get hot chocolate. You want to go ice skating?"

"Hell no! I want to eat!"

"Never change, Dominick. Never fuckin' change."

While Detroit had certainly changed a lot since Dominick had lived here, it still wasn't New York. The last time the two boys had seen each other in person was when Troy had visited New York three years ago. The New York Dominick showed to Troy left him with what he thought were unattainable standards for his own hometown. Detroit had all-night coneys but no all-night pizza or Jamaican or Chinese. Detroit had its gay bars but not nearly as many as Manhattan. And while the Detroit Institute of Arts was world-class, even Troy, an unabashed art lover, had been overwhelmed by Dominick's suggestion that they hit the Guggenheim, MoMA, and the Cloisters in one day. Ice skating in a public park was the most New York activity Troy could think of in Detroit that could satisfy a true town mouse like Dominick.

"How about these food trucks? This one," Dominick said, pointing to a barbecue truck, "was recommended in Best of *Detroit Hotline*, 2018."

"Uhhhh, no. It's so not good, the macaroni is nasty and unseasoned trash. I wouldn't trust *Detroit Hotline*'s endorsement for anything."

"Why's that?"

"There are exactly four people that work at *Detroit Hotline*. And every one of them is white and from the suburbs. Four white people," Troy said, voice rising, "tell an entire Black city what they think is best *for us*. No joke."

"Damn, it's like that?"

"You see all these white folks around?"

"I've noticed. Goddamn, what happened?"

"These white people are on some other shit, I'm telling you. They're rude as hell, they walk all over the sidewalk," Troy laughed, and Dominick joined in.

"I noticed. You know my mom has white neighbors now? Off Joy Road!"

"She lives on the nice part of Joy Road," Troy said. "They'll be in the hood soon enough."

"Well, New York is nice, so would it be so bad if it happened here too?"

Troy sat on a bench and sighed.

"My worry is that it won't be a Black city anymore. That it's not going to belong to us like it used to. White people have started moving here in droves. Every time you look up—Dan Gilbert! New restaurant! New this, new that! And my thing is, I'm looking at my kids at Mahaffey and their families, and I know they won't be able to keep up when it hits."

"Is it going to hit them?"

Troy thought about telling Dominick about everything that was happening at work: Mahaffey's possible closure, the way a brand-new neighborhood of townhomes and condos was just springing up around it lot by lot, the artisanal shop that had opened nearby that *only* sold macarons, and his thoughts about just quitting it all and asking his dad for a job to take things easy. But the night was just getting started. There was time to get into all that later.

"It will and it won't. Like, look at it like this," Troy said, drawing an imaginary diagram with his hands. "You have the people that won't be affected at all, like . . . your mom. I mean, your mom is not going to be a victim of gentrification, and she's not going to be hit when all these higher-paying jobs come here. She's good. I mean, a lot of people in Detroit are good. But the inequality between my kids and the new white people . . . that's just going to get worse. That's what makes this so complicated because it's like *ugh*, I just want everybody to be stable."

"Sharing the wealth." Dominick said.

"Exactly."

"Hmm."

"I know where you're going with this. I see that look."

"I didn't say anything."

"I know what you're thinking," Troy said. "That I'm just a fucking hippie Marxist about to start a protest or some shit."

"You've always been a little Marxist," Dominick said with a slight hint of concern.

"I just, you know, want the world to be happy."

"We all do. Unfortunately, you need money to be happy. So what can you do?"

"Let's get food."

"I thought we were ice skating."

"There's something I want to show you first."

Troy tucked in his lips, inhaled deeply, and looked around. He took off his gloves and reached inside his left jean pocket and pulled out a small bag of white powder.

Dominick looked down at the baggie, looked up at Troy, and then looked down again and laughed.

"Oh, really?" he asked.

"So you're not surprised?"

"I am surprised, actually. Troy . . . since when?"

"Not long. Maybe like a year at this point."

"Troy, this . . . this is wild."

"You've done it!"

"Yeah, but I don't *buy* it. And I don't *do it*, do it. How often do you do it?"

"Don't ask me that. Come on, let's go."

"Are you asking me to do cocaine with you, Troy Clements?"

"I am asking you to do a tiny bump with me, Dominick Gibson."

"Oh, my God. Are you serious? OK, just for you."

"One thing, though. When you meet Remy, you can't tell him. He doesn't know."

"I can't believe you."

"Anyway, I only do it with my white friends."

"You just said—!"

"I know, shut up."

"All right, come on. I can't even believe this. You know, I left New York to get away from this shit, and here *you* go."

The fact that one landlord controlled most of the buildings in downtown Detroit made it a near-cartoonish monopoly that only existed in the fictional towns of daytime soap operas. That same landlord had contracted security officers to patrol most of the streets downtown, and it was no surprise they tended to gravitate to where the Black folks were—the basketball courts near the center of downtown or the still-low-income apartment buildings. Every winter, though, the downtown development authority constructed faux winter wonderland fantasies inside greenhouse globes down the grassy median of Woodward Avenue. They were unlocked, just large enough to pass through but not large enough to make yourself comfortable, as every downtown entity was cognizant about how to prevent the homeless from sticking around any place too long. Inside one of these snow globes, next to two foam snowmen and surrounded by ornament-adorned dried branches, Troy dipped the tip of his house key inside the baggie and held it up to Dom's nostrils as he sniffed. Dom reciprocated.

"I guess this is Detroit now," Dom said. "Come on, let's eat."

CHAPTER FIVE

A few days later, Troy got to Motor City Wine at exactly 5:45 p.m. His mentality had always been that drinks at 6:00 p.m. sharp left room for one more hour of happy hour but also meant the bar wouldn't be too crowded. He wondered how his two closest friends would react to meeting each other for the first time.

Dominick scurried in just before 6:00 p.m. And before Troy had time to think, Remy arrived in unmistakably Old Detroit glam uniform: a cognac-shade mink bomber jacket, a tan Ralph Lauren knit cap, and Carties with brown tinted lenses. Beneath the Motor City excess was downtown Detroit simplicity: a black cashmere sweater, gray wool pants, and classic Ferragamo loafers. Everything was new except the shoes; Detroit men, gay or straight, cherished their years-old Ferragamos, proving to be just as attentive to their Italian shoes as they were to their cars. Remy removed his buffs, placing them inside their white case, and strolled to the table.

"Bonjour, bitchessssss!"

"I see it's mink season already," Troy said.

"Just pulled it out of Dittrich's storage this morning," he replied, turning to Dominick. "Dominick, the famous Dominick I've heard so much about?"

"Remy, the famous Remy I've heard so much about?"

"Give me a hug. We're family at this point."

The two men embraced like cousins who hadn't seen each other for years. Dominick ran his hand across Remy's mink sleeve.

"C'mon now!" he said. "What is that, velvet?"

"Just a lil' sumthin', you know, you know."

The three men sat down, the bar around them beginning to fill up with people coming in after work. There was New Detroit and Old Detroit, and if Motor City Wine was New Detroit, it sure didn't behave like it. New Detroit consisted of anything built by white people when the city was at its lowest point. Corruption in the mayor's office, rampant crime, a recession, and, finally, municipal bankruptcy created a perfect storm for hipsterpreneurs to swoop up cheap property on half-empty commercial strips and make their own kind of mayhem. Their patrons were the extended but closed-off circle of white millennials and late Gen Xers who had flocked to the city in droves—just like Black folks in the Southern Migration except they didn't bring soul or seasoning with them when they came.

Old Detroit was the product of that Southern Migration, this city's conglomerate. They say New Yorkers are South Carolinians in Timbs, and Chicago is made up of Mississippians in winter coats. Detroiters, then, are 'Bammas wrapped in fur. Old Detroit never went away during the corruption and the recession, but it was having to adapt as New Detroit made itself comfortable. But Old Detroit still owned businesses, still was at church every Sunday, and still made sure its music was melodious in every hood—even in Corktown, where Motor City Wine, a relatively new neighborhood addition, had jazz or Detroit house going every night. Plenty of Old Detroiters had reciprocated by adopting the wine bar as their own.

Dominick ordered cheese chimichangas. He wasn't supposed to eat them, but he really wanted to have something he'd loved back in the day.

Troy ordered the shrimp quesadilla. He wasn't supposed to eat that either, but it was inexpensive without being obviously cheap. Remy definitely shouldn't have ordered enchiladas topped with cheese and a side of sour cream, but he wasn't in the mood for something heavy like fajitas. All three men were lactose intolerant and in denial about it. It hits all Black folks at some point. For each of the three men at the table, it had all struck them sometime after they turned thirty.

Turning thirty really was a bitch, though as gay men, Remy, Troy, and Dominick were very much in tune with their health. They had no other choice because for decades, both pop culture and public service had inundated them with the threat of disease—and the warning signs that could cause it. Fever? AIDS. Fatigue? AIDS. Night sweats? AIDS. Compound that with being Black and cowering from every disease that's ever struck anyone of African descent since they've been in America, and these three men had never had a morning where they could just wake up and be healthy.

"Which high school did you go to?" Remy asked.

"Don't judge. U of D Jesuit," Dominick said.

"Ugh, I dated a guy, *briefly*, that went to U of D. But he was a hoe. Truly a man for others."

"What you trying to say?" Dominick laughed.

"So where in New York do you live again?"

"Don't change the subject! Hell's Kitchen."

"Oh, nice. I've always wanted to spend some time in Harlem."

Me too, Dominick thought. But after he and Justin moved in together farther south, Justin had forbidden them from ever going north of 110th Street again.

"I'm actually really excited to be back home, though," Dominick said.

"I heard," Remy said, turning to Troy.

"I told him a little bit of what's going on, not the full story," Troy said.

"Well," Dom said, taking a gulp of his Piesporter, "to make a long story short, I caught my boyfriend in *our* bed with another man on the exact same day the agency I was working for shut down. So yes, let's just say I'm happy to be anywhere but New York right now."

"First of all, I'm sorry to hear that. Second of all, I know some niggas on East Warren if you want to go back to New York and handle it. I'll even pay for the flights."

"I'm good," Dominick laughed. "But I do appreciate the offer."

"How long were you together?"

"Eight years."

"My God. Are you still with him?"

"We haven't talked since I came home."

"Would you ever . . . talk to him about it?"

Dominick looked at his glass of wine, finger-tapping each side. At this point, only two people other than Remy knew he had stolen away from New York City in the dead of night: Troy and his mother. Neither of them had asked about forgiveness.

"I don't know if I can. We were supposed to be monogamous. Key word, *supposed* to be," he said, feeling the wine kick in. "I told him from the beginning that my father cheated on my mother and that's why they divorced. I was trying to break the generational curse and have something happy. And what the fuck happened? This."

"Wait, were you married?"

Dominick paused again, looking down into the bottom of the wine glass and focusing on the stem.

"No. I wanted to, but we weren't."

Dominick sometimes wondered if gay Black men were even the marrying kind. Only 10 percent of all the gay men in America were married to each other. It seemed like there were always lots of Neil Patrick Harrises and Lance Basses and Jesse Tyler Fergusons. The few Black gay celebrities that were married . . . well, they took beautiful portraits in well-tailored suits, and the photos were circulated across the internet so much that you might know them just as well as you know your own friends. Gay

Black men certainly had their hashtag relationship goals. They just had to idolize the same five viral couples repeatedly.

Dominick thought about the musical number "Somewhere That's Green" from the film version of *Little Shop of Horrors* quite a bit. Yes, it was an overwrought campy parody—Ellen Greene with the perfectly coiffed hairdo and all, pining over a life of TV dinners and Tupperware. *But goddamn, it would be nice to have that life*, Dominick thought. To be a spouse, to be loved automatically, and to have some predictability. To be a Mr. So-and-So carrying a brown bag lunch, to quibble over games of Monopoly, to go to sleep in the suburbs hearing only the wind outside. All while having the kind of sex that would shift tectonic plates, of course.

"OK, let's do a Boomerang," Remy said, hoping to lighten the evening. "To celebrate our new club."

"Are we in a club?" Troy asked.

"Yeah, this is a little clique now! We should have a name."

"I don't do cliques. Not since 2002," Dominick said.

"So what do we call this, a threesome?" Remy said. "Come on, it'll be fun."

"I told you he was crazy," Troy said.

"I could use another friend," Dominick said.

"I already know we're going to be friends," Remy said. "You and Troy have it, me and Troy have it, but now we've got a third."

"A third!" Troy and Dominick laughed.

"Not like that, you dummies," Remy laughed. "A bitch is a little tipsy right now, but please just indulge me."

"Well, if we're a club, we have to have rules. Like the Little Rascals," Dominick said.

"The who?" Remy asked.

"OK, rule number one . . ." Troy said.

"Rule number one: Don't be a booty call!" Remy sang.

The boys couldn't help but roar with laughter, ignorant of the folks around them.

"OK, but for real though," Remy said. "Rule number one is . . . shit, I forgot what I was going to say. I need a minute, but until then, let's do a Boomerang!"

The boys lifted their glasses and, per Remy's instruction, toasted on cue. The image looped to his liking, so he tagged each of them and posted it to his Instagram Story.

Remy had been using his Instagram Story a lot more ever since he'd seen that Roland was watching them. Roland barely used social media—something Remy had confirmed on his own after searching every platform for his name; Roland's Instagram was the only thing that turned up. Remy followed him, and almost immediately, Roland followed back.

Still, it was hard for Remy to stay in touch with Roland elsewhere online. Sure, they texted, but Roland was insistent about not joining other platforms. When Roland wasn't in town, him watching Remy's Stories from time to time was the only connection they had. It meant something. So Remy still wanted to show Roland what a fabulous life he was living. He also wanted to drop the 5,000-pound hint that Roland was welcome to join this life whenever he wanted to. Five minutes after posting the Story, Remy checked to see if Roland had viewed it. Only two people had so far: a friend from high school and a white dude he'd curved some time ago on Scruff.

He is not watching your Instagram Story, he thought. *He's smashing the cakes of a far more good-looking man than you'll ever be, giving that man the best stroke you'll never have because HE is giving YOU the bare minimum, right?*

To Dominick, who was three glasses of wine in, it was starting to feel like New York. This was the kind of interaction he had craved, reminiscent of when he had first moved to the big city, before—as he explained to Remy and Troy—Justin began micromanaging their existence right down to the clothes Dominick wore, the food they ate, and how much money they collectively spent. And for the first time in a while, Dominick could discuss this with men just like him; in New York over the last year, his and Justin's social circles had been growing increasingly whiter.

After dinner, the three boys piled into the back of their Uber. Remy began composing a drunk text to Roland but then paused so he could half-rap along to 42 Dugg, the driver's choice for the evening and someone Terrell had introduced him to. The undergirding of Detroit hip-hop always sounded like the ominous horror film piano playing in a haunted house—if that haunted house was on the corner of Seven Mile and Morang.

"Y'all having a good time?" the driver called to the back.

"Oh, we're having a real good time," Remy said. "You smoke?"

"Remy!" Troy laughed.

"Yeah, I get into a little something," the driver said.

"Well, we're about to smoke at my house. You should come through."

"Nah, I'm working."

Both Troy and Dominick tried to muffle their drunken laughter. Anyone in the life knows that when a Black gay man asks another man, "You smoke?" he's flirting.

"Is this the place?" the driver asked, turning onto St. Paul.

"Yeah," Remy said. "You sure you don't wanna smoke with us? My shit is nice."

"I'm good. Y'all have a good night."

The trio moved inside and took off their coats.

"Take off your shoes before you walk across my Pewabic floor," Remy said, heading to the breakfast nook to uncork a bottle of wine. "Let me check to see what I have. If we need anything else, my weed man also takes Venmo and will deliver."

"In this weather?" Dominick asked. He and Troy made their way to the couch.

"Welcome to New Detroit," Remy scoffed. "White folks don't get cold."

"I'm surprised Mr. Detroit has a weed man."

"There's a lot the public doesn't know about Mr. Detroit. My weed man's actually an artist. I used to mess with his homeboy. Who is Black by the way, OK? But besides all that, art does not pay the bills, so he sells weed to get by. Y'all want Backwoods or this vegan paper?"

Remy always had plenty of weed to share, and he and Troy had near-weekly smoke sessions. If they were bored? Smoke. Boy problems? Smoke. Just wanted to vent? Smoke. And quiet as Mr. Detroit kept it from the public, he'd sometimes take a hit alone before showings and client meetings.

Backwoods allowed the THC to seep in their bloodstreams quicker. The wine gave speedy escapism. Remy commanded his Alexa to play a best of Labelle playlist. They were floating in no time.

"Do y'all ever think about weddings?" Dominick asked. They'd been sitting in silence for who knows how long.

"Oh, shit," Troy said.

Remy burst into uncontrollable giggles.

"Niggas ain't trying to get married."

"This nigga is," Dominick said.

"Can y'all not say . . . never mind," Troy said.

"You and your half-Asian ass," Remy said between giggles. "You're more Black than you ain't so you can say it."

"I choose not to."

"Can y'all answer the question?" Dominick asked.

Though it wasn't top of mind for now, Remy did in fact have an image of what he wanted his wedding to look like. Pushing through the haze, he poured out a half-slurred version of it. It would be on Belle Isle. Early summer, before the sun came around in August and Detroit became unbearably hot, with the skyline in the background. The song: "Ribbon in the Sky"—not Stevie Wonder's original but the cover version by Intro. Both grooms would be fly: each in tailored, gray sharkskin, leaving no indication of who was the top or who was the bottom. (Not that it mattered if guests knew. Remy just didn't want folks spending the whole afternoon trying to guess.) Gators? Maybe, if they could find a pair that looked just right without looking like Easter Sunday at Wayne T's church on Grand River. Both grooms would read vows, and a preacher— preferably a woman, because Black male preachers would definitely drag that shit out—would do the honors. Lamb chops as the main course during the reception, and no time for vegetarians; they'd just eat the side salad or die. But above all else, there would be no traditional first dance (though if Remy's groom wanted one, it would be Miki Howard's "Love Under New Management") but instead a first Detroit hustle, where the newlyweds and all the guests would pour onto the dance floor to Stevie Wonder's "My Eyes Don't Cry," followed by Janet Jackson's "Feels So Right" and Kirk Whalum and Wendy Moten's "All I Do."

"And you, sir?" Dominick asked, turning to Troy.

Troy had already consigned himself to the idea of perpetual bachelorhood. Had he ever seen someone who looked like him as the better half of one of those gay influencer couples on the Instagram Explore page? A Black gay man? A gay South Asian man? Never mind both. Who would ever settle for a mixed man where both parents were of color, a man with a love of social justice and the betterment of children's lives, a gay man with a bare-minimum appreciation for fashion, and a man who was cynical about, well, everything?

But all boys dream of weddings, even the cynics. And when Troy thought about his, he sometimes imagined a ceremony that combined the best of both his cultures. It would have the vividness of a Bengali wedding—which he'd seen through the bootlegged Dhallywood films he sometimes watched with Suhas—decked in turmeric shades of orange and with glittering metallics on silks, but it'd also have a Black wedding's soul. *Imagine jumping the broom in a tunic. That'd really fuck with people's minds*, he thought. Two men at the altar, however, seemed highly unlikely. Not a Bengali man, not a Black man, not any man. And even if Troy could find someone who was willing to put up with him, they'd probably just settle for a courthouse wedding in nice suits.

"And what about you?" Troy asked, looking at Dominick.

"Let's change the subject," Dominick said.

"Fuck you!" Remy said, back to his rabid fits of laughter. "You make us confess our deepest feelings and now you want to get quiet? You're a dog. All men are dogggggggssss!"

"You know what?" Dominick said, taking another gulp of merlot. "Why do we compare men to dogs? I *wish* I had a dog. Dogs are fuckin' loyal. They're happy to see you when you get home, they cuddle 'n shit, and they love you to death. You know what men actually are? Giraffes. Like who the fuck needs a giraffe? They look good, and maybe they have a big dick—at least I'm assuming a big-ass bitch like a giraffe has a big-ass dick. But at the end of the day, they're pointless."

"A giraffe? Nigga, you high as fuck," Remy said.

"High as a giraffe, perhaps," Troy said, having now caught the giggles.

"Both of y'all," Dominick said, trying to stifle his own laughter, "ain't shit!"

"Let's just face the fucking facts," Troy said. "Men like us don't get married. We don't get happiness. We get . . . I don't know, but we don't get weddings."

"Somebody will marry you one day," Dominick said.

"Maybe I don't want to get married," Troy said.

"Is that because you think you won't or because you haven't found the right one?"

"I'm tired of looking."

"What about Roderick?" Dominick asked.

Remy snorted.

"Excuse me?" asked Troy.

"You talk about a dog? That nigga is a full-bred canine," Remy said.

"Remy, stop," Dominick said.

"The word you were looking for is *purebred*," Troy said, rolling his eyes.

"I'm just telling the truth. He stays out all night, doesn't text you back. Get rid of him, Troy. I keep telling you."

"Why don't you check your phone again to see if Roland texted you?" Troy asked.

Dominick stumbled over and sat on the floor next to Troy's chair, just as the playlist flipped to "Isn't It a Shame?"

"Don't listen to him, Troy," Dominick said. "He's drunk."

"And you are, too!" Troy said. "While you were in New York having the time of your life on Broadway, we've been struggling over here!"

"I struggled too. I was in a relationship with an unfaithful boyfriend I thought I was going to marry. And that's why I don't want to talk about weddings."

Troy burst into full-blown laughter.

"You the one who asked about weddings, dumbass!" he said.

Remy and Troy laughed while Dominick's eyes started to warm.

"Are you crying?" Troy asked.

"No," Dominick said. "I'm fine. I'm fine."

He turned away from the two boys and squinted his eyes hard. It was the first time he'd started to cry in years. And damn if Patti, Nona, and Sarah weren't right on time.

Isn't it a shame you have to laugh before you cry?

CHAPTER SIX

You know, when Coleman Young said for all the pushers and muggers to hit Eight Mile Road, I wish he would've included these dusty, emotionally unavailable, won't-text-back-ass bums with them. Neither Roland nor Terrell has responded to my messages, and I'm irritated. I don't know what type of time they on. I mean shit, you ain't fuckin' with no broke-ass dude without a job here. My ass is good, the dick is good when it wants, I stay in shape, I'm never out here looking like a rat, I'm pleasant to talk to, and believe it or not, I actually am a nice and considerate person. How these dudes have their phones on all day and can't text back? And me, double text a man? *A man?* You got me real fucked up.

And as if I wasn't already worked up today for this meeting with the McQuerry son to talk about the new development. He's younger than me, but he's always going on about how he and I are the same age. He doesn't know there's a huge difference between us eighties millennials and those from the nineties. But my plan is to go to the barber, then scope out the site for the townhouses this morning—they're right next to Mahaffey and I wonder if I could stop in and see Troy during his planning period—and then meet the McQuerry son for lunch. I'll get an Asian salad, and he'll probably order all appetizers and sides and talk about how cool the bar is down the street because it's also an arcade. And if this muhfucka don't look exactly like Chris Farley, chile. I just keep telling myself it's about the money and the business. Nothing else.

I can't get to where I need to be unless I have meetings like this, with white suburban men like this.

But before that, I need to get prepared. I always get breakfast at the fancy bagel shop in Corktown even though I know I'm going to be one of two Black people in the whole place. I'm going to be the only one in line, too, and I'm guessing some white woman from the suburbs will try to cut in front of me because I'll be standing just a little too far away from the person in front of me (I cherish my personal space, and plus I don't want these folks to be all scared that a Black man is getting too close to them—such is life), and I'll have to say, "There's a line here," and she'll give the, "Oops, sorry 'bout that!" and nervously walk behind me. I'll order strawberry schmear—God, when did we start calling it that?—on a plain bagel, with a sea salt chocolate chip cookie and a blood orange Pellegrino. The whole deal will cost sixteen dollars because that's how much bread, water, and spreadable cheese costs in New Detroit.

When I finally place my order, I can practically hear the cashier's laugh lines stretching along the edges of her mouth as she smiles. She's one of those white girls who's so nervous about making a mistake and being called a gentrifying racist that she's going to go all the fuck out to make sure this strawberry *schmeeeeear* bagel comes out just right. I feel sorry for her but only just a little bit—maybe this is some form of reparations.

Just when I think there's no one here that I know, I feel a tap on the shoulder and turn around to see Felix Gianopolous in line behind me. I keep forgetting he lives in Woodbridge, not that far away. Part of me wants to say a quick hello and leave, but for some reason, I feel obligated to be a little nice.

"Hey, man. What's going on?" he asks.

"Not a whole lot," I say. I take my can of Pellegrino out of the fridge and move to the side while I wait for my order. "You having breakfast?"

"Yeah. Want to join me?"

I knew he would ask.

"You sure you have time?"

Felix Gianopolous is not the kind of guy who should be attracted to me, but for some reason, he is. He's half-Black, half-Greek, and he grew up in one of the Grosse Pointes. I don't even know how you come up with someone with his lineage, 'cause it wasn't *that* long ago you couldn't even be in an interracial marriage in GP. But then again, this is Southeast Michigan, ground fucking zero of beige babies. That's what my grandmother used to call them, and if you think that's offensive, take it up with her and not me.

Since Felix socializes mostly with white boys, I assumed that's who he's attracted to. But he followed me on Twitter about a year ago and slid into my DMs soon after that.

"I really like your thoughts on Detroit. You make people like me think and see things differently. Your voice is needed.—Felix G."

Then, later that day, I got another message, this time on Grindr, from a headless torso.

"And you're handsome, too," it said.

"Who is this?" I responded.

"It's Felix, better known as @giannybgoode. I messaged you on Twitter earlier."

I considered blocking him right then and there. The fuck? But I was intrigued. Neither his Twitter nor Grindr had any readily identifying information, but I knew there couldn't be that many Felixes in Detroit, so I punched his name into Facebook, and when I saw "Felix Gianopolous" pop up with fifteen friends in common, I connected the dots. His profile photo was black and white, and he was holding a bass because, after I googled him—his Facebook account was so locked down I couldn't find out much—I saw that he played in a local band, the Kinsmen, which *Detroit Hotline* had ordained as the heir apparent to the White Stripes.

That "you're handsome" threw me for a loop. I mean, hell yeah, a bitch looks good. But this guy who thought so? Beyond the hair, he had nice eyes, nice eyebrows, and nice skin. His body wasn't so bad, either.

Troy said Felix looks like somebody named Shuggie Otis, but I think he's got this DeBarge thing going on. Problem is, I've been trying to feel the beat of the rhythm of his night for a minute now and can't seem to close the deal. We started the usual dance to the melody: back-and-forth Grindr messages (no nudes), and he added me on Facebook. Then the music stopped. We'd been making plans to see each other for like, three years now, but he always ghosted, which made me wonder if he really had time to have a bagel with me today.

"I do have time," he says. "Let's sit down."

"You know, if I sit down now, I'll never get up. I hate to eat and run, but I've got to get a haircut, and then I've got a meeting."

I could just see the younger McQuerry's face if I strolled into the restaurant twenty minutes late. This deal was already delicate, and I didn't want to make it any harder than it had to be.

"Oh yeah, you're a busy guy," Felix says.

"So are you! It seems like you're always on tour."

"Yeah, we're actually going to Europe in two weeks."

"Really? Wow." I'm faking it.

"Yeah. Our manager gets us a lot of shows outside the city. People outside Detroit love Detroit bands. When I come back, we should get that drink we've been talking about," he says.

"Yes, that drink *you've* been talking about for how long?"

"Yeah . . . I know. But really this time."

I've been "sup'd" and "how are you tonight-ed" by numerous guys on the apps. But I'm special. Not the average kind who'll accept any line. Felix is one of the few who have made it to Facebook friend status. And even though he's annoying, he's persistent. And I *still* haven't been on a real date in God knows how long. Men in Detroit just don't believe in taking each other out for a good time. And if this guy from the suburbs is even giving me the slightest inkling that we might go out together in public, I'll take it.

It was inevitable. I knew once I started getting my hair cut at a place advertising itself as "DETROIT'S BEST BARBERSHOP FOUR YEARS IN A ROW!" despite having only been open for exactly four years, a white man was going to end up cutting my hair. In thirty-three years on this earth, I've never let anyone other than a Black man touch this head.

I've never been faithful to one particular barber. If anything, most of the barbers I go to aren't any different from half the men I've dated: unreliable, full of excuses, all talk, and only available at their convenience. But I've always stayed with Black barbers. Just like I've always stayed with Black men, even if they're disappointing sometimes.

Still, I come to this shop just because it's the Detroit thing to do now. It's the Detroit thing to go to conference buffets at Slows, to go on dates at Ottava Via, and now, for me, to get my hair cut where Black and white barbers coexist and where the white customers wear flip-flops while getting their Machine Gun Kelly trims. The fuck is this, some interracial BoRics?

When I get to the counter, the guy at the front desk—and I never could have imagined going to a barber in Detroit with a front desk—tells me my regular dude has called in sick today. But he says another barber, Harley, can line me up. The name sounds ambiguous, and I pray that he's Black, but when one of the tatted-up white guys comes out to greet me, I think I'm going to swallow all the oxygen in the lobby. There's no turning back though. Mr. Detroit cause a scene in this we-are-the-world salon? Lord knows if I were to pitch a bitch, someone would capture it on video, it would go viral, and *Detroit Hotline* would get a bunch of pageviews off my name. Let me just get this over with.

They make all these beard balms and oils here, and the place smells like lemongrass and a bunch of other "essential" shit. I'm so used to what a real, Black barbershop smells like: hairspray, grease, and whatever's in the takeout container someone's eating. I've always loved smelling the heat from the clippers—you know how you can smell heat? That particular hot smell where it doesn't smell like paper or fire burning, but you feel something in your nose that suggests these clippers might go dead if they get any hotter. In this barbershop, there are no posters of all the different Black haircuts, and there's no pressed-wood coffee table from the mid-1990s with stacks of *BLAC*, the *Chronicle, Ebony, Entertainment Weekly* (addressed to one of the barbers' wives), and a few stray *King* magazines from 2004 that had somehow survived. Never in my life would I have expected to see dudes getting tapered to the tune of Peggy Lee coming out of Sonos speakers, but here the fuck we are.

I can't help but feel that if this McQuerry deal goes through—and they seem pretty dead set on making it happen—that I'm just clearing space in the city for more barbershops like this. In this neighborhood now, except for Motor City Wine and the little ramen place next door, I hardly feel welcome. Almost every neighborhood in Detroit has an identity because it knows exactly what it is. Corktown doesn't know *what* the fuck it is. Half the people who live here are angry all the time because rents keep going up and Ford is moving into the train station, and the other half don't even know Detroit. They're in their own little Corktown world, unaware of the rest of the city around them. The only Black people who live here are still in the projects, and you sure enough don't see them buying $15 cocktails at Sugar House.

Getting your beard done up at a Black barber is the closest thing to a hood spa treatment. It's basic as all fuck: all they do is steam a damp towel, get it as hot as they can, and wrap it around your face to soften the hairs. It's brief, maybe about a minute and a half, but it always brings me that much needed calm. Then they put on the shaving cream—also warm—and massage it in just enough before going over your sides with the razor. And it glides so smooth.

Harley is too quick. Instead of a razor, he uses electric clippers over my face, moving up and down as if he were sanding wood. By the time he's done with my head and face, I'm off the chair in fifteen minutes. I guess I look good.

I leave the shop. Because of Harley's quick work, I know I still have plenty of time before I have to meet Chris Farley McQuerry for lunch, but I check the time on my phone anyway.

When the screen lights up, I see a text from Felix: "Show me a pic of the cut?"

I send him a selfie. A few seconds later, he reacts with a tapback heart. Fine. Maybe I'll give him another chance.

CHAPTER SEVEN

Ever since Roderick and Troy had discovered the joys of fucking each other while they were high on cocaine, they decided to make it a Saturday morning tradition. Roderick had only tried coke a few times but felt comfortable using it with Troy. And Troy mandated that the only time they'd do it was on Saturday mornings. No more than that, even though it was common knowledge that coke was passed around Roderick's warehouse to keep up with Amazon's demand.

The first time, they snorted if off Troy's nightstand. Once, midway through intercourse, Roderick pulled his dick out from Troy's ass, wiped it off, and set a bump on his still-erect shaft. Another time, they mixed poppers and coke, which led to them fucking in a haze for about an hour and passing out for twice as long.

This Saturday, they skipped the ritual, though. Roderick couldn't stop talking about his name-change ceremony at Taking Back Detroit, an activist group that had been taking up more and more of his time of late.

The group had started with a Facebook video. Four years ago, a hooded man, the thirty-seven-year-old Diallo Holmes, beard specked with gray, held his arm outstretched, filming himself as he stood in front of a dilapidated house on Manistique Avenue, where his grandmother lived.

"My grandma has lived here all her life!" he said. "Since 1958! And they're kicking her out because she didn't pay her water bill!"

The water department had been such a mess for years that hundreds of residents had stopped paying their bills but hadn't been disconnected from service. After the city's bankruptcy, though, every department in the city was looking at their revenue collection systems with new eyes. The water department had begun cracking down on residents with missed payments, sometimes even putting liens on homes where folks hadn't paid up.

"This is what they want for the new Detroit," Diallo said, as court-ordered workers in blue jumpsuits moved his grandmother's possessions into the street. "They prey on people who have given their blood, sweat, and tears to the city of Detroit and kick them aside like dirt. Like garbage. Like their lives never mattered. And now you have another empty house. This is all part of the grand plan to kick all the hardworking African Americans out of Detroit in favor of the new Detroit. *Down*town. *Mid*town. And what do you see in those places, Detroit? What do you see? You see white billionaires down there living it up like it's nothing. Folks are out here struggling, hungry, getting put out of their homes for three dollars and some change. All for what? So that the white people can take over. They got a whole plan downtown in city hall and Detroit Future City to push all the Detroiters, the real Detroiters, out so they can bring the new Detroit in. Old Detroit out, new Detroit in. Well, I'll tell you this, not again. It's time for us to take back the city. Take back Detroit!"

A few weeks later, a loose collective of equally angry east-side Detroiters, led by Holmes, began meeting at an empty storefront on Jefferson Avenue. They made plans to run candidates for public office, wreak havoc at city council meetings, raise money for the poor, and even load up on weapons for war (should it come to that). Holmes officially changed his name to King Musa, echoing Mansa Musa of Mali, and encouraged his followers to adopt African names that recalled power, wealth, and pride. Taking Back Detroit was distrustful of corporations and suspicious of the foundations that now had their names across every new project and initiative in the city. And they were growing, their latest recruit being a young Amazon warehouse worker named Roderick Still, who was deeply interested in spreading the group's gospel in Romulus.

Once, before they were official, Roderick had taken Troy to a Taking Back Detroit meeting as a date. They got coney after. In between their meal of wingdings, all flats, fried hard, with coney ranch on the side, Troy couldn't stop talking about what King Musa had said. He was hooked and wanted to become an official member. After all, he had tried getting involved in other ways to have a say in Detroit's future, but it seemed like all the loudest voices lately were white.

And now, as whispers about the Mahaffey School's fate were getting louder, Troy was thinking seriously about joining Taking Back Detroit too. The school was close to where some of the moneyed Detroiters like Troy's father lived, but it was also in proximity to Eastern Market, which was changing fast. Development was creeping northeast from downtown to Eastern Market to the exact lot where Mahaffey stood. It seemed that after every discouraging meeting with the principal or the school's board members—more bullshit talk about strategic plans and feasibility studies—Troy would drive home and see a new sign saying "Coming Soon" or "Leasing Now." One by one, the buildings around the school were all getting sold. There was talk about a teardown, which would mean the kids would be dispersed to other charter schools around the city that were willing to absorb them. Troy was beginning to think it was only a matter of time.

He had already been to meetings with the Islandview Residents' Association, the Charlevoix Street Block Club, and the People for McDougall-Hunt. And when Marlie and Noelle had invited him to another neighborhood meeting at the big Catholic church on Mt. Elliott, he soon found out it had been organized by the Detroit Coalition for Action and Progress, whose founders were all white.

It was at that meeting that Troy realized that the white millennial socialist in Detroit cares not for Black liberation but only for the vanity of Black association. In the last few years, he'd seen these kind of upstart white Detroiters everywhere, playing trap music at Honest John's, pissing in the alleys between Corktown bars. They were the ones on Facebook ranting about affordable housing, completely unaware that their own presence was the reason the goddamn prices were going up. On Reddit they'd ask if anyone knew of any cheap rentals in Islandview, Midtown, or Woodbridge. "They're just so friendly over there," people would post, but Troy knew that was just millennial white code for "these Blacks probably won't rob you."

These millennial white socialists wouldn't last a day in Remy's old hood, he thought. *They'd be shook going down Hayes, and they'd clutch their pearls if they ever went deep into Southwest down by Dearborn Street, where the rhythm of truck traffic and the coughs of toxic smoke towers have been in asthma-inducing harmony for decades.*

The truth, which came closer to light the more Troy thought about it, was that these people only wanted to liberate a certain kind of Black person—that is, the convenient kind. Their mission always began with the Black people right around them, whether those same Black folks accepted the mission or not.

Other than the few white friends he had, Troy was reaching the end of his patience with Caucasians. But it finally felt like things were aligning in a good way, even if it was a bit fraught. Dominick was back, which meant Troy had one more Black friend. And he and Remy were close, though as Troy saw it, Remy sometimes seemed more interested in preserving his relationship with money and getting laid every other night than in maintaining their friendship. Remy was dismissive of Troy's growing concerns about Detroit's future, about the east side's future, and about Mahaffey's future. Troy had noticed that when he and Remy got together for drinks, his friend talked less and less about work—he just said things were busy and changed the subject. Troy couldn't help but feel that Mr. Detroit might even be one of the people behind all the changes going on. He encouraged Remy to make sure the majority of his clients were buyers of color, but every time he looked up, it was another gay white couple buying in Boston-Edison, a single white woman buying in Lafayette Park, or an empty-nester older white couple buying downtown.

"Remy, can't you, for once, try to sell to people like us?" he had pleaded. "Can't you stop talking about commissions and champagne? And if you're so focused on trying to nail down that flight attendant and so hung up over that dullard you went to high school with, why are you still taking dick from all over the city?"

Dominick would never. Dominick had sense. *If only I could get Remy to think more like Dominick*, Troy thought. Then it would just be about figuring out what to do with Roderick.

Because even though Roderick was over the moon about today's Taking Back Detroit meeting, Troy couldn't help but notice his hesitation when Troy suggested he go in support. Roderick finally gave in, but he said he was going out with some of the Taking Back Detroit warriors after, so they drove in separate cars.

———————————

"Roderick brought me here," Troy told King Musa, excitingly dapping him up as people began filing into the meeting. "I teach at Mahaffey, and we could definitely use some help. I'd also love to have you come speak to the kids one of these days."

"Brother Troy," Musa said, placing a hand on his shoulder and pointing to Roderick. "When a brother or sister joins Taking Back Detroit, they take a name that reflects the African within. In these walls, Roderick is Kiburi."

"Kiburi?"

"That is his name now. Didn't you know about his naming ceremony?"

"I thought it was today. That's why he brought me here . . ."

"Maybe there's confusion. The naming ceremony was last night, in one of our members-only meetings. Today, Kiburi is being presented as a board member." King Musa paused. "But you should know, just as a precaution, this business of yours is not welcome here, brother."

Troy took a small step back.

"What do you mean?"

"Kiburi's lifestyle is not something we discuss. He is welcome because he will advance the cause in Romulus. You're welcome because of your role at the school and your clear desire to see real change in Detroit. But you should know that one of our primary missions is to advance, strengthen, and protect the Black family."

"I'm not sure I understand."

"The Black family unit is this: The Black man leads. He provides food and shelter. He trains up the child to become the leader."

Troy could feel the heat rising in his face.

"And what does a Black woman do?" he asked.

"If I may finish."

"Please."

"The woman protects the house. She raises the children. She provides for her family but in a different way. She is the guardian of the legacy. She walks behind in the shadows."

Troy looked at him quizzically. Out of the corner of his eye, he could see Roderick talking to a few other folks.

Is he ignoring me, he thought. *Did he know this would happen?*

"External forces for centuries have tried to destroy the Black family," Musa continued. "Slave owners sold us away. Now the government tears us apart, and the police kill us. In order for the Black race to progress, we must return to the unit. The family unit. That is what we're about here."

"I agree Black families are under siege," Troy said, "but I'm not sure what this has to do with me getting involved and helping the cause."

"If you are a homosexual, there is no way for you to create a family. So you can be down, but know that we do not discuss those lifestyles in these walls."

"There are other couples here."

"Yes. Those couples will make families."

"So I have to have a family in order to get respect?"

"You have my respect. Everyone has my respect. And if you were to make a family with a Black woman, that would be admirable. But in order to protect the Black family . . ."

"I get it," Troy said, walking off to find a seat.

After the meeting, Troy returned home to sit alone in his bed, cold and limp. He'd gone bloodless after Musa's rejection and Roderick's refusal to come to his support. He'd driven home in silence. Roderick had texted that he was getting some green tea shots at Minnie's downtown with some TBD folks and that he'd meet up with him later for dinner. Hours had passed since then. He called Roderick twice—no answer. He texted, "please call me if you get this," but there was no sign Roderick had read the message.

Troy's stomach rumbled, a stern reminder that he hadn't eaten anything all day. He dragged himself out of bed and got some Better Made Hot BBQ chips from the kitchen. The bag was near empty—Roderick's doing. It was too late to order food from one of the delivery apps; drivers in Detroit didn't stay out late, and there weren't enough restaurants in the city to support the app-delivery economy anyway. He considered going on a quick run through the McDonald's drive-through. Then he remembered he had a boyfriend in a car out there on the road somewhere.

He texted, "Could you bring me some food on the way back from wherever you are?"

That "wherever you are" was meant to start an argument. Because as soon as Roderick came through the door, Troy would have questions at the ready. Top among them would be either "Where the hell have you been?" or "You couldn't say anything?" He was still trying to decide which one he would ask when he heard Roderick's key in the lock an hour later.

"I got food. Popeye's," Roderick said.

"Thanks. Where were you?"

Roderick sighed and put the food on the dining room table, unpacking its contents.

"You know how those shots at Minnie's are. We drank a little too much, so one of them drove my car to his place in Livonia so I could sleep it off. I got a nap in."

"All you did was sleep?"

"Yeah, I swear."

"Sleeping. In Livonia. I didn't even know you had friends in Livonia."

"I have a lot of friends. You just haven't met them," Roderick said, cracking open a biscuit and putting honey sauce on it.

"So while I was worried about you, wondering if you were dead in an alley somewhere, you were sleeping in Livonia. I was calling and texting you over and over, and you were sleeping in Livonia. I was over here going crazy, driving myself insane and wondering what the hell was wrong, and all the fucking while, you were sleeping in Livonia."

"I'm sorry, OK? We were just chilling and then, all of a sudden, I woke up on the couch because I was dead asleep."

"I'm sure."

"You don't believe me?"

"How about you just go back to wherever you were in Livonia then?"

"You're throwing me out?"

"Hell yeah, I'm throwing you out. Get your shit and leave. Want me to get it for you?"

"You're being ridiculous, bro. Calm down."

"Calm down? You need to get your shit before," Troy said, pointing at Roderick as he walked closer.

Roderick grabbed Troy's arms and pulled him in for a kiss.

"What are you doing?"

"Chill," Roderick said.

"Get off me! What do you think this is?" Troy said, pushing him away.

"Come here."

"Not gonna work this time. Get your shit."

"Come here."

"You think this is a game? Shit, I'll show you better than I can tell you."

Troy walked to the kitchen, pulled a Hefty bag from under the sink, and went into the bedroom. One by one, he loaded up T-shirts, jeans, shoes—anything that belonged to Roderick.

"Fuck are you doing? Don't do that!"

"I just told you, if you don't get it, I will!"

Roderick took the bag from Troy's hand, grabbed him by the arm, and shoved him hard into the closet door, holding him against it.

"What's wrong with you?" he screamed.

"Get off me!" Troy yelled.

Roderick wrapped his hand around Troy's neck and pushed hard, his full weight pressed up against Troy's body. He slowly moved his hand up to Troy's jawline, shutting his mouth. Roderick's eyes widened.

"Say I won't, bitch," he said. "Say I won't."

Troy struggled. He kicked. But Roderick was standing on his feet, and his weight was too much. Troy had nowhere to go. He was trapped. All he could do was stare into the combustible look in Roderick's eyes.

Ten minutes later, Troy was arranging two lines of coke on a perfume mirror that had belonged to his mother. Roderick was gone, and the street outside was still. Troy reached for his phone and dialed. Ignoring the fact that it was nearly midnight, he could always rely on Gregory—or Gogo as everyone called him—an old boyfriend who hadn't worked out, though the two of them had stayed friends.

"Hello?"

Troy startled at the unfamiliar voice on the other end of the line.

"Uh, hi—I might have the wrong number. Is this Gregory's phone?"

"It is. Who is this?"

"This is Troy. Who's this?"

"Don't worry about who this is," the voice said.

Troy heard another voice in the background, this one more familiar. Then he heard a muffled, "Who the fuck is Troy?"

Gogo's voice finally came through.

"Troy, I'm sorry. Can I call you back?" he said.

"I'll be OK. Have a good night."

"Troy, wait—"

Troy ended the call. Five minutes later, he got a text: "That was Anthony, the new boy. I'll tell you about it later. Don't be upset, but he gets jealous. I'll call you in the morning after I calm him down. I already know what you're thinking, but don't."

Troy switched his phone to silent, turned it over, and put it on the nightstand. Then he snorted two more lines, looked in the mirror above the dresser, and stared at himself for exactly six minutes before he lay down on the floor in front of his bed and groaned an excruciating, elongated "fuuuuuuck!" Then, bewildered over his current circumstances, he started laughing hysterically.

CHAPTER EIGHT

For almost as long as he'd been in the advertising world, Dominick had been subjected to regular diversity trainings, minority employee seminars, and inclusive networking events. Larger corporations wanted to put on a good face to show they cared about recruiting (and occasionally, if they were in the mood for it, retaining) people of color. And Tandy and Simms had been no different. As part of all this, Dominick had once volunteered at a job fair for Black advertising majors at Howard where he met Monique Chambers, who worked in human resources at GearWorks, a Tandy and Simms subsidiary so named because of its proximity to the Motor City. Monique was from Detroit, which meant she and Dom hit it off right away. They added each other on LinkedIn and promised to keep in touch if anything professionally interesting ever came up.

Now Dominick was cashing in on that promise. At a gas station on the Pennsylvania Turnpike on his way from New York to Detroit, he had messaged Monique. He didn't tell her the exact circumstances of his new situation, and she was surprised to hear he was interested in coming back to Detroit. But she said GearWorks had a temporary opening, and she would take care of him.

"Have you written for any automotive-related accounts before?" asked

Caroline Werth, the fortysomething, autumn-bobbed head of HR at GearWorks.

"I have, actually," Dominick said. "When Tandy and Simms won the Cadillac account, I assisted on some campaigns there."

He was dressed simple and clean: Plain white oxford—none of his Bleecker Street finery for a job interview—with a black-and-white Ben Sherman plaid tie with streaks of lavender and teal, and black slacks over Donald J. Pliner loafers. He kept his feet flat on the ground just in case someone tried to make out the name on the soles.

"I see your background is primarily in luxury accounts," Caroline said.

"True. I know there's a stigma around luxury, but every brand has a story. We really did a lot, in my opinion, to make luxury more accessible to everyone by showing the real story behind each brand. It's about making it relatable."

"Oh, of course. I just want to make sure you know what you're getting into here."

Deep down, Dominick knew it didn't matter if you wrote copy for tool lubricants or anal lubricants. Good ad writers were the chameleons of the ad agency, people who could quickly make themselves knowledgeable about any subject and spin verbal gold.

He also knew why he was getting subjected to extra questioning. He was a single, male New York ad writer coming to the Midwest. In this industry, the only ones who moved inward from the coasts were married women who followed their husbands to another city and settled for a new job at the first available agency. Dominick had no kids and no wedding ring. Why would someone with two silver medals from Tandy and Simms want to slum it at GearWorks, situated in Birmingham, a dull, moneyed suburb a full half-hour from downtown Detroit?

And what to make of a Black copywriter, of which there were so few across the industry to begin with? Locally, GearWorks was not known for retaining Black employees. Although, as Dominick noticed when he walked through the building and saw a sea of gray hair, they also didn't look like they were known for retaining any employees born after 1980 either.

Monique had warned Dominick about all this in advance. She was selfish; another Black coworker in the office meant one more person to kee-kee with in the office cafeteria, one more person to head-nod with in the hallways and trade gossip about the Potomac housewives. But she also remembered how kind and earnest Dominick had been when they'd first met, how he was unlike some of the other brothers that worked in the field, those who pulled the ladder up behind them. *Dominick Gibson won't leave us behind*, she thought, and after she walked him to his car and said good-bye, she immediately went to Caroline's office and implored her to hire him. A day later, Caroline made Dominick an offer over the phone and asked him to come in for orientation on February 1.

One hell of a diversity hire, Dominick thought, *starting on Black History Month*.

The headshot he took for his ID badge was listless, worse than any driver's license photo, but when the photographer asked if Dominick wanted a reshoot, he declined. Dominick then signed a tome of paperwork without looking at any of it: the IT policy, the parking policy, the trade secrets policy, the release for filming in case he was filmed, even the allergy-to-pets policy for Bring Your Pets to Work Day. Then came the unnecessary swag from HR: an orange, recyclable-mesh tote that included a GearWorks-branded golf polo (size XXL), a GearWorks-branded miniature portable speaker, four GearWorks-branded pens and a GearWorks-branded journal, and—new!—a GearWorks-branded rubber card pocket that could affix to the back of a cell phone.

Monique navigated him through a sea of cubicles to his desk. He set the bag of swag by his computer and sat down. He was now an official GearWorks employee.

He logged in to his computer with no direction or task and instinctively opened Microsoft Outlook. His email had already been set up, and he saw four unread messages, including one with a subject line screaming "WELCOME!!!!"

> Hello, Dominick! I'm Krystin Powers, and I'm an account manager for MarineTech, one of GearWorks's priority clients! I understand you're filling in for Sally while she's on maternity leave. MarineTech was one of her beats, so let's chat today at some point when you get settled in. Please stop by my desk on Lafayette Avenue at 11 a.m.
> Best,
> -KP

To ensure everyone knew GearWorks had authentic ties to the Motor City, all the workspaces were named after prominent Detroit streets. Lafayette Avenue was accounts, Vernor Highway was the creative studio, and the copywriters sat on Fort Street. There were maps posted all around the building with these details, though they looked nothing like an actual map of Detroit. Dominick also noticed that none of the street names were anywhere on the west side or too far east—the *hoods*. Joy Road? Dexter? Cadieux? *Forget it.*

To prepare for his first meeting, Dominick googled MarineTech and learned they produced amphibious vehicles that could travel on land and in water. *Who buys these things?* he thought, but before he could investigate any further, there was a tapping at his cube.

"Hi, there! Are you . . . Dominick?"

"Yes."

"Hi! I'm Esmeralda. I'm going to be handling traffic for you."

Besides Monique, Esmeralda Maranado was one of the few people of color at GearWorks, and her sunny face, much brighter than the miles of fluorescent tubes that hung overhead, was a welcome sight to Dominick.

"Good to meet you," Dominick said. "Yeah, I'm just getting settled in. . . . It looks like I'm working on MarineTech?"

"Yeah," Esmeralda said with a slight laugh. She leaned in. "They're struggling with this account. I'm so sorry you got stuck with this. I hope you don't mind, but I peeped your LinkedIn this morning. How'd you end up moving to Detroit?"

Dominick readied the answer he'd been practicing ever since he'd left New York.

"I missed it here," he said, "and I missed my family. Plus, New York was getting expensive."

"Your family's from here?"

"Yeah, my whole family lives here. My parents are starting to get older now, so."

"But you don't look so old."

"I—well, if you say so."

Dominick had a keen sense of when a woman was flirting with him. And he had developed a practice of safe rebuttal before finally answering the inevitable question about a significant other with male pronouns. The fun part was tallying the distance between the woman's first glance and his first disclosure.

"I'll introduce you to Krystin and Kristen," Esmerelda said, as they walked back through the sea of cubicles. She lowered her voice to a whisper. "They manage the MarineTech account. I know, right? Krystin and Kristen! Two basic white girls, but you'll learn the difference."

"Uh, speaking of," Dominick said in an even lower tone. "How many . . . how many people of color work here?"

"Look around. You, me, and my little circle over there," Esmeralda said.

She pointed to her desk in a trio of cubicles where Dominick saw two other women, both Black.

"The other two traffic managers over there," Esmerelda said, "Crystal and Fallon."

Dominick, Crystal, and Fallon, Dominick thought to himself, the opening horns of the *Dynasty* theme now playing in his head. We're all eighties babies, and Black women who became mothers in that decade are undefeated.

"I take it you met Monique in HR. And there's another Black writer, Will. We also just hired this Asian girl to work in art, but she doesn't really speak English and barely talks to anyone. And, well, that's about it for this floor."

"How do you deal?"

"I'm Puerto Rican and they still think I'm Mexican," Esmeralda said. "But every time I try to get into another agency . . .." She stopped and threw her hands up. "What can you do, you know?"

They walked and talked, and Esmeralda was able to squeeze in that GearWorks wasn't all bad—the benefits were good and sometimes the cafeteria had good soups. She also let Dominick know what to expect on the MarineTech account: the company needed a new product guide for the new Landphibian 5000 model; new copy across the MarineTech website landing pages; copy for a flotation device warning label; and a dozen lines for various social media ads. In one of Dominick's last assignments for Tandy and Simms, he had brainstormed a campaign for a Sonoma County vineyard, a lengthy process that had included a two-week sojourn to Northern California. Now, he was writing instruction manuals and warning labels for floating cars.

Esmeralda leaned toward Dominick's right ear, just close enough to pick up a scent, his usual YSL Rive Gauche Pour Homme.

"We've got company," she whispered.

Coming down the aisle, Dominick saw two white women of equal height, blonde hair-length, and build. As they approached, he focused on their eyes and noticed an age difference. Both had crow's feet, something Dominick scanned everyone for, as it was a worry for himself (*all the white gays in Chelsea probably own stock in Clarins*, he thought), but one had deeper lines than the other. He pegged the smoother one at about twenty-seven and the older one closer to his age.

"Ez," one of them said, "do we have someone new in the office?"

"Yes, Krystin—this is Dominick. I think you're scheduled to meet with him now?"

"Oh, you're Dominick! I'm Krystin Powers," said the younger of the two. "Did you get my email?"

"Uh . . ." Dominick said, realizing he had to lift out of his morning-long fog. "Yes, I did. Nice to meet you."

"I'm Kristen, account manager," said the older one. "Welcome aboard!"

"Krystin and Kristen, both account managers?" Dominick asked.

"*Right?*" they said in unison.

"I mean, total coincidence," Krystin said. "But Kristen here is my rock. She knows it all. I'm just following in her footsteps."

"Oh, stop," Kristen said. "You're a boss and you know it."

"Ez, my dear? Can you do us a quick favor and reserve the St. Aubin pod for our meeting with Dominick here?"

"Once I get back to my desk, I can make sure it's not already reserved, or if you just wanted to check . . ."

"I know, Ez, but could you just do it on your phone quickly? It's almost 11:00 now."

Almost 11:00 now? Had time passed that fast? Dominick thought.

"Sure. You know what, why don't you just go right in? I'll take it from here."

"You're the best!" Kristen said as she made her way into the small conference room.

A few seconds later, Dominick's phone vibrated.

"This is Esmeralda," the text read. "I got your cell from your paperwork. Now you see what it's like for us here! Even though they do it, please don't call me Ez. I hate it so much lol."

The next ping on Dominick's phone that morning came from Facebook

Messenger. He opened it as soon as he left the meeting with the Krystin-Kristen duo.

"Hey you," it read. "Saw you were back in town. How long are you here for? Would love to catch up . . ."

The dot-dot-dot was annoying—*men who end sentences with ellipses need to get to the fucking point*, Dominick thought—but for Rico Martin, he'd forgive it. Dominick took a deep breath and tried to think of a proper, timely response to the man who had taken his virginity fifteen years earlier.

• • •

Dominick Gibson
How'd you know I was back?

Rico Martin
I follow Remy Patton on IG
He tagged you in a story
Didn't know you had fancy friends like that lmao

• • •

There were things Dominick had tried to forget about the summer he'd turned eighteen: the cracks in his parents' marriage growing visibly larger, his fear for his friends who entered the military after 9/11, and Platinum Fubu cargo shorts. But he'd never forget Rico. They had met on Black Gay Chat—Dominick often sneaked up late at night to the computer in his parents' home office to log on. Rico was an Eastern Michigan University senior home for the summer. He had a Lincoln LS—Dominick still didn't know how he was able to afford it—that he drove all over the city. They started chatting a week after Dominick's high school graduation, and two days after their first online communication, they exchanged cell numbers.

The emotional state of an eighteen-year-old baby gay can best be compared to a squirrel on a power line: moving far too fast along a tightrope with no preparedness for any kind of shock. On their first date, they went to see a movie at the Star Southfield. On their second date, they walked around Fairlane Town Center. On their third date, they started off at the walk-up Dairy Queen on Oakman and Wyoming, but then Rico said his mom was away at a conference with her church's congregation, so they went back to his house on Birwood and Thatcher and fucked.

Even if a gay man realizes he's a top after more experience, he never forgets his first dick. To this day, Dominick still kept Jennifer Lopez's "Secretly" in his music library, the song that was playing in the background as Rico, fully aware it was Dominick's first time, eased inside him after foreplay. There were a lot of firsts that night. Dominick's first kiss with a man. Dominick's first time performing oral (he was terrible, accidentally scratching Rico's penis with his teeth twice) and receiving it in return. Dominick's first time getting his asshole rimmed, even though he was too shy—and nervous of what lurked beneath—to reciprocate. And, as Rico's favorite slow jams played from Limewire, the first time he bottomed—face down, lying flat on Rico's bed, with enough Vaseline for a hood boxing match.

That summer, Dominick got his tongue pierced at Greenfield Plaza and hid it from his parents. He started long-distance chatting with another gay dude in Saginaw and bragged about his newfound sexual prowess. He stayed out late with Rico, smoked a lot of weed with some of his U of D classmates, and went to the Woodward for the first time.

That fall, he enrolled as a freshman at the Mecca. He kept in touch with Rico and made sure to get as much dick as he could during trips back home, and they had a magical winter break together. But that was their last hurrah. By sophomore year, Rico had moved to Chicago, and Dominick, who had stopped wearing his silly tongue piercing, wanted to try other dick, and maybe ass, too.

Thanks to Facebook coming around in Dominick's junior year, the two had technically never been disconnected, though it had been years since they'd seen each other.

Dominick sat at his desk in the GearWorks office. His computer screen was full of pictures of army green amphibious cars. They were some of the ugliest things he had ever seen.

He picked up his phone.

I bet he's still fine, Dominick thought, as he typed out another message. *And maybe I could bottom for the first time in God knows how long.*

They decided to meet at a pie shop near Remy's townhouse that the local foodies had been raving about. It felt good to take to Detroit roads again, and on his way there, Dominick gripped the wheel of the Marauder, blasting his own music through the aux cord in one of the baddest rides to ever come out of the Motor City. In Detroit, Dominick could drive how he wanted, when he wanted, where he wanted, and unlike driving through Pennsylvania and Ohio, he knew exactly where the state boys would be hiding. He could do ninety on the Lodge if he wanted to. Cruise along Outer Drive if he wanted to. Maybe fuck around and take 94 all the way to Chicago if he wanted to. But for now, it was just 94 to Van Dyke, all the way to the east side.

At the pie shop, two white women with pixie cuts—*Manic Pastry Dream Girls,* Dominick thought to himself—scurried around the open kitchen, kneading and creasing dough made from organic flour, peeling Georgia's juiciest peaches and coating them in ginger to the beat of St. Vincent playing from portable speakers. In the windows, through the bars that stretched their entire height (a reminder that any New Detroit spot is never too far from the Old Detroit hood), Dominick saw succulents potted in thrifted coffee mugs, along with the requisite "#blacklivesmatter" poster that hung in any Detroit restaurant owned by white people.

There was just enough whimsy in the shop that Dominick secretly wished he'd have a meet-cute there, that instead of meeting Rico, he'd run into his actual true love who would have to stop in front of the shop to fix a flat tire. Then again, do Black gays ever get the meet-cute? It's such a white, BuzzFeed-y thing, a romanticized image taken straight from the movies that has somehow become fodder for millennial writers in Brooklyn. But when he thought of himself and his friends, Dominick couldn't think of a single Black relationship that didn't have digital origins.

Dominick's phone pinged—a message from Rico.

"Running a little late. Be there soon. . ."

Still such a pretty boy, taking his time to get ready, Dominick thought.

He ordered a pour-over coffee and sat down. He pulled out his phone to remind himself what Rico looked like now, more than a decade after he last saw him. Light, smooth skin, and eyebrows with a distinctive, natural arch.

I can smell the Acqua di Gio already, he thought.

Twenty minutes later, with tepid coffee in hand and an urge to go back to the west side, Dominick got another text.

"Hey at the corner of Van Dyke and Vernor b there soon."

Did he get pulled over? Dominick thought. *OK, let's not overthink. Maybe he's got a good excuse.*

"OK. I'm here sitting inside," he texted back.

Three minutes later, Rico walked through the door.

"It's good to see you again," he said, giving Dominick a warm hug.

"Long time, no see. Want some coffee?"

"I would. You know, I've never been here before."

"Oh, where do you go?"

"You know what's good? The buffet at MGM Grand. We should go there."

Dominick laughed, albeit nervously.

"Maybe next time," he said.

"Oh, so there's going to be a next time?" Rico smiled. Dominick noticed he was missing a side molar.

"Uh . . . I assume so."

They each had slices of ginger-peach pie. Rico complained about the crust, then said it wasn't sweet enough. After four bites, he gave up.

"I can't wait for you to finally meet my mom," he said. "Now *she* can throw down on some peach cobbler."

"Your mom?" Dominick asked.

"Yeah, you're going to meet her real soon. She's the reason why I moved back from Chicago."

"Oh, really?"

"Yeah, really," Rico said, looking straight at Dominick. "You know, you're still so handsome. I'm so happy you came out to meet me."

"I am, too."

"Is that it?"

"What do you mean?"

"Do you think I'm handsome? Do you think I'm cute?"

Dominick found himself trying to compartmentalize several things at once: the man sitting before him, that man's distaste for what was actually an excellent slice of ginger-peach pie, and that man's already formed plans to introduce his mother to a relationship that didn't actually exist in the present moment—at least not to Dominick. And to boot, this man, who no longer had the devil-may-care attitude he had had at twenty-one when Dom first met him, but was now very much a man almost forty, might also be such an insecure narcissist that he needed to be told about his looks right here, right now, instead of assuming that because Dom was on the date in the first place, physical attraction was implied.

Dominick looked him in the eye. He was quick enough to realize that if their two faces weren't squared up, he'd be branded a liar.

"You are handsome, Rico," he said. "Very much so."

"Why did you hesitate?"

"I was caught off guard. You know you're handsome. You don't need me to tell you."

"But I do need you to tell me," Rico said, sipping his coffee. "I need you to be honest with me."

And I need you to show up on time, motherfucker, Dominick thought.

"I will be," he said. The words started to feel like wedding vows offered under duress.

"I've been lied to before by so many men. They only want one thing."

"Oh, I know," Dominick said.

"So what do you want?"

This was the question Dominick hated to answer. 'Cause to be real, at this point? The only thing Dominick *wanted* to do was fuck, because even though Rico's insecurities were projecting at warp speed, there was no denying that, missing tooth aside, the rest of him was aging into his late thirties just fine.

"It may sound kinda corny, but I want to feel like I'm valued."

"Is that it?"

"That's it," Dominick smiled.

"Come on."

"That's it," he laughed, trying to flirt and keep some semblance of mystery—but also as a defense. "What do you want?"

"I want someone to grow with. And maybe I could grow with you."

Dominick took a sip of his coffee.

I don't want to grow with a man. I want a grown man, he thought. *But maybe my biggest problem right now is overthinking things.*

———————————

Dominick followed Rico's truck to a familiar address. They parked side-by-side in the driveway, a Dodge Durango and a Mercury sedan. Straight up Detroit shit.

Maybe we'd have one of those three-wheelers in the garage for fun one day, Dominick thought. *Maybe this is my version of a meet-cute. Maybe now we're mature enough to not spend an endless amount of time talking and*

getting to know each other. Maybe, like the movies, this is where the two old
lovers reunite and pick up right where they left off.

Except, which movie was there where two Black men were doing this?

He tried to stop overthinking again as they made their way to the same bedroom where, in a way, it had all started. They were nude within seconds, hands and lips all over each other, their sweat building up despite the chill in Detroit's air outside.

"I've been thinking about this ass for a long time," Rico said.

"Mmm? Well, it's been a long time since I've bottomed. A *long* time."

"So it's tight?" Rico asked, moving the tip of an index finger inside Dominick's anus.

"Uh . . . yeah. So maybe we can just . . . " Dominick said, moving his hand away and leaning in for a kiss, "keep doing this."

They kissed again, fondling, limbs moving against each other. Rico bit into Dominick's bottom lip and held it in his teeth.

"*Ow!*" Dominick said.

"Man, you got soft," Rico said. "But I kinda like it, though."

Rico had never been this rough before.

But maybe I could learn to like it, too, Dominick thought.

Rico slapped Dominick's ass.

"I'mma have this again," he said.

"Until then, let me just . . ."

Dominick pecked Rico's neck, then each of his nipples. He moved his mouth down to his belly button and then began to suck Rico's dick.

"Yeaaaah," Rico moaned. "Hold on."

Rico reached inside the nightstand by the bed and took out a lighter, a half-smoked blunt, and a tube of cherry-flavored Anal-Ese.

"For later," he said.

"Anal-Ese?" Dominick said, incredulous. "You still use that?"

"It always works."

"I mean, I guess it worked when I was eighteen, but we're grown now.

Don't you have a silicone-based lube or even a water-based one?"

"What's your problem? You never used to complain before."

Dominick sighed.

"Light the blunt."

Maybe if I smoke, I'll relax, he thought. *Maybe I'll get him used to using a grown-up lubricant. Maybe I'll have to start being vers if this works out. Maybe I'll just ignore that disgusting strand of hair wrapped around the cap of fucking cherry-flavored Anal-Ese.*

"Keep sucking my dick while I take a hit. I love that shit."

Dominick obliged.

"Look up at me."

Dominick gave his best porn star gaze as Rico palmed the back of his head with one hand and took long pulls from the blunt with the other. It didn't take long for the room to be hotboxed—nor did it take long for Dominick's jaw to feel stiff.

"Baby, let me take a break," Dominick said.

"I was just about to come!"

"No, you weren't," Dominick said. "I know I'm not that good."

"Take that dick and hit me in the face with it."

"For real?"

"Yeah. Come here."

Dominick straddled Rico's chest and complied. Even though it seemed a little out of the ordinary, he figured it might lead to something better on a future date.

"Come on my face if you want," Rico said, smacking his own penis toward the crack of Dominick's ass.

"Let's come together."

"Can I come inside you?"

"*Maybe.* One day, when we get there, you can stick it in a little."

"Bet."

Dominick moved his hand up and down his shaft, positioning the head of his dick over Rico's mouth, his tongue out and ready to receive it.

"I'm close," Dominick said in a loud whisper.

"Come on," Rico said, furiously stroking his own dick and flicking his tongue.

Just as Dominick exploded all over Rico's face, the bedroom door swung open.

"What did I tell you about smoking in my house?!?"

Dominick awkwardly dismounted and covered himself with the first sheet he could find. Rico, his face now streaked with cum, covered his crotch with a pillow.

"Mom!" he yelled.

"This shit again? I told you about bringing these men over here!"

"Mom, get out!"

"This is my house, Ricardo! Clean the fuck up and get that boy out of here!"

"OK, I'm sorry!"

"It's nice to meet you, young man. I'm sure you're nice and all, but you need to leave."

Dominick fumbled around for his briefs but could only find his slacks. Through a haze of pot smoke and apologies from Rico, he made the split-second decision to go commando.

Ten minutes later, he was hitting speeds so high on the Lodge, he could have even outrun a state boy if he dared.

CHAPTER NINE

I always try to do my part along the way, so this time, instead of meeting the McQuerrys at one of those new open-concepts in Midtown, where you're forced to look at the line cooks in the kitchen like zoo animals, I insist we meet at this new Black-owned spot by Eastern Market. Now here's the thing about this new place: it's been open for a little bit now, but nobody talks about it. When I say "nobody," I really mean white Detroiters. We know about it because all the new Black restaurants in Detroit get famous through Instagram. It's like our own little secret negro network—a local *Green Book* if you will.

At least the playlist isn't bad. They're in here playing Phyllis Hyman's "You Know How to Love Me," a fucking *bop*, and when I look behind the bar, I see my girl Lonnie has his phone plugged into the sound system. If you go into a newer restaurant and hear some old-school bangers from the unsung divas on the speakers, you just know it's probably a gay Black man with the aux cord.

I order the white wine salmon burger with a Hennessy glaze—you know niggas love a salmon burger, so every Black restaurant has one. By the way, I don't drink Hennessy, or really any kind of brown liquor like that. And no, I ain't one of those "I'm not like other Black people" people either—I just don't like the shit. But I appreciate this place for having Hennessy at the bar 'cause you know how most of these *other* New Detroit places are: if they don't have Hennessy at the bar, they don't want your Black ass there. Think about it.

The father orders a pear and walnut salad with a Ciroc peach vinaigrette. And his son, my goodness. He orders the parsley butter parm calamari, the Crown Royal-infused sweet potato fries, stuffed mushrooms, two orders of Patron-lime crab cakes, and a side of Honey Jack mac and cheese.

"So this is what's going on," says the father, who's got slicked back salt-and-pepper hair. He's got on a navy blazer and just looks like he knows what the fuck he's talking about. "You know about the townhouses already, but I wanted to talk today because we're working on something new. For the plot of land next to the townhomes—and let's just say we're . . . in the process of acquiring the land right now—we've got a great idea. Picture this: a two-hundred-unit high-rise of microstudios."

The son smiles at me with the goofiest smile I've ever seen before diving back into his macaroni and cheese.

"Microstudios," I say. "I didn't realize that was part of the plan."

"Just came up. At this point, it's still very contingent. But it's a killer opportunity, and we just had to grab it."

"Interesting. Why those?"

His son stops stuffing his face long enough to actually contribute something to the conversation.

"Microstudios are hot," he says. "All the kids our age love them."

Here he goes with our ages again.

"Everybody wants to live small now," he continues. "We have the money to build now, and we're going to get it all back from these kids who want like some Japanese bedroom shit where everything is in one room and you got a tiny toilet."

"My son gets a little enthusiastic with his descriptions," the father says. "Don't worry about the microstudios—they'll be easy to sell, and the commissions will be out of this world. And in this market, we're thinking the townhouses could go for 300K each. Final price, of course, would be determined by the agent of record. So, what do you think?"

"Are you offering me to be the agent?" I ask.

"That's exactly what I'm doing. You know this neighborhood, you know this area. There's absolutely no one else we'd like to partner with on this deal."

I had had a feeling this was all going to happen, but now that it is, I am a little taken aback.

"I'm . . . I'm flattered. Wow. I've never been the agent of record for a new development."

"Really? You're a fucking rock star. You're Mr. Detroit!" the son says.

"I don't know what to say."

"It's easy. Say yes!" says the son, his mouth full of food.

"Well, yes, of course, yes," I say.

"Fantastic, Remy. Fantastic," the father says as he reaches his hand across the table. I shake it, impressed with myself that I haven't screamed right here in this restaurant. I can already see myself toasting about this tonight with the boys at Motor City Wine.

"All right, so," I say, "we're going to need a marketing campaign. Had I known that you were going to bring me this offer, I would have had some materials ready to go."

The father leans in toward me.

"*Well*," he says, "we've been trying to keep this low-key for now. I'll be perfectly up front with you. This development won't be popular."

"What do you mean?"

"We're going into a challenged area. You've seen the comps. Everything except West Village and Indian Village are below market over here. But with the way things are going downtown, we know eventually things have to come north. We want to get in on this now."

"So why won't it be popular?"

"This will be 100 percent market rate. We're not going to the city for anything. You know, the city will give you a break if you make some of new residences affordable. We do not want affordable at this time."

"Why not?"

"Look around. Housing here is already affordable. If people aren't taking advantage of it now, why should we go out of our way to make our new places affordable? Plus, we think the incomes we bring in with these new residences will balance out the neighborhood. We're talking about two hundred units—that's a lot of moneyed people moving into the area."

"You've got a point."

"That, and we're still trying to acquire the property for the second phase of the development."

"It shouldn't be that hard," I say. "Pretty much everything over there is empty except for the Mahaffey School."

The two men go silent.

Shit, I think. *Shit. Shit. Shit.*

"You're . . . you're going to build the microstudios where the school is?" I ask.

"I said this wasn't going to be popular. But that school is a teardown anyway—have you ever been inside? And U of D Mercy's strapped for cash and thinking of off-loading it," the father says.

"My friend teaches at that school."

"It's a charter school. They can easily relocate. Hell, maybe once we sell these places, we can even build a new school for them!" the father laughs.

"Two schools even!" says the son.

"Remy, listen," the father tells me. "This building could be a real gamechanger for this part of Detroit. How long has that part of the neighborhood been sitting there? Ten years? Fifteen? It's an eyesore, and we want to help."

Daddy has a point fasho. The hood isn't going to fix itself. We need more people to fix the hood. And besides, I got folks all the time who want to move into Indian Village but don't have Indian Village money. Troy's daddy has it. But these folks who come to me don't. And when I try to tell them to look outside the Village, they just run away.

White guys from the suburbs gotta save this hood. Goddamn. Well, they're not going to save it, like, *duh-da-da-daaaaaa! Super Caucasian!* It's just . . . damn. A Black developer could knock this shit out the park if he or she just had the means. But now here comes this no-job-too-big-no-job-too-small-we're-father-and-son-we'll-do-it-all duo to build these expensive-as-fuck-for-this-neighborhood townhouses. And they're asking me to be their Trojan horse.

I try everything I can not to look at the situation this way, but fuck it. I decide to do it. Troy will never let me hear the end of it, but what else am I supposed to do? Not make a living? And if I take my chance to get in on this, won't I at least be able to make sure Old Detroit stays in the game somehow? I tell myself to remind Troy that he's not paying diddly shit for the place he has now. Nobody is going to gentrify his building. And the McQuerrys are right—Mahaffey can move. It would probably be better if it did. The building is run-down anyway. The kids didn't deserve that. This is just one development, one market-rate thing. And hopefully, it will be the thing that gets everyone else in the neighborhood to get their shit together. Besides, a new development run by this Caucasian father and son is better than some empty building U of D Mercy's probably going to abandon anyway, isn't it?

The stuffed mushrooms that ol' boy is eating look good as hell, so I flag down the waiter and order a second round. I also ask him to bring over three bottles of Bell's Two-Hearted Ale to celebrate. White boys love that shit.

I had kept the rest of the day clear for family. There's nothing else I leave money on the table for. I drive to Annesha's house on Promenade and pull all the way up the driveway 'cause I'm not trying to have my windows busted out. Annesha greets me at the back door.

"Ooh, girl, you need some WD-40 for that screen," I tell her.

"I ain't got no time for that right now, come in," Annesha says.

I know she's about to go somewhere because her hair's in a high ponytail and she's wearing a shirt with buttons—which are holding on to her titties for all they're worth—on a weekend. All the women in this family ended up with big titties and asses, and fortunately for me, I got just enough smidgen of ass that I can pump up a little if I do squats when I go see my trainer. But Annesha only dresses up when she goes to church or the club. All the other times she's in her LPN scrubs.

"So, how are you?" I ask.

"I'm good. They keep trying to play me scandalous at work by giving me shifts they know I can't be on, but that's going to change. I'm looking at nursing school."

"Look at you."

"I'm serious," Annesha says, handing me a bottle of water. "Paris is getting older. I gotta pay for his college somehow. He's asking me for all kinds of things now I can't afford."

"Do you want me to—"

"I didn't say that," she says, cutting me off. "He is taken care of. Today I just need you to ride around with him for a little bit while I go to this block club meeting."

"What block club?"

"Apparently to get the mayor's attention, you have to start a block club, so some district manager from the city, someone or another, was over here going door to door, trying to get us to think about putting one together, so we're going to. The point is, a few of us want this neighborhood to get better, and the only way we do that is if we get together and solve some of these issues."

"I know you fuckin' lying."

"What?"

"You? Doing community service?"

"Shut up! Leave me alone."

"I'm just saying. Cognac queen, taking the crown off?"

"I'm trying to set an example. Shit, Paris is getting older now, and I don't want us to have to leave this neighborhood yet."

"I've been telling you, those co-ops over on Larned . . ."

"Not those. I still want a real backyard for my son to play in like we have now, and plus, I won't even be ready to buy anything until I start making more money, and I won't start making more money until I go to nursing school. I got a plan. I'm going to move to Westland as soon as he's old enough to start high school."

"Girl, ain't nothing good ever came out of Westland. Can we aim a little higher?"

"*Somewhere* off this block. And you can do what you want with this house. Either way, at least I'm going to try and make things *a little* better while I'm here."

"So why can't Paris go with you? To see the new and improved you?"

"Shut up! Can you just take him, please? I don't ask for much, but I need you to just this one time, Remy."

"He must be acting bad," I say, taking a sip of my water. I'm still a little tipsy from my celebration with the McQuerrys. "Paris! Come see your cousin!" I hear steps clomping down the stairs and Paris, who's eight, appears in the doorway and comes over to give me a hug.

"How's school?" I ask.

"It's good," Paris says. He's missing a tooth and is a little shy about his smile. "My teacher gets on my nerves sometimes, but I'm doing good."

"You too young for a teacher to be getting on your nerves."

"I'm grown," he says.

Me and Annesha start laughing.

"Boy, put your shoes on. You're going to go in just a minute," Annesha says.

"Paris, where do you want to go today?"

"Can we go to a sushi restaurant?"

"Where in the world did you get that idea from?" I ask.

"Because he's smart," Annesha says, putting her arms on Paris's shoulders. "Take him to that one place you took me. Downtown. Maury or whatever it was."

"Maru? OK, we can go to Maru." I look over at Paris. "You do know that sushi is raw fish, right?"

"So? I like raw fish."

"Go put your shoes on," Annesha says.

Paris runs back upstairs. I look directly at my cousin.

"How does this child already like sushi?"

"Because he saw you eating it, genius."

At Maru, I watch my eight-year-old cousin read each item on the menu as if he's reading an encyclopedia. I wonder if I was ever this intense at his age.

"And what will the young man be ordering?" the server asks.

"Could I please have the spider roll, the crispy wontons, and a Diet Coke?"

"You drink Diet Coke?" I ask.

"You have to drink Diet Coke, Cousin Remy. It's what everybody drinks."

All I could do was try not to laugh, because Dominick posted something in the group chat about white gays in New York and two kinds of coke: "In their twenties, they like Diet Coke. In their thirties, it's just coke."

"Well," I say to the server. "You heard the man."

"And for you, sir?"

"The caterpillar roll and two of the salmon roe. And we'll do edamame for an appetizer, thank you."

Paris pulls out his phone and turns the screen to me.

"Do you know this group? It's called LOONA. I love the choreo in this video."

"The choreography?"

"What's choreography?" he asks, sounding it out.

"That's what choreo is short for. Choreo and choreography are the same word, basically. What do you know about that?"

"It's dancing, duh! I know what it is."

As he's watching, I send a quick message to the group.

•••

> **Remy Patton**
> Y'all heard of this group Luna?
> Asian girl group with "choreo" according to my little cousin

> **Troy Clements**
> Korean girl group. Some of the kids
> at the school talk about them

> **Dominick Gibson**
> OMG, it's LOONA, not Luna. They're one of the
> biggest K-Pop girl groups in the world
> "Singing in the Rain" and "Egoist" are fucking BOPS
> #StanLoona

> **Remy Patton**
> My cousin seems to be obsessed

> **Dominick Gibson**
> She's got good taste

> **Remy Patton**
> He

•••

"Cousin Remy, I have a question," Paris says, putting down his phone. I can't even understand why this child has a phone in the first place. Who do eight-year-olds be talking to?

"What's that?"

"What's it like to be gay?"

I nearly choke on my Pellegrino.

"What do you mean?" I ask.

"Well, I asked Mom what it was like to be gay, and she said to ask you because you're gay. I just want to know what it's like."

I look everywhere around the restaurant except directly into my little cousin's face: at the ceiling, at the people next to us, at the chefs behind the bar. And then it all begins to add up. The Diet Coke, the stanning of a Korean girl group, the reason why we are here in this restaurant.

"Well," I say, taking a deep breath, "let me just say that being gay was not my choice. I was born like this. Everyone who is gay knows that they are when they're a kid."

"How did you know you were gay?"

I don't have the energy to tell him that in sixth grade, when I was going to that raggedy-ass Catholic school, the building was so decrepit that the boys didn't use the locker room to change for gym class and instead used an empty classroom, and that I always caught myself trying not to stare at the other boys in their Fruit of the Loom briefs. Nor did I tell him that when I had my first wet dream later that year, a girl wasn't in it.

"There wasn't really an exact moment when I knew, but I just did," I say, trying to find the right words. "When you know . . . you have to tell yourself that there's nothing wrong with it."

"What's wrong with it?"

"Absolutely nothing! It is completely normal and fine and perfect to be gay."

Just as I say that, the server lays down our sushi.

"Would you like chopsticks, or is silverware OK?" he asks.

"Do you know which ones gay people use?" Paris responds.

"We'll have both," I say before the server scampers off. I look Paris in the eye. "Paris, it's not polite to tell strangers that other people are gay."

"But if there's nothing wrong with it, why not tell them?"

"Do you know what *imply* means?"

"What?"

"When something is implied, it means you don't have to say it because everyone can figure it out for themselves. It may not make sense now," I say, realizing this is going to be my refrain with Paris for a long time, "but it will when you get older."

"OK, so back to being gay. Why can't I tell other people that you're gay?"

He has some aggressive wrist movements aligning with his speech. Oh, Lord. Suddenly I feel like I'm back in middle school, the first time when somebody called me a fag. *You're not a boy. You're just a little girl.* I broke down in tears in gym class and everyone laughed. I had to toughen up that day, and for the rest of middle school, I just laid low and didn't say much. I opened up just enough in high school to make friends, but still kept low. Just enough until I got to college, though even then, being out wasn't always easy. All told, it was almost ten years of hiding. A whole-ass decade. I had to hide who I was for that long.

"I tell people I'm gay all the time," I say. "I'm not ashamed of it, but there's another thing I want you to learn. It's called *knowing a time and place*. There are some times and some places when I tell people I'm gay. And then there are times and places when I don't think it's the right time to tell people I am. Now, you may not understand this, but you're Black, and I'm Black, and you probably don't have to think about being Black because this is Detroit and everyone around you is Black. But when you're like me, and you're gay and Black at the same time, you just have to be extra, extra careful about the gay part."

"OK."

"Where is all this coming from?"

"Well, I thought I might be gay because someone at school called me gay, so when I got home, I looked it up on Wikipedia and I think I am."

Is it that easy now?

"What did Wikipedia say that made you think you're gay?"

"After I clicked on the gay page, I clicked on the page for homosexual, and it said a homosexual is someone who is attracted to the same gender, and I think that's me because I'm attracted to the same gender as me."

"You like boys."

"I think so."

"Well, Paris, you either like boys or you don't. Now, when you say you like boys, do you mean . . . like, you like boys because your friends are boys? Or is it like, would you give a boy a valentine on Valentine's Day?"

"Well, I wouldn't give a valentine to a friend of mine. But I'm afraid of what people would say if I gave a valentine to a boy that's not my friend that . . ."

"That you *like*?"

"Oh my God!" he says, giggling and hiding his face.

"Don't be shy around me, boy! Do you have a crush on someone?"

"No!"

"I know that look. Trust me, I've been there."

Paris stops for a second because he knows I'm about to drop some knowledge.

"Let me tell you," I say. "When I like a boy, I start to feel really nervous because I want him to like me too. It's a funny feeling because I start to think of him all the time, and then I start to figure out the things he likes so I can like them too."

"But what if he doesn't like the things you like? You shouldn't stop liking your favorite things if he doesn't like them."

Damn if this boy isn't making some sense. He low-key might have to join the group chat.

"Well, it's not that easy," I say. I can't help but think about Roland and Terrell. "You see, sometimes, when you're gay, you have to make sacri—well, let's say *changes* to who you are to get people to like you."

"Mom said I should never change who I am."

"Your mom is absolutely right," I say, and internally, I thank God that girl has some sense. "But . . ."

I sigh. I don't even know how to navigate this conversation. I want to ask the group, but where would I start? *Help, my little cousin is gay, and he wants his big gay cousin whose life is a complete mess to help him out?*

"Let's talk about something else," I say. "Do people make fun of you?"

"Everybody makes fun of everybody," Paris says. "This one girl at school always has this beat-up old Michael Kors purse and it's not even real."

"Paris, do you know what *shade* is?"

"Duh, that's when you sit under a tree! What does that have to do with anything?"

"No, honey. First, I'm going to show you how to use chopsticks," I say, getting up from my seat to sit next to him in our booth. "Next, I'm going to explain shade. But just remember, there's always a time and a place."

———————————————

Before I take Paris home, we stop by the Nike store and I get him a pair of gym shoes off the clearance rack—I don't want him to be spoiled just yet. I ask him what he wants to be when he grows up. He says he doesn't know anymore, because at first, he wanted to be a pediatric cardiologist—that's what all kids say when they find out how much money they make—but now he wants to be a farmer.

I tell him he can be whoever he wants to be and that he has years to figure it out. I don't tell him that he'll probably still be figuring himself out at my age, that the boys he likes will probably have phones like his but won't know how to use the goddamn text-messaging function properly, that he'll like his job, and he might like his friends, but that one day, a big decision might come along that will threaten those two parts of his life.

We take a walk along the Riverwalk, not minding the weather, and it hits me that Paris has never been across the border. He's been on the Riverwalk several times, but I watch as he stares across the water, transfixed by the headlights easing down the riverside road toward the traffic signals. I stop to watch with him. The obnoxious red neon of Caesars Windsor is to our right, but the little homes with lights shining from their second-story windows are far more captivating. To me, Windsor is starting to look like an escape.

Before 9/11, you could run back and forth to Canada with no hassle, and today, even the strict border agents at the tunnel or the bridge are a pretty minor inconvenience for Detroiters who want to travel internationally without setting foot on an airplane or cruise ship.

Windsor is more American than Canadian. They don't punctuate sentences with "eh" and shit like that there. But it's still an escape. Why would you ever go to the suburbs when you could go to *another country?* Detroiters love to turn eighteen in Canada and drink the night away there. Beyond booze and universal health care and the better-but-not-absolute acceptance of people of color (Drake is a hero there, right?), though, that spot across the river looks, in this moment, like a chance to escape everything here and start over. Slaves saw Detroit as the last stop before crossing the river into total freedom in Canada. And right now, Canada has the freedom I'm looking for.

London, where Roland is, has it, too. Roland's ask—"*Why don't you just move here?*"—is weighing heavier and heavier on my mind. I have a crush, and he's winning. Terrell is just on some other shit. And I still haven't been out with Felix, despite playing text tag for weeks.

But does Roland like the things I like? How can I even know unless I actually go over there and find out? It's easy. I could disappear in Windsor, disappear in Toronto, disappear in London . . . disappear anywhere but on this side of the river.

––––––––––––––

"Did you have fun today?" Annesha asks as Paris and I take off our shoes at the front door of the house on Promenade.

"Mom, we did everything! We had sushi, we got new gym shoes, we went to the river, we used chopsticks!"

"Go upstairs and lay out what you're going to wear to church tomorrow."

Annesha and I walk into the living room and sit down.

"I know what you did," I say.

"What?"

"Don't play dumb with me."

"Whaaaat?" Annesha says, coy.

"He asked me."

"Asked you what?"

"He asked me if he thought he was . . ."

"He asked me too. I mean, I always knew he was. But I wanted him to figure it out for himself and then tell me. But damn, I didn't know he was going to do it right now."

"So how do you feel about it?"

"The same way I felt yesterday or the day before or the day when he was born. I don't care. That's my son. I'm his mother."

"You know you'll have to sit down with his dad."

"Fuck that nigga. I wish he would tell me how to raise my kid, and if he does have something to say, I will personally beat the fuck outta him."

"You're a good fucking mother."

"Shit," she says, high-fiving me. "Who you telling? Paris has got all As and one B. I don't play about my child."

"Aren't you worried he might get bullied?"

Annesha sighs.

"It'll toughen him up if it does," she says. "I mean, I don't want it to happen, but it's probably going to. And when it does, I'll be here. And you'll be here, right?"

I think about dropping the whole microstudios deal, ghosting the entire thing, and just taking off. In my mind, I can see Roland and London and planes and freedom again.

"Of course," I say.

I might be telling the truth now, but I know the right time and place will come.

SPRING

SPRING

CHAPTER TEN

The board of the Mahaffey School called an unscheduled meeting. Troy didn't have time to change. Had he prepared, he would have had his shirt and tie, but now he was in usual drag, wearing a navy hoodie over a white collared shirt, paired with plain tan pants and navy blue Chuck Taylors.

"I don't know what this meeting is about exactly, but I'm not expecting good news," Dr. Shandra Fluker, the school's principal, said to Troy in her office. "But I wanted to prepare you. One of the parents may have complained about your change to the morning affirmations."

"What did they complain about?" Troy asked.

Shandra was in her late forties, had neat brown braids with honey blonde highlights, and wore gold-rimmed glasses that partially obscured the freckles on her almond-brown face. "This . . . stolen land thing you've got the kids saying. The affirmations are supposed to be positive reinforcement."

"These kids need a reminder that this school and everywhere in Detroit is *on* stolen land. This land was the land of the Anishinaabe tribe, specifically Meskwahki-asa-hina. Without acknowledging that, we're being ignorant of history."

"Well, one of the kids thinks their mama stole the land their house is on, and he's going around telling everyone she's a thief," Shandra laughed. "This might be too much for them to handle in sixth grade, Troy. You know how strict the board is about curriculum changes and the school's mission."

Troy thought about the growing rumors about Mahaffey's closure and scoffed.

"Does this board ever act in the best interest of what this school's mission is?"

"I don't want to argue that right now, but until we know the full extent of what this meeting is about, can you try to tone it down? For all of our sakes, please?"

"Dr. Fluker," a secretary's voice called over an intercom. "They're here."

"Please take the hood off, Mr. Clements."

Troy followed Shandra into the auditorium and surveyed the crowd, which was larger than normal. He saw the parents who were regulars at gatherings like this, but there were new faces as well. Remy's cousin, Annesha, was there. Troy spotted people from the neighborhood who were too old to have children at the school. He also saw a few younger men and women in the back he had met briefly at his first Taking Back Detroit meeting. And standing behind them, leaning against the wall of the auditorium, were two white guys—the younger one overweight and immersed in his phone—who looked like they could be related.

Community board meetings had never begun with prayer until Rev. David Boyce III had taken over as board president. A perennial mayoral candidate, perennial state senate candidate, and perennial state representative candidate, the best elected position the reverend could get was chair of this board, which, truth be told, he didn't particularly like serving on. But it helped keep his name, the third in a line of legendary Detroit preachers (and he was the least legendary of the three), out there in the community. After saying "amen," Rev. Boyce got down to business.

"Let us move straight to the matter at hand," he began, as the auditorium quieted down. "I don't come to this meeting with good news. The outlook of the Mahaffey School is, quite frankly, bleak. As many of you know, this school's long-term sustainability depends on enrollment.

And while enrollment is stable now, five years down the line, there will be fewer children for this school to serve."

Troy was sitting next to Marlie and Noelle, and the three of them glanced at each other. Having worked at the school for years, this was the first time they'd ever heard this. The rest of the teachers and support staff took quiet breaths.

"And unless there is a plan to boost enrollment immediately—with clear, assessable steps in place—the board is considering closing the school at the end of this spring," Rev. Boyce said.

A few shouts rose up from the audience as parents voiced their disapproval. Scattered questions filled the air and Rev. Boyce pounded a wood block on his table to restore order.

"Rev. Boyce," Shandra interjected. "If I may, enrollment is, quite frankly, not only one of the highest priorities for this school, but something we've been very successful at. Our students largely come from this neighborhood, but we have kids from all over the city. We had a long waiting list last year and had to turn families away."

"I understand that, Dr. Fluker, but we are not talking about last year, we're talking about the near future. The fact is, more families are leaving Detroit than coming here, and our operator, who has to pay attention to the best ways to allocate its limited resources, feels it may be best to continue their mission at the Mahaffey School at a different facility . . ."

"A different facility?" Troy asked from the audience.

"Excuse me, young man?"

"Is it a different facility or are they closing the school?" he asked, standing up.

"Well, we don't know for sure yet," Rev. Boyce said, evasively. "The university says it wants to have a school, just not necessarily here."

"It's the land they want," a parent yelled from the audience. "Everybody knows that!"

"Fucking vultures," Troy muttered. He had only meant to say it loud enough for Marlie and Noelle to hear, but a number of other staff members turned and looked at him.

"Did you want to say something, young man?" Rev. Boyce asked.

The noise in the room died down. Troy faced the reverend and felt a rare moment when he could stand up for himself in front of someone who, unlike Roderick—wherever *he* was—wouldn't push or choke or throw a punch.

"It's no secret developers are targeting this area and trying to buy everyone out. We know all of the buildings up and down the block are going up for sale one by one. And we know from our parents right here in this neighborhood that people are pressuring them to sell their houses. *You all* know enrollment has nothing to do with it. Enrollments have been good. They'll stay good. The university *now* only wants to sell this building to make a profit. That's what their 'allocation of limited resources' is about. It's about cash. And it's gentrification in full force."

Troy heard a smattering of applause and supportive shouts behind him.

"Now you wait a minute," Rev. Boyce said. "I've known you since you were a little boy. Me and your daddy go way back. *Way* back."

"My father doesn't have anything to do with this," Troy interrupted. "The issue at hand is this board's lack of compassion and common sense when it comes to protecting this school and the families in this neighborhood."

"Mr. Clements," Shandra said. "Let the reverend finish. Please."

Troy sat down, silently mocking Shandra's command in his head. He had first flirted with atheism when Suhas died and had fully embraced it two years after finishing college, and for him, the false idolatry Detroiters made out of preachers was one of the things he disliked most about his city. The other thing he hated was when anyone suspected him of nepotism because he was Bill Clements's son. Another thing he hated, of course, was actually *being* Bill Clements's son.

"The reality is," Rev. Boyce said, "unless this school produces a sustainability plan to the university—again, with clear, measurable outcomes that the board can assess—before the end of the spring that can convincingly demonstrate enrollments will remain steady five years from now, then the university will be reconsidering its investment in the school."

"Reverend Boyce, if I may?" Shandra asked.

"Go ahead, Dr. Fluker."

"Not only will we have a plan, but we'll have it well before the spring. You have my word on that."

Rev. Boyce fielded questions from parents, giving the pat nonanswers and evasions Troy had come to expect from meetings like this. He didn't listen. He just sat in his chair, angry and defeated. He looked around the room and saw parents and neighbors who were upset. A number of them were looking down at the floor, stunned. In the back of the room, Troy saw the people from Taking Back Detroit sitting stone-faced in their seats. The two white men were both furiously texting away.

•••

Troy Clements
I need a drink
A stiff one

Remy Patton
Come by the house and smoke instead

Dominick Gibson
The roads are too bad for me to drive
BUT
Let's go to the Woodward tomorrow?

Troy Clements
Remy HATES the Woody lol
He's too bougie for it now

> **Dominick Gibson**
> Lol I haven't been in years
> When you said "stiff drink" that's immediately what I
> thought of

> **Remy Patton**
> For you, Dominick I'll go
> And you too Troy
> I guess I'll go to the ghetto for one night

• • •

Remy considered the Woodward to be Detroit's last resort for nightlife. He hated its aesthetics. Everywhere else in the world, gay bars were obviously gay bars, with their billowing rainbow flags hanging in the windows and the TV screens sometimes airing pornography visible from the sidewalk outside. Not so with the Woodward.

The entrance was in an alley behind the bar's adjoining, more prominent storefronts on Woodward Avenue. It felt so underground, so closeted, Remy thought, like it never truly wanted to show gay pride. It almost felt like negroes having to enter through the kitchen instead of the main entrance. Mostly through Troy's consistent prodding, though, he was a frequent patron. After all, there were only a handful of "safe spaces"—a term Remy loathed but that Troy frequently bounced around—for Black gay men in the city.

"Do they have places like this in New York?" Remy asked as they made their way inside. "I've only been to clubs in Atlanta."

"Yeah. Sometimes the hole-in-the-wall places are the best places to, you know, get a drink and just kind of hang out if you're not trying to be . . . all that." Dominick said.

"All that. Like?"

"You know. This is a place to be low-key. Not trying to impress anyone."

"Shit. This is one of the few places in Detroit where you actually have the opportunity *to* impress someone."

"I don't understand."

"You've been away too long. This all we got here. The Woodward. Menjo's. Adam's Apple, where the old white queens go, Gigi's for the young gays, and . . ."

"The Hayloft. Where the bears go," Troy said.

"I've been to Menjo's. It's been forever, obviously, but I've been," Dominick said.

"And probably the same niggas there back then are the same niggas there now," Remy said. "This? Right here? Is all we got. And this shit is trash. Same niggas. Same music. Same bottom shelf-ass liquor. Maybe if they built some new shit here then we'd have better options. And as a matter of motherfucking fact, why aren't we drinking right now? Let's get some Long Islands because I don't even want to remember this shit when it's done."

"Don't . . ." Troy said.

"Don't what? Drink too much?" Remy said.

Troy eyeballed him.

"I'm *not*," Remy said, dropping his voice to a near-whisper. "Leave me alone."

"OK," Troy said.

"I smell chicken. Do they cook here?" Dominick asked.

"Yeah. You want some?" Troy asked.

"Why not?" Dominick asked. After years of carefully planned meals just to please Justin, and after weeks of pouting around his mother's house, eating deep-fried chicken cooked by the same guy slinging drinks felt revolutionary.

"Y'all go head. I already ate," Remy said.

"You are too bougie for words," Troy said.

"I don't eat random fried chicken. But y'all go head."

Over stiff Long Island iced teas, and before the bar got too loud and crowded, Troy detailed exactly what had happened at the meeting. As the spirits set in, Dominick wondered aloud if Mahaffey's staff and Shandra could go over the board's head, either appealing directly to the university or asking the neighborhood to take action in some way. Remy, who was wavering between distraction, annoyance, and drunkenness, simply offered that it might be best for Troy to prepare for the worst, polish up his resume, and find something else.

"You've been at that school for years now with no promotion or anything. It's time to move on," Remy said. "They're building all over that neighborhood anyway."

"I can't just get up and go," Troy said. The music was louder now, and the boys were yelling. "Do you know anything about what they're building around there?"

"I don't know specifics," Remy said. "Probably just your run-of-the-mill townhomes. Those are the cheapest and fastest way for developers to turn over a property in a neighborhood like that. They don't look amazing, but they bring in revenues. And that can actually be good for the neighborhood if you look at it the right way. I mean *look* at Midtown."

"Yeah," Troy said, "and meanwhile, my kids will be taking the bus across town for school."

"It's happening all over Detroit, Troy. It's not just your school. I don't know why you don't just find something else. Or even go work for your dad. He's old. You can take over Clements Printing. I wish I had that kind of hookup, shit. Plus, you wouldn't have to deal with any of this shit."

"Wait, is this a Tamia song?" Dominick asked, confused at why the slow-singing Canadian chanteuse, of all artists, would come on midway through a DJ set at a gay bar but seeing an opportunity to cut the tension nonetheless.

"My shit!" Remy said, relieved by the distraction. He raised his glass in the air.

The night's DJ emerged from the booth, clutching the microphone to his mouth as if he were going to fellate it.

"Now I want all my real Detroit niggas to get on the floor and do what the fuck you do. You know what the fuck it is!" he shouted as the first lyrics for "Can't Get Enough" flowed over the speakers.

"What's going on?" Dominick asked. "I'm *so* confused right now." He thought this was a *lot* for a Tamia song.

"You'll see," Troy said. "Watch Remy go. It happens every time. He says he hates it, but then the liquor kicks in and all it takes is one good song."

The Woodward's patrons formed in single-file lines—old men, young men, trans women with good wigs, trans women with bad wigs, studs, femmes, and a few heteros along for the ride. They moved to each of Tamia's syllables—"close the *door*, bed or *floor*, I just want *more*"—doing a slight hop, without completely lifting off the ground, and a shuffle to the right, left, front, or back each time.

It's definitely a Detroit hustle, Dominick thought, attempting to watch and memorize the steps through a drunken haze. *And they definitely aren't doing this in Harlem or Bed-Stuy*.

Remy, in the middle of it all, raised his glass in the air, mouthing along the words with everyone else—"stomach muscles gettin' tight, skin so wet my fingers slide"—and not missing a beat. This was a heightened Detroit hustle, more than just the step-to-the-right, step-to-the-left half-turns of Dominick's youth. The most complicated thing back then was bending down to pick up imaginary dollar bills on the ground during "My Eyes Don't Cry." But now, muhfuckas were crisscrossing and hopping? To *Tamia*?

"Looks like fun, doesn't it?" a voice said, startling Dominick and Troy from behind.

Troy turned around, and his heart dropped to his stomach. It was Roderick, who before Troy knew it, was holding his face and kissing his lips. Dominick looked on quizzically.

"Roderick!" Troy said. "Didn't know you were here, babe."

"I guess we both had the same idea," Roderick said. Troy could smell cigarette smoke. And tequila. He could also see Roderick's pupils were much wider than usual.

"This is Dominick," Troy said as Roderick sat down and slung his arm around Troy's shoulders. "Dominick, this is Roderick."

"New York!" Roderick said, pointing at Dominick, who was still trying to size up the hustle going on in front of him. "The one he's known since summer camp and who works in advertising? Troy thinks I don't remember these things, but I remember. I remember everything, don't I, boo?"

"You sure do," Troy said, unsure what to make of his rapidly beating heart.

"And you two are living together! How's married life?" Dominick asked, so focused on the hustle that he couldn't see Troy's discomfort.

Roderick laughed.

"You know, we get along much better now than when we weren't living together. Troy used to clean up his place, but I knew that wasn't the real him. I told him everything doesn't have to be crystal clean for me. He doesn't have to fake it anymore."

"I'm glad to hear that," Dominick said. "With everything going on at the school, Troy needs all the support he can get."

"What's going on at the school?" Roderick asked.

"I didn't tell him yet," Troy said, glaring at Dominick. "But we'll talk all about it when we get home."

Roderick pecked him on the cheek and went to stand in the drink line.

Dominick rested his elbows on the table and propped his hands under his chin, cocking his head and looking directly at Troy.

"I know what you're thinking," Troy said.

"I didn't say anything," Dominick said coyly. "But he is handsome, I'll give him that."

———————————

"Do we have to gooooo? Can't we go somewhere else?" Dominick asked, slurring his words.

"Text your mom and let her know you're sleeping on my couch," Remy said.

"I'm having such a good tiiiiiiiime!"

"We can tellllllllll, bitch!" Remy said, gently mocking him. He turned to Roderick and Troy. "Are you two going to be all right?"

The four of them were outside on Milwaukee Avenue, waiting for two separate ride shares.

"We'll be good," Roderick said.

All four turned to catch an angry voice a few feet away from them.

"I don't give a fuck! I don't give a fuck! Try me! Try me! Try it if you want to, bitch-ass nigga! Nigga, try me! With yo' bitch ass!"

"What's going on now?" Dominick asked.

"Niggas. Fighting," Remy said, taking out his dab pen. "Probably started inside, as usual."

"Are we just going to stand here and watch?" Dominick asked.

Remy took a long draw and exhaled a plume of white smoke.

"Might as well," he said.

A spry twentysomething man, wearing skintight ripped jeans and wielding a baseball bat, charged toward a Dodge Avenger pulling out of a parking space and struck the back windshield with it, nearly shattering it.

"Ooh, shit!" Remy said, chuckling. "Safelite repair, Safelite replace!"

"This is ghetto!" Dominick said, his sobriety starting to overcome his dizziness. "How far away is the Uber?"

"Five minutes, chill."

Then, gunshots.

The driver of the Avenger fired three shots into the sky from behind the steering wheel.

"Down!" Roderick yelled, pulling Troy to the ground. The four of them crouched low beside the brick wall that led to the Woodward's entrance, and Roderick covered all of them.

"You see why I don't come here!" Remy said.

"It's not always this bad!" Troy yelled back.

"Our Uber is here, babe," Roderick said.

"It's not safe to go out there!" Dominick said.

Roderick poked his head around the corner.

"It's cool, they pulled off," he said.

Dominick sat on the ground, bewildered and covering his forehead, as if—in his current state of inebriation—he thought his hand could stop a stray bullet from piercing his skull. Remy, meanwhile, brushed himself off while Roderick helped Troy to his feet.

"Let's just all go together," Roderick said.

"He's right," Remy conceded. "Thanks for protecting us just now. You didn't have to do that."

"I'm not so bad after all, right?" Roderick said, glancing back at Troy, who wasn't quite sure how to respond.

CHAPTER ELEVEN

It was never supposed to come to this. But here Dominick was anyway, sitting in the dark of his mother's house, deep down in this hole he wasn't sure who dug, about to look for love on his phone again.

Dominick was old enough to remember a time when online dating was new and capricious, how risky it used to feel to meet a stranger through fiber optics. Roger Troutman, Shirley Murdock, and Charlie Wilson sang about "Computer Love," but that shit wasn't supposed to be real.

Things were different now. Desktop matchmaking had moved to the smartphone, and Black Gay Chat, Adam4Adam, and Manhunt were all but fossilized in amber. And Dominick was nervous because after eight years of not having to log in to find love, here he was again, new to all this.

"Otters are in *style,* honey," Remy had told him, attempting to boost Dom's confidence. "Besides, every gay man in Detroit is like two degrees of dick away from each other. You're fresh meat. They'll be all over you."

The profiles Dominick swiped through day after day were all over, all right. Recently, his left swipes had included, in no particular order, Elon Musk fanboys, guys prefacing their profiles with "perks of dating me," Black men who described themselves as "spiritual," men looking for "my king" or "my prince," quote-unquote sapiosexuals, men with no discernible means of income who described themselves as "self-employed," skinny white boys who used the word "thicc," men whose profiles included only pictures of feet, scary white men with busty blonde women looking for threesomes, bare-minimum white boys who posed with an askew peace sign above their head, Black men dressed like pastors, Black men in Steve Harvey suits, Black men who posed in photos as if they were at a Sears Portrait Studio in 1992, and those who advertised "surprise butt touches" as a selling point.

Dominick took a swig of the Honig he'd pilfered from his mother's wine rack and sighed.

I'm sitting in my mama's house with a glass of cabernet, swiping though men, hoping one might make a husband, he thought. *Is this how eternity begins? With a woof or a right-swipe?*

It had been eight weeks since his return to Detroit. Dominick had had 103 matches on Tinder in a radius of more than fifty miles. Of that 103, only forty-six had led to conversations, and of that forty-six, fifteen had progressed past "hey." There was a clear script everyone had memorized. Usually, it would start with the exchange of a "nice pic, handsome," and then a "same to you" and a "what's up?" If it moved past pleasantries, the guy would ask Dominick about hanging out sometime—"hanging out" could either mean "hooking up" or maybe just something less forward— and Dominick would mindlessly answer "sure" (it was "sure" for white gays and "OK" for the Black ones, because the code-switching never ended). At this point, it didn't really matter to him.

They'd go out once, have drinks, and talk aimlessly about Detroit and work—Dominick rarely got into how bad things were going at GearWorks. They'd avoid all questions about marriage and kids, talking instead about the latest streaming phenomenon or Azealia Banks's latest tirade. Then they'd go to one of their places and fuck.

Sex became comedy. Or melodrama. If his partner was less-than-appealing, Dominick would try to beat a new record each time, aiming to come in under five minutes. The sooner it was over, the better. But the men were always so happy to have a dick inside them, and they were always sure to thank Dominick profusely afterward. Say his partner's head wasn't that good, and then Dominick would fake a few moans and deep breaths, giving his best Golden Globe-worthy performance. With younger hookups, Dom even sometimes saw it as a teaching moment. He would take their hand and bring it across his cheek, signaling that there needed to be a test of intimacy. After they leaned in for a kiss, Dominick would take the lead again, moving their hand down toward his crotch. *The kiss*, he would signal with his movements, *leads to making out, then leads to some other body part*—maybe that hand again—*grazing this hard dick*. The point was, as Dominick showed them charitably, they needed to know this dick was ready and wouldn't be around forever.

Once, a man asked Dominick to keep his dick inside him while he got off. As the man furiously jerked his erect penis and moaned, he was sweating enough to make Dominick damp. *This is the part I hate*, Dominick thought, trying to will some blood flow to his penis to keep it stiff enough to squish inside the man's asshole. When the man finally came, he was a shooter, ejaculate pole-vaulting a half-foot into the air and landing smack on Dominick's left pectoral, warm as maple syrup on a pancake. Once he dismounted, the man immediately put his arm around him, preventing Dominick from grabbing something to wipe the viscous spunk off, leaving it to dissolve into clear liquid doing the Blade Dance down the side of his chest. As the man talked about how good it felt to come with a dick inside him, the only thing Dominick wanted was to dive into the Dead Sea and let the salt cleanse his body and perhaps bring him closer to God—or maybe cannonball into a vat of isopropyl alcohol.

This can't be the path to marriage before thirty-five, he thought.

After the sex, he and whomever he'd fucked would go their separate ways after an awkward kiss. The next day, they would text each other about how they should do it again sometime. Maybe they'd follow each other on Instagram, and maybe they'd abruptly cease all contact and never speak to each other again, unless you count viewing each other's Instagram Stories but never really interacting as "speaking."

Perhaps, he sometimes thought, *this is actually a good deed. Maybe I'll see heaven just by delivering good dick to the needy.*

Dominick eventually lost count of how often this had happened and was now only half-informing the group chat with Remy and Troy about whoever's hole—*ugh, couldn't gay sex terminology be a bit more congenial*, he thought—he'd most recently visited.

There had been Neil, the art teacher who was two inches shorter than Dominick and who lived in Southwest Detroit. ("Like Neil from *The Young and the Restless*," Dominick had quipped, though Neil hadn't gotten the reference.) He was twenty-three, which made them ten years apart, which was, by Dominick's summation, just the right cutoff before a gay relationship looked sketchy. ("You don't want to be a Charles Pugh in these streets," Remy once posted in the group chat.) There had been the match who had scared him a little with his opening conversation ("Do you have any fears? What are your fears? What's your biggest fear?" he'd asked, wide-eyed, over Mexican beers and lengua tacos) or the one who, after just two sips of wine, had blurted out, "I can already tell you're the nicest guy I've ever met!" Even after Rico's mama had caught him with Dom's load on his face, he still kept trying to hit Dom up too. Dom hadn't responded, but at least the incident had taught him to carry a travel-sized bottle of Astroglide with him on dates.

To keep it lively, and to keep from completely drowning in his misery over both his love and work life, Dominick started nicknaming some of the boys he came across, which was more fun than thinking of the TV characters they shared names with. There was the Colombian Tour Guide, the white boy who confusingly adored guided tours and insisted they take one at the Detroit Institute of Arts; he also insisted they do a bump of coke in the bathroom beforehand. There was Young Al Pacino, who thought a good first date idea was to watch the movie *Cruising*, about a gay slasher in New York, before inviting Dom to his bed, which was adorned with Pacino-print pillows from some internet company. There was Neville Tallbottom, a spindly, bespectacled otter-type who was still obsessed with the "Harry Potter" franchise at his big age. (He was Ravenclaw, FYI.) And then there was Bedwetting Bloomer, the horticulturalist who got so drunk on their date that he passed out in his Casper bed and urinated on the mattress. And based on the maize and blue flannel blanket, dry yet scented with urine, that Dominick used to keep warm that night, it wasn't the first time.

Are these the same men Alicia Myers was thanking the heavenly father for?

Once, after struggling through yet another small-talk goodbye with yet another disappointing match—plans for the rest of the weekend, a light hug, a peck on the lips—Dominick stood on the steps of the apartment building and finally decided to try something he'd seen numerous Black folks do in the movies: have a little talk with God.

"Lord God almighty, I need you," he said, looking up toward the stars, "to take time from your busy schedule to send me a bottom. I pray for a bottom that's at least halfway good-looking and can ride on top for more than three minutes. I pray he looks at me as more than just my penis, I pray he has good credit, I pray he can host, I pray he is between twenty-three and thirty-five—no wait, Lord God, better make that twenty-eight and thirty-five—and I pray he isn't already taken or in an open relationship with a white man and just looking for some Black dick on the side. And Lord, would it be too much to ask that he have a clean ass before we make love? I've seen the abundant blessings you've laid upon our good sis Ciara and I'm praying for my Russell, too—in bottom form, of course. In Jesus's name. Amen."

Scruff and Grindr kept chugging along, though—they always did. And on nights like this, when Troy was hanging out with Roderick, and Remy was out with either Roland or Terrell, Dominick would sit alone at his mother's house—on a date with his device. Some nights, it became a sport to swipe through all of Detroit's limited selection of men until none were left. On others, the circumferential beam emanating from the icon at the end of swiping seemed like an SOS signal.

It was enough to give you a kind of identity vertigo. As Dominick swiped through photo after photo, sometimes so fast his phone looked like the flipbooks he would make as a child—each profile blurring into the next—it made him wonder what he was really looking for in a partner. When he and Justin first met, his only type was "must be horny and able to take dick." Now, though, it was a question he had to think about, because for the first time in eight years, he had options.

When he'd first started, Dominick had scrolled through each app repeatedly, first figuring out what he didn't like. At five-eleven himself (though he always said he was six feet), any potential guy had to be no more than two inches taller or five inches shorter than he was. He didn't want a scrawny little twink, either.

Some of these little boys on here look like those hairless cats, he thought, *no meat on the bones, no brawn, no . . . scruff.*

As a top, Dominick thought about the kind of guy who would straddle him, bend over for him, or lay down under him. How big (or small) did he want the ass to be that he would be burying his face into? He'd never had to think about this before, though he did think about all the ways he had pleased Justin and how he'd probably have to carry that over to the next man. The whole thing made him feel conflicted.

You read all the time about how vain and cruel gay men can be, he thought, *demanding "no fats, no femmes," and damn, am I becoming one of those gay men? But is it really wrong to have a preference? I mean, as long as my preferences aren't racist, right?*

Most of the signals that popped up on Scruff came from horny men who lived way outside Metro Detroit, but every once in a while, a new person would show up on the grids inside the city. They were almost always white.

Dominick knew some of these white boys only dated Black men for the novelty. It was one more thing he had to suss out, which made interracial dating even more laborious. But he was more concerned about what everybody else would think about it. Remy seemed to be dead set on only dating Black men, and even though Troy didn't seem to care one way or another, the majority of his past flings and hookups had been Black. Dominick knew that if he started dating a white guy, he'd never lose his two closest friends because they'd know the whole story, but to everyone else, he was worried that if he crossed that color line—a barbed line that zig-zags, trembles, and sways all at once—he'd run the risk of being seen as just another cliché brother who got a little money in his pocket and started playing in the snow.

But wait, I love Black men. I mean, it's not that I wouldn't date a white guy, or any other race. But if I have a choice, I mean if I really have to Sophie's Choice *it here, I want a man who looks like me. Someone I can crack jokes with without pretext, someone who knows where I'm coming from at all times, someone who I don't have to think twice around. I do that enough with people from work. Do I want that energy in my personal life?*

Besides, Dominick knew that if he were to get into an interracial relationship, he'd have to answer the same batch of questions again and again: *What is it like? Why did you do it?* There was a healthy contingent of Black gay men out there that despised Black men who got into same-sex relationships with white guys. Sellouts. Uncle Toms. The worst names any Black man could be called by one of their own. Dominick knew he'd get it tenfold from these messy queens. But after being asked a million times, "how do you make this relationship *work?*" with a Black man, maybe he'd at least be a little prepared for them.

Plus, it happened all the time! A Black gay man reached that status in life—his career on point and his bills on autopay—and he inevitably

ended up with a white partner. One look at any famous gay Black man—
the few, *the very few,* who comfortably existed in the public eye—and
they're almost always in an interracial relationship. Professional athletes,
actors, rich Black gays—all the same. Why did Dominick think he was
any different?

Preferences. Goddammit, I have them, he thought. *I'm not going to
apologize for this shit. I was with a Black man, just shorter than me and built
like me, for almost all of my twenties and a little bit of my thirties. I put in
a lot of time for Black love. Would it be a sin—no, a crime—to date a non-
Black guy for once?*

The profile photos scrolled by in waves, and Dominick couldn't help
but think of the strange way that as he stared at the screen in the dark,
looking through this tiny window at all the little people inside who were
hungry to fuck, those same people were also looking back at him. That
forced him to wonder who he really was. Or was trying to be.

Upon first signing up, these apps felt like surveys prior to a doctor's
appointment. Both Scruff and Grindr wanted to know what kind of
body Dominick had, how much it weighed, and how much hair was
on it. Dominick had never really thought much about his exact weight.
He kept in shape. No abs, but no belly either. Perfectly acceptable for
a thirtysomething gay man who ate healthy most of the time, held a
mandatory-for-a-Manhattan-gay Equinox membership, and jogged
regularly in Central Park.

Tinder didn't ask for his height or weight, but Dominick saw that
its gay male users put them in their bios anyway. Before he uploaded any
pictures, he had stripped down to his underwear and looked at himself in
the full-body mirror in the bedroom.

*How do I describe this body? I'm hairy, but am I very hairy? Am I athletic,
or a jock? I have arm muscle definition, but no visual abs. My pecs poke out
a little—average? You can see them when I wear a tight enough shirt, I guess.
Am I tall? What's my shoe size—twelve? That's pretty average. But thirteen*

would indicate something else—a bigger dick, maybe. Some of my twelves are pretty tight on my feet, but sometimes thirteens are too big. Should I lie and say thirteen? Can I lie on my dick like that?

Chrisette Michele's "Love Is You" came on iTunes shuffle. Dominick snapped out of his scrolling reverie.

"Delete this shit," he mumbled to himself, half-drunk, immediately clearing the song from his library. It reminded him of Justin. It was one of the potential songs Dominick had imagined playing at their wedding, a Black-ass celebration of nuptials that was now never going to happen.

As a matter of fact, Dominick thought, *let's just delete all the wedding songs off this motherfucker.*

He went to his playlist titled "Me and Him," which he'd put together to possibly play during their ceremony, the first dance, and the big family blowout on the dance floor. Miriam Makeba's "A Promise," deleted. Anita Baker's "Love You to the Letter," wiped away. Marvin Gaye and Tammi Terrell's "Your Precious Love," Lil Mo and Fabolous's "4 Ever," gone. Kacey Musgraves's "Golden Hour" (*Even that bitch got divorced,* Dominick thought), O'Bryan's "You and I," Sade's "Kiss of Life," that goddamn "Cha Cha Slide" for the reception, a song Dominick secretly hated but acquiesced to at all Black functions—all purged from his library forever.

His eyes were warm. He wanted to cry. The loneliness and the lostness still felt new. After all the lessons about how to not be a fucked-up adult—from his parents, from his friends, from reading *The Coldest Winter Ever*, or watching countless episodes of *Living Single* and *Girlfriends*, or replaying *Waiting to Exhale*—here he was, out here looking stupid. Boo-Boo the Fool. Whodunit, and why. And this was all new to him because he didn't know how to plan for the kind of disappointment he'd worked so hard for the past eight years to avoid.

Because even after all this, there was still no clear playbook for young, Black gay men coming up in this world. There was no hip-hop-and-R&B soundtrack of back-to-back bangers to be their chorus, no Gabrielle Union subplot or Taye Diggs line to sum it all up. T. D. Jakes and Steve Harvey hadn't written a relationship book for them. Iyanla couldn't fix their lives. All they got was barely two seasons of *Noah's Arc* and Chiron crying about a hand job on the beach. Any other lessons were in heteronormativity.

But I got the degree, the job, the money, and I had the man. I should be able to get another one just as quick, Dominick thought. *Right?* After years of reading and watching other folks' mistakes, he should be able to handle this, even if the characters in his narrative were all male. *Keep playing along? Adjusting the rules as we go?* If Black folks have had to do it all this time, Dominick thought, then hell.

He finished the last of his mother's wine. He'd have to buy her a new bottle tomorrow. He stared out into the dark living room, his eyes still half-seeing flickers of the profile images that had flashed across his screen.

I'm single. I'm alone. My professional life is at absolute zero and my love life may as well be too. I don't know what the hell I'm doing. It's like if all 101 dalmatians took a shit at once right on top of me, and I just want to cry. Just let me cry, just let me cry.

But the tears wouldn't flow. Dominick tried to think of the last time he had cried over a man—the last time he had really cried at all. He hadn't cried at his grandfather's funeral, or when his mother had said her breast cancer had gone into remission, or even at the end of *Hamilton*, when the audience was bawling at Alexander and Eliza's epic love. He hadn't cried about losing his job at Atomic Ranch or all the shit Justin had put him through. It had been far too long, and if there was ever a time to do it, Dominick knew it was right now. But the tears wouldn't come. All he could do was sit in his mother's house, drunk by himself.

In the darkness, his phone screen lit up. Dominick picked it up and saw a new woof from Scruff, followed by a message.

"Never seen you here before," it said. "I'm Felix."

CHAPTER TWELVE

It used to be easy for Troy to keep up with the comings and goings in his building because there hardly were any to begin with. Like a lot of other places in Islandview, almost all the residents in his apartment complex were in their senior years, and most had lived there for twenty years or more. But then the old folks started to die. At first, folks like Troy took their place, but that was only until white Detroiters decided West Village was too expensive and that Islandview was just perfect. The change was becoming clearer and clearer to Troy, like the afternoon when a white woman with short brown hair and bangs asked him in the laundry room, "Do you really need both of those washers?"

"Pardon me?" Troy asked.

"You only put one towel in that washer and a bunch of clothes in the other, and I was just wondering if I could use one of the machines?"

Troy, holding a basket with a jug of Seventh Generation detergent at his side, paused and leaned on the washer that had his bath towel inside. He could hear it filling up with water.

"The reason I'm washing this towel separately is because there's feces on it. See, I'm usually cleaned out when my boyfriend and I have sex, but last night we were in a rush, and I didn't want to leave any traces on the sheets. And I don't want to mix this towel with my shit on it with the rest of my clothes. Hashtag gay problems!"

The woman looked down at her white Keds and tapped her fingers against the laundry basket clutched to her chest.

"Oh," she said, barely above a whimper. "I can wait. I'm sorry. It was nice to meet you . . ."

"Troy, eighth floor."

"I'm Sandy."

"Oh? Like the squirrel, and like from *Grease*?"

"Yeah, you could say that. Well, nice to meet you. Have a good day!"

The tactics were simple: scare the new white people in any way possible. If they wanted to be in Detroit, they would have to accept it all.

I bet that bitch has a cat that walks on her kitchen counters, Troy thought to himself.

And then he remembered why there were feces on the towel to begin with.

Roderick had spent the night with Troy after the shooting at the Woodward and after he'd apologized at least twenty-five times for choking him. Troy didn't say it out loud at the time, but he missed Roderick. He had gotten used to his scent of African black soap and patchouli. Most of all, though, he missed Roderick's warmth. They decided Roderick would move back into the apartment the next day. Roughly ten minutes later, he was truly back home, inside Troy.

"Are we good?" Roderick asked, stroking Troy's face.

"I told you, I'm fine." Troy knew he had a worried look on his face, and he couldn't help but look away.

The night after that, though, Troy cooked biryani for dinner. And by the fourth day, they were back to their usual routine of recreational cocaine and sex. Since moving back in, Roderick had been helpful, eager, and always home on time. When Troy wanted to cook dal, Roderick soaked just the right amount of lentils. Instead of leaving his Black nationalist books in boxes, Roderick displayed them on a small bookshelf he built in the living room. And when Bill invited Troy over for dinner, Roderick asked if he could come along.

"I'm not sure what's going on with my dad, but I don't think it's a good time to meet him. He's been out of character recently. I can't put my finger on it. But something's not right."

"I thought we were trying to grow our relationship?" Roderick asked. They were in each other's arms, lying in bed. "Wouldn't it be good for me to meet the man who made you who you are?"

"He didn't make me who I am," Troy said, wiping the lenses of his glasses. "I've been on my own without his money since college. The only thing he's given me is this mattress and that's because he felt guilty."

"What did he do that was so bad?"

"It wasn't one thing. He was just a terrible father. After my mom died, he clocked out. Everything with him is business, a transaction. Shit, he probably thinks I owe him something for this bed. And now's just not a good time to go through all that."

"Well, it's a nice bed, at least."

A desperate man will do anything to earn forgiveness. Troy knew this. But there was still fear. Troy knew that with Roderick back, any day could potentially begin or end with some varying level of violence. The choke was one thing. Maybe next time Roderick would shove or punch him. Or worse.

I should have told Remy and Dominick what happened that night, he thought. *They would have saved me. But I don't need Dominick to come to my rescue again. And Remy's got his own problems. I'm a big boy, I can handle this.*

He watched as Roderick, disappointed about not getting to meet Bill, skulked into the kitchen to start dinner.

———————————

The next night, they were in bed again, spooning after Roderick had tried, but failed, to climax after roughly twenty minutes of sex.

"You know my friends Noelle and Marlie?" Troy said. "They're coming to dinner tomorrow so we can discuss a plan to keep the school open."

"Those two white girls you go out with?"

"Yeah. I just realized you haven't met them, so . . . you can meet them tomorrow if you're around."

"What do you mean *if* I'm around?"

"I mean . . . if you weren't planning to go out or something. I don't know your plans. I guess this would be me asking."

"Why can't I have dinner with your father?"

"I told you, I don't think he's well. I don't know what it is . . . he doesn't talk . . ."

"I'll tell you what it is. He's a Black man missing his son. And you're denying him that privilege."

Troy sat upright.

"What do you mean?"

"Remember the code of Taking Back Detroit? About men training their children to become leaders?"

"You took that oath, not me. They won't even let me in the meetings."

"You could come to the meetings if you would just be yourself."

"What's that supposed to mean?"

"I hear how you talk on the phone to those girls. You code-switch. If you quit that and were more of the true Black man you clearly are, then you'd be welcome at TBD."

Troy got out of bed, found his glasses, and put on a pair of gym shorts.

"I'm . . . not sure where this is going," he said, "but I think we should end this conversation before it gets out of hand."

"Come back. Sit down," Roderick said.

"Roderick . . ."

"Kiburi."

Oh, so we're back to this shit again, Troy thought.

"I'm just going to go to the living room."

Roderick stood up and walked toward him. Troy immediately threw up his hands in defense.

"Don't!" he yelled.

"I'm just putting on some clothes!" Roderick said. "I told you, that won't happen again."

"OK, I'm sorry."

"We have to code-switch around everybody," Roderick said, putting on a pair of flannel pajama pants. "I can't be too gay around my male relatives because they'll laugh behind my back. I either have to be a Black woman's gay best friend or act perfectly straight so she won't condemn me to hell. I have to talk like a white boy in front of white boys and talk like a white girl in front of white girls. I can't be too hood in front of *any* kind of white folks, but I gotta be just hood enough to prove I'm actually from the hood even though I don't live there anymore. And I can't talk shit about being gay in front of anybody professional. Shit, I'm tired. The only place I can be my actual self is at Taking Back Detroit."

"I mean, we all have to code-switch a little at some point," Troy said, "but I . . . I don't do all that."

"You do, actually," Roderick said, lighting a 12th and ViV candle. "Especially around those girls. And we both should stop."

"You're masculine. You can get away with a lot. I can't just turn *this*," Troy said, moving his arms up and down, "off. If I didn't wear heavy shoes, I'd float away."

"You're not that gay," Roderick laughed.

"What does that even mean, 'not that gay?'"

"You know exactly what I mean. You're not all flingy and, you know," Roderick said, twisting his hand side to side and waving his fingers.

"Oh, I'm not *a fag*?"

"I didn't say all that."

"Yes, you did. You can't see it in yourself because you carry yourself as a man. People can see you as straight. That's a privilege."

"But the fact is I don't hide the fact that I'm gay from anyone."

"You clearly do when you go to those meetings."

"Troy," Roderick groaned, "You don't get it."

"I do get it. And besides, it's not that easy because we're living in a white man's world."

"Ok, yeah, fucking tell me about it."

"Niggas have had to survive all kinds of shit since we've *been* in this country," Troy said, briefly taken aback at his own use of the n-word. He swore he would never use it, but here he was, and it had rolled off his tongue with ease. He thought how much he was sounding like his father. "All the shit we have to deal with for just being Black period, but now I have to go through all this? Something has to change. We all got to deal with being Black. I'm not about to let being gay complicate that. Period."

"You say that now. But you still code-switch."

"I really don't have a fucking choice, Roderick. What do you want me to say?"

"What I want you to say is that you're proud to be Black. Proud to be yourself."

"And what I want you to say at those meetings is that you're proud to have a supportive *Black boyfriend*."

"It's not happening like that."

"Why not?"

"Just forget it."

"You started it!"

The tang of curry spice hung in the air long after it was cooked. Troy didn't use it often, but he didn't mind it because it reminded him of the rich meals Suhas would make. Bill said that as an Arkansas boy, he could handle anything spicy. That didn't deter Suhas from challenging her husband on just how much heat his taste buds could stand. If it wasn't peppers, it would be gourds and root vegetables—potatoes, daikon, radishes, turnips, bittergourd, sinqua—that she'd dice and stir-fry with chicken, or stew with pork fat or beef. But she always came back to her curry dishes. Curry and coconut chicken, curry potato, mung beans in spiced milk, chana masala. Troy, a quiet child, watched his mother cook everything while Bill sat in the living room and waited. Now, so did Roderick, who Troy could tell was beginning to loathe the smell of anything curry.

When Bangladeshis started moving to Hamtramck and opening restaurants, Troy always surprised the servers with his adept knowledge of menu items and requests for specific dishes. Soon, they came to expect him, and they treated him like family once he explained his background. Hamtramck was the only lifeline Troy had to Bangladesh. Visiting his mother's home country always seemed like one of those "one day" things. *One day, when I have the money. One day, when I work up the courage to reach out to my relatives there.* But Bill was all the blood family he had now. And without him, who else would Troy have in the world? A bunch of waitstaff in Hamtramck?

Lonesome Troy held tight to the very few who could see him for who he really was. Dominick. Remy. Marlie. Noelle. Gogo. Now, Roderick.

Nobody else but Roderick minded the smell of curry, though.

Marlie and Noelle were going to stop by to see if they could come up with some plan, anything, to keep the Mahaffey School from shutting down. There were talks about a community petition, getting their city councilperson involved. And when the girls found out Roderick would be there, they even began brainstorming ideas about how to collaborate with Taking Back Detroit.

Troy ordered a deep-dish pizza stuffed with seafood from Pizza Papalis since there'd finally be enough people in the house to share one of those big-ass things.

"Can you do me one favor?" Troy asked Roderick, scrubbing dishes in the sink. "Please just be nice. Noelle and Marlie really do just want to help so the kids can keep their school and we can keep our jobs."

"I'll be good," Roderick said, pecking Troy on the forehead. "Look, I know I said some shit about them before, but I understand now. They're allies."

"You promise?"

"Scout's honor."

Roderick pulled Troy tighter into him and kissed the back of his neck.

"Love you," he said.

But before Troy could respond, Roderick had released him and scurried into the bathroom. Troy set a plate to dry in the rack, rinsed off his hands, and took a sip of the riesling he'd poured earlier, still feeling the sudden tingle on his neck and wondering how true the words were that were now repeating in his ears.

Marlie and Noelle arrived about a half hour later with a legal pad, two six-packs of Ghettoblaster, and a baggie of snow. Roderick gladly partook in a line of the latter before the first slice of pizza was served.

Halfway through dinner, Marlie, who'd taken just a tiny bump, thought she had it figured out. She suggested to Roderick—who had explained everything that Taking Back Detroit was about—that the school's staff link up with TBD and stage a massive protest at the University of Detroit Mercy, calling out their hypocrisy for being a school that supposedly supported social justice but that was now robbing Black and Brown kids of a future by selling out to developers. To guarantee a higher impact, they could even do it on Accepted Students Day, when the school would have its best face on for the incoming class and parents. TBD was guaranteed to cause a ruckus, and Roderick said the group was looking for ways to engage in children's welfare throughout the city. He said he would bring the idea up at their next meeting.

Troy had decided to keep his nose clean at the get-together, but his heart began to race anyway. His friends and his boyfriend were all getting along. If only Dom and Remy could see this.

"To be honest, though," Noelle said, after going through the plan, "I just don't have much faith in Shandra. She's a fucking doormat for the board, and I don't think she'll stand with us if things get rough."

"I'm sorry, what do you mean?" Roderick said.

"Nothing," Noelle said, backtracking a bit. "I mean, she's great at her job. She's an excellent administrator. But she loses her backbone when it comes to the goddamn board . . ."

"Pardon me," Roderick said, "but this Shandra you speak of. She's a Black woman, correct?"

"She is, babe," Troy said.

"Kiburi. My name is Kiburi," Roderick said, his tone suddenly shifting. "We talked about this."

"I'm sorry," Troy said. He felt the fear in him rising.

"And with all due respect," Roderick said, looking back at Marlie and Noelle. "I don't appreciate that kind of talk about my African sister. This school largely serves African boys and African girls, right? Before people like you started moving into the neighborhood, most of the people who lived there were African, were they not? So shouldn't it be the voice of the African woman in charge of this operation that is the loudest?"

"I don't think anyone meant any harm," Troy said, his heart now sliding toward the depths of his belly.

Marlie and Noelle were both looking down at the slices of pizza that remained on the coffee table. Roderick looked back at Troy.

"I find it interesting that you never spoke an unkind word about your principal all this time but now have an issue with her after your friends mentioned one."

"We didn't mean anything by it," said Marlie.

"And now, suddenly these two girls come here with an idea about a single protest and printing up some yard signs, and you're in their camp? These are surface actions, Troy, code-switching civil disobedience. They make white people feel good while still making sure they get to dictate what's best for Black Detroit and its African people!"

"Just calm down, Roderick," Troy said.

"Don't 'calm down' me!" he said, getting up from the couch. Marlie and Noelle's faces turned pale. "And I just told you, call me Kiburi. Respect my name in this house."

"This is my house, and I'm," Troy said, burying flashbacks of when Roderick's hand was around his throat and trying not to see his friends out the corner of his eye. "I'm going to ask you to leave."

"You're telling me to leave?"

"I am asking you to leave."

"Maybe we should go," said Nicole.

"No. You're good," said Troy. "This is enough, Roderick, please just go."

"Fine, I'll go. You bootlicker, you sellout. You'll jump and skip for these white girls over here but not be the Black man you claim to be. You're not even all the way Black. You just want to be."

"What the fuck are you talking about?"

"You're not one of us. You'll never be. You weren't born into this. You haven't earned this legacy like we've earned it. Your Bangladeshi ass is only half of us. You don't deserve what we're working for."

Roderick stormed out. Troy slumped into the couch, trying to catch his breath. Both Noelle and Marlie were crying.

The meeting had been a disaster, and even though he'd apologized to Marlie and Noelle, and even though they had tried to put together some plans for the protest at the school the following Saturday—though they now knew Taking Back Detroit would not be participating—they knew things were pretty much over.

Troy needed laughter and warmth. So he drove over to Gogo's apartment in Palmer Park. Gogo, whether he was between boyfriends or not, was always there for an old friend. His quizzical look when something was off had always made Troy laugh, and the way he'd make playful puppy-dog eyes when he was wrong couldn't help but feel heartwarming.

"I've basically got a fucking pharmacy," Gogo said, talking about his newest job handling daily operations at a coworking space in Midtown. "Everybody there is on something and we just trade. But I'm stockpiling," he chuckled. "What do you want? Flexeril? Xanax? I might even have a Valium left."

"Any cigarettes?"

"Trying to quit."

"Look at you!"

"Yeah, I know. How's your dad?"

"Don't ask."

"What's going on? You're more bitter than usual."

"I'm not bitter," Troy laughed. "Everything's a mess. This new boy I told you about, Roderick . . ."

"Uh-oh."

"We fight all the time."

"Physical?"

Troy looked away, fixing his eyes on Gogo's *Lady Sings the Blues* poster on the wall. "Once," Troy said.

"Oh, Troy. I'm sorry. Have you told anyone?"

"No."

"Oh, God," Gogo exhaled, swallowing half a Xanax and then chasing it with a whiskey shot. "I mean, when you had mentioned that he was with Taking Back Detroit, I knew they were on some bullshit. That whole 'man is the head of the household thing' they're on is just . . . where is he now?"

"Gone. I put him out."

"Good. Does he have a key?"

"Yes."

"Get the locks changed."

"I will," Troy said, though he knew he was lying. In a few days, Roderick would apologize, and they'd be right back where they'd started.

"Where are you sleeping tonight?"

Troy looked at Gogo.

"The couch is all yours," Gogo said, leading his friend to a hand-me-down La-Z-Boy sectional. "I'm going to get some good oil and massage your neck."

Gogo came back with a small, label-free bottle of amber-colored oil, rubbing a bit into his palms before going to work on the back of Troy's neck.

"You know I'd still do anything for you, Troy. You're one of the sweetest people on this earth. This dude is turning you into something ugly. And you're too cute to be ugly."

"I'm cute?" Troy asked.

Gogo knelt next to him.

"Too cute for your own damn good," he said, "and you know it. You still know who the fuck you are, Troy. Don't you?"

CHAPTER THIRTEEN

"I've got a date with him tomorrow," Dominick said, passing his phone to his friends over glasses of Syrah at a newer restaurant around the corner from Remy's townhouse.

"Oh, Lord. I know him," Remy said.

"Did you date him?"

"No."

"Hooked up?"

"God, no. He's one of the Yacht Club gays."

"The hell is that?"

Remy rolled his eyes and sighed.

"Literally the most wannabe group of status-seeking, nouveau riche, faggy airheads in this city who sit around the pool at the Yacht Club all day and listen to Duolingo and eat sushi," he said.

"He means *Dua Lipa*," Troy said, laughing.

"I barely keep up with these new girls. They're all just Britney knockoffs, anyway." Remy sighed again, stabbing at his Maurice salad. "Anyway, it's business. When you reach a certain . . . level, I guess, you just have to be friends with everyone in Detroit."

"I don't understand," Dominick said.

"I don't like their asses. But occasionally, in the summer, I have to go to the Yacht Club and hang out with them."

"We're old as fuck," Troy said. "First we go to Belle Isle to get on the Giant Slide, and next thing you know, you're at the Yacht Club."

"Anyway," said Remy, "when I see these girls out and about, yeah, we'll be cordial. But really, they're like starting to—I don't know—move and shake the city. And I'm in these circles sometimes, but I don't really feature them. I just have to fake it."

"This is giving Hyacinth Bucket," Dominick said. "You're putting on airs to impress people for no reason. Keeping up appearances."

"Hya-what now?"

"Never mind."

"You've been in New York too long," Remy said. "You were surrounded by professional gay men. You could afford to burn a bridge there. Here, you can't."

"*You* can," Troy said. "You just worry too much."

"Of course I worry. I have a name," Remy said. "And Detroit is full of these folks nowadays, these faux-cialites with no discernible income. Fuck the dude and be done with it."

"What else do you know about him?" asked Dominick.

"He's Lebanese, but he claims he's white."

"I could tell he had something in him. I would've guessed Italian."

"He's one of those kinds of Lebanese that says white unless it's convenient for them to say otherwise. All his friends are white. They probably don't even know he's not white-white."

"I'm surprised he swiped on me, then."

"Girl, listen. Lebanese dudes will fuck you sideways, but don't expect a relationship. Their mamas only want them to bring home women."

"I don't think we should be having this conversation," Troy said. "We're not of this culture, and none of us here are educated enough about it to speak on it."

"Fuck all that," Remy said. "I mean, I ain't trying to be offensive, but it is what it is. This city is full of closeted Arab men, and yes, they *are* Arab—I don't care what they say, they're from the Middle East—who love our Black dicks and Black asses but won't have Black relationships.

All these religion and color complexes and daddy and mommy issues got them more fucked up than us."

"I mean, do you want a Lebanese boyfriend?" Dominick asked.

"Not necessarily, but at this point, all men have potential," Remy said. "I don't care if he's Arab, Mexican . . ."

"Latinx," Troy corrected.

"You know what I mean. Just not white. Or white-passing."

"Are these Yacht Club gays mostly white?" Dominick asked.

"Most of them, yeah," Remy said. "I hate it here sometimes. We're the majority, and it still feels like all the ones who are getting the power aren't."

"So what are you going to do about it?" asked Dominick.

The McQuerry father and son flashed across Remy's mind for a split second. He saw himself at a rooftop bar as the sun was going down, pouring out champagne for the three of them.

"I just have to fake it until I get mine," he said.

———————————

At GearWorks, Kristen and Krystin asked Dominick for some creative help on a pet project the company had taken on at the behest of one of the agency's global creative directors, Chad Dombrow, a recruit from Silicon Valley who had moved to Detroit three years ago and made it GearWorks's mission to help local, "authentic" companies who needed assistance with branding and exposure.

"Who's the client?" Dominick asked. "What are we selling?"

Krystin sighed.

"I don't know," she said, "It has something to do with paper airplanes, I think?"

"Paper airplanes?"

"This is such a nonpriority for us, but Chad wants to introduce everybody to some influencer we're thinking about bringing on board for this. It's one of the urban ideas projects we take on. Honestly, you just have to listen to Chad's spiel and see if you want to donate your time to it."

They went into the conference room and found seats. Dom felt a tap on his shoulder.

"Oh hey, Esmeralda!" Dominick said. "You're in this, too?"

"Yeah, I've actually got time to check one of these things out," she said, opening an aqua Shinola journal. "How's it going?"

"Ez," Kristen interrupted, "are you sure you have time for this?"

"Oh, don't worry Kristen, I've got time."

"This is really a meeting for creatives, Ez," Krystin said. "It might not be for you . . ."

"Chad said this could be all-hands. I'd like to try, especially with any of the Detroit projects," Esmeralda replied. "I'm from Detroit."

"I thought you were from Mexico?"

"Southwest Detroit. By way of Puerto Rico."

"Well, it's one thing to be from Detroit, but to actually sell Detroit is a different thing," Kristen said.

"I've got the time," Esmeralda said.

"Well, OK. Anyway, things should be getting started."

As Krystin and Kristen turned around, Dominick took the pen from Esmerelda's hand and wrote on the blank page of her journal, as if they were in a tenth-grade note exchange session: "*I can't believe these silly white bitches are that dense.*"

When he turned around and looked toward the front of the room, he saw Chad, who headed up GearWorks's urban projects—Dominick hated when anything was labeled "urban"—chatting with a bored-looking Black woman dressed in an African headwrap, gold bracelets, and a loose, flowy dress. Her eyes widened when she caught sight of Dominick, the only other Black person in the room.

"Wait, Natalie?" Dominick said.

"Dominick! You work here?"

"You two know each other?" Kristen asked.

"Yeah, we went to college together. H-U!"

"You know!" Natalie hollered back. The rest of the room fell silent.

Natalie Oladapo had graduated from Renaissance High, the academic powerhouse on Detroit's west side. It was cool to be a smart kid on the west side, and it was cool to go to Renaissance—though the female population there preferred to date the preppy boys who went to Dom's school, three miles away. And Natalie was one of the coolest of them all. Whenever Dominick saw her at basketball games or dances or leading a group of her friends at Northland Mall, you couldn't help but notice the artillery she'd built up: a wardrobe of Nautica jackets and Nike Air Maxes, a Visa Buxx card, a Motorola two-way pager, a custom-made Gigi Hunter dress at junior-year homecoming, a tangerine-orange Hyundai Tiburon, and approximately three hundred tons of weave.

After graduation, she'd gone to Howard and then become a hugely successful lifestyle influencer. Like every other Black person Dominick knew, he followed her on Instagram, watching as she scurried off to NYC or LA to party with the likes of Selita Ebanks and Millie Monyo. In the last few years, she had reinvented herself as a budget travel maven, seizing Instagram by the throat as she trotted around the world, staying in hostels, eating "like the locals," and mailing beautiful silks and beadery back home.

Renaissance High alumni, ever a gossipy bunch, wondered how she did it all. No one could figure out how she could afford it. *Are her abs showing because she works out, or is the bitch starving to death?* they wondered. And when she'd been spotted back in Detroit recently, local tongues had been wagging again. *Was she sick? Was she exiled from somewhere? Was she broke?* She and Dominick had always hit it off, but one thing was for sure: Natalie was cold. (Not temperature or personality-wise—the Detroit definition. Ask a real one.)

After their greeting and the awkward silence from the room that had followed, Natalie tried to shirk back into a regal poise. Dominick planned to stay silent the rest of the meeting.

"Wow, that's really great," Chad said, finally breaking the silence. "People always told me Detroit has that small-town feel and it really does! OK, well, thanks for dropping in, everybody, it's really appreciated. I'm sure you all know that one of our core missions at GearWorks is to uplift and amplify homegrown products, and today we've got one of Detroit's finest right here, Natalie Oladapo. Some of you, like Dominick, may know Natalie from her Instagram account, @gonataliego, where more than 500,000 followers track her exploits around the world. How many of you here follow her?"

Dominick shot his hand in the air. But when he looked around the room, he realized he was the only one. He tried not to look directly at Natalie, who was obviously mortified.

"OK, well, you will!" said Chad, as cheerfully as he could. "I thought it would be great to bring Natalie in on this exciting new project we're working on. Now, what we need for this are few deliverables," continued Chad, "like a tagline that really drives home the Detroit message. Then we'll need product copy, further campaign work around the Detroit image, and maybe future talking points for the client."

"God, are we doing speechwriting now?" Krystin whispered.

"But before we do all that, let's talk about the spec video I sent around this morning. It's obviously *very* spec, but did anyone have thoughts?"

A young woman with cropped blonde hair raised her hand.

"I think it's one of the better videos to capture, you know, the spirit of Detroit in one message, that I've seen," she said.

"Yeah, it's hard to argue with how, I don't know the word, maybe compelling? Yeah, compelling. How compelling the video is with the voiceover," said Chad.

"It's very Chrysler, but better," chimed in another voice.

"Do we want it to be Chrysler?"

"Well, it works, right? There's no use reinventing the wheel.

Detroiters love this town, and you show the town they love."

Dominick raised his hand.

"Excuse me, may I . . . may I cut in here?" he asked.

All eyes turned toward him. He had promised himself he wasn't going to say anything, and now he was engaging in the politics of interruption. Black boys are taught "excuse me," taught to wait until the conversation is over. In corporate settings, you have to jump in where you can, but those Black boys, who are now Black men, have to do it with grace. It has to be prefaced. You have to have a hint of that politeness you're taught at a young age. You still have to be aggressive, but not in a way that comes off as too intimidating to the white people in the room. All of this, just to get a word in.

"Sure, Dominick," Chad said. "Has everyone here met Dominick? He's a killer new hire. He won a bunch of medals working at one of our sister offices in New York."

"Thank you, Chad," Dominick said. "If I can be honest, I don't know if this video feels Detroit at all to me. It's very *downtown* Detroit, but Detroit is so much bigger than that. It doesn't show any of the neighborhoods, any houses, or any trees, or color. There's no Belle Isle, no Giant Slide. You know, the Giant Slide? You ride it . . . backwards . . . with your eyes closed?"

"That's right next to Hipster Beach!" a young woman sitting a few rows up said.

"Uh, yeah, if that's what it's called now. But this video really just shows everything downtown that was built, like, a year ago. And you don't even have any . . . I'm not sure how to say this . . . ."

Here Dominick paused, knowing that his next critique needed to be framed perfectly in order to be taken seriously, in order to not shut down the entire conversation.

"Go on," Chad said.

Dominick quickly once-overed the room, realizing he was the only one of two among his peers and not the guest of honor. For a split second, he locked eyes with Natalie.

"Well," he said, "the video doesn't have any Black people in it, and Detroit is a majority Black city."

Save for the gurgles of someone drinking from their water bottle, the room sat nervously quiet for about ten seconds before Natalie spoke up.

"I'd agree with Dominick," she said, "and when I think about how this video might play with the Detroit folks I follow on Instagram . . ."

"We tried to look for people of color," Chad said, "and that's something we'll need help with for the campaign going forward. Would you and Dominick potentially want to help us take that on?"

"This is an ad for a bespoke paper airplane company," Dominick said. "I'm not sure why we would need to show emotional visuals about downtown Detroit for that? And, no offense to you, Natalie . . ."

"None taken, believe me, love," Natalie said.

"But I'm not sure how an influencer of her stature would help with this—the two things just aren't running in the same circles."

"Well, at GW, we always come back to the idea that the city of Detroit is your clever coconspirator. You've got a sense of adventure, and Detroit is here for the ride."

"I'm not . . . I'm not sure I understand."

"Well, the concept of a clever coconspirator here at GW is someone who doesn't take the spotlight but is a key supporting player."

"But Detroit is the focus of this visual," Dominick said.

"Right. It's supporting the Detroit Paper Airplane Company, on its journey."

"The ride?"

"The journey. As a coconspirator."

"And . . . so the influencer would be a supporting player . . ."

"Coconspirator," Chad said.

"Right . . . would Natalie be a coconspirator as well?" Dominick asked. He could feel the room deflating around him.

"Absolutely," Chad said. "But if you're thinking we need stronger visuals, then . . . ."

"Or maybe," Esmeralda said, raising her hand, attempting to save Dominick, "could we add some visuals of Clark Park into the draft materials as we go deeper into the campaign? It's a big, open space— perfect for flying paper airplanes—and you'd have plenty of diverse faces there, if that's a concern."

"We already do quite a bit with Clark Park," Krystin said. "I don't think we want to create any favoritism with one place. But there may be other places around the city that might work? Ez, maybe you and Dominick can brainstorm some more in a separate meeting?"

"I'm afraid we're at time," the other half of the Kristen-Krystin duo said. "Chad, any final thoughts?"

"Not right now, but we do want to thank Natalie again for coming out. We're really looking forward to working with her on this."

Tepid applause and a few "thank yous" rose from the room as people began making their way out. Dominick, unsure of what to make of the last half-hour's activity, watched as his coworkers quietly exited. Just as he rose to go back to his own desk, Natalie stopped him.

"Hey, what are you doing back in Detroit?" she asked. "It's been so long, love!"

"I should be asking you the same thing!"

"It's . . . let's just say I felt a need to come back and . . . refresh. But Dominick . . .," Natalie said, lowering her voice. "What on God's green earth happened just now? What am I even doing here?"

"You think you can hang around until five when I'm off, and we can get a drink?"

"I'm not sure I can wait that long, love," she said. "I desperately need to get out of this building. I can feel the life draining out of me. But hey, we're both back here for a reason, and I suspect it might be the same thing."

"Everything OK?"

"Send me a DM, love. I've got to be at the Shinola Hotel in an hour, and I barely remember how the freeways work around here. But . . . we should *definitely* catch up."

Joseph Thomas had suggested he and Dominick have a late dinner at La Dolce Vita on the edge of Palmer Park. They shared eggplant parmigiana and bucatini carbonara, and afterward, Joseph suggested they go to the Eagle, a gay bar Dominick had never heard of on the other side of Woodward. When they got there, the bouncer at the door stamped their hands, and Joseph immediately took Dominick's hand and guided him toward the back.

Doesn't every city in America have a risqué gay bar called the Eagle? Dominick thought. *And isn't it interesting that a symbol of American pride—white American pride?—is the adopted name for each one? Do white men choose everything? Stop overthinking, Dominick.*

This place had all the telltale signs of an "Eagle" bar. The walls were paneled with painted black plywood and covered with posters of men in skimpy lumberjack attire. A fog machine belched white mist against two spotlights, one with a pink neon bulb, the other orange. Every inch of the place looked like it could fall apart at any moment. Shoddy craftsmanship, conveying just the seedy message its owners were hoping to send. This was not a place for romance. This was uninhibited sleaze. In the dark, behind walls, where strangers could dance without judgment but nonetheless maintain their discretion.

Joseph pulled Dominick around a corner and pushed him against a makeshift wall, leaning into his face and kissing him. Dominick reciprocated, pulling Joseph in closer and putting his hand on his crotch.

"Let's go back to your place," Dominick whispered.

"Not yet," Joseph said.

Joseph moved to the floor and rested on his knees, unbuckling Dominick's belt and opening the fly of his pants. He pulled out Dominick's dick and worked it in his mouth.

Dominick looked down, laughed nervously, and then tapped Joseph on the shoulder. He wanted to say, "that's enough," but he started to tingle. He was feeling it. He put his hand behind Joseph's head and nudged it closer. Dominick closed his eyes, the bass from the music now pulsing through the soles of his feet. When he opened them again, he caught sight of a fat bearded man staring at the two of them, jacking off.

Dominick gently pushed Joseph's head away.

"Let's finish this at your place," he said.

His belt was still unbuckled as he got behind the wheel. Joseph lay limp in the passenger seat, massaging Dominick's erection through his jeans. They crossed the border into Ferndale, and when they arrived at Joseph's front door, they nearly knocked it off the hinges before snatching each other's clothes off.

"Want some?" Joseph asked, handing Dominick a small, brown bottle with a red and yellow label.

"You know, I don't really do poppers, because isn't that . . . kind of bad for you in the long run?"

"Nah," Joseph said, pressing the uncapped bottle to each nostril and inhaling deeply. "It's just a little rush. Not like you'll faint every time you snuff."

Nearly forgetting that he had done a bump of blow with his best friend not even a full week after being back home, Dominick took a quick sniff.

"Do you have any lube?" he asked.

"Fuck, I just ran out."

"Uh . . . do you have any lotion?"

"Hold on."

Joseph scurried out of the bedroom, his pancake ass flopping behind him. Dominick, feeling dizzy, heard the creak, and then the slam, of a cabinet. Then, footsteps.

"This might work," Joseph said.

"Come here," Dominick said breathily. "Let's take a look."

Joseph pulled a yellow spray can from behind his back, and when Dominick saw it, he snapped out his amyl nitrated-induced haze and nearly jumped out of the bed and up to the ceiling.

"*PAM?* Are you fucking crazy?"

"What? It might work?"

"I'm not about to fuck you with vegetable oil in a spray can!"

"Let me spray this on your cock and we'll try it."

"You're not spraying PAM on my dick. That is not going to happen." Dominick felt his erection starting to deflate like a dollar-store balloon.

"OK, maybe I can take it. Let me see, if I just . . ."

Joseph straddled Dominick and immediately shoved his penis inside him. This was a red flag for Dom. That easy? No hesitation? He must have been fucked recently, and maybe that shit about being too loose was true. But how recently? Two hours ago?

This guy is loose, he thought. *Or maybe he's just a natural. Don't overthink this right now, Dom. All men have potential.*

"God, I love your big cock," Joseph said, grinding on Dom's crotch.

Dominick closed his eyes and said a silent prayer in his head: *Please, Lord, don't let him say it. Don't let him say it.* He opened his eyes and pulled Joseph in for a kiss. Joseph slowed his grinding, their torsos and mouths now moving in sync.

Joseph closed his eyes, and Dominick glanced around the room, taking a quick inventory. Blue-gray paint on the wall with white crown molding bordering the ceiling and door jambs. Matching nightstands on each side of the bed with lamps that matched the fixture above. Clean floors. And the bedsheets, a nice cotton blend with a good thread count from what he could tell.

He's living all right, he thought. *I wouldn't have too much work to do.* Joseph pulled up off him and rolled over to his knees.

"God, you get so deep," Joseph said. "I love your big, Black cock!"

Goddammit, Dominick thought.

"Fuck me doggy style, handsome," he said.

Dominick obliged and mounted him, but then he caught a faint smell and felt his dick push on to something hard and jagged.

Shit. Literal, actual shit, he thought to himself.

"Keep going," Joseph said.

Hell no, I can't keep going, Dominick thought. *I just touched your stool. What in the Toni Morrison hell? I can't fucking believe this. Shit, shit, shit.* His dick started to soften as he realized God hadn't answered his prayers for clean ass.

He grabbed his penis and put it back in, and sure enough, when he wiped his hand on the sheet, it left behind a brown residue.

The smell grew stronger, and so did Dominick's thrusts as he tried to get it over with. He closed his eyes and held his breath, gripping the sides of Joseph's waist harder, pushing until he came. He let out a few grunts for aesthetics (though ejaculation still felt good) while Joseph tried to tighten his sphincter around Dom's dick. It didn't work. Dom pulled out, looking down at a pale brown streak across the condom, like honey-Dijon mustard on a kielbasa.

"Do you mind if I use the bathroom?" he asked.

"No, go right ahead. It's down the hall."

Some fucking nerve, he thought. He unrolled a mile of toilet paper, wrapped some of it around his hand, pulled the condom off, and immediately flushed it. Then he took the remaining toilet paper and wiped his dick off. He looked around and grabbed a hand towel (at least one that clearly wasn't decorative—you have to have some hookup etiquette). He wet the top half with warm water and soap and scrubbed around his dick, balls, and crotch, being careful to move in the same motion so as to absorb the shit and not rub it in. He used the other half to dry everything off. Then he urinated what little was inside his bladder and repeated the birdbath with another hand towel for good measure. His crotch now smelled like milk, honey, and almond instead of shit.

Have bottoms always been this foul? he thought.

Dominick swore when he had first started fucking, this was never a problem. What could it be? The apps? Did this dick-on-demand culture give access to men who wanted it now, right now? Was everything so immediate that they didn't have time to practice basic, prehookup hygiene?

"I usually try not to come so quick. But it's been a . . .," Dominick said, exhaling deeply and attempting to save the night with some banter, "rough week at the office."

"Oh."

Dominick's eyes darted back and forth, waiting for more from Joseph. He decided to go on anyway.

"Yeah, I'm a writer at this ad agency. I mentioned that at dinner, right? Anyway, it just seems like they have these outdated ideas about how the city is, and I just feel like, you know, I'm actually from Detroit and I have some valuable insight, but when I try to say something—which is hard, because you know, I'm new there, and I'm not really, uh, ingrained, I guess is the right word, in the culture there—but aside from that, I just know that if I were to say something, it would automatically get shut down, and it's like, well, what can I do? And even if I do put in all this work, I might never find my way into the culture of this place. But anyway . . ."

"Yeah, that is a lot," Joseph said, stretching his arms outward. "Well, this was fun, handsome, but I've got to be up early, so . . ."

"Right . . . well, you're right . . . I have an early morning, too," Dominick said, putting on his underwear. "Maybe we can do this again sometime."

"Yeah, because I need to feel that cock in me again."

Dominick wanted to say more. But he swallowed his words and sent them to the bottom of his stomach. He knew he'd only come off as angry. It was better to just hold it in and try to keep up appearances.

CHAPTER FOURTEEN

The McGregor Center is absolutely one of Detroit's most gorgeous buildings. Minoru Yamasaki really did that shit. I've been here a few times for events, fundraisers, and shit like that. Today I'm here for a career fair before some afternoon showings. It's insanely bright in here all the time because the building is covered in glass, and the sunlight reflects off the white marble on the first floor. But when I'm at the top of the second-floor landing, I can't help but think about falling over the railing and landing headfirst onto the marble, my blood and brain matter splattering everywhere.

It's beautiful, but I dread it because lately, that image is all I can think about. Today, I'm supposed to be on a panel for these college juniors and seniors, hopefully convincing them not to make terrible career choices. They'll fall asleep listening to what I'm talking about because no one their age cares about selling real estate. And who knows? I've got so much on my mind with Roland and Terrell and this McQuerry deal and Troy acting all sad about Mahaffey closing that maybe I'll stop listening to myself.

I walk slowly up the stairs, making sure my entire foot lands on each step while I grip the handrail as tight as I can. I stay away from the balcony so that nothing—me tripping over my feet, an unexplained gust of wind, whatever—could knock me over onto the marble. And still, all I see in my head is my own demise. I promise I'm not suicidal. I don't even like to think like this because what if I'm foreshadowing? But I can't explain why I keep having these visions, why I'm curious about what it would feel like if I fell.

I keep trying to tell Troy about the McQuerrys, the microstudios, and the school, but I know he'd kill me. I tried to find a way to tell him that night we were all at the Woodward, but my hints didn't take. And I can't just, like, drop into the group chat and tell him that it's basically a done deal that the Mahaffey School is done. Ever since he started hanging with those white teachers at his school, he's changed. Now everything is "Eat the rich" and "Guillotine!" That's how all these new white people are in Detroit now. But I'll be damned if some white socialists, anarchists—whatever kind of -ists they say they are—who just fucking moved here are going to say something about everything I've worked my ass off for years to get. I just never imagined Troy would fall into all that. You'd think he'd see his dad—the way his money helped Detroit even if he had to get his hands a little dirty—and see that as a possible option rather than just messing around with Marielle and Natalie, or Marlie and Noelle—whatever their names are. Bill Clements understands that everybody's just out here getting theirs, that the thing driving this city is money, and that if you don't get out here and take it, somebody else will. Shit, if I'm not having lunch with the McQuerrys, somebody else sure as hell is gonna be there. At least if it's me at that table, I'll have a say on how Detroit might look in the future and not just be screaming my head off in front of city hall, holding some flimsy sign while the real paperwork's getting inked inside.

Whenever people call me to do shit like this talk today, they're like, "You're a *hero* for Detroit!" Whatever. I'm just a nigga from the east side who had to make it. I didn't ask for all this. I should probably have more confidence, as Troy might say. I should probably be, like he would say, an ambassador for marginalized *el-gee-bee-tee-cue-eye-ay-plus* people of color. But I just can't do that. I don't want to be anyone's hero. That's the thing about living here. Niggas here have done this city so wrong, any young Black person with a voice is supposed to be a leader. I really don't want to lead anybody, because half the time I don't even know where we're leading to. You're not supposed to feel burdened by the city that made you who you are. I don't want kids looking up to me, I don't want old ladies lusting after me, I don't want these men in my face talking about "Man, I'm just trying to get like you!" All I want is peace, money, and good dick.

After the fair, your Detroit hero is now on the corner of Calvert and the Lodge in a neighborhood that doesn't quite have a name. It's not Boston-Edison, the nice neighborhood with the mansions that everyone on the west side of Detroit has coveted for years. And I don't know if it's really Dexter-Linwood either, which is named after two of the hoodest streets ever known to man. That's Detroit, though—the hood-hood is always right next to the rich hood. We're all in the quote-unquote struggle, though, and this afternoon, I'm trying to convince this young Black couple they should buy this house on Calvert and the Lodge because it's in this gray area between the hood and not-the-hood. I try not to smoke in the Charger, but I roll the windows down and take a hit before I go in, making sure to spritz on some Tom Ford Black Orchid to cover up the smell.

"As you can see, it does need a little work," I say, pointing to the cracked crown molding above us in the living room and fully aware of the frayed carpet. "But you can get a first-time homebuyer's grant, or a renovation grant. There are so many ways to get money now to fix up an old house in Detroit."

"I don't know," the wife says, drumming her fingers across her Goyard clutch—I see she couldn't afford the whole tote, but I ain't judging.

"What's the ROI in this neighborhood? What's going on with homes on Edison or Longfellow?" the husband asks.

"May I be honest with you?"

"Please," the husband says.

"I'm not going to tell you what's going on with Edison or Longfellow because you already know. A few years ago, you could get a house there for

$25,000. Now you need $350,000 just to get in the door. Next year, it's not going to be $500,000 *yet*, but it *is* going to be at least $400,000. But here's the thing," I say, leading them to the kitchen, which has been patched over with peel-and-stick linoleum on the floor and builder-grade cabinets. "You can't afford Boston-Edison. I have your numbers and you aren't approved for $250,000. You're approved for Rosedale Park, but you say you want to live close to downtown. So I'm trying to show you this area outside of Boston-Edison because guess what? If we go one block over to Glynn Court, which is just like Longfellow, then you're going to see a whole bunch of white transplants sitting on their porches at houses that look exactly like the one we're standing in right now. You would never think white people would be out here off Linwood or Dexter, but here they are, and you know why? They're not afraid anymore. This economy has got things so fucked up that white people are looking everywhere and anywhere they can afford to live because they don't want to live in the suburbs anymore. They want to have an *authentic* Detroit experience on their terms and with their own money, so they're buying these $25,000 houses on Glynn Court, on Collingwood, on Lawrence, on Burlingame, and on Elmhurst. And guess what? They're buying right here on Calvert because they're not afraid. They come into these neighborhoods and mind their own business just like our aunties and uncles have done for years. They don't sell drugs, but they buy them, just enough to stay high but not enough to cause trouble. They don't go where they're not welcome. They drive cars that won't get stolen. And they don't walk around with thousand-dollar Goyard bags bringing attention to themselves. They're going to gentrify each and every one of these streets right under our noses. And you know what's going to happen? Folks like *us* are going to be lamenting how much the hood has changed while sitting by our fireplaces in Birmingham, paying two and three thousand dollars a month for mortgages we can barely afford because we wanted to make something of ourselves by owning a house, because that's what the American Dream tells us to do. Well, I'm giving you this chance to own a house—it's even got a damn fireplace—and you can be one of those rare Black Detroit couples that actually takes back the hood and makes it worth something before the white people do it their way. And you can have this house, or any of the rest of the comps I can show you with a quarter of the cash it would take to buy some eight-hundred-square-foot piece of nothing on Fourteen Mile just so you can send your kids to an all-white school where they'll be called a nigger three times a week in the cafeteria."

I know I've gone on a tangent. But I have to be real. And there they are, standing dumbfounded in this kitchen with plywood covering the windows and paint peeling above us.

I won't make a fucking dime off this commission if I sell it. I won't have any dings to my reputation if they run and tell everyone I made fun of Miss Mamas's little Goyard bag, either. What I do know is that I'm standing my ground and trying my best to get these Black folks to buy a house in the middle of the hood when everything around the hood is starting to change.

"We need a moment. Do you mind?" the woman asks.

"I'm going to head upstairs to make sure there are no surprises," I say. It's true. With these old houses, it might be a possum or some shit living in the closets. But I also need to text Terrell to confirm plans for later. Felix said he wanted to finally go out on Saturday, and that's the only night Terrell is free. So I'm trying to move Terrell to Sunday. I love the dick, but damn if I don't feel like a prostitute scheduling two dicks into my agenda.

"Can you do Sunday morning?" I text, knowing there's a chance I might still be worn out from Felix the night before, but I don't care.

"Gotta take mom to church. What's wrong with Saturday?" he texts back.

I don't respond right away.

He texts again. "Another dude?"

I text back, "What if it was?"

•••

Terrell Puryear
Hmm

Remy Patton
We're not exclusive

Terrell Puryear
I didn't say all that

Remy Patton
So what's the issue

Terrell Puryear
I'm just saying

Remy Patton
Elaborate

Terrell Puryear
Never mind

Remy Patton
If you want to use some big boy
words, now's the time

Terrell Puryear
Just never mind. Have fun on Saturday and
I'll see you when I see you

Remy Patton
Lol why are you being so emotional?

Terrell Puryear
I'm not emotional

Remy Patton
Whatever, I'll ttyl

•••

"What do you think?" I ask, making my way back downstairs, being sure not to put too much weight on the rickety banister.

"I mean, you didn't have to come for my Goyard like that," the woman laughs, "but I hear you. We're going to think about this one, but we'd also like to see some other comps in the neighborhood."

"Of course," I say. "Follow me upstairs. The master bedroom has so much potential."

———————————

On Friday, Felix texts me to cancel for Saturday—a last-minute gig came up in Cleveland. Surprise, surprise. At first, I think about texting Terrell to see if he wants to keep our original plans, but the truth is, I'm in the mood to suck new dick. But my phone is dry. Was an email sent out across the city that I was damaged goods or something? Am I unattractive? How the fuck am I supposed to feel? This mouth is platinum. This mouth has a 750 credit score. This mouth is God's Storehouse of Eternal Love.

So, as usual, after I make my texting rounds and see none of my regulars want to come through, I check Scruff with my blank profile for new prospects. And per fucking usual, I see the same old faces in the grid, the same usual suspects:

Hood gays. One time, I had a dude over who wanted to dilute my very expensive bottle of pinot grigio with the only other thing I had in the fridge at the time, Pamplemousse La Croix. Then he asked if I had fruit punch so he could mix it up some more. I put him out. That's every nigga on the east side, in a nutshell.

Church gays. Have you ever given head to someone with Karen Clark-Sheard playing in the background, and then when they nutted, they did a Karen Clark-Sheard run themselves? These damn Church of God in Christ gays. Drop a bomb in Gilead.

Alden Towers gays. It's a damn shame what happened to that building. One of Detroit's nicest exteriors and they let that bitch get raggedy as fuck on the inside. Niggas there be having bedbugs and box springs on the floor. Pass.

Ferndale gays. Just a horny bunch of old white guys who fantasize about Black men but don't want to live near them. They need to rebuild that Eight Mile wall in my opinion.

Roland was such a breath of fresh air when I saw him on the grid for the first time. But now, I see that he's on the grid again.

Oh? Oh.

His profile says he's five miles away from me, which means he's most likely at the Marriott, his usual place. Why didn't he tell me he was coming? Maybe he had a last-minute schedule change. But still, why wouldn't he tell me that?

I ain't asking the man to marry me. *Yet.* I just want to know where we're going with this, whatever this is. And the fact that he's in town without telling me, after all we've been through, well, I have an issue. So I text him to let him know I saw him—I know, I know. He at least *says* it was a last-minute change and he's headed back to London in the morning. But he says we could meet up at the Volt Bar inside the RenCen. And yes, since I know it's only a short walk and an elevator ride to his hotel room, I douche before I leave the house.

———————————

"So, uh . . . why didn't you tell me you were here?" I ask him.

"Like I said, it was last minute. And besides, we don't have to see each other every time I'm in town now, do we?"

Roland sips his martini, straight up with a twist. Like a Black James Bond.

"We're not obligated to, but . . . I don't know, not even a text?"

"I thought it was clear we weren't going to get emotionally involved in this."

Don't get emotionally involved. Don't get attached. Yeah, this motherfucker *had* said that. But you know what else he said? "When we" and "if we" and "let us" and "all our." And now *we're* here. And *we* seem to be having an argument.

"I know. But then why do we keep seeing each other like this?" I ask.

"I enjoy your company, mate. It's fun."

"And I enjoy yours." I take a long sip of my wine. "I still think about London."

"I told you you should move there. Then we could pursue *something*. But until then, we can't get too caught up now, can we?"

"I can't just move to London."

I can't. I mean, it would be nice. But you know how people talk. For most Black men—oh, he must be running away from something. *You know he only moved to another state to get away from child support, right?* It ain't always that, but that's always what they think. The Black gay man, though? *Oh, he was too good for us? Something must've happened. He fake. He bougie.* Niggas will tell your biography without opening to the first page, won't they? And on top of that, I can't afford to just move around like that. I'd have to start from the bottom again. The Black men who don't leave Detroit move upward because they stay. You try going somewhere else with the same credentials and getting the same kind of offers a white man does.

Still. That "*until then*" Roland said. That part. That's where I'm at. That's where I'm stuck. Maybe he's right that he doesn't have to hit me up every time he's in town. Maybe I *do* need to make a move that clearly indicates I'm serious about . . . whatever this is. And that "this" won't have a definition until I—or *we*—make it so.

"Have you ever been to Palm Springs?" Roland asks.

"No. I've always wanted to go."

"Same here. Ex-boy wanted to go. But I'm still going 'cos it turns out my route is taking me to LAX later this year. Maybe you and I could have a little trip?"

I look down at my empty wine glass, not just because of my own feelings for Roland but also because I hate that he's always bringing up his ex-boyfriend, Lou. Some white boy he was with, which didn't quite match up with his "keep Brixton Black" persona.

"Roland. I'm confused. I have . . . something for you. I can't explain what it is, but you say you don't want it. But then you ask if I want to go to Palm Springs. If we're casual, we shouldn't be taking trips like this."

"Don't you enjoy them? Didn't you like coming to London?"

"I loved it."

He leans over, looks me in the eye, and places one of his dark hands on my thigh.

"Well, now I want to fuck you in Palm Springs," he says.

I knock his hand off.

"And then?"

He sighs.

"And then, I don't know. But maybe after Palm Springs, you'll think a little more about London."

––––––––––

Less than twenty-four hours later, I find myself at Capers with Terrell.

Now, I don't take a man to Capers unless he's worth it. My mama would only take me there on special occasions. Now that I can afford it, I take her there on Mother's Day, her birthday, and anytime she wants, really. It's the best steakhouse in Detroit, even though it's right next to a used car dealer and it looks like a cabaret or some shit from the outside. I took my longest relationship, Quentin, there once too. But we broke up three weeks later. Ever since, I've pretty much kept Capers to myself.

Seeing as Terrell came up on the east side, though, I know he's been here a few times. But now we're here together.

"The plant's probably not going to be making combustion engines in twenty years," he says between sips of his Miller Lite.

"Are you still going to be working at Chrysler in twenty years?"

"I don't know. Right now, I'm trying to plan in case everything gets automated. I still want to do my thirty and out. I'm halfway there, and I hope I can make it. But just in case, I've been coming up with a backup plan."

"What's that?" I ask.

"You promise not to laugh?"

"What? Tell me."

"OK," he says. "I want to open a butcher shop."

"A butcher shop?"

"Yeah. I'm going to make homemade sausages, preseasoned cuts of meat, all that."

"Are you serious?" I ask. I really can't tell if he's serious or not.

"Yeah!" he says. "Go down to Eastern Market. Who's been there all this time? The butchers."

"True."

"You probably didn't know I had an interest in that, did you?"

"I didn't."

"Well, I told you before."

"When?"

"Remember when I brought those brownies to your house?"

Shit. That night he brought those edibles that knocked me out for damn near a whole weekend. I remember we split one before he fucked me to sleep.

"You were out of your mind," Terrell laughs. "But we talked all morning."

He stuffs a bacon-and-cheddar potato skin in his mouth.

"Shit is good," he says.

I honestly don't remember what we had talked about. But now that I'm thinking about that morning, it crosses my mind that it was the only time he'd spent the night and stayed with me until the next day.

"I made breakfast," he says.

"I remember," I say. "Steak and eggs. I told you not to use my Delmonicos because I was saving them for company."

"Wasn't I company?"

"Wh—never mind, Terrell."

I cut into my T-bone and take a bite. Now it's quiet between us—not the calm I'd been hoping for—even though every table around us is buzzing.

"Why do you like wine so much?" he asks.

"I don't know," I say. "It's classy. It's grown-up. You could learn something. I mean, bro—you're drinking Miller Lite with a steak."

"That's how I like it."

"It's immature."

"What?"

"Look, if you really want to be an entrepreneur and open a business, the way I do? Every day? You've got to step it up. Wear better clothes. Go nicer places. Drink better . . . drinks."

"You know what your problem is? You're too uptight, always trying to run people's lives."

"I am *not* uptight, and I am *not* trying to run anyone's life."

"Yes, you are. You know how you talk about your friend, Troy? How you always think he can do better than that one guy he's with?"

"That's because he *can* do better. I know Troy. I know he's better than that bum-ass nigga."

"Your definition of better isn't the next person's definition. I mean, damn, I'm trying to tell you about what I want to do with my life and you're going in on me over some beer."

Don't tell me this nigga is in his feelings over a damn Miller Lite.

"I was just playing," I say. "I'm sorry I hurt you and your little bottle of beer. Enjoy what you like. I won't judge."

"And for the fuckin' record, I do wear nice clothes. You didn't have to buy me that suit."

"I did. You didn't have one."

"I do, but that's beside the point." He takes a long sip of beer. When he sets the bottle down, he starts peeling the label on the neck with his thumb.

"This is fuckin' crazy," he laughs. "We're fighting like we're a married couple or some shit."

But I don't see shit funny.

CHAPTER FIFTEEN

"I just want someone I can walk into a room with," Dominick said. He, Troy, and Remy were back at their normal happy hour table at Motor City Wine.

"What do you mean? Like, make an entrance?" Troy asked.

"I mean, just someone you feel comfortable walking into a room of people with. You look good together, and there's no doubt to anyone else about what you are. He's dressed nice, he smells nice, you're holding his hand, or you're arm in arm, and you just look so damn good with him. Like yeah, we're walking into this room, and we're owning it."

"NeNe Leakes," Troy snickered, taking a sip of California zinfandel.

"No, not NeNe, that's not what I'm saying."

"You just quoted an Atlanta housewife," Remy said.

"You motherfuckers know exactly what I mean."

"I mean, it's a little superficial to base it entirely around looks," Troy said.

"Is that wrong?" Dominick asked. "You ever seen a bummy couple? Do they look happy? They don't look happy because they're not happy. And yes, maybe I do want us to look good together at any age. In our thirties, forties, whenever. I'm going to stay slim."

"What about him? What if he loses his hair or gains weight? And you over there talking about dating white boys, knowing they the main ones who are in denial about going bald," Remy said.

"First of all, I said dating a white man was an option, not my mission, and second, I said I'll cross that bridge when *we* get to it. I'll love him as long as he can, you know," Dominick paused and gestured toward his crotch.

"Lord help us all," Troy said.

"I'm right there with you. I mean, shit, just because we get old, we gotta stop fucking? Hell naw! I'mma still be putting my legs up over my head with a fake hip and a knee replacement."

"Y'all are too much. I can't," Troy said.

"Take those dentures out and slob on this knob, nigga!" Dominick howled.

"Stop it!" Troy said.

"Boy, take them Depends off and let's go!" Remy said.

Troy couldn't help but laugh and join in.

"Eating wrinkled ass looking like chitlins!" he said.

All three boys, red-faced and near tears, roared.

"You know that after you date one white guy, they all look the same after you break up with them. And they all remind you of what you were supposed to have," Remy said.

"How do you know? Because *you've* dated one?" Dominick said.

"No," Remy said, suddenly regretting this disclosure.

"Yes," Troy laughed. "Yes, you have, lying ass!"

"He didn't count," Remy said, looking away while taking a sip.

"You liked his ass, don't lie."

"I know you fuckin' lying. You were sprung over some white dick?" Dominick asked.

"It was one time. A short time, the only time, and the last time," Remy said.

"A Black dude from Detroit caught up over some white boy from the suburbs," Dominick smiled. "It's giving *The Boys in the Band*."

"*Patrick*," Troy said, swirling his glass and affecting a sing-song voice, "was from *Toledo*."

"Nigga. Ohio?" Dominick asked.

"He lived in Detroit before he moved there. I'll give him credit for that," Remy said.

"What, would y'all meet up to ride that bicycle tightrope at the COSI Museum?" Dominick asked.

"There might have been rope involved at some point," Troy said.

"Both of y'all can die a slow, painful death," Remy said. "Look, I was willing to try it one time to see what it was like. I had fun; it didn't work. And that's that on that. My anti-white-boy stance remains."

"But . . ." Troy said.

"But nothing," Remy said. "*Nothing.*"

Troy glared at him.

"Just tell Dominick. This is a safe space."

Remy sighed.

"All right," he said, now taking a healthy gulp of his malbec. "He had the biggest dick I had ever seen in my life at that point."

Dominick jumped back in his chair and covered the squeal escaping from his mouth. "Whaaaaaaaat?"

"Yeah, yeah. Judge not, lest ye be judged. I couldn't help it. It was, like, Rocco Steele big. I wasn't ready!"

"I'm not judging. I've seen *some* big dicks on white boys—I mean, nothing I can do with them except, you know," Dominick said, clicking the inside of his cheek and pointing to his mouth.

"Enough with all this," Remy said. "I mean, is a white man going to pluck the ingrown hairs out your beard? Because that's love. That's Black love. You can't get that with a white man, and that's why I'm one and done."

"I've consigned myself to the possibility—not the reality—that *maybe* I'll end up with a white man," Dominick said. "What I'm saying, Remy, is that sometimes it's not all that bad and maybe if I keep an open mind, you know . . ."

"You're the most sensitive top I've ever met," Remy said. "No offense, boo, but damn. You have more emotions than dick."

"Excuse me?"

"I'm saying, Dom. Tops are masculine. You're not. You're so deep in your feelings all the time. You want to be swept off your feet, but as the top, you're the one who's supposed to do the sweeping."

"Can you get your boy? Get your boy," Dominick said, turning to Troy.

"Remy, that's a very narrow way of looking at things," Troy said.

"You sound just like my damn ex," Dominick said.

"Is that why y'all ain't together?" Remy asked.

"Now hold the fuck up . . ." Dominick said.

"Hey, hey, boys, listen. Y'all are doing a little too much right now, chill."

"Explain what you mean, Remy."

"Y'all might call it old-fashioned or whatever, but I think tops should be masculine and bottoms should . . . have a little more leeway. I mean, shit. I ain't exactly GI Joe over here and never will be."

"But . . ." Dominick said.

"But that's it. I mean, if I'm gonna be with a man, I need a man. Someone to look out and take care of me."

"Take care of your damn self, Remy. You're already doing that," Dom said. "Look the fuck around you."

"What do you mean?"

"You rich-ass bitch. You don't need a man to do for you. You're clearly doing for yourself."

"That's different. This is my money, this is my career, my bag. I'm talking about in the bedroom."

"Don't worry about what I do in the bedroom," Dominick said. "Just know I handle it."

"I bet you cry when you cum," Remy laughed.

"Bitch, fuck you," Dominick laughed, putting up both middle fingers. "You ain't shit."

"I see what Remy is trying to say," Troy said. "But we shouldn't have to live in gendered norms forced on us by the patriarchy."

"Here we go with the academic shit," Remy said.

"Yeah, bitch, here we go. How are you gonna sit there and talk about Dominick being too . . . whatever you think he's too much of, when you get mad when someone calls you too sissy or faggy? You gotta put bass in your voice every time you show one of these white folks a house just so you can get paid . . ."

"Oop!" Dominick said.

"How about this, Remy?" Troy continued. "How about we all just live in whatever skin and voice and action and intent we're most comfortable with and stop worrying about what other people perceive us to be?"

The table went silent.

"Damn, Troy. You cut kind of deep," Remy said.

"I'm sorry," Troy said.

The crowd at Motor City Wine was getting larger now. Two white girls in beanies slid past their table, asking if they could just squeeze through.

"First of all," Remy said, "I'm going to always wonder what people perceive me to be because I'm a Black man in America. They can shoot a nigga in the suburbs and guess what, they can shoot a nigga in Detroit too because of these crackers on the police force coming from the suburbs."

"I could get shot just as well," Troy said.

"It's different for you and you know that," Remy said. "You grew up in fuckin' Indian Village!"

"Yeah, because my father chose that for me. I had no control over that. But in your job, you do. If you made half the effort to try and sell Black people houses there . . ."

"You don't think I try? Goddammit, Troy. You and this socialist bullshit! It never fucking ends. I'm going outside for a minute. I can't take you right now."

Remy took out his dab pen and headed for the door. As he left, two white men came in and took a seat at the table next to them.

"Al-fucking-ready," Troy said, looking at them. "The Ford bros are going to take over Motor City Wine when they get here. I swear to God, they can have everything they want in Detroit, but they can't take my favorite bar," Troy said.

"What's with all . . . all this? Those kids got you stressed out?" Dominick asked.

"Dominick, I'm pissed. Pissed all the way off that Remy enables the kind of gentrification that's going to kill the city. That's going to kill the Mahaffey School."

"I'm confused."

"That new development Remy's in on? It's going to kill Islandview. It's going to make all the rents go up everywhere, including mine. All the parents at the school probably won't be able to afford to live there."

"What development?"

"Remy hasn't said anything, but I know. I found out. It's Detroit. You can't keep a secret here. I don't know why he won't tell me, but I know. Sneaky motherfucker. They break ground next spring. It's going to be announced soon. He's supposed to be my best friend too."

"Shit."

"Yeah."

"So, what are you going to do?"

"I can't do shit! The whole neighborhood is about to be gentrified the fuck out and Remy's leading the way with this rising-tides-lifts-all-boats bullshit. He's cosigning gentrification with this fucking evil McQuerry group. He knows what this will do to the neighborhood. First the luxury townhomes, then the Whole Foods."

"You said Detroit needed Whole Foods!"

"Yeah, but this is how it starts. Just like the Whole Foods in Harlem you talked about. White folks with money are going to move into those new townhouses, then white folks with money are going to move into my building and everywhere else. The school might as well close now."

"Slow down. What do you mean?"

"Our charter operator's pulling out. Parents are already pulling their kids. They're moving to River Rouge. Mahaffey hasn't told anyone officially, but any parent who sticks with us is going to be shit out of luck come next fall."

"I don't get it. The test scores and everything are good, right?"

"Yes, the test scores are good. The kids are smart as hell, but it's not enough. It's never enough compared to these white people with money. I should've never taken this job."

Troy got up to go to the bathroom. His hand was already in his pocket.

"You need to get off that shit," Dominick said.

"And you need to leave me the fuck alone."

Troy walked off and Dominick sat, stunned. He knew Troy wasn't really mad at him—he was just blowing off steam. But it still hurt. He looked around the bar. Almost every table was full now, and almost everybody except him was white.

A few minutes later, Troy came back to the table.

"Remy just texted me," Dom said. "He's taking an Uber home."

"Good. Fuck him."

"Troy. Stop."

"You just don't know, Dominick. All the shit we've been through together, and now he's just . . ." He slumped in his chair. "Whatever. I don't want to talk about it now. I need to get home before Roderick says something."

"Like what, Troy?"

"Just leave me alone, Dominick. You don't know."

"You and Remy are something else, you know that? One of y'all running behind some dude like a battered wife, and the other one is chasing random dick across the ocean. If these are the type of niggas y'all wanna deal with, maybe me fucking a *white boy* isn't so bad."

"Then go get you a white boy, Dominick. Do whatever the fuck you want. I don't care."

Dominick stood up from the table, ready to spill his guts to Troy and then go home in his own Uber. Instead, he looked down at his defeated friend who was staring into his last few sips of wine. Dominick buried what he knew he shouldn't say.

"Text me when you get home," he said.

CHAPTER SIXTEEN

•••

Troy Clements
Dom, I want to apologize
I was tripping the other night and you didn't deserve that
I'm sorry

Dominick Gibson
It's OK, Troy. I still love you
Are you going to Remy's thing tonight?

Troy Clements
What thing?

Dominick Gibson
Some Detroit Young Leaders Association
mixer at MOCAD
He's getting that award

Troy Clements
I don't know if it's the best idea for me to be
hanging with Remy right now

Dominick Gibson
You've got to see him sometime
You're just going to ghost him after
fifteen years of friendship?
And anyway, he said there's free wine

Troy Clements
OK, I think Roderick's working tonight
I'll be there

...

It had been a week and a half since the dustup at Motor City Wine. Dominick and Remy texted separately, as did Dom and Troy, but Troy and Remy had been silent with each other.

Remy instead sought counsel from Roland and Terrell. Terrell suggested that Remy should give Troy some space and that if they'd been friends for this long, they would survive a few days of not speaking. Roland, texting back two days after Remy's inquiry, sent a shrugging emoji and a flirty pic of him in River Island briefs with three eggplant emojis. (Remy, albeit frustrated, still couldn't ignore that Roland had a dick longer than Patti LaBelle's run of flops between "Lady Marmalade" and "If Only You Knew," so he responded with a pic of his ass tooted in the air captioned, "I think it should be here.")

Remy had finally invited Troy, though he sent the invitation through Dominick, to come watch him and nine other Detroiters under the age of forty get an award for, really, just being a Detroiter under the age of forty and having a name and status in the city. Remy treated these events like networking socials, making sure he had plenty of business cards to pass around and top-of-mind knowledge of all the comps in every Detroit zip code, even if it meant another dull evening overall.

When Dominick got there, he was in awe of the museum. He was surprised that in the years he'd been in New York, his hometown had added one of those exposed-brick spaces that could be cut and pasted over any one of the New York galleries he'd schmoozed at for the last decade. After scanning a photograph of a homeless Black man pushing a grocery cart through the abandoned Brewster Projects—*God, do all these Detroit artists love to capitalize off broken, destitute Blacks or what?* he thought—he turned around and waved at Remy from afar. On the other side of the room, he could also see Troy in line for hors d'oeuvres.

He once-overed the room again and counted the Black folks. A few years ago, a newspaper column had caused a stir in Detroit when it concluded that Black people were nowhere to be found in the city's new downtown. (Troy had emailed it to Dominick with the subject line "This is low-key true now . . .") In New York, Dominick had hardly ever felt self-conscious about being one of the only Black people in the room; it was just the norm in his industry. But after doing a quick head count, Dominick saw just how stark the disparity was.

Seven of us among about a hundred folks not-us. This is not supposed to be the norm in a city like Detroit, he thought. *No wonder Remy's drinking like he is.*

The eighth Black guest came in the form of Natalie, now draped in a wrap dress she'd picked up at a Turkish bazaar. Jeweled bangles from Ecuador jingled on her wrists.

"We never did get that drink, love," she said, coming up behind Dominick.

"Natalie! You scared me."

"The two of us are probably scary to everyone here."

"So you see it?"

"What's happening to Detroit? Did everything just turn into *Dawson's Creek* while we were gone?"

"Not quite. I was dodging bullets at the Woodward the other night."

"You know, I'm still not over that atrocious video at your agency. A whole video about our city and no Black people in it?"

"Unfortunately, that's the ad industry in a nutshell," Dominick said, turning on an accent that sounded like Oprah in *The Color Purple*. "All my life I had to fight!"

"Why'd you leave New York for this?"

"Long story. Broke up with my ex. Moved in with my mama. Why'd you leave . . . wait, where were you last?"

Natalie half-smiled.

"I don't know. I'm feeling called home for some reason. I haven't had a permanent address for a decade and a half. I just need to like, cool my heels and figure out what to do with this platform I have."

"In Detroit?"

"I guess so. By the looks of it, they need people like me. People like us. What were you doing in New York that you couldn't do here?"

They walked toward one of the drink stations.

"Truth be told," Dominick said, "I was working for a startup that imploded right before I broke up with my ex. I don't know, I guess I'm good at advertising, but I can't help but think I could be so much better if I didn't have to deal with situations like that meeting where it felt like I was the only one. Like where I have to think before I speak, and think before I give an idea, and think about talking about why Black people should be in a video in Detroit. We never had to think about this shit at Howard or in high school."

"You did go to U of D, love."

"Still! I grew up on Joy Road!"

"The *nice* part of Joy Road, love. Let's get that drink."

"What'll you have?"

Dominick looked the bartender up and down, a brown man with chestnut eyes and his hair tied back in a ponytail.

"I'll catch up with you later, love," Natalie said, quietly taking an available champagne glass from the bar and moving off to another corner of the gallery.

"I was drinking merlot," Dominick said, "but I think I'll switch to that IPA."

"The brewery that makes that is kind of racist. Are you sure?" the bartender smiled.

"Hmm. Do you recommend something else?"

"Hold on a sec," the bartender said, pulling out some lime juice and shrub vinegar from under his station. "I've been meaning to try this. I'm a little new at making drinks."

"Oh yeah?"

"Yeah, I just started doing this. I work in service for a few places when I'm not playing with my band. Usual Detroit hipster stuff," he said, mixing a few of the ingredients with seltzer and vodka.

"What's your band?"

"The Kinsmen. We're not that well known . . ."

"I've heard of you! I work for an ad agency out in Birmingham, and we're on this whole support-local-business kick, so we're always listening to songs by local artists for potential commercial placement."

"Word? My songs could be in a commercial?"

"I'm pretty sure I remember seeing your band's name. Maybe?"

"I'm Felix, by the way. Lead singer."

"I'm Dominick," he said, extending his hand. Their handshake lingered a bit too long, and Dom felt the calluses on Felix's fingers.

"Bass or guitar?" he asked.

"Bass," Felix laughed. "Are you . . . new to Detroit?"

"I'm from here, but I haven't lived here in a while."

"I think I might have seen you somewhere," Felix said.

"Oh yeah?"

Felix leaned in.

"Dating apps? Quote-unquote?" he asked.

Bingo! Dominick's gaydar never failed.

"You woofed me a few weeks ago!" he said. "Now I remember."

"I've got a break coming up," Felix said. "Join me for a cigarette?"

After a lifetime of Truth ads and warnings from the surgeon general, successful young Black men don't smoke tobacco, but Dominick felt the allure of spontaneity.

"I saw a trailer out back," he said. "Is there something there?"

"A pop-up exhibit, but it's closed," Felix said. "Or is it?" He reached into his pocket and produced a key. "It's where our boss made us change into these get-ups."

"Can't be too long, though. I'm here with my friends, one of whom is getting an award tonight. Fun's fun, but my boys come first."

"It'll be quick. Promise."

Maybe this is it, Dominick thought. *This could be the meet-cute.* His mind wandered a bit as they made their way out the back of the museum. *He's smart. He's talented. He's got gorgeous eyes. He's got presence. He's got an interesting job. He can make a drink. He's*—Dominick looked up, then down at Felix on his knees, his hands wrapped around Dominick's bare buttocks, then he looked up at the ceiling again—*swallowing every drop of cum I'm pushing out, effortlessly.*

—————————

"So you might finally meet Terrell tonight," Remy said to Troy. He'd seen Troy walk in, and though the two of them had tried their best to avoid each other, the awkwardness got to be too much. Besides, they had to talk about something once they realized neither one of them knew where Dominick was.

"Which one is Terrell?"

"*Which one?* Damn, Troy, what are you trying to say?"

"Nothing! I didn't mean anything by it."

"Bullshit. You know, you can be so shady."

"Remy, can we move on?"

Remy exhaled.

"Terrell is my plant dude, remember?"

"Right. Sexually fluid. I thought that was his name. I just mixed up the names, that's all."

"I've been thinking about that, and I don't think he is. He likes me. He likes *this*. And he's not in denial about it, unlike your man."

"What are you trying to say about me and Roderick?"

Remy sucked his teeth.

"Never mind," he said.

"Come out with it."

"I might as well just say it," Remy said. His mind was jumbled with hazy thoughts. He didn't feel like fighting with Troy again, but the wine had taken over. "You lowered your standards for this dude. He's running you into the ground. You should leave him, cut him loose. And the fact that you had to wait until he was at work so that you could hang out tonight—Dom told me. Me, who you've known for how long? For you to put me aside for . . . for this . . . bum?"

"This isn't just about Roderick," Troy reminded him.

"Anyway," Remy said. "You let your desperation outweigh your common sense."

Remy was right, and Troy's insides burned anytime his best friend's suspicions proved true. There was absolutely discord between Troy and Roderick, and Remy was reading. Yes, he and Roderick had moved in together too fast. And yes, Troy knew better. But when their initial conversations about cohabitation started to grow louder, it sounded like sweet music because for once, Troy could feel complete in a way Remy couldn't. He'd been happy—working his little job and coming home to his little life—and here was his best friend, reading it all. And now Remy was getting an award for gentrifying the fuck out of Troy's neighborhood, and Troy was supposed to be happy for him.

Terrell, tall and dark, approached the two of them.

"Hello there, sir," Remy said, giving him a peck on the cheek and opening Terrell's jacket. "This looks like H&M, which you don't normally wear to an event like this, but you still look good."

"I wasn't aware there was a dress code," Terrell said.

"I think he looks fine," Troy said, his ears still burning from Remy's comments about Roderick. He wanted to hurt him. He held out his hand.

"You must be . . . Roland," Troy said.

"Terrell," the man corrected.

Remy swallowed air and buried his bubbling humiliation.

"Terrell, the program's about to start and you should find a place to sit. Troy and I just have to find Dominick. Can you hold a couple seats for them?"

"Of course," Terrell said, quickly. "I'll . . . just see you in a minute."

Remy smiled as Terrell walked away, then turned to Troy and tore into him.

"How dare you, Troy. How fucking dare you?"

"I'm sorry. I got confused."

"You son of a bitch. You know what the fuck you did. It's not cute."

"And if you weren't fucking two men at the same time and spreading your ass all over the city, you wouldn't have this problem," Troy said. "At least I have the comfort of knowing I can go to bed with the *same* man every night. And at least I know that the money I'm making at my job isn't coming off the backs of Black folks who have made this city what it is."

A woman in a black turtleneck approached them.

"Excuse me, Remy, we need you up on stage," she said.

Remy looked coldly at his friend.

"Congratulations again, Remy," Troy said, extending his hand. "It's so well-deserved. Thanks for everything you've done to help New Detroit become New Detroit."

January 2006. The winter icebreaker for Oakland University's ASE—All Students Equal, the campus's gay and lesbian organization—was poppin' with "L.O.V.E." by Ashlee Simpson blaring from the speakers at the Bloomfield Hills home of organization president Gabe Lowenstein, whose parents were vacationing in Naples. Troy was nineteen, wearing beige Tommy Hilfiger corduroy pants, brown Kenneth Cole loafers, a red and navy blue argyle sweater-vest over a white oxford pilfered from his father's closet, and thick lenses wrapped in Polo Ralph Lauren frames. He was a Carlton Banks of the new millennium, and he'd been dragged to the party by Raina Willingham, one of the handful of out Black lesbians at Oakland who shared Troy's affection for *Sailor Moon,* Xanga, and Hitchcock films.

Troy made his way through the crowd—art fags, goth hags, blonde twinks, and exactly one Asian—to the kitchen to grab a beer. At least he assumed there was beer there. Growing up the way he had, he'd already tasted it all—a sip of pinot noir at dinner, a don't-let-your-mama-see-this taste of Red Stripe at backyard barbecues. He had never seen, however, what white folks in the suburbs drank.

Oh, look, here's a Smirnoff Ice Black, he said to himself. *That'll do.*

Gabe, clutching a bottle of the same, beamed toward Troy.

"Hiiiiiii! I'm Gabe! Welcome! What's your name?"

"Troy. Is this your house?"

"No, it's my parents. But thanks for coming! Are you new to ASE?"

"Yeah, my friend, Raina, wanted to come."

"Oh, niiiiiiice. So are you . . .?"

Troy tucked his lips in and nodded. He still wasn't comfortable being asked if he was gay. Nor was it something he was quite confident telling someone he'd just met.

"Ohhhhhhh, great! Well, welcome! We're a lot of fun, I promisssse. We meet every other Thursday night in the student center, and our main goal is to support all of OU's gay and lesbian students. That's the mission, and I'm president!"

Just as Troy had had enough of Gabe's hackneyed Paris Hilton impersonation, he caught sight of four Black men in the next room. With that sight came sound, and Troy marveled that he hadn't hear them earlier. He made his way over to the doorway and peered at them. They already had too much swag compared to his argyle and corduroys. He suddenly wanted to be invisible.

"Oh, heyyyy," one of them said, spotting Troy. "Come on over, don't be shy."

The words poured out of the man's mouth like cheap maple syrup, runny and undiscerning. Troy hesitated, but he locked eyes with the man who had called him over. He was wearing an OU hoodie and Abercrombie and Fitch jeans, and he was clutching a red cup. A Black frat boy if anyone ever saw one, except his voice had a feminine lilt, Troy noticed.

"I'm Remy."

"Uhh, wassup everybody?" Troy said, lifting a hand to wave.

"Hi," one of the other men replied, dry as gravel.

"Y'all, don't be like this," Remy said.

"Chill," another of the four said, grabbing the back of Remy's hoodie.

Remy's voice suddenly deepened.

"Don't be grabbing my shit like that!" he yelled.

"Well, it was nice meeting you guys," Troy said, backing out of the room.

"You as well. Have fun," one of the men said.

Troy went to find Raina, who he found in the living room chatting up one of the goth hags.

"Troy, come sit with us!" she yelled. She was already two bottles of Smirnoff Ice in.

"Did you see those guys back there?" Troy asked.

"No, who?"

"Those other Black guys. In the den."

"Oh, no, I didn't. Is something wrong?"

After a few minutes, Troy saw two of the men make their way to the living room to tell Gabe they unfortunately had to go because they'd promised to go support one of their favorite performers who was in a drag show in Pontiac. Troy watched them leave, excused himself from Raina under the guise of getting more booze, and wondered what had happened to Remy and the other man. But when he wandered over to the archway to see if they were in the den, they were gone.

Troy saw another door leading away from the kitchen. He guessed it might have been a pantry, but when he opened it, he discovered a staircase. He tiptoed up the stairs, careful not to be heard and unaware of what he'd find. Something about Black folks potentially creeping around a mansion in Bloomfield Hills was daring. Troy wanted in on the action.

At the top of the stairs, with the party's din still going on below him, he saw a closed door on the left, light peeking from underneath, and approached it. Hands shaking, stomach tingling, he got close enough to put an ear to the door but couldn't make out a sound.

I'll just say I'm looking for the bathroom, he thought. *That'll be my excuse, I'm looking for the bathroom.*

He opened the door.

There, lying on the bed with his jeans down to his ankles, was Remy. The other man, who was naked and had a condom on his hard dick, was slobbering on Remy's erect penis.

"Get out," the dick sucker said.

Troy's private thoughts clumsily verbalized.

"I was looking for the bathroom. Let . . . Let me watch," he said.

"Get the fuck out right now."

Troy's heart rate diminished a bit, and so did his own erection. He saw that Remy, who just a few minutes ago had warmly asked him to join his social circle, wasn't moving at all. His penis was hard, but he wasn't speaking.

Only one man in this room is awake, Troy thought.

"What are you doing?" Troy asked.

"I told yo' ass to get the fuck out!"

"OK, OK, I'm leaving."

Troy knew what was going on, and he knew he needed to find Gabe. Or Raina. Or anyone else. But he also knew that would take too long. From the urgency in the man's voice, Troy knew he had to work quickly.

He left the two men with the door open and went into another room. On a bookshelf, he found a globe a little bigger than a softball, carried it down the hallway, and heaved it as hard as he could at the conscious man, who was still on his knees. It missed him to the right and awkwardly skidded across the floor.

"The fuck?" the man said, looking back at the doorway. He pulled up his pants and chased Troy down the stairs into the party.

"He's a rapist! A fucking rapist!" Troy yelled as loudly as he could.

"What the fuck is wrong with you?" the man yelled.

They were outside now. The would-be rapist had caught up with Troy, knocked him down, and was kicking him in the ribs. Raina ran outside, going to Troy to help him off the ground while three other partygoers did their best to hold off a Black man whose arousal had been replaced with rage.

"What the hell happened?" Raina asked.

"That guy was about to rape the other guy! Remy!" Troy screamed. "I saw it!"

"Are you sure?"

"Look upstairs!"

By now, the music had stopped and someone had already gone upstairs and found Remy, still passed out.

"My parents are going to fucking kill me," Gabe said.

"You have to call the police. He could die."

"I'm not supposed to be having this party!"

"Remy just got fucking raped in your bedroom, Gabe!" Raina yelled.

"Can't somebody take him to the hospital or something? Can we just wait?"

"I'm calling the police, you selfish prick."

Minutes later, an ambulance came to transport Remy—who, as one partygoer described it as a preemptive cover, "had a little too much at our friend's birthday party"—to Beaumont Hospital. Troy wanted to ride with him; the situation had calmed since the would-be rapist had left after a few white girls at the party had told him, "The police are gonna come here and take your Black ass to jail!" The paramedics wouldn't allow Troy in the ambulance, so he and Raina followed in her car.

In the waiting room, Troy tried to piece together everything that had happened. Raina told him that Remy was a junior who'd been part of ASE since his first year at Oakland. He attended every meeting, served on committees, and had wanted to be vice president but was too busy with his business major and work to make that kind of commitment. He lived on Promenade Street in Detroit but rented an apartment near campus.

The doctors found GHB in Remy's bloodstream. A higher dosage, one doctor told Troy, and Remy could have been killed. He woke up at 8:30 the next morning, Troy and Raina asleep at his bedside.

"What happened? Where am I?" he asked.

Remy's eyes widened at the IV in his arm. He groaned and reached for the bright red panic button but paused when he recognized the familiar boy with the thick glasses.

"You were at a party last night," Troy said. "Some guys poisoned you."

"They what?"

"Some guy put GHB in your drink and was going to rape you."

"Where's my phone, where's my wallet, where's my keys? I don't even know you."

"And I don't know you," Troy said. "Do you remember the guys you were with?"

Remy began to piece things together. One of the men, Robert, was an Auburn Hills local. He and Remy had met on BGC. The other two men, the ones who had left the party and essentially left Remy for dead, were two OU sophomores, both transfers, who Remy had tried to recruit to join ASE. They were new to campus; Remy was desperate for a social circle, and he wanted to introduce them to the networking opportunities ASE provided so they wouldn't feel alone. So much for a good deed.

"It must have been something in that punch," Remy said. "This never happens to me."

"Everyone was drinking it. Nobody was crazy drunk," Raina said.

"I had another cup of the punch after that Mike's. There was something in it because . . ."

Remy covered his face with his hands and loudly exhaled.

Robert was the one who must have roofied him. He was the one who had brought him the second cup of punch. And now that Remy thought about it, maybe Robert wasn't even his actual name.

But Remy also remembered another crucial detail from the party. He'd never seen Troy before the previous night. And he recalled the fleeting thought of having another gay Black male friend at OU, even if he was dressed like Steve Urkel after a trip to the Somerset Collection. In his drunken, chemical-addled brain, he saw potential peeking from that doorway. There was brightness before dark. And now, here at his hospital bedside, that brightness was again.

Raina relayed the whole story of how Troy threw the globe at Robert and how he also probably needed to see a doctor after the fight. Troy was a little sore, but it wasn't anything close to Remy's headache. The doctors found no evidence of penetration anywhere. Remy was given a prophylactic just to be on the safe side and was discharged the next day. A week later, he saw Troy having lunch by himself in the student union and thanked him for saving his life.

"You know what? Fuck you, Troy. Fuck you forever. I don't need this shit," Remy said.

He held a plaque in one hand and a glass of white wine in the other. The crowd was beginning to thin—after Troy's embarrassing name mix-up, Terrell had come up with an excuse for why he had to leave early—though a photographer was still snapping pictures of the people who were left.

"Well fuck you too, Remy. You've been acting like a bitch ever since I started talking to Roderick."

"This was my night. All you had to do was support me. I thought you'd be a better friend than this."

"You want to talk about being a better friend?" Troy asked.

"What did I miss?" Dominick asked, rejoining the other two men. He was still euphoric from Felix's blowjob and was completely unaware of everything that had transpired.

"I'm leaving," Troy said. "Dom, you want to go to the Woodward? If we go now, we don't have to pay cover."

"Seriously, what's the problem?"

"You know what the problem is?" Remy asked. "The problem is that Troy is being a bitch-ass and I don't have time for all this. He's acting like I'm the only one out here getting dick and making money. But I'm not going to apologize for any of that. I'm happy doing what I'm doing. And I didn't see you up on stage tonight receiving any applause. So Troy, you go do whatever it is you need to do, and when you're ready to stop acting like a bitch, let me know."

SUMMER

SUMMER

CHAPTER SEVENTEEN

Some might say it's Rouge and some might say Clark Park, but if you're from the east side like me, you know that summer in Detroit formally begins on East Jefferson Avenue. Every year, soon as the forecast hits the D with eighty-four, folks from all over the city pull their old school out from under its polyester cover, shine up the chrome wheels and tire walls, take it through the $3 car wash one more time for good measure, and then ride up and down the strip. When we were coming up, before the state took it over, "the strip" used to be on Belle Isle. Now it's Jefferson. When you ride up and down Jefferson, you smell charcoal and weed. Folks actually start barbecuing at seventy degrees. If it gets to be eighty, the whole damn city is a cookout. But folks are going to be riding high in any weather anyway, so. I just know that when you have both scents at the same time, summer is here.

Me and Troy used to ride up and down the strip together, but we haven't talked in over a month. So now I'm linking up with Dominick to go to the Yacht Club and bringing Paris along for the ride. I miss Troy sometimes. But then I remember that night at MoCAD. He still hasn't apologized. And I definitely can't apologize to him. Apologize to him for what? For making money? Making something of myself? Things are still going strong with the McQuerrys. They've already razed one old building that was halfway torn down anyway, and the shiny new sign is up, advertising the future home of "The Studios @ Isl@ndview"—they insisted on two @ symbols—and there's a lot more to come.

Anyway, I just think it's wild how time flies because I used to only go to Belle Isle for the Giant Slide. And the old zoo for field trips. And when I was in my twenties, riding around the Isle with boys . . . well, I'm not going to get into that right now, but if you know, you know. Dominick told me once that there's a part of Central Park named after Diana Ross, and she wanted it to be the kind of place Belle Isle was to her when she was little. The fact that shit has influence all the way in New York? That's what the Isle means to us Detroiters.

But now I just go there to go to the Yacht Club when I need to see the Yacht Club gays. You know the ones I can't stand but have to network with anyway? Just like me, they're at the Yacht Club pool every year on schedule. That's where summer for *all* the upwardly mobile Detroit gays starts.

And damn. I could fuck up a chicken pita with ranch right now, but I've been starving myself for weeks in advance of this first poolside confab.

One of the ringleaders of the Yacht Club gays, and one of the few Black ones period, is this stump-jumper Foster Jones, who had made up for a lifelong Napoleon complex by reinventing himself as the city's millennial political insider-to-the-stars. He went to Cass—a Cass Tech nigga won't let you forget they went there—and then to Michigan. He had a job in the mayor's office but quit it, blindsiding just about everybody who'd assumed nothing was wrong. Nothing *was* wrong, but Foster knew he could play the Black-man-quitting-the-white-mayor narrative to his advantage.

Why do I know all this? Because it's Detroit. Bitches talk.

"Bottoms in Detroit only love two things, and that's dick and scams," I tell Dominick right after I sign in with the guard and pull into the parking lot. Luckily, Paris has his AirPods in and can't hear me. "Not me though, I just love dick. But you gotta watch out for this queen, Foster. Everybody's ran through him and he's always chasing behind my leftovers. I date someone, next thing I know he's up on them three business days later. Short little fuck."

"Oh, boy," Dominick said.

"He's got a hole in his ass the size of a CD."

———————

"How are you, sir?" I ask, greeting Foster with a one-armed hug, still leaving considerable distance between us.

"Brother, I'm blessed. Blessed and highly favored. But always just trying to get like you."

"Oh, really?"

"Yeah, man. I see you out here."

"Hmm, well, you know, you know, blasé-blasé."

"We haven't met," Foster says, turning to Dominick. "Foster."

Dominick introduces himself and before I know it, Foster has pulled him close and is rubbing both hands slowly up and down his back. I try hard not to laugh as Dom signals with his eyes, *The fuck is he doing?* I know what this is.

"It's important for brothers like us to show that we love and care about each other, and to build community value. This is the concept of Adodi," Foster says, finally releasing Dominick. "Are you familiar?"

"That shit you put on Mexican food?" Dominick asks jokingly.

"No, silly. Ado-di," Foster says, stretching the word's final syllable. "It's a practice among same-gender loving Black men like ourselves to reinforce community."

"That would presume I'm a same-gender loving man."

"You're not gay?"

"I'm kidding. I am," Dominick says, bending his wrist. "But . . ."

"You're right, I apologize. I should not have been so presumptuous. I just saw you here with Remy, and . . ."

"We're friends," I say, cutting him off. I'm trying my best to hurry this conversation along.

"Oh, nice. As I was saying about Adodi . . ."

"It's this retreat Black gay men go on every year where they spend time in nature getting to know their true selves," I say, "and also sharing intimate moments among themselves, *nude*."

"Well, Remy, when you say it like that, it sounds like an orgy."

"I didn't say it was, Foster."

"I'm intrigued. Add me on Facebook and we'll talk more?" Dominick asks.

I drop my Jack Spade tote on the chaise lounge, send Paris over to the snack stand to get a Faygo, and pull Dominick out of earshot after Foster walks away.

"Are you serious?" I ask. "You want to do that orgy with them?"

"Hell no. Calm down," Dominick says, pulling sunscreen from his bag. "I was only faking nice. You should try it sometime. You got me burning up with all this heat you're giving."

While Paris plays in the shallow end of the pool, Dominick and I take our places with the rest of the Yacht Club gays. There's "Big" Randy Chen, a Singaporean pop-up chef, who rotates around five recently opened bars in the city under the business name KitChen. The "Big" doesn't relate so much to his muscle definition as it does to the fact that he's considerably taller than his boyfriend, "Little" Randy. They've got a couples TikTok now that's kinda blowing up, and I might be the only one who remembers the time Big Randy was on Facebook asking if cotton sprigs were appropriate decorations for a dinner. In Detroit, this Black-ass city. *Anyway*. Next to them is Todd Jason Berman—like any white gay who uses all three of his names, you *have* to say all three—another realtor who does most of his business in Oakland County, and then Dietrich Lange, a German expat designer at Stellantis who started as an intern way back when Mercedes used to own them. Both of them are cool, and we've always had good rapport, though still not at the same level that I had it with Troy.

"Paris in a month, baby!" Big Randy shouts.

"What's there?" Dietrich asks.

"Our anniversary. I figured since it's been two years, we should do something special, right, babe?"

"You'll love it," Foster says.

He's sitting in the middle of it all because of course he likes to be in the center of a bunch of scantily clad men. "It's my all-time favorite city. The last time I went, I stayed in this cute pied-à-terre. Had a little gentleman caller, you know."

"A *little* gentleman?" Todd asks.

"Well, there was *nothing* little about him," Foster says, leaning over to me. "Have you been to Paris, Remy? You do have a French first name, unless you were named after the liquor."

I know what this is and where it's going, but I answer anyway.

"I can't say I have, Foster."

"You'll get there. Someday. I mean, you're making decent commissions. You don't travel? Come on, when's the last time you've been out of Detroit?"

"Well, as a matter of fact," I say, applying Black Girl Sunscreen to my arms and legs, "I'll be headed to Palm Springs in a bit."

"Oh? Tell us more."

"Aht-aht, boys. You know how I am about discussing pleasure instead of business."

"Well, you'd love Paris if you ever got there," Foster continues. "Especially if you love Detroit. Detroit *is* the Paris of the Midwest."

"I don't know why they call it that," I say, "'cause ain't no motherfuckers around here speaking French."

I get all these fags to laugh out loud while Foster silently adjusts his prescription Warby Parker sunglasses in disapproval. Once again, I'm in control. But the only part of this competition I like is letting Foster think I'm an active player. I couldn't actually care less about the rest of it.

"It's the street patterns," Dominick says.

The fags turn to him, curious about the new arrival's first words.

"What about them?" Todd asks.

"If you've ever been to Paris," Dominick says, "the streets converge to a point like a bicycle wheel. Detroit's the same way. Campus Martius is downtown, and the streets are diagonal from there. Grand River going this way, Gratiot going the opposite way, then Woodward going straight up?"

"Have you been to Paris?" Foster asks Dominick. Clearly he's trying to regain control.

"Several times, actually. My partner, well, my ex-partner now, I guess, and I used to go once a year. I also went a few times for work."

"Wow, so you're quite the expert."

"I wouldn't say expert. I think it's a little overrated."

The fags gasp in homosexual horror.

"What makes it overrated?" Todd asks.

"Because it's Paris. It's so cliché, like, 'Oh, I'll fall in love in Paris, it's so romantic.' Whatever, French people are rude and racist—no offense if any of you boys are French—and they smell. The whole place is touristy as fuck. Us Americans need to appreciate the other European cities." Dominick peers over his Topman sunglasses directly at Foster. "Have you ever been to Milan, Foster?"

I'm enjoying this.

"No," Foster says.

"Oh, you have to go. Milan's the new Paris. Everyone's going to Milan now because it hasn't been gentrified and it's still cheap. How about Copenhagen? Or Prague? Ever been there?"

"No."

"Tell me you've at least been to Lisbon. Everybody goes to *Lisbona*, as the Italians say. And the men are fucking gorgeous there."

"I haven't been there, either."

"Oh, girl. See, that's the issue with us Black folks—no offense to you boys over there. We're so happy to have these passports but are barely using them. Why go to Paris for the umpteenth time when there's a whole globe to explore? Wasn't James Baldwin enough?"

"Who's James Baldwin?" Little Randy asks. Big Randy shushes him down.

"I wouldn't say it's just a Black thing," Foster says.

"Copenhagen really is beautiful," Dietrich says, his German accent proudly coming through.

"*Wunderbar, mein freund, ich liebe es*!" Dominick says without missing a beat.

My eyes are bulging, but you can't tell behind my Saint Laurent aviator frames—this wasn't a moment for any of my buffies. Since when could this nigga speak German?

"So wait, why would you go to Paris every year if you hate it?" Todd asks.

"My ex loved it. You make sacrifices in relationships, and if an annual trip to Paris is my sacrifice? Bet."

Big Randy has a Bluetooth speaker going and after "Levitating," the "Levitating" remix with DaBaby, and the "Levitating" remix with Madonna—*kill me, please*—a vaguely familiar indie rock song comes on.

"Who's this?" I ask.

"It's the Kinsmen. Did you see that video they made on the Detroit Princess? This is that song."

"And that cute bass player Felix who's always around," Todd says. "He's actually a good songwriter."

"That's not the only thing he's good at," Dominick whispers, leaning over to me.

"What do you mean?" I ask him, making sure the other boys can't hear us.

"Well, you remember the night at MoCAD . . . well, actually, never mind. But anyway, me and Felix have been, kinda, maybe, you know . . ."

"Are you dating?"

"Not really, but we have been messing around. Do you know him?"

"Hmm," I say.

Dominick pulled Felix just that quick, and I couldn't after all this time?

"Can't say I do," I tell him.

The truth, which Dominick tells me after Foster has gone home, is that he's only been to Paris once during a study abroad trip, though he stayed there long enough to take it all in. He's been to Milan briefly for work. He hasn't ever been to Lisbon, but a designer friend had lived there for a short while and told him all about it. He's wanted to visit Prague and Copenhagen since he was fifteen. And he only knows a handful of conversational German phrases thanks to studying old Donna Summer interviews on YouTube.

"I dealt with queens in New York for years," he says. "This is light work."

"Cousin Remy, can I ask you a question?" Paris asks. He's done swimming and is laying out on the chaise lounge next to us, sunglasses on and everything, watching TikToks with this girl and hollering about "my coconuts."

"Of course. What's on your mind?"

"Are all your friends here gay, too?"

"What do *you* think?"

"Well, it looks like you're friends, but you're really mean to each other."

"One day," I say, "I'll explain the concept of *frenemies*. But until then, let's indulge in something gay men like to do most."

"Ketamine?" Dominick snickers.

"No! I'm talking about *self-care*."

I order a Shirley Temple for Paris and take a sip from my own margarita. Still a little high from seeing Dominick put Foster in his place,

I snap an Instagram Story pic of my feet with the pool in the background, captioning it #pooldaze. I can't stop checking to see if Roland has watched it. He doesn't, but Felix does, and when I see his name pop up, I send a selfie directly to him with my drink in hand.

"You should join me one of these days," I text him.

CHAPTER EIGHTEEN

A peculiar thing that's happening in New Detroit is white millennials getting together in dive bars to dance, or at least try to anyway, to the music that Black millennials' parents grew up on in the sixties, seventies, and eighties. There was one regular gig around town where it was all Motown cuts, playing to a crowd that probably couldn't differentiate between Mary Wells and Mary Wilson. But that's always been a thing for white people, hasn't it? Rediscovery, then profit.

On Thursday nights, over at UFO Factory in Corktown, just five blocks from the boys' regular spot at Motor City Wine, a few white DJs, some of whom Troy knew, would play late-seventies disco and eighties post-disco at a de facto queer gathering, even if UFO Factory wasn't a gay bar. They'd go surprisingly deep with Dynasty, A Taste of Honey, or Alton McClain & Destiny. Maybe a few foreign-language versions of American hits. But to keep the crowd going, they'd also play the more basic favorites.

"Goddammit," Dominick sighed to himself. He was sitting next to Troy at the bar, surveying the scene and sipping from a can of Hamm's lager as the opening electronic percussion of Whitney Houston's "I Wanna Dance with Somebody" pulsed through the speakers. This party was called Penny Thots, and the bizarro, warp-speed appropriation of a term Black men used to mock Black women's sex positivity into a basic white gay term for iced-coffee manics who treated their holes like Michigan Bell switchboards was too much to Dom's disliking. Why was it that "I

Wanna Dance with Somebody" was the only Whitney song white gay men liked? Did old-school radio in Detroit even play this song? No, there it was always "You Give Good Love" and "I Have Nothing" and "Saving All My Love for You."

But here we are again, Dominick thought, *a bunch of gay white men in ill-fitting Zara screaming, "Iiiiiiiiii wanna dance with somebody!"*

"Troy, why are we here again?" he asked.

"Because tomorrow's the last day of school," Troy said. "All I have to do is run through the morning affirmations and then hit Play on a video before summer vacation officially begins."

"How are you feeling?"

Over the last few weeks, Dominick had sensed his friend growing more and more depressed. Troy seemed weighed down—either from work or Roderick or some combination of the two. Summer's arrival, which usually gave the teachers at Mahaffey a jolt of giddy energy, seemed like it was hitting this year like a cloud of doom.

"I feel like shit," Troy said, defeated. "But what can I do? It's done."

"Y'all never did do that protest."

"Roderick . . . thought it was a bad idea."

"Wasn't he all for it?"

"He was, but . . . never mind that."

"So what are you going to do?"

"To be honest, I don't know. I mean, there's this other charter that got in contact with me last week—it's in Hamtramck and it's STEM focused. DTE runs it."

"And?"

"Well, they'd heard about everything going on at Mahaffey and they said if I wanted to, I could start there this fall."

"Troy, that's good!"

"Yeah." Troy paused and looked up at his friend. "They also want me to be assistant principal."

"What?" Dominick shouted. "That's fantastic! I mean, it's still awful about Mahaffey, but I'm so proud of you! Hey, bartender, open that bottle of prosecco. We've got to toast, even in this dingy-ass bar."

"Trust me, the beer is fine. Cheers," Troy said, lifting his can.

"So are you gonna take it?" Dominick asked. "It sounds like a real step up."

"Is it?" Troy said bitterly. "I'd basically be working at the whim of DTE Energy. And guess what? They're also ugly capitalist swine that take advantage of the most vulnerable Detroiters. Who knows? Maybe they're thinking about selling out now too. Talking about 'resource allocation' and 'DTE's core mission.' I wouldn't be surprised if they've been holding meetings with Remy, too. I'm tired of it all being so hard. Maybe I'll just be AP there for a year. It's a job, and then I'll move on. It's not worth it anymore. And maybe Remy was right."

"When's the last time you talked to him?"

"Don't ask me that."

"Well, let's at least celebrate a little now—I mean, short-term this is a good thing, and . . . oh . . . oh God," Dominick said, trailing off while looking over at the DJ booth. "Remember that guy I hooked up with? At MoCAD? He's right there, on deck to take over the turntables."

"Felix? You're messing with Felix?"

"Yeah! He's nice. He plays in a band, too. And gives great head."

"You and every guy in Detroit agree."

"He follows me on Instagram, though."

"He follows every Detroit gay on Instagram, and often sleeps with them, too."

"Has he slept with *you*, Troy?"

"No. But he's got a thing for Remy. It's weird."

"Does Remy like him?"

"He told me they've been trying to hook up for a while. Felix always ghosts him."

Dominick thought back to Remy's muted reaction at the Yacht Club when Felix had come up in conversation.

"Oh, that's why . . ."

"Why what?"

Dominick paused.

"Oh, I was just thinking of how we have those same kind of guys in New York, too. The ones who just collect gays on Instagram like Pokémon."

"Except here we're stuck at Generation One."

Troy felt his mood lift a little as both boys, once teenage gaymers, laughed heartily.

In Detroit, one can usually tell a lot about a man by whom he follows on Instagram. If a white gay man only follows other white gay men, they're the only kind of men he dates. The same holds true for a Black man who only follows white gay men. If there's not a healthy amount of other men of color in his list, then he's a Black guy that only dates white guys. Now if he's Latino and follows other Latino gays, or an Asian who follows other Asian gays? Well, as Remy once surmised in the group chat, those groups tend to follow each other in packs anyway, so one would actually have to ask them to see where their preferences lie. If they're living in Detroit and have no pictures of themselves with any Black gays? Well, they're just not into you.

"Have you been seeing Felix?" Troy asked.

"No, we've just been messing around. Well, we *were*. I asked if he wanted to get a drink a few weeks ago, and he never responded."

"So what are you going to do now?"

"I'm going to go say hello."

"Don't. He's not worth it."

"I'm just going to say hello," Dominick said.

Felix was thumbing through a crate of records, pulling out what he might play for his set: Sister Sledge, the Pointer Sisters, Mariya Takecuchi, Deniece Williams.

"I didn't know you were such a man of many talents," Dominick said, coming up behind him.

"Oh, hey!" Felix said. "What's up?"

"Nothing. Long time, no hear."

Felix set the albums down.

"Yeah, uh . . . yeah. I'm sorry I didn't contact you lately, I've been a little stressed because, uh . . . my friend is in a coma."

"A coma?"

"Yeah. Well, we actually kind of used to date, too. His family wanted me to visit him, so I have . . . from time to time."

"Can I . . . ask what happened?"

"It's a coma. He's just . . . in it," Felix shrugged.

"And you used to date him?"

"Dating is . . . kind of a strong way of putting it?"

"But close enough where his family asked you to visit him?"

"Uh . . . yeah."

"You could've told me you had a friend in a coma!" Dominick yelled, just loud enough for a few queens on the dance floor to turn a head and raise an eyebrow. Over the speakers, Rebbie Jackson was emoting over a hot, horny centipede crawling in the moonlight.

"It's just a weird situation. Sorry. I've got to go on in a second, so . . ."

Great, now I'm the weird boy, Dominick thought. *I'm the crazy, clingy one. I'm the "God, remember that one guy you dated?" guy. You spend all this time trying not to be someone else's crazy story, the one he thinks about when he's too drunk and has to come up with a story to one-up someone else at the bar, the one who, when you run into one of his friends, they get that look on their face of "oh . . . him." Well, I'm him.*

"Anyway . . . it was good seeing you again," Dominick said. "I . . . I'm going to get another beer at the bar with my friend," he said, pointing back to Troy.

"Oh, that teacher guy! You're friends with him? I follow him on Instagram. Tell him I said hello."

Dominick breathed deeply, turned around, and took a long look at the images moving on the wall behind him, summoning the strength to make it back to his barstool. He took a few steps and then felt a splash of liquid on his foot—warm beer, spilled from a bottle of Bud Light. Then he saw Joseph Thomas's familiar face.

"Oh hey, there. Didn't see you! How's it been?" Joseph asked.

The last time I saw this man, he wanted to spray canned vegetable oil on my penis, Dominick thought.

"I'm good," he said. "I'm just . . ."

Suddenly, the rest of the dance floor came into focus. The Colombian Tour Guide was out there, in a friend circle with the bespectacled Neville Tallbottom. Off in the distance, Young Al Pacino was sitting in a booth by the ATM and the pinball machine. Dominick quickly counted four other men from various apps who had all invited him into their bedrooms, screwed him once or twice, and never spoken to him again. He made his way back to Troy, walking past the Bedwetting Bloomer, who was scrolling his phone at the end of the bar.

"Troy," Dominick said, "I want to go home."

"What is it?"

"I have slept with every guy here," Dominick said. "Him, him, him. I've talked about all of them in the group chat and on wine nights, but Jesus fucking Christ, they're all here. Half this bar has seen me naked. Has had," he gritted his teeth, "my dick in their shitty assholes."

"Dominick," Troy laughed. "That's Detroit! It's OK! Everyone here, well, except for me," he smiled, playfully putting his arm around Dominick and bringing him in for a hug, "has been with each other. What is Detroit, if not a big city and a small town? It's just like Remy said . . ."

Troy caught himself. His best friend who he hadn't spoken to in weeks was back in the conversation again.

"Two degrees of dick away," Dominick said.

"Perk up," Troy said, pulling out a baggie and handing it to Dominick.

"Tonight's supposed to be a celebration of my maybe new job, remember?"

They were sitting at a table under string lights, the hum of a cab company on the other side of iron gates behind them mixing with the chatter of gays in fake vintage band T-shirts and skinny jeans in front of them.

"Fine," Dominick said, taking his key and dipping it in. Once. Twice. A third time. And then the postnasal drip got a little too bitter. "I'm enabling you, you know that, right?"

"I'll be good tonight," Troy said. "Don't let anyone here get to you. We needed to get out."

"Seriously, though. When's the last time you talked to Remy?"

Troy took a drag from a cigarette he'd bummed from one of the guys outside.

"I said don't ask me about him," he said. "You want a cigarette?"

"Last time I had one was . . ." Dominick thought, at first thinking it was back in New York. But then he remembered having one right before Felix blew him.

"Never mind," he said.

Troy stuffed the baggie into his jean pocket.

"You have no idea how much I appreciate your friendship, Dominick," he said.

"Don't get sentimental, motherfucker. Come on, we're having a good time," Dominick said, snapping his fingers in rhythm.

The bar got quiet as the track changed. "How Much I Feel" by Ambrosia came on. UFO's white gays loved their dad rock.

"It's not good with Roderick," Troy blurted out. "I don't know what's going on."

"Fuck, Troy. What?"

"I just don't feel . . ." Troy said, looking up to find the words. "I'm not in love with him, but I don't want to stop trying to make it work."

Work, Dominick thought. *Again.*

June 20 was actually Troy and Roderick's one-year anniversary—three in gay years—if they based if off the day they'd made things official. Living together for six months, dating for twelve, and with only one physical incident the whole time, for which Roderick had profusely apologized, Troy thought he might have been beating the odds. It could always be worse than this. And because Roderick hadn't been physical lately, Troy didn't have to lie or conceal anything. He could look anyone in the eye and say his boyfriend wasn't violent. Many men can't. Troy couldn't stand to be one of those desperate boys living in silence, hiding wounds with makeup, always coming up with excuses. And ever since he'd apologized profusely for his blowup that night with Marlie and Noelle, Roderick had been good for the most part.

For the most part.

You ignore the signs that you might be involved with a habitual coke user. Maybe you even start by calling him a "coke user" and not an all-out "cokehead." You avert your eyes as he evolves, and you begin to accept new normals. You get used to being jolted out of your sleep because his occasional teeth-gnashing sounds like metal on grooved pavement, and then you get used to him saying in the morning that it must have been a bad dream or stress from work. You no longer question why a man in his early thirties uses Cialis because he sometimes can't get it up. You know at a party when he's snuck off and used some because his mood swings immediately: he gets embarrassingly loud, telling deeply personal stories to strangers, taking off his shirt at inopportune times, sweating profusely.

But at least Roderick had been faithful. Or at least Troy assumed he had. Roderick hadn't stayed out late. There had been no unexplained absences or disappearances. No surprise STIs, no phone calls from side pieces, no suspicious texts in the middle of the night. For that minimal set of gay standards, Roderick had cleared the bar.

Still, Troy felt stifled. Trapped. Unsupported. When he brought up the ongoing problems at Mahaffey, Roderick barely paid attention or just asked, "So what are you going to do about it?" Roderick still didn't like Troy going out with Marlie and Noelle, but they compromised when Troy agreed not to complain when Roderick hung out with his friends in Livonia.

Somewhere down the line, though, Roderick had stopped helping with dinner. No more soaking lentils in advance, no more spontaneous trips to Eastern Market to pick out vegetables. Troy hadn't made any of his Bangladeshi dishes in weeks. And for some reason, Roderick hated everything now. The chicken was never seasoned enough, the spaghetti sauce wasn't thick enough, and the Kool-Aid wasn't sweet enough. Troy tried to cook better. And he tried to cook healthier, because along with all this other criticism, Troy was also getting a little too doughy for Roderick's taste.

They compromised, somehow, on Roderick being called Roderick at the house. Because out and about, among everyone they knew, he had fully transitioned into Kiburi. Kiburi, who was now director of community outreach for Taking Back Detroit. Kiburi, who appeared on a Let it Rip segment on Fox 2 with King Musa to talk about a gas station takeover, in which members of Taking Back Detroit stormed an Arab-owned gas station on Seven Mile after the owner purportedly disgraced a Black female customer. Kiburi, who said on air that no one was more important than the Black woman. Kiburi, who that night at home, did not touch his Black boyfriend.

But the fear of losing Roderick drove Troy to keep him around. Other than Dominick's years-long thing—whatever it had been—with Justin, no one in the trio of friends had been in a relationship longer than the one he had now. Troy thought any milestone was bound to come with obstacles. Long-term relationships weren't supposed to be easy. There had to be compromise and patience. Gay men didn't have it easy. Black men didn't have it easy. And gay Black men had it even harder than that.

Ever since Dominick had been back in town, Troy had listened to him and Remy trash every man in Detroit. Dating here seemed to be just as frightful as getting carjacked. With Roderick around, Troy was free from all that. Free from undefined relationships with British flight attendants. Free from the worry of ever walking into a New Detroit bar and seeing a bunch of old flings all at once. Free from the disaster of gay dating period.

He had the dual income since Roderick was now paying his half of the rent. He had the regular fucking. And now, past year one, it was time to make things good with Roderick. To pray that he wouldn't be an asshole anymore, to wish that he'd start to listen, to ask for more consolation. To make it work.

Just as Dominick's high kicked in, he and Troy left the Penny Thots party and Ubered to the Woodward. Dominick wanted to dance, and although he normally wouldn't mind white gays and eighties pop, he wanted to get buck and be around more Black people.

They paid their cover, held hands going past the bar, and pushed their way to the dance floor, where the DJ had Roddy Ricch going—damn near the whole club was out on the floor doing a Detroit hustle to "High Fashion." And when Roddy yelled over the track, "*You ain't gotta deal with none of these niggas no moooooore!*" everyone put up their hands and sang along.

It wasn't lost on Troy that the Woodward was where he'd first met Roderick and that now his boyfriend was nowhere in sight. He'd waited all week to see if Roderick even knew it was their anniversary, but the topic had never come up. Instead, Roderick had said he wanted to go out with some of the Taking Back Detroit crew tonight. Troy said he would go out with Dominick, and they both agreed that if they ended up spending the night elsewhere because they were too high or drunk, it would be fine. No texting "where you been?" or "where you at?" At least, Troy thought, they were building some modicum of trustworthiness.

Maybe anniversaries were heteronormative anyway. Maybe, Troy thought, as he watched Dominick buzz back and forth, drink in hand and dancing with whoever gave him even the slightest look, Roderick just didn't believe in old traditions and thought it was time to build new ones. Maybe he didn't think to ask about anniversaries, or maybe he thought their official day was another day farther off and *was* planning something. But wasn't Roderick the one who had declared the official day their relationship had started? Maybe he just didn't feel it was important enough to remember.

Or maybe I should have reminded him. But if I reminded him, Troy thought, *I'd be undermining him. Insulting his intelligence. And then he'd get mad.*

And then Troy knew Roderick would have yelled, just like he would whenever Troy checked him on something. So Troy, as usual, kept the peace.

You've always kept the peace, Troy thought. *You've never wanted to disturb anyone. You've stayed out of your father's way. Now you're staying out of Roderick's. And now, with a whole year passed in a relationship, a whole year added onto this thirtysomething life—these thirtysomething years of keeping yourself small—you want more?*

Troy's speeding train of thought was halted when he felt a hard object pressed between his shoulder blades.

"Run yo' pockets!" a voice shouted behind him.

Troy jumped, thinking, *oh shit, some bullshit again at the Woody,* but when he turned around, it was Gogo pulling a practical joke on him with a highball glass.

"I'm just playing with you," Gogo laughed, setting the empty glass down on the bar.

"You scared the shit out of me."

"What are you doing here by yourself?"

"Dominick's out there dancing. You're here by yourself, too?"

"Yeah. Anthony and I broke up."

"Oh, Greg, I'm sorry."

"I think we're on a break? I don't know. So . . . where's your Mister Man?"

Troy shrugged.

"Hell if I know," he said.

"You don't know where your own boyfriend is," Gogo responded flatly.

"He's a grown man. I don't keep him on a leash."

"All right. Scared of you," Gogo said, taking a sip from a new Long Island the bartender had set in front of him.

Troy reached into his pocket and felt the baggie of cocaine, trying to decide whether to pull it out and offer some to Gogo. Before he could, Dominick came back off the dance floor.

"Who's your friend?" he asked.

"This is Gogo, my . . ." Troy said.

"Oh, you're Gogo! Oh-ho-ho-ho!" Dominick said, a mix of awareness, stimulation, and good-natured bravado hitting his circuits at once. "Well, I'll just leave you two heeeere, and I'm going to go talk to that boy I was dancing with . . ." He playfully held up a hand to Gogo's face to cover it up, leaned into Troy, and whispered loudly, "Go. Have. Fun."

Tamia's "Can't Get Enough" came on. Ever since Dominick had seen the Tamia hustle the first time, he'd been watching YouTube tutorials in his room and practicing. He was ready.

"Your friend is hilarious," Gogo asked, smiling tenderly. "But still . . . your own Mister Man isn't here?"

You wonder where he is, Troy thought to himself. *And then you wonder how, exactly, you got to where you are now. And then, maybe, you begin to find your way out.*

CHAPTER NINETEEN

In his grandfather's Marauder, Dominick circled the building three times before pulling into the parking lot. There wasn't much to look at on this side of the city. Most folks in Detroit didn't grow up here. They grew up on streets with brick houses and played in nearby parks. But this area, where Body Zone, a bathhouse, was located, was industrial—the parking lots surrounded by metal fences topped with barbed wire. Lots of warehouses, not all of them active. Behind the warehouses were broken-down wooden homes, most of them clinging to dear life.

This, Dominick thought, *is the Detroit they like to talk about in the news. The ghetto. The poverty. The Black folks in peril that white folks love to gawk at.*

He sat behind the wheel and exhaled as he backed into a parking space. His grandfather's Marauder fit right in with most of the other vehicles there, which clearly belonged to older people. Cadillac SUVs, German sedans. Dominick swallowed air as if it were infused with Vernors, trying to dissolve the unrest in his stomach. Were any millennial guys going to be inside this place? There was only one way to find out.

Inside the front door, he was greeted by a short, bald man behind four-inch bulletproof glass with a few holes punched through it for sound.

"Welcome!" he said. "Need your ID, please."

Dominick complied. The man examined his New York license.

"You're a long way from home," he said.

Dominick quickly came up with a lie on the spot: "I'm here for a conference but figured I'd have a little fun while I'm in town."

"Of course. Do you need flip-flops? A larger towel? Toiletries?"

"Uh..."

"Shoes aren't allowed, so when you get inside, you'll have to be barefoot or in socks. But you can take home a pair of these flip-flops if you want. They're $15."

Reasoning that rubber flip-flops were usually no more than $5 at Old Navy, Dominick declined.

"What were the other things?" he asked.

"You can upgrade to a larger towel that, you know, has some more *absorbency* than the standard towel. But there's a charge for it. And toiletries. We can give you some soap, shampoo, and one douche, but trust me, you don't want to pay for that. You'd be better off going to CVS and coming back."

"I think I'm good," Dominick said.

The clerk handed Dominick a thin white towel, barely big enough to wrap around his waist and cover his crotch, and pointed him toward the locker room.

I should have splurged for the damn flip-flops, Dominick thought, feeling the carpet, which was somehow hard and damp at the same time, once he had undressed. He walked lightly down the hallway, briefly poking his head into each room as he passed.

In the various rooms, he saw two Lebanese men, obviously friends who had come together. There was a short Japanese man. A Vietnamese man. A fat Mexican. A slim Indian. *It's fucking "We Are the World" in this bitch,* Dominick said to himself. All these men, Dominick thought, come from cultures where they're not out. Or they come from cultures that are not desirable to the white majority. The only way they can be themselves, and be viewed as sexual beings, is in this dank space.

In one room, where a TV was playing porn, two men sat on a bench, jerking each other off. Inside the sauna, Dominick saw a large man sucking off another one in front of an audience of three in the dry heat. The door handle to the sauna was filmy. *God, please just let it be steam*, Dominick thought. He walked by a room with a swing in it, stopping to observe a masked man on his back, spread-eagled on a thin black vinyl mat that was hanging from chains bolted to the ceiling.

"Have at it," said another man, standing nearby.

"You just . . .?"

"Yeah, go right in."

Dominick adjusted an imaginary shirt collar, worked up his dick to erection, put on one of the condoms the man behind the front desk had given him, and prepared to fuck a masked stranger. He let down his towel and slowly went inside the man's hole.

"Ohhhhhhh yeahhhhhh, daddy," the man groaned. "Give it to me hard."

Dominick gave five thrusts before he lost his grip on the man's sweaty legs.

Okaaaaay, that's enough of that, he thought to himself. He wrapped himself back up.

"Awww, that's it?" the other man asked. "I was hoping for a show."

"Yeah, I'd like to . . . keep checking things out."

"Maybe you and I can try something."

The man, a trim Latino with a receding hairline and a bit of a paunch, had a broad smile that Dominick couldn't help but notice.

"You've been here before?" the man asked.

"First time actually. Have you?" Dominick asked, adding some bass to his voice. He was trying to sound like Don Cornelius—if Don Cornelius were cruising.

"It's been a while," the man said. "Are you sure you haven't been here? You look familiar."

"Maybe I just have one of those faces."

"What about that cock?"

"What about it?"

"Do you have one of those?" the man asked, reaching toward Dominick's growing bulge and stroking it through the cloth.

"You got a room?"

"Yeah. Let's go."

The room they went to was about the size of a walk-in closet. A seven-foot-long vinyl cushion sat on a platform that took up half the room lengthwise. A small cubby on the other side had just enough shelf space for whatever guests wanted to lay there. In the case of the slowly balding Latino, it was a strip of condoms, two bottles of Rush poppers, and a bottle of Swiss Navy lubricant.

As they started making out, Dominick's dick sprang upward as his new partner undid his towel, letting it drop to his feet. The man sat bare-assed on the vinyl cushion, cupped Dominick's balls, and sucked his dick for a few minutes before he reached for a condom, slipped it on Dominick's dick, and lubed it up. The man lay on his stomach, snorting the fumes from one of the bottles of poppers while Dominick eased him in. Soon, though, Dominick realized he could act upon a bit of fantasy and pulled the man up to his knees, put him in a slight headlock with his right hand, and pounded him from behind until he came. After he slipped out, the man took the condom off Dominick's dick, put it to his mouth, and slurped the semen out from inside. Dominick winced and tried to keep his stomach from turning at the repeated thought, a looping image now seared into his mind. He laid down next to the man on the slim cushion, trying to create something, anything, resembling romance.

"You feel so damn good. But I can't stay too long. I've got to teach a class tomorrow."

"Oh yeah? Where do you teach?"

"I teach Spanish at a community college—Wayne County."

"I took Spanish all through high school."

"Really? That's amazing."

Dominick now wanted to sound intelligent. He wanted this man to know he was more than a good fuck.

"I loved the language," he said, "and still do, but honestly, I've always been better at reading it than speaking it."

"Did you . . . you said you're from New York, right?"

"Well, I lived in New York for years, but I grew up here."

"Where'd you go to high school?"

"U of D Jesuit."

"No shit? I taught there for a year."

"Really? When?"

"2001. I was in between schools, but I went over to Grosse Pointe Academy and taught there for a few years before going to WC3."

Dominick sat straight up.

"Oh my God," he said.

He looked at the man in horror, pushing him away to remove any sort of physical contact between them. Suddenly, it all came together.

"You were my teacher in tenth grade!"

The words fell out of Dominick's mouth, but his brain couldn't comprehend them. He had just come inside one of his high school teachers. One of his high school teachers had just drunk his semen out of the free-clinic-brand condom that had been too tight on his dick. Dominick was now taking hurried breaths, naked, sitting next to one of his high school teachers, who was also naked.

"Wait, what's your name?" the man asked.

"It's Dominick."

"Oh! Domingo! That's why you looked so familiar!"

Dominick stood up and wrapped the first towel he could find around his waist, no matter how small or slimy it was.

"Domingo was my Spanish name," he said, "but can we go back a second? I just fucked my high school Spanish teacher!"

"Well, we're both full-grown adults, *Domingo*. And you were good," he said, stroking Dominick's arm. "Really good."

"Oh my God. This is not cool. Not cool."

"Calm down, Domingo. It's not like I preyed on you or anything. I didn't even know it was you!"

"Still! Oh my God!"

"It's awkward, I know. But don't worry, you were not attractive in high school."

"What?"

"I mean, what I'm trying to say is, I wasn't attracted to you, or any of you students, in high school. Only guys my age, my whole life. Swear."

"How old are you?"

"I'm forty-five. I was a young teacher, remember? And I was a lot chubbier back then, which is why you probably don't remember me. I also wasn't out then."

"This is so fucking weird, Mr. Santos."

"Do *not* call me that. I'm Miguel, OK? We're adults. And your dick wasn't weird just now. That shit felt amazing."

"Mr. Santos!"

"No, no, no, por favor. No señor. Yo soy Miguel. Y tú eres Domingo, y tú eres un hombre. Un hombre adulto. ¿Verdad?"

Dominick sighed.

"Claro."

Dominick eventually calmed down and exchanged numbers with Mr. Santos—Miguel—and fake-promised that he'd keep in touch, even though he fully intended to block the number as soon as he got home. Miguel texted him a few minutes later: "That was amazing, but I completely understand if you feel uncomfortable. You don't have to text back. But if you want to, and only if you are completely and unequivocally OK with it, we can see each other again. Take care."

Dominick, reading the text as he sped down the freeway, realized again that he was behind the wheel of a car, speeding away from a place he was trying to forget. But because it was one of the kinder messages he'd received in months, he decided not to block Mr. Miguel Santos quite yet.

A half hour later, at the back door to his mother's house, he inserted his key in the lock, hoping she wasn't waiting up for him. Her car was in the garage, so he quickly prayed she might be on the couch, asleep from watching Netflix. But then he heard the hum of an engine pull up to the house and what sounded like the bassline to the Jones Girls' "Nights Over Egypt" and caught the flash of headlight beams. He heard his mother's voice say, "Please don't forget to call me as soon as you get home" before he heard a door slam.

Tonya was out and about. She entered through the front door, laying her red Coach handbag on a side table. She met Dominick waiting for her by the stairway. He was looking concerned.

"Who was that?" he asked.

"Well," she said, slipping off a white pashmina, "you're in a mood."

"Mom! You were obviously with a man. And you're wearing red lipstick!"

"Ooo-oop!" she said, forming her two hands in the shape of a triangle, index fingers meeting at the pinnacle and thumbs meeting at the base. "Did you forget?"

"And I can smell the whiskey on your breath."

"And you," she said, sniffing him, "smell like you've been swimming. Why do you smell like chlorine?"

The phone rang.

"*Oliver Lewandowski calling. Oliver Lewandowski calling,*" a robotic voice said from the kitchen.

Tonya, still a bit tipsy, ran to the front door and onto the porch and hollered across the street, "It's all right, Oliver! We're good!"

"Mom!" Dominick called.

"It's my house. And I live here!" Tonya said. "Remember how I used to play that song for you? You always did like *the Miss Ross*."

Now I know where I got the dramatics from, Dominick thought.

"Never mind that," he said. "Who was that man?"

"*That man* was Bernard. He was an Alpha at U of M, but we've known each other for years. I've known him since we were back on *The Scene*. Maybe he's on YouTube, I should check . . ."

"Was it a date?"

Tonya walked into the kitchen, the stiletto heels of her black Stuart Weitzman booties clicking against the tile floor.

"Not really. There was a fundraiser at the Alpha House, and I was his guest. I took an Uber there. And Bernard gave me a ride back."

"You still go to the Alpha House?"

"Yes, I *still* go to the Alpha House," Tonya said. "I see where you're going with this. I'm not dead, you know. And if you really want to know, Bernard and I have been talking about seeing each other."

The talking phase? People over fifty have that? Dominick asked himself. But he was still stuck on the fact that his mother was hanging at a fraternity house at her age. The Alpha House in Detroit was a well-kept historic home, and it was natural for sorors like Tonya and her crew to go there, but all Dominick could think about was the number of men there who were probably just like his father: overgrown Black frat boys who were likely trying to fuck every woman in sight. *But then again, a woman needs love just like you*, he thought. And if Dominick could inadvertently fuck his Spanish teacher in a filthy carpeted bathhouse, the latest in months after fucking every man in sight, his mother talking to an acquaintance she had known since before he was born really wasn't all that bad.

"OK," Dominick said, desperately wanting to shower off his bathhouse shame. "Well, I'm going to bed."

"Come here," Tonya said, pulling a bottle of Black Girl Magic merlot down from the countertop wine rack. "Have one glass of wine with me before you go to bed, and let's talk. Come open this."

Dominick shuffled toward the kitchen drawer for a corkscrew. He took the bottle from her hands and twisted out the cork while Tonya rinsed two stemmed glasses.

"Bernard was on the track team at U of M before he got injured," she said as Dominick filled the glasses generously, "so then he went into engineering. We all thought he would go to the Olympics, but, you know, God must have had other plans. So he worked at Chrysler, then went to General Motors until he retired. Now he flips houses, does some consulting, started writing a book, coaches little league, whatever he can to stay busy. But he was one of the first people to reach out to me after your father and I finalized the divorce."

"How did he know?"

"You remember Nat Morris? The producer of *The Scene*? He had a reunion for the show every year. Your dad and I used to go, but after we finally separated, I went by myself. Bernard was there. It wasn't the right time for me to start dating again. I was still, like you kids say, in my feelings. Your grandfather had just died and your aunts and I were still dealing with all that, and I was," she exhaled, taking a long sip of the merlot, "thinking about you in DC and worried because you had just come out, and I didn't know who or what you were doing out there because I knew you were smart, but DC had so many people with AIDS and I knew you would be protecting yourself, but . . . anyway. *Anyway!* You're fine now, right? I mean, you are getting regularly tested and . . ."

"Yes, mom, I'm HIV-negative. I got tested right after I came back and I take PrEP."

"Well, your dad, he just moved on so quick and I'm just sitting here like!" she said, throwing her hands up in the air, blowing a slight raspberry with an astonished look on her face. "OK, my turn! I'm almost sixty, but I'm not done. Life doesn't end at . . . how old are you? Thirty-five?"

"Thirty-three," Dominick laughed.

"Damn, I'm aging myself. Shit," Tonya chuckled. "Thirty-three, OK, OK. Life doesn't end at thirty-three, Dominick. I know you wanted to be with that boy Justin, but listen. I could not *stand* him. *Whew!* Can I say that out loud? You can say what you want when you've been through what I've been through. There were so many times I wanted to tell you, you know, to play my mommy role, but I just kept telling myself, 'OK, he's grown. He doesn't need me all in his business.' But you kept me locked away for so long, I wasn't . . ."

She exhaled again, then pushed her hair back.

"You weren't . . .?" Dominick asked.

"I don't know," Tonya said, her voice now cracking slightly. "You barely came home, and you were so short on the phone whenever I called. You were so quiet at your granddaddy's service. I didn't know if it was you or *Justin* or what. I thought maybe it was something I did."

"You didn't do anything."

"I was thinking that because of the divorce you had some resentment toward me."

"It wasn't that. It was . . ." Dominick said, realizing he had to choose his words carefully. Black mothers can be volatile. Black sons have to be clear with what they say.

"Justin. It was Justin," he finally said. "I don't want to talk about it now but he just . . . he had a very specific vision of how he wanted us to be."

"That didn't include me?"

If Justin had hated Tonya from the start, Dominick knew it had been mutual. "I don't think your mother likes me," was something Justin had repeated to Dominick a *lot*. Maybe the three of them should have had more dinners together. Maybe Dominick should have flown his mother out to New York more. Maybe Dominick and Justin could have come back to Detroit for more holidays. Maybe, maybe, maybe.

"Mom, it wasn't you. It was him, and I'm sorry. I'm sorry for . . . all this. I'm going to keep you in the loop about everything from now on."

"Well, since we're in the loop," Tonya said, refilling her glass, "let me finish telling you about Bernard. He's divorced. He's two years older than me. And he wants to take me to his condo in Albuquerque for a long weekend. He's thinking of retiring there full time."

"You're not ready to retire, Mom."

"No, not yet. I still have a lot left in me. But when you get to be my age, and all I've been through so far, you think about it more and more. And from what I've seen, New Mexico is nice. I mean, not a lot of Black folks, of course, but Bernard isn't the first one to have some property down there."

"Mom, can I ask you a question?"

"OK . . ." Tonya said, preparing for something embarrassing.

"Are you happy?"

"Am I happy?"

"Yes. Are *you* happy?"

Tonya swirled her glass before taking another sip.

"I have . . . the most wonderful son in the world. He has a father that loves him unconditionally. I'm still all here," she said, pointing a red fingernail to the right side of her temple. "Some folks don't even know they're here. And . . . I'm not playing around with Bernard. You get to a certain age and you just can't play the same kind of games you were playing back in 1977. So, am I happy? In some definitions, yes. I'm not where I want to be exactly, but I feel like I have time to get there still, even at my age, which *is about to be sixty*. Oh, Lord! If you would've told me that one day I'd be creeping up on sixty! But," she said, setting down her wine glass and reaching over to place her hands on Dominick's shoulders, "like I said earlier, baby! Life doesn't end for you right now! You are still so young! Stop walking around here like you don't have time!"

Tonya's purse started buzzing, a noise so audible they both could hear it.

"Is that Bernard?" Dominick asked.

"Probably. Can you go in my purse and get that for me?"

Dominick fetched the purse and handed it to his mother unopened. Tonya huffed. "What's the point of having a gay son if he won't even go in my purse?"

"Mom!"

"I'm just teasing you."

Tonya glanced at her phone, typed a short message, then placed it face down on the counter.

"I've always wondered," Dominick said. "Did you and Dad ever want to have any more kids? You know, after . . . you know."

"You mean after the miscarriage?" she asked.

Dominick tapped the sides of his wine glass. His voice dropped to a near whisper.

"I just wondered," he said.

"Well," she said, "we didn't try again. At first I was upset at myself. And your father, well . . . for the record, he never put any pressure on me, on us, to have another one. But maybe that was just God telling us that you were always enough. And Dominick, you'll always be enough."

CHAPTER TWENTY

I'm halfway out the door of the 2501 Agency, late for another lunch with the McQuerrys, when my phone rings.

"Hello?"

"Ah, hello, Remy, my name is Vivian Young, and I'm a reporter with *Detroit Hotline*. I'm wondering if you have time to chat about the new high-rise development slated to go in on the site of the Mahaffey School."

"I'm actually on my way to—how did you get this number?"

"It's on your Mr. Detroit billboards."

"Right. Well, I'm not the developer of that project . . ."

"But you are the agent contracted for the units' eventual sale, correct?"

"Well . . . yes, but what does that have to do with . . ."

"The microstudios are being listed for more than $500,000 each in a neighborhood where the average income is less than $20,000."

"Yes, and . . ."

"Do you think that's fair for the existing residents already living there?"

"Existing residents are not buying these units."

"You're excluding them?"

"No, I'm not—where are we going with this? Is this going to be printed?"

"On your show two months ago, you also said all Detroiters should have the opportunity to find housing within their budgets. Do you think these $500,000 units are within the budgets of the people who'll be living next door to them? Or what about the closure of the Mahaffey School? Can you comment on that? It also serves a number of families in the neighborhood."

"I've got another call. Can I call you back?"

"My deadline is noon today."

"But you don't have a full story."

"I'll just tell you, if you don't call me back, the story will reflect what you've told me now and what I've gotten from other sources. I would love for you to have a chance to tell your side."

"OK, I've got another call. I'll call you back," I say, pressing End. "*Bitch!*"

"Mr. Patton, I'm still here."

"Fuck!" I whisper to myself, pressing the End button firmer this time.

POPULAR REALTOR "MR. DETROIT" PEDDLING PRICEY MICROSTUDIOS IN IMPOVERISHED EAST SIDE NEIGHBORHOOD

In just a few short years, Remy "Mr. Detroit" Patton has become a local icon.

With billboards across town that rival the likes of Joumana Kayrouz and Mike Morse, the stylish real estate agent often seen around Detroit's hot spots in furs and Cartier sunglasses has thousands of Twitter followers, steady appearances on local shows like *Flashpoint* and *Detroit Today*, and his own half-hour weekly talker on 910-AM. Despite his outward appearance, Patton's charm and affability comes largely from his rags-to-riches story and his relatability to Detroiters as a die-hard east-sider.

But a new Islandview development may be at odds with Patton's message of equality for anyone wishing to buy a home in the city, raising questions about how authentic that message actually is.

Detroit Hotline's eyes and ears were wide open Monday night when playboy developer scion Thad McQuerry II was spotted making the moves on a young woman at the Candy Bar in the boutique Siren Hotel. The son of Novi developer and noted slumlord Thad McQuerry—you may remember the father-son pair from a 2010 *Vice* documentary that showed them gobbling up Detroit homes for pennies during the foreclosure crisis and then renting them back to their current owners in distress—was visibly inebriated, according to our source.

But our source notes that the younger McQuerry was quite chatty, rambling on about "a multimillion-dollar development on the old Mahaffey plot" and having "Mr. Detroit come in and clean up our image in the city."

According to Wayne County records, the site of the Mahaffey School changed hands in March and is now under the ownership of an entity called McQuerry Land Holdings, LLC.

Reached by phone, the younger McQuerry confirmed the company is planning to build "microstudios" on the property and to "look for the press release when it's out there" but referred further comment to an attorney. The attorney did not return repeated calls from *Detroit Hotline*.

Reached by phone Tuesday morning, Patton also confirmed his involvement with the development, saying that current residents in the area—where annual household incomes average less than $20,000—"are not buying these units."

Compare that with Patton's declaration during a late-March episode of his 910 show, *The Real on Real Estate* with *Mr. Detroit*, where he said: "All Detroiters have the opportunity to buy in Detroit, and all Detroiters have a birthright to that opportunity by nature of everything we as Detroiters have been through just to be in this city."

Patton, who referred to this reporter as a "bitch" before abruptly ending the conversation, offered no further comment on the development.

• • •

Dominick Gibson
Are you OK?

Remy Patton
I take it you saw the story

Dominick Gibson
Yeah, what the hell?
You talked to her this morning and the story's already up?
Goddamn that was fast
How are you feeling?

Remy Patton
I'm feeling like I want to call a lawyer
You can't just take what I said over the phone and print it without my consent

Dominick Gibson
I'm saying this as a friend
You were on the record as soon as you answered that phone

Remy Patton
Is that how it happens?

Dominick Gibson
Did she identify herself as a reporter?

Remy Patton
Yeah

Dominick Gibson
Unless you say something like "we're off the record,"
then it's on the record

Remy Patton
What does that term even mean?
Isn't everything technically on the record?

Dominick Gibson
Think of it this way
Remember when you were telling that story about the
threesome you had with two Lebanese guys and you made me
promise not to tell anyone?

Remy Patton
Not the time, Dominick

Dominick Gibson
Lol sorry I'm trying to cheer you up

• • •

I have a showing at 9:30 a.m. I sleep until 9:15.

I took a long bath last night. Soaked myself in some sake oil and made some chamomile tea before I went to bed. So technically I'm clean, I guess.

I thought the oil and the tea would help me sleep, but the truth is, nothing seems to help now. I'll go to bed at 10:00 with good intent, then wake up at 1:00, scroll through every app until 4:00, try to sleep again at 4:30, and go through this cycle, or whatever, until I finally need to get up for work. I'll curl up in a ball and hug my comforter like it's a real person. I'll think about something that's past its deadline, some little bit of paperwork the McQuerry son's badgering me for, and my whole body will shudder. And just when I feel like I'm going to fall asleep, something will creep into my mind, fictional or real. In those hours, I'll think about the night I was almost raped back at Oakland, or about being hit by a car, even though I've never been hit by one.

I know I need to get this looked at. But I just don't have the time. It's not some too-proud or too-manly or too-Black thing. Hell, I know Black men have trouble with controlling their emotions and all that, and I know we have trouble admitting we need help. But that's not me. I mean, I'm from the fuckin' east side, and I know I don't have any trauma or PTSD or any of that shit. I know the first thing one of these Caucasian-ass therapists would ask me is if I got shot or if someone I know got shot on the east side. That ain't me. Shit, it's the east side. Whatever it is, it is, but I know what it *isn't*, and it *isn't* that for me. Period.

Then they would ask me if it was because I grew up partially without a father. Look, just because I don't talk to the nigga that much doesn't mean I'm a worse person now because of it. My mother did good raising me. Me, a Black man who didn't end up in jail or making her a grandmother—not like I could—before her time. Never brought her any trouble, never made her mortgage the house for some dumb shit. Lest we forget, I also bought her a condo, and I don't throw it in her face either. So no, Mr. Psychoanalyst, it ain't that.

Then they'd ask me if it's because I'm gay, and whether I have some *traumaaaa* from that. They'd probably assume some old man or nasty cousin touched me when I was little. Wrong. That ain't it either. Because I've searched and searched through the deepest corners of my mind just to be sure I wasn't, you know, repressing anything like that, and nothing.

That's not to say that men my age who were molested have some sort of defect or anything like that. It's just that I'm gay because I was born this way, not because someone made me this way. Wait, wait—Troy wouldn't like that. I don't know how to put it. It's like, damn . . . let me put it this way. Nobody preyed on me, I guess, because they sensed I was gay. God, I hope I'm saying this right. God, please let me just find the right words to say *whatever* it is I'm trying to say.

What I know for sure is that I don't want to be mentally poked and prodded. Black people have it hard enough. Again, it's not the whole, "Oh, Black people don't deal with their mental health and don't go to therapy and they hold their feelings inside until it kills them" type of thing, no. It's just that I know these motherfuckers will have all the answers just looking at me. A white therapist will blame it on me being Black, and a Black therapist will blame it on me being gay.

Well, what if I got a Black, gay therapist?

Like I said, I just don't have time to stop what I'm doing. The moment I slow down is the moment I lose. And as a Black man in America, I can't lose. I have to keep moving. I have to push through. I can't slip. I can't fall. We already have chains on to begin with, and if we slow down, we have to catch back up even more because we're already behind. If we fall down, we fall harder. And we have to get back up from below the ground. And I can't ask *Dear Prudence* about that shit.

CHAPTER TWENTY-ONE

As Dominick's plane began its descent into JFK, he went through his two objectives for the trip one more time for good measure. First, he had to attend the Catskills wedding of his friends, David and Ryan, the third attendance to upstate nuptials of conventionally attractive white gay men in just as many years, but hopefully without having to answer any questions about why he was attending alone. Then, he had to take one last, long look at New York City and accept the reality that he'd never live there again. The wedding was the easy part. The saying good-bye, to the city and possibly to Justin . . . not so much.

It had been seven months since he'd left, and, being back in Detroit, he'd gotten used to driving again. There was a renewed sense of freedom in having his own transportation, being able to get up and go—escape—at his own discretion without being held at the mercy of the subway system. There were other things he'd gotten used to. The relative silence of sleeping in his bedroom, no clanging radiators, no dog shit on the sidewalks. "Rent control" and "broker fees" and "$56 Uber rides just to cross a fucking bridge" were foreign terminology back in Michigan. There were a normal amount of people walking around, hardly any of whom were taking photographs. Being back in New York now, he remembered how suffocating it could be. In Detroit, Dominick could breathe.

He was committed to only doing things he enjoyed on this farewell tour. For the next few days, he'd be crashing on Jonah's couch in Brooklyn—the two had started at Tandy and Simms around the same time. And oh, how Dominick loved Brooklyn. No longer restricted by the dietary choices Justin made for them, Dom wanted to pig out at Smorgasbord in Prospect Park. He wanted to browse the Brooklyn Public Library at his own leisure.

"And don't forget," Jonah said, as they strolled down Tompkins Avenue, a Black-owned business strip that brought to mind Detroit's own Avenue of Fashion, "that we definitely have to go to that Mariah vs. Ariana party at C'mon Everybody. And if I leave there early with some little bottom boy, just, you know, try to keep your ears covered when you come back to the apartment."

"I brought my AirPods," Dominick laughed.

A pair of white women jogged past them at the corner of Halsey and Tompkins.

"What's going on here? Is this still Bed-Stuy?"

"All the white culture writers got bored with Crown Heights, so they came over to this side of Fulton," Jonah said. "Give it time. Brownsville will be next."

Jesus, it's everywhere, Dominick thought.

"Speaking of," Jonah continued, "if you moved back here and lived in Brooklyn, I'd actually stay because I miss you! Tandy is just not the same now. And you could move back here by yourself! You didn't do what all the other New York gays do and cohabitate until the lease was up. You left and never looked back. That's still a boss move. Would you ever consider living down here?"

"Maybe, but things are so cheap in Detroit, and I actually like it. Maybe *you* should move *there*."

"Can you still buy a house for a dollar there?"

"Not *that* cheap, booboo."

Though he spent most of his time wandering around and seeing old friends in Brooklyn, Dominick knew he'd have to take one final trip to Hell's Kitchen to clean out his $2,750-per-month apartment. And early on Thursday afternoon, when he figured Justin would be at work, he took the A train into Manhattan.

He unlocked his old door and stepped inside, alone. Justin hadn't touched anything since he'd been gone. Sure, the apartment was a perfect facsimile of what gay men should have in their household. He saw the bookshelf was still stacked with its volumes of David Sedaris and Augusten Burroughs before sitting down on their Room & Board couch. His-and-his Turkish cotton robes still hung in the closet, and Jonathan Adler ceramic bric-a-brac rested on each side of the glossy white credenza that held their fifty-inch Sony flatscreen. But if it weren't for the photo of the two of them on vacation in Provincetown, encased in a Neiman Marcus frame lined with mother-of-pearl, you'd have no idea that the gay men who lived here were Black.

There wasn't much more for Dominick to take back to Detroit because, in building his New York coexistence with Justin, he'd already purged so much of that past life. When they had first moved in together, the James Baldwin and Langston Hughes books Dominick had begun collecting at Howard were shipped back to Detroit. Then it was his copies of Toni Morrison and Zora Neale Hurston. Then Gloria Naylor, E. Lynn Harris, and Terry McMillan.

"You read these in high school," Justin said. "We're grown-ups now. Come on! Let's try some new authors who have published in this decade."

Justin hated clutter and loved new technology, so Dominick's CD collection had been shipped back to Detroit, too. Brandy's entire discography, the one-hit or no-hit girl groups like Before Dark and Changing Faces, even the bootlegged DJ Assault mixtapes he had bought from the bootleg boy at U of D—all sent back home. Instead, Justin's music, neatly stored on an iPod—Bluetoothed through their Alexa speaker—reigned supreme in the living room, leaving Dominick to curate his collections on his own devices, none of which were played when company was over.

His collection of *GQ* and *Vibe* had all gone to recycling. His old T-shirts from Howard, which Dominick had barely saved from a Goodwill pile Justin had started once, were, like everything else, shipped back to Detroit. The one thing he had managed to save was a full-page poster of Aaliyah the *Detroit Free Press* had printed after she died. His parents had laminated it for him, and it had followed him from his bedroom to the Howard dorms to his first two apartments—Justin had begrudgingly allowed him to hang it in the closet of their home office.

They hadn't had much art when they first moved into this apartment, and Justin picked all of it when they settled in. Mass-produced photos of flower arrangements, a generic print of the New York City skyline, a few posters from IKEA—nothing that suggested any inkling of originality, or Blackness. Everything borrowed from the aesthetic of a suite at the Hampton Inn.

What did Justin want us to become? Dominick thought. *All this Pottery Barn, Williams Sonoma bullshit.*

Dominick found the Aaliyah poster, then loaded up a box with a few other personal effects, including the USB drives he thought he'd forgotten. He paced from room to room, walking in circles, taking things off shelves and putting them back.

It almost felt like home once.

He realized—remembered, actually—that this had been such a clean break because he had actually been planning it for a while. Seven months ago, Dominick had been texting Troy about how irritable Justin had been recently, how snappy they had been to each other, how he had been spending more time at Atomic Ranch than at home because he dreaded being in his own apartment. He had already moved some of his clothes out of the bedroom and into the closet of their home office. He'd started separating his toiletries to one side of the medicine cabinet too. Dominick had been planning his getaway in plain sight and Justin hadn't even noticed.

As he was taking one last look, Dominick heard the door unlock. He stood tall as Justin walked into the living room.

"What are you doing here?" Justin asked, setting his briefcase by the door.

"I came to get the rest of my stuff. That's all."

Justin caught his breath.

"I can't believe this is still happening," he said.

"Don't worry, I didn't take anything that belongs to you."

"Dominick, sit down."

"I don't have time for this, Justin."

"Please."

Justin walked over to Dominick and hugged him, burying his face into his chest as he sobbed.

"I'm sorry," he said. "I miss you so much. Please . . ."

Dominick stood still, looking up at the ceiling to hold back his tears.

"I'm sorry. All I can say is I'm sorry," Justin said. He looked up at Dominick, eyes shiny from crying.

Dominick wiped a tear away from Justin's cheek with his thumb. Then he pulled Justin's entire body into his embrace. The heat and Justin's familiar smell had Dominick's dick rock hard. And as he quickly found out, Justin's lips were still pillow-soft, his thighs still like velvet, and his ass still had that jiggle and bounce. They kissed, finally, and Dominick remembered something that had been missing for months. All it took was one touch, and then one look. Dominick did not go back to Jonah's that night. He stayed at his apartment to sleep in the bed he and Justin had split the cost on, the two of them side by side for the first time in months.

"So, how are you feeling?" Justin asked.

It was late the next morning. Justin had called in sick and the two men had yet to get out of bed.

"About what?"

"You know. Last night?"

Dominick couldn't find the words fast enough. He couldn't deny that sex with Justin felt damn good. It was everything that had made their relationship great.

It might've been the only thing that made our relationship great, Dominick thought, though he had to admit to himself that sex had always been one of the only activities they shared where Dominick was fully in control. It was the only time when Justin was submissive, the only time Dom felt like, for lack of a better term, the man in the relationship.

"I don't know," Dominick said, after a half minute of agonizing silence. "I don't know."

"Are you confused?"

"Maybe."

True.

"Are you angry?"

"No."

A lie.

"Are you sad?"

"No."

A lie, again.

"Do you regret what happened last night?"

"I never have regrets."

A lie, again.

"You're feeling something. Tell me."

"I don't know what I'm feeling. And honestly, I don't know if what I'm feeling now is how I'll be feeling later," he said.

That was true. Right now, one thing that was definitely on Dominick's mind was whether he'd be showing symptoms of an STI in two to fourteen days after having raw sex with his cheating boyfriend.

"So what is it?"

"I don't want to talk about my feelings right now."

"And see, this is why we have an issue," Justin said, changing his tone.

"*This* is our issue?"

"Don't raise your voice."

"Don't talk to me like a fucking child, Justin," Dominick said through gritted teeth. And just like that, any new thoughts he'd had of marrying this man dissipated.

"Calm down. Relax."

"Justin, stop. You do this all the time. You talk down to me. You act like a parent. I am your boyfriend, remember?"

"Oh, are you? I thought you wanted to end this."

Dominick said nothing and looked down.

"Do you?" Justin asked.

"I won't say yes, and I won't say no. What I will say is that if we continue this—if!—then some things will have to change."

"I know I have to change some things. I know you have to change some things. But if we both change, this will work."

"That's the thing. I don't know what 'this' is anymore."

"It's us. It's you and me. It's Dominick and Justin, Justin and Dominick. The way it was, forever."

"It seems like it's Dominick, Justin, and the first Tom, Dick, or Harry you meet on Grindr."

"It was only one time!"

"One time that you had sex?"

"Yes."

"How long did you know him before you did?"

"For four months."

"*Four months?* And you only had sex with him once?"

Justin sighed and looked down.

"Answer my question."

"He was the only one! I swear to God. It won't happen again. Promise."

"You can't just . . . you can't just get an 'I'm sorry' here. It doesn't work like that. You know how I feel about cheating."

"So do you want to break up with me?"

"I just want to know why. Did I do something?"

"You ignored me."

"What do you mean?"

"It was you and your job and your friends and your mom and everything else. You lost track of me and us."

"What are you talking about? I gave you everything! I let you take my money to buy anything you wanted, to decorate the house, to spend on you and your friends . . ."

"I have my own money. Don't do that."

"We agreed it was our money, but you spent a lot of it," Dominick said, folding his arms.

"And you didn't? All of your shirts and shoes that you bought?"

"Are you fucking kidding me?"

"Don't curse."

"I did that because you said you were embarrassed to go out with me in public because I couldn't dress!"

"I know, I know. But you don't know your limits."

"See, you're doing this thing again where you put everything on me, as if I was the one who cheated and put us into debt."

"We're not in debt. Yet."

"Well, since you got so much money, fix it."

"I am fixing it. Now, are you ready to talk like an adult?"

Dominick sucked in his bottom lip. Just to get the conversation over with, he nodded.

"OK," Justin said. "So, I talked to your old coworker, Constance, at Tandy and Simms. I told her the whole situation. She said they missed you there and were willing to offer you your old job back."

"Wait, what?"

"You heard me. I got you your old job back."

"How did you do that? What are you trying to do?"

"I'm trying to fix this. I want our life back. So you're going to start back at your job, you're going to move back in, and in a few weeks, we're going to go to the Hudson Valley like we used to and we are going to get back on track."

"This is not going to happen. I'm not going back to Tandy and Simms."

"You are. And if we play it smart, we won't have to do a lot of explaining at Ryan and David's wedding."

"I don't care about no damn Ryan and David right now. That's the thing. You're so busy trying to keep up with everybody, and the everybody you're trying to keep up with is trying to keep up with somebody else."

"Look, it's obvious that we're . . . too toxic for each other right now, so how about we have dinner tonight? One more time. Just to go over . . . everything."

"Fine. I want to go to Amy Ruth's."

"You know I don't go to Harlem."

"It's my choice, Justin. For *once*," Dominick said, getting out of bed to get dressed. "Be there at 7:30 or we're finished."

That afternoon, Dominick decided that if he was going to break up with both his boyfriend *and* New York City, it was going to be in the Blackest way possible. Justin could have Broadway. Dominick wanted Lenox Avenue.

For too long, Dominick realized, he'd been living Justin's white sneakers and iced coffee version of New York City instead of the Strivers'

Row fantasy he'd imagined. Dominick would sneak to Harlem when Justin wasn't around to browse at the Schomburg Center, chow down on plates of chitterlings at Sylvia's, perhaps steal away to a hole-in-the-wall jazz club on Lenox, or journal in Marcus Garvey Park.

"I don't want to get robbed," Justin always said about Harlem.

The red flags were always there, Dominick thought. *Why would anyone, even a Black person, move to New York and not have some inkling of fear?*

Being back in Detroit reminded Dominick of just who he was. Seeing his mother interact with her sorors and still going to the African Methodist Episcopal church he grew up in. Head-nodding 'til his neck was sore to every Black man in the street. Seeing beautiful Black women who always looked glamorous, whether their hair was done or in a bonnet on their way to being done. Feeling Troy's unbridled passion for wanting the kids in his school to do well, or seeing Remy doing the damn thing against all his odds. Black excellence was what he relished in Harlem. In Detroit, it was all around.

Now, having finally found some courage to look his Black partner in the eye, Dominick felt uncomfortable. Inside Amy Ruth's, he stabbed aimlessly at his fried catfish, trying to find the exit to something he thought was the promised land. Here were two young, successful, Black men in a relationship, dining in Harlem at last, living what may have been Langston's dream. Only in this case, it was really more of a messy gay nightmare akin to Tennessee Williams.

"Just tell me, Dom," Justin said, "Why don't you love me?"

"I do love you."

"Do you?"

"I do."

"Let's backtrack then and see where we end up. Why?"

"Well, if I have to go through all the sordid details," Dominick said. "We just had a lot in common. We're both from the Midwest. We both had East Coast educations."

"OK."

"And we both just . . . we were both on this same path, I guess. We both wanted to be in New York and do the whole New York thing, and we were doing it together."

"You love me because of what we had in common?"

Dominick looked down at the white tablecloth. He closed his eyes, seeing clearly the truth he'd been avoiding. There was no true love to be had in this relationship. Only opportunity. Only something to make work.

"I don't hate you, Justin. I never could," he said. "I don't want this to end with us hating each other."

"You can't stand to look at me right now."

"Because if I look at you," Dominick said, stifling a cry. "If I look at you . . . I won't. . ."

"Look at me," Justin said. "Open your eyes, look up."

"Justin, please."

"Look at me, Dominick Andrew Gibson."

There were only two people who were allowed to call him by his first and middle name, and those were the two people who had procreated to make him.

Never, Dominick thought, *never again will this man treat me like a child.*

Dominick looked up and tried not to blink. All those empowerment songs about not letting your opposing party see you cry echoed in his mind like calls to prayer. But then Justin blinked, and tears fell down his cheek. Dominick blinked back.

"I'm never going to hate you," Justin said. "You are going to go on and do great things. You're going to be big—bigger than Tandy, bigger than New York, bigger beyond your wildest dreams. You always had it in you, you just never knew how to reach for it."

That's the thing, Dominick thought. *You always held me back from reaching for what I wanted.*

Dominick wanted desperately to say this. He swallowed air three times, keeping the words from falling out. What little hate he had for his ex-partner had dissipated but was now roaring back in a five-alarm blaze.

All of the missed potential to be the best person I could be, he thought, *or at least try to figure out because I was too ready to minimize myself for him. And once again, I'll have to. Because I don't want to cause a scene, and the last thing Black gay men should do is be messy in front of Black heteros. Keeping up all these goddamn appearances.*

"Say something," Justin said.

Dominick let the air out from his lungs.

"You're right," he said. "I'll be better."

Justin placed his hand on top of Dominick's.

"We'll be better," he said.

"*We* won't," Dominick said, snatching his hand back. "I will."

He stood up and placed his napkin on the table.

"You need to move out that apartment into somewhere cheaper," he said. "And if you need help, I will give you help. I don't hate you. I never could. We're still on the same path, but we're not . . . we're not holding hands on this path anymore. You are also going to be bigger and better, and I hope you find someone who supports you in getting to where you want to go. But just remember that *you* need to support *them* as much as they support you. And I'm always going to be rooting for you. Because I still love you. As a friend. Only a friend, from now on."

"Do you not want your dinner?"

"No, I'm good. I'm going back to Brooklyn. Now. Right now. I'm going to David and Ryan's wedding alone, and after that, I'm going straight back home."

"Dominick, sit down."

"No. No. No. Not this time. Let it go, Justin. I'm done with the relationship, but I'm offering my friendship. You're not obligated to take it. But I am offering, because despite everything else, you've helped me grow as a person. And I know I've helped you. So either this could be the end of our season or the beginning of a new one."

"Fine," Justin said, rising from his seat, "I'll be your friend."

They hurried down 116th and found Dominick's rental car.

"One more thing," Dominick said. "Who was he?"

"Who was who?"

"You know. Your four months."

Justin sighed.

"A flight attendant. He's from London."

Dominick stopped dead in his tracks and furrowed his brow.

It can't be, he thought.

"Wait. What's his name?" he asked.

"If it's that important," Justin said, "His name was Roland. Roland Braithwaite. He worked for Virgin Airlines and flew Heathrow to JFK once a week. Satisfied?"

CHAPTER TWENTY-TWO

Troy poured a tiny hill of cocaine on top of the desk in his father's office, lined it with the end of Bill's Montblanc pen, and snorted, using a Kleenex to clean up any evidence.

The office was his father's pride and joy. A big, black, quilted office chair and oak desk stood on a burgundy oriental rug. Sconces were low lit along the walls—pairs of white tubes topped with miniature lampshades that matched the light in the ceiling's center. When he was younger and bored, Troy would lay on the rug and count them repeatedly. Everything in the room was a frozen portrait. The whole house itself could have easily doubled as a compact version of a museum.

Troy looked up at the large oil portrait of Bill's grandfather, Claude, lit up under an antique brass, wall-mounted light on the wall opposite the desk.

"He was the first one in our family," Bill had said to Troy so many times, "born in Reconstruction. His mother was a slave. He told me about her. I'm that close to slavery. You're that close to slavery."

Now Troy was staring at the portrait alone, his father's muffled voice on the phone in the next room, waiting for the cocaine to kick into his system so he could make it through the evening.

I'm that close to slavery, he thought.

Bill had invited him to dinner. It had been a while, and he'd also mentioned that he "wanted to talk about something," whatever that meant. When Troy arrived, his father was busy talking to a client. Troy had quickly excused himself to the office, whispering that he wanted to look at the portrait of his great-grandfather.

Back in the living room, Troy nursed a glass of wine as he and Bill sat in silence. Sporadic noises filtered in from the kitchen—the chef putting the final touches on the night's meal. The lack of conversation made him twitchy, and he nearly bolted out of his blue velvet wingback chair when the doorbell chimed.

"We're having company?"

Bill hobbled up without saying anything and went to answer the front door down the hall. Even in such a large home, the screen door squeaked like any other house in Detroit.

"OK, hunchback. I know you're not that beat down."

Troy caught the voice. *Aunt Gwen?* he thought. He stood up and made his way to the foyer.

"Well, look at my nephew all grown. Let me just look at you for a minute. Mmm," she said before turning to Bill. "I still see Suhas all in him."

"He always had her face," Bill said. "Here, let me take your coat."

"I'll handle it. You go sit down, old man," Gwen said, taking off her maroon jacket and silver sequined beret and hanging them in the closet underneath the stairwell. "I was just saying your father is over here walking around like the hunchback of Notre Dame. Mother would be so disappointed if she didn't see us stand up straight."

Gwendolyn Clements—then Gwendolyn Sanders, then Gwendolyn McCoy, and now Gwendolyn Parker—was Bill's younger sister. She'd also come up from Palestine, even though she had just been a baby then. While Bill had stayed in Detroit, Gwendolyn had moved to Harlem, then Chicago, then Indianapolis, then back to Detroit again before finally settling in Los Angeles, picking up—and then leaving—a husband in almost every city along the way.

"I didn't know you were coming back home, auntie," Troy said. "When did you get in?"

"Last night, and I stayed at this raggedy hotel on the riverfront. They said it's Black-owned, but this place? It smelled like mold, and it barely had a minibar. Your daddy here could have put me up in a better place."

"I thought by now Bobby would have had that place cleaned up," Bill said. "We did the graphic design for them, you know."

"Next time, put me at the Book-Cadillac," Gwen said. "Troy, baby, how have you been?"

Troy wasn't quite sure how to answer. He hadn't seen his aunt since he'd graduated from college.

"I'm . . . I'm OK, I guess," he said.

"Hmm," Gwen said. "Just OK?"

"Just OK," Troy said. "Nothing new, really. How long are you here for?"

"'Til we get whatever business straightened out that we need to get straightened out, I guess."

"Can I get you something to drink?" Bill asked.

"Whatever Troy's got looks good, if you don't mind."

Bill went to get a glass of wine for his sister as she and Troy headed back to the living room.

Business, Troy thought. In the Clements household, it was always business. Even those rare times Bill had visited Troy at school and taken him out to dinner, he'd always found a way to write it off as a business expense.

And with all the room in this house, Troy thought, *he couldn't even invite his own sister to stay in one of the guest bedrooms? Did he think she was a client?*

"Do you have a fever, boy?" Gwen asked.

"No, I'm fine," Troy responded.

"You're sweating a little. Everything OK?"

"It's the wine," Troy said, tapping his glass. "It always gets me like this."

"None of the men in our family hold their liquor quite well," Bill said, handing Gwen a glass of merlot. "Daddy was a drunk. I'm always careful with it. And now this boy over here has to do the same."

"Hmm," Gwen said. "Daddy was a lot of things."

"A real son-of-a-bitch from what I've heard," Troy said.

"That is correct," Gwen said. "And I'll drink to that!"

"Well, auntie, you definitely didn't come all the way from California to have a drink. What's going on?"

Gwen sighed and looked at her brother.

"Well?" she asked.

Troy realized his father wasn't drinking.

"Are you having any wine?" Troy asked.

Bill swirled his empty glass as if there were some inside. He reached for a bottle of Pellegrino he had brought back with him from the kitchen and poured that instead, then turned slightly in his chair and made it plain.

"I'm not well, son," he said.

Troy had been oblivious to his own sweat at first, but he could now feel large beads forming on his forehead.

"What's wrong?" he asked.

"For one, he shouldn't be drinking that wine you offered him to begin with," Gwen said.

"Excuse me," Bill said, cutting his eyes to his sister, who threw up a dismissive hand and swallowed her next interjection.

"I'm confused," Troy said.

"I am, too, Troy," Gwen said.

"You don't know?"

"Hey, I'm just here," Gwen said, lifting her glass. "Having a drink."

"So here's the deal," Bill said. "I *can't* have the wine. But I'm going to be fine. The doctors have all said there's a good chance . . ."

"Doctors? What doctors?" Troy asked.

"But in the event I don't . . . I don't . . . in the event that things don't work out, I have a business. And I need that business to be taken care of, son."

"What are you talking about? The printers?" Troy asked.

"Yes, son. The business that's given us all this and the business that, for reasons only God knows, you hate me for."

"I don't hate you, Dad. Where the hell did that come from?"

"The way you walk in here, like you don't give a damn about all I've done, all I've built for you! You're so damn selfish. Your mother would be so disappointed if she saw all this."

Troy couldn't contain himself.

"Well, my mother is the only one who ever loved me," he said. "You never did."

"Where do you get this from, that I don't love you? That I didn't put everything I ever goddamn had into the company to . . ."

"That's the thing, goddammit! Everything with you is the fucking business! What about me? You were the one that put me to the side when Mom died! You did everything you could to keep me out your way. And now what? These half-ass dinners and family reunions are supposed to make up for all that? Are you really dying? Is it just guilt? Are you feeling guilty?"

Gwen folded her hands under her chin and cocked her eye toward her brother.

"Are you?" she asked.

Bill picked up his glass.

"I'm not dying," he said. "But I will someday. And I've been thinking about the business and who's going to take over when it happens."

"Jesus fucking Christ," Troy said.

"One of you . . ."

"I can't fucking believe this."

"Troy, stop!" Gwen said. "Just stop. Your father is trying to say something."

"Well, why didn't he say this shit when I was fifteen? That would've been the time, auntie."

"I'm not dealing with this shit. You two need to talk. I'm going out back for a cigarette, shit," Gwen said, cussing and fussing her way to the hall closet to fetch her coat.

The two Clements men sat opposite each other in silence. Troy stared at the ceiling, in partial disbelief that the bougie Black family blowup had finally made its way to Indian Village, while Bill fixated on his glass of sparking water.

"So?" Troy asked, avoiding eye contact.

"I never, ever didn't love you. Just know that," Bill said. "My father was the son of a bitch, not me. I made sure to never treat you the same way he treated me. I tried. And I don't know why you're always so angry, but you're still my blood anyway."

Troy stood up.

"Tell Aunt Gwen I'll see her next time," he said. "I'm going home."

"Sit down, Troy."

"I've got to go, Dad. We'll have this conversation later. When I'm not so angry, like you say."

Troy knew his father was hiding something. Any Black man who's showy about his wealth hides like a turtle in a shell when things aren't going well. That had never happened before in the Clements house. And now that it had, Troy was torn between the layers of disdain he'd accumulated for his father over the years and the deep sympathy he felt for someone he actually loved and who, despite it all, he certainly didn't want to lose.

Just before the 2008 recession, when Troy was a junior at Oakland, Clements Printing had been forced to lay off some of its staff. That Christmas, when he tried to bring it up at dinner, passive aggressively making comments about his father's employees who *weren't* lucky enough to have a nice meal that night, Bill had been silent about it. But six months later, after the initial shock had calmed, he hired everyone back.

"You got to love your own people, 'cause don't nobody else do," he said.

On the first day everyone was back at work, Bill's executive assistant suggested he bring in champagne so the whole staff could toast with Dixie cups.

Troy thought about all the Black folks his father had put to work for decades. How people were able to provide for their families because of his father, how a future generation—like the kids he taught at Mahaffey—had it just a little bit easier in a world unfriendly to his own people because someone was bringing home a regular paycheck his father signed every other Friday.

Black folks had to overcome so much. Bill Clements had risen from Arkansas dirt and survived the Black Bottom and then helped other Black folks overcome too. He had given them some hope. Given them some opportunity. Given them a champagne toast. Remy, too, had made it from something. He too had overcome.

Goddamn, Troy thought. *That close to slavery.*

That night, Troy couldn't fall asleep. His bed was empty again—he had no idea where Roderick was. And he was restless from the mix of cocaine, wine, and coney wings he'd picked up on the way home. So he got into his car, drove over to Jefferson Avenue, and walked toward the Belle Isle Bridge. He walked on one of the sidewalk paths toward the middle, staring out into the dark river below. Every year there were stories about a few folks who jumped off the bridge when they couldn't overcome anymore. For a fleeting moment, Troy considered joining those ranks. It'd be such a relief, wouldn't it? No more worries about family, friends, students, or money. No more Mahaffey School or Taking Back Detroit or microstudios or fights with Remy about what was best for the neighborhood. Leave that to everyone else. After all, everyone else was taking care of it already.

All I'd have to do is climb up, close my eyes, and let it all go, he thought.

But he knew he couldn't. His mind wasn't that far gone, and suicide would be a bad example for the kids he saw every day. Even just the thought of it brought him to the clarity he'd been searching for since he'd stormed out of his father's house. Tonight, Bill had had something to hide. He'd been hiding it by hiring someone to prepare meals for him, disguising it with the new concern he was showing his distant son. Troy, sober and clear, didn't want to believe his new suspicion but had no choice but to consider the possibility. Bill Clements was more than not well. He was sick. Very much so. But what he was sick from and how grave the situation might be were thoughts Troy never expected to cross his mind. But now, as he walked back across the bridge to his car, here they were.

"So where were you?" Roderick asked him when he got back to the apartment.

Troy, in his current mental state, had completely forgotten about his boyfriend, the one who was now sitting on the couch in their living room, questioning his whereabouts.

"At my father's house. I thought you went to Union Street."

"Well, guess what? They closed."

"What do you mean?"

"A new owner just bought the building. Told you the shit was going to be gentrified."

Fuck, Troy thought. *It's happening in the whole fucking neighborhood.*

"I have some bad news, I think," he said.

"Were you really at your father's house?"

"Yes. I was. And I think something's happened."

"Stop fuckin' lying. You weren't at your dad's house. I know."

"What?"

Roderick handed Troy's MacBook Air to him. The messaging app was open.

"You want to tell me who the fuck Gogo is?"

Troy was having trouble keeping up. It was as if he and Roderick were having two different conversations.

"You know Gogo. My friend Gregory—what's wrong with you? My dad . . ."

"I was using your laptop to make some flyers. And when I opened it, your messages were right there. You've been seeing this nigga Gogo behind my back."

Shit, Troy thought.

"Roderick, listen . . ." he said.

"Listen to what?" Roderick shoved Troy against the wall, knocking down a picture and sending the MacBook crashing to the floor.

"You said you wouldn't do this again!" Troy yelled.

Roderick sat back down and buried his face in his hands.

"You were the one saying I was cheating, but you were out here this whole time?"

"Gogo and I don't do anything. We've never had sex. I just see him when I need to talk to someone. You're never here!"

"No, no, no."

"You're with TBD all the time."

"Oh, this is on me?"

"You come in and out of *my* apartment like it's a damn hotel."

"I pay bills here too!"

Troy stopped to consider what he might say next.

"Do you think we should break up?" Roderick asked. "Seems like you want this Gogo dude more than me anyway."

Troy remained silent.

"What did I do to deserve this, Troy?"

Troy found words. They weren't necessarily what he wanted to say, but he needed to.

"You pushed me again," he said. "That's one time too many. We have to break up."

Roderick went into the bedroom and slammed the door behind him. Troy followed. "Open the door, Roderick," he said. "You know we need to discuss this."

Troy pushed against the door and found it wasn't locked. Roderick was sitting on the edge of the bed.

"So what are you going to do?" Troy asked.

"Can we please just . . . work on this?"

Troy quickly considered what work might mean in this context. Couple's counseling? When had anyone ever seen two gay Black men do that? Advice from Roderick's oh-so-beloved TBD members? Troy wasn't welcome there. Advice from friends? It had been months since the one person in the world who would know exactly what to say and do had spoken to him. Advice from his dad? Certainly not. But then Troy paused.

Perhaps Dad could be a temporary refuge, he thought.

He picked up his laptop and packed it into his messenger bag, along with his chargers, his lesson plans, a toothbrush, another pair of glasses, and an envelope with his passport and birth certificate in it.

"I'm going to leave for a while. You should think about where you might want to stay because I don't think we can work through this," he told Roderick, who hadn't moved from the bed. "We can talk about this tomorrow. I might be back."

"Where are you going?" Roderick asked softly.

"I'm going to my dad's house. You should know that he's ill. I just found out, so . . . I need to spend some time with him. But like I said, you should think about your next steps."

"Troy," Roderick said.

"What?"

"Love you."

Troy sighed and looked at the ceiling.

"Love isn't work."

He closed the bedroom door, not wanting to see Roderick's face again as he made his way out, leaving his miserable apartment to what might be his father's hospice.

CHAPTER TWENTY-THREE

Two days before we're supposed to meet in Palm Springs, I finally hear from Roland. By now, I've reserved the hotel and made dinner reservations for our first night there. I emailed him the whole itinerary. I spent days online shopping for just the right outfits before I finally settled on some cute stuff from Farfetch. I even got a bottle of Double Scorpio—coincidentally, just like our zodiac signs—just so we could try it, even though it's not my thing.

This trip has been the only thing on my mind, but then Dominick, ever the peacemaker, texts the group chat—I still haven't talked to Troy since MoCAD—and asks if all three of us can go to Somerset before I leave for California. He thinks it would be fun if we all got drunk on white wine in the food court and made amends. Nigga what? Can you imagine Troy, at Somerset? Truth be told, I still miss Troy. I hate that we've been avoiding each other, after all we've been through.

But he doesn't respond to the group chat, so Dominick and I plan to go alone.

We go on a Saturday after my only morning showing, a white couple from Plymouth interested in one of my listings in Islandview. Dominick is all too eager to drive, but I later find out that it's because he wants control of the aux cord. This nigga's shit is all over the place: Trey Songz fades into

Patsy Cline, which fades into Oingo Boingo and then Das Racist, then into Melissa Manchester and Count Basie and Britney Spears. If it weren't for Shazam, I wouldn't even have known.

"OK, this is a banger," I say, as "It's Britney, bitch!" comes over the speakers. I pretend to hold an invisible microphone. "Ooh, here's my part! *A center of attention, even when we're up against the wall . . .*"

My parents are Black. Every man who I've loved and been disappointed by is Black, and I live in the Blackest city in America. But I promise you this. There isn't a single Black gay millennial on earth that doesn't like the Legendary Miss Britney Spears.

When the song is done, my mood subsides again.

"We are drinking first, right?" I ask.

"Yes, Remy," Dominick says, as we pull in the parking lot. "Come on, let's go."

I don't mean to be a bitch. But now I'm slightly irritated that we came all the way out here . . . to do what exactly?

"I should tell you about Felix," I tell him. "Don't waste your time with him."

"Yeah, Troy said he had a thing for you, and I could tell by the pool the other day you had a thing for him too."

"How'd you do it, Dom? You just walked into town and started pulling hoes left and right?"

"You're the one that said I was fresh meat!"

"Right," I conclude. He's right.

"Anyway," Dom says, "don't even worry about it. We went on a few dates, and he's really good at giving head. But that's it."

"I know we didn't come all this way for hoe tales."

"Well, I really wanted to talk about Palm Springs. Just how well do you know Roland?"

"See, this is why I didn't say anything, because I knew you two would judge."

"I barely know anything about him because you never talk about him. All I know from Troy is that you've been seeing this flight attendant guy who lives in London and you took a trip there once."

"We've been at this for almost two years. We just see each other when we can."

"Has he given any kind of indication that he wants to keep this going?"

"He calls me his 'Motown Man.' Troy said I should call him 'my weekend boyfriend.'"

"This is a situationship, Remy."

"This is not a situationship."

"Yes, it is. You're in a long-distance situationship. Y'all fucking, y'all living together, y'all keep on doing all the things boyfriends do. But you don't have an actual relationship yet."

"Situationship" is one of those new-age Twitter terms I don't know the exact definition of. It seems to be exactly what Dominick is describing: dating and dating and dating, playing house without a mortgage in sight. Situationships don't evolve into relationships, monogamous or otherwise, and they certainly don't lead to marriage. There's never an ex-boyfriend in a situationship because there is never a boyfriend. With a no-strings-attached situation, you can just agree to no longer fuck each other, which is how most of these things end. You can naturally drift apart. You can even just ghost. Because situationships have no clear beginning, an ending can be just as elusive. But I *know* that's not what me and Roland have.

"So what do you have to tell me?" I ask.

"Remember how I caught Justin cheating? And I never saw the man? Well, when I was in New York, I asked Justin what his name was, and it was . . . Roland. Roland Braithwaite."

"There are a ton of Braithwaites in London. It's a common name there. Maybe Roland was this guy's middle name."

"This guy was dark-skinned. Justin said he was a flight attendant on Virgin."

"I'm telling you, it can't be him. That's too much of a coincidence."

"Are you two going to be monogamous?"

"We are going to be after this trip."

"Are you sure about that?"

"I'm honestly losing my patience with you, Dominick. First, you throw Felix in my face. Next thing you tell me is that my man is sleeping with your man, and . . ."

"Your man? You're calling this a relationship?"

"I mean, we're in an open relationship. He's free to have sex with anyone he wants."

"Do you hear how you sound right now?"

No, I am not hearing how I sound. Because for the first time in my life, I have the chance to be truly happy. I mean, yeah, it's not a picture-perfect situation but it is what it is . . . for now! I'm going to Palm Springs to make it official. I'm going to take a chance. No one in Detroit is worth getting into a relationship with, so why shouldn't I try it somewhere else? Troy and Dom can take care of themselves. They're grown men. I've been taking care of myself for years. This is what Detroit does to niggas—birth them, build them up, and eat them alive. Well, not me. I know when I get on that plane to LAX, I might not ever come back.

I don't tell Roland, of course, but I sneak a picture of him at dinner while he's reading the menu. The lights from above hit just right, showing his dark hands on the cover of the menu while he studies it. You can see the crinkle above his nose and the way his eyes squint when he's really deep in thought. Right then and there, he's in his element. I post it to my Story— close friends only—with Instagram's little "like" sticker above it, and I tag the restaurant's location. I am in love. I am going to claim this man. And he is going to claim me.

I decide not to directly broach the subject of moving to London tonight. At this point, it should be implied. I flew all the way to Palm Springs. I'd go anywhere with him now. You remember what Anita Baker said? "Ask me to go with you, you know I will?" It's my favorite lyric of all time. That feeling of giving yourself to someone, trusting them whole, letting them lead. I won't *let* him lead, of course. I'm still my own man. But I don't want to chart my course alone.

The wine gets us in the mood. We decide to forgo another drink and go straight back to the Airbnb. We can't stay off each other, but I want a shower. The desert heat is dry, but I still feel dirty. I want to run through my insides—he can shower after me if he wants to. He does, and I lie in bed waiting for him.

This is it. After this, I'll never have to think about anything else back home again. It'll be hard leaving Annesha and Paris, but they're in a good place. I'll come back and visit them, of course, and make sure Paris grows up into the proper gay man—out, proud, and Black—that he's destined to be. Mama's in a good place with the condo, and I can rent mine out and use that as income until I steady myself in London. Those hideous microstudios can go up and the McQuerrys can bank another few million and people can complain and Detroit can just go on doing whatever inevitable thing Detroit's going to do. Mr. Detroit won't be there for it.

Roland's phone is on the bedside table, and I see it light up. At this point, we're more than lovers, so I don't mind checking it. I click the screen.

"Just saw the news on Facebook!" the notification reads. "Congrats, mate! Best of wishes to you and Lou."

Lou? The ex-boyfriend?

All right, let me breathe for a second. Roland has always told me he wasn't on Facebook. Maybe he is and just said he wasn't because he never used it, like Instagram? Maybe he's just started a profile? But what's this news? I try to unlock his phone. Four-digit passcode? It's always the birthday or the last four of a social security number, and since they don't do social security in England, I try his birthday. It doesn't work—but then I remember that they switch the days and months in England, and when I try it that way, boom.

And there I see it: the Facebook icon, with twelve notifications in the corner. He *is* using it. I open up the app, and the first thing that pops up is "Engaged to Louis Featherstone."

Lou. The ex, the *white* ex. The one Roland was still seeing when we first met but that he said he was done with.

I can hear Roland in the shower as I scroll through the other apps on his phone. I open up his photos and see pictures of him and Lou hugged up, laid up, and kissed up, a video of Lou sucking Roland's dick, Roland in his flight attendant uniform, and way, way, way back in the history, a picture of me sitting across from him at Selden Standard. When I go back to Facebook, I see congrats after congrats after congrats on the engagement. The date of the engagement: Exactly one week ago. Back to the photos: All recent dates. In his text messages, I see Louis's name with a heart emoji next to it, then some names I don't recognize, and then a thread that's just a number with no contact.

It's my number. And I'm on *Do Not Disturb*.

———————————————

And now here I am, all the way out on the West Coast, looking stupid. It feels like I'm halfway across the damn globe, but I'm just four hours from home. *Home*. Everyone loves me at home in Detroit, but I *can't* get the one person that I thought mattered most to me—and who I thought I mattered the most to—to love me back. A fucking superstar working my ass off, and I'm just a toy he can cast aside. I'm a Looney Tune now, looking in the mirror and fading into the shape of a lollipop with SUCKER written right across the middle.

While Roland's still in the shower, I pack as fast as I can, get into the rental car, and drive to a Costco parking lot where I cry my eyes out for an hour. My phone's going off—yes, it's him—but I don't answer. Through my tears and a spotty cell signal, I look for flights from LAX to Detroit, trying to figure out how soon I can get the fuck out of this place. I end up paying almost $1,000 for a last-minute flight on Delta.

You'd think I'd be smarter than this, but the truth is, I let this happen, and I can only blame myself. I wanted to believe my heart, but the heart's got no logical reasoning or critical analysis. That's what your brain is for. And I haven't been using my brain. My heart doesn't have common sense. And neither do any of these men. They don't even have just plain old sense—they just have dicks. And I got fooled by one of those, too.

I feel foolish. Finding that out cost me the plane ticket and the Airbnb, but at least I'm finding it out, right? Big baller, nothing to a boss? I could've kept this money and put it literally anywhere else other than the promise, the *expectation*, of a good fuck or two and some palm trees. Because that's all this was really going to boil down to, just fucking around in all these different cities with no end goal. At the end of this thing, this whatever it is, I'm walking away with nothing. Roland can go do whatever the peachy fuck he wants to do. All I have is an empty heart and a dusty brain.

Is he remembering the most important things I told him? When he said, "You're fine, babe, don't worry about your weight," or, "I like your body just the way it is," did he really care, or was he just saying that? I never wanted to think twice about any of this, but here I am. I had told him everything about me. And looking back, I barely know anything about him except the basics. I realize that now.

Fuck, Dominick was right. And I can't even talk to Troy about this. And now I'll have to tell people this story for the rest of my life—that

Mr. Detroit got played by some charming fucking douchebag on Scruff.

I'm too old for this shit. And you'd think it would hurt less at this age, because you think once you get here and you've been through some shit, you can take it. I can't. Why did I think I'd get any sort of commitment out of this? Why do these men think they can just string you along instead of just manning up and saying what they really want? And ain't I a man? That's the thing about this gay shit. It's not like, oh, men are trash to these women or women keep playing games with these men. With two men, it's a staring contest where no one blinks. We're just expected to read each other's minds and build . . . something, whatever, from there.

Gay Black men have to look out for themselves, but the shit gets lonely. Nothing is more heartwarming than a "we." Every day is walking a fucking tightrope, and instead of holding one of those long poles, I've got weights dragging down both of my arms: this Blackness, this gayness, my ambition, my love, my loyalty, my responsibility, my respectability, my skepticism because of my circumstances, and my optimism that things might change. And I'm walking this rope with nothing and no one to catch me if I fall. We all are, until we finally reach a path where we're no longer alone. But it looks like my rope is reaching all the way from Detroit to fucking Palm Springs, and I'm tired. This is where I fall.

I'm deleting every dating app, switching my personal Facebook page to strict business, and giving up Twitter once and for all. From now on, it's business and business only. I'm getting refocused on growing the firm and making these deals. I'm not gonna chase. I'm going to let come what may. If someone's interested, they are going to have to court me. And I'm gonna use my brain instead of my heart. I'll learn to be lonely, I guess. But it for damn sure is better than being played again.

———————————————

A week after Palm Springs, I'm doing fine. OK, so I haven't given up Twitter like I promised I would. *Whatever.* But then Roland shows up again, staring out at me from the magenta ring around his profile picture on an Instagram Story. The one app I'd forgotten to block him from.

He's never posted to Stories before. When had he started? Or has he always been there and the algorithm has just decided to start showing him to me now? I'm so glad I see it's him before I click—I don't want to leave any trace of myself. But the hardest thing I have to do now is block him. At first, I just mute his Stories. But then I keep checking his profile anyway. Checking to see his tagged pictures—they're still the same. Checking to see if he's viewed one of my Stories. And then I realize I'm going crazy over some stupid fucking app, so I finally take a deep breath, go to his profile one last time, and press Block.

As soon as I get back to the city, I keep my promise to focus on business. I line up three new listings—two in Palmer Woods and a third in University District. I usually don't do that part of the west side. But the people there are older and starting to move into one-floor condos. I also have showings all around—in West Village, some condos on the Gold Coast. I do a radio show talking about the dangers of refinancing. The Links club has a silent auction raising money for Focus: HOPE, and I buy a vintage ashtray.

Everybody knows that in this city, you hustle. I've had my episode. I've had my tears. But in Detroit, we don't cry out loud. We keep it inside and learn how to hide those feelings—stupid song from Dom's Frankenstein-ass playlist. So no, I am *not* going to therapy. Not now. I don't have time for it. I might go when my schedule frees up. But this week isn't good, next week is busy too, and the week after that, I might look into hiring a second broker because I'm getting more listings than I can handle. Plus, talking about Roland in therapy will just keep him around.

I've been hurt by men. By my dumbass father trying to be a kingpin. By that piece of shit who tried to rape me back in college. And now by this damn flight attendant. So yeah, I have to hustle to get over the hurt. It's all I know how to do.

And now look at this. Dominick is calling *again*. The fuck does he want?

CHAPTER TWENTY-FOUR

Eight days was all it took for bile duct cancer to make short work of Bill Clements. Secretive until the very end, Gwen and Troy didn't find out until the doctors told them Bill had been battling it for over a year. But Tonya, who had been Bill's anesthesiologist the day he was rushed into Henry Ford Hospital for surgery, told Dominick to tell Troy he should go to the hospital right away. Troy spent three days at his father's bedside, waiting for a recovery he knew would never come.

Having never planned a funeral, Troy found orchestrating one to be surprisingly easy. He overcame grief with delegation. He started by informing Bill's relatives in Palestine, sending Facebook messages to a handful of relatives and asking them to spread the word. He copied and pasted the same note to each one: "I'm sorry to say that my father, William, has passed. We're holding a funeral in Detroit later this month for all who would like to attend." The words were hollow. So, too, were some of the responses. Generic "My deepest condolences" and "How did he pass?" replies popped up in Troy's feed, but, nonetheless, everyone said they would come up north as soon as they could.

In the days between Bill's death and the actual service, Troy set up shop at the house on Burns to handle all of it. He asked Dominick to stay in one of the guest bedrooms. Troy knew there needed to be life in the house. Predators in Detroit were smart about knowing when big houses were empty, and the last thing Troy wanted to deal with in addition to his father's death was a burglary.

Bill's will left everything to Troy and Gwen, with the lion's share going to Troy. He got the house, control over Bill's accounts and, should he want it, immediate ownership of Clements Printing. He asked to meet with the staff prior to the funeral to determine next steps. He figured he'd first let the office manager run the day-to-day until he could figure out a line of succession. It bothered him that he didn't immediately know what he wanted to do, but Dominick reminded him that in less than a week's time, Troy had found out that his father had cancer, that the cancer had killed him, and that he had become a multimillionaire overnight. It was OK to not have every little detail figured out.

Bill would have wanted a true Detroit funeral, so Troy arranged a meeting with Swanson's—it's called Swanson, but all the Black folks in Detroit made surnames possessive—because they used classic Cadillac hearses. Since Bill didn't hold membership in any church, Troy decided to hold the service at Greater Grace like a lot of prominent Black folks in Detroit did. Fortunately, the pastor was one of Bill's frat brothers; he could easily officiate.

He asked a few more of Bill's fraternity brothers to serve as pallbearers, and three of them, along with Aunt Gwen, agreed to deliver remarks. Dominick asked his mother to help Troy curate some Black funeral hymns and spirituals to play (her choices: "Amazing Grace," "It Is Well with My Soul," "Oh Happy Day," and "Going Up Yonder"). Rather than spend money on a new suit, Troy picked one of from his father's wardrobe, making sure it would complement the brown casket he'd selected. Bill had already set aside a plot right next to Suhas at Elmwood Cemetery, where all of Detroit's elite were laid to rest. Troy called up Brazelton's for floral arrangements and went with simple white rose displays for both the service and the burial.

Had Bill died in the winter instead of July, folks wouldn't have been hot sitting in the pews. But on the afternoon of the service, Troy could see they were uncomfortable. *Just like my father to do things on his own terms, even at other folks' expense*, he thought.

He sat with Gwen in the front pew with some of Bill's Palestine cousins. Dominick and Tonya sat one row behind them, and behind them were Gogo, Marlie, and Noelle. In between handshakes from well-wishers, Troy occasionally looked back at Dominick and threw some classic gay shade. *She's giving me female Luther Vandross. Uncle Ben-looking-ass-motherfucker. Did my dad even know him?* Troy occasionally caught glimpses of Tonya smiling. It had been almost twenty years since she'd seen her son and friend play around like big kids.

Dominick's phone buzzed and he saw a text from Remy.

"Hey, I'm here," it read. He turned around and saw Remy, along with Annesha and Paris, in a pew toward the back. While Troy was busy talking with someone else, Dominick gestured for them to move forward to sit with him, but Remy shook his head.

•••

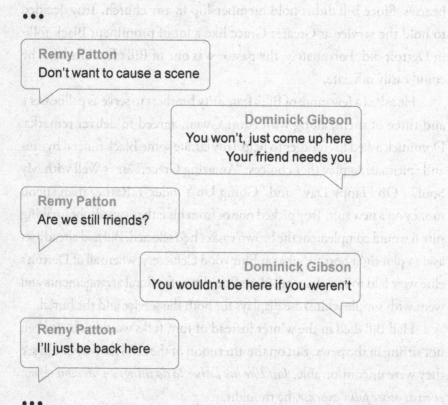

> **Remy Patton**
> Don't want to cause a scene

> **Dominick Gibson**
> You won't, just come up here
> Your friend needs you

> **Remy Patton**
> Are we still friends?

> **Dominick Gibson**
> You wouldn't be here if you weren't

> **Remy Patton**
> I'll just be back here

•••

If it's one thing Black Detroiters are going to do, it's have a grand but long as hell funeral procession across the *whole* city. So from Greater Grace on Seven Mile, the big, classic Swanson's hearse, affixed with orange flags on each fender, led a caravan of cars all the way down to Woodward Avenue, then to Grand Boulevard and Elmwood Cemetery.

Somehow, Remy avoided being seen by Troy. He, Annesha, and Paris left for the parking lot as soon as the pastor was done and skipped the processional, instead making their way to the cemetery early. They joined the other mourners, blending in the back to avoid conflict. And when Bill Clements was lowered to the ground, they quietly left and went back to their car.

Gwen also left early to prepare to host the repast at the house on Burns. Some of the Palestine cousins hadn't seen the house in years. Some hadn't seen it at all and were shocked to learn they had a rich cousin in Detroit. Troy, unusually upbeat, and without the help of any substances, entertained all of them, sharing the best stories—there were only a few from his perspective, but he mustered up some—of how William Cordell Clements had left his mark on Detroit and his small family. Dominick, ever the observer, wondered how much longer his friend could keep the show going.

Remy dropped Annesha and Paris off at their townhouse and walked, rather than drove, to the house on Burns. It was only about fifteen minutes. But he needed the time to contemplate whether it was the right decision to show up at his best friend's dead father's mansion after everything that had happened between them. His best friends—now, best friends, plural—had been right about so much: the deal with the McQuerrys, his situationship with Roland, his disastrous trip to Palm Springs. And now he wanted to console Troy. He wanted Troy to know he was there, but he just didn't know if now was the time or place.

Remy was so lost in thought, he didn't realize he was already at Bill's front door. Gwen was standing there to greet him.

"Come in, young man. Are you a friend of Troy's?" she asked.

"Yes, ma'am. You must be his Auntie Gwen. I've heard of you."

"*Lord.* Now what did that boy say about me?"

"That you," Remy said, grasping her hands, "are his dad's little sister, right? And that you are so beautiful, you can have any man that you want. And that you've had quite a few, is that right?"

"*Oh!*" Gwen laughed. "You know what? My nephew is something else. You must be good friends if you know that."

"I like to think we are."

Dominick was making his way to the bathroom near the foyer when he saw Remy and Gwen chatting at the front door. He immediately changed course, and the two men embraced, tightly.

"I didn't know if I should come," Remy said.

"You made the right choice. Troy is in the living room."

"I'm not ready to see him yet. He's probably busy anyway, right?"

"OK, maybe later. You came. That's what matters. How are you? How was . . . Palm Springs?"

"Oh, girl," Remy said, looking up at the ceiling, feeling the emotions rushing back and trying not to cry. "I fucked up. I fucked up so bad. I don't want to talk about it right now . . ."

Dominick looked around, pulled Remy close, and lowered his voice. "You got niggas on East Warren. I got cousins on Puritan. And we can all roll the fuck out to beat Big Ben's ass if you want."

A casual threat of violence elicited just the slightest smile from Remy as he tried to fight back tears, something Gwen noticed as she came back with a cup of punch for him.

"Well! So are you two . . . you know . . . partners?"

The boys laughed and put an arm around one another's shoulder.

"No, Miss Gwen. This one here isn't my type," Dominick said.

"Oh, I'm not?" Remy said, feigning shock.

"Yeah. 'Cause I don't fuck with you crazy-ass east-side niggas!"

As the guests started trickling out of the big house on Burns, Dominick and Gwen cleaned up while Troy gathered contact information from relatives and colleagues, making promises to keep in touch. He still hadn't seen Remy, who'd stayed out of sight the entire afternoon. But as the crowd thinned, Dominick took Remy into Bill's office and told him to think about what he wanted to say, then returned to the living room where Gwen and Troy were collecting cups and plates.

"You sure you'll be all right by yourself?" Gwen asked Troy.

"Dominick's going to stay with me. You go enjoy the hotel."

"Well, thank you for putting me in a *suite* in the Book-Cadillac," Gwen said, affecting a posh voice. "Your daddy never would've sprung on me like this."

"It's OK. I know. I know you want to go prance around that suite."

"Put me up for a few more weeks and I might try to get you a new uncle."

The three laughed. Gwen grabbed the keys to her rental Navigator, another splurge from Troy.

"One thing I'll say though, and I'm done," she said, "is that your father might have been cheap sometimes, but he did have a big heart. He just didn't always show it. You, on the other hand, are the opposite. You have a big heart. You love everybody. But you show it differently. You don't think you're like him, but you are. I can see it in you. I can see it in your face."

"You always said I looked like Mom."

Gwen cupped his face.

"I see you, and I also see *him*," she said. "One day, you'll look in the mirror, and you'll see him too. He took care of me, you know."

"What do you mean?"

"When I was . . . in between some things. I didn't even have to ask. He took care of me. Didn't complain, either. He was like that. He didn't have a lot of friends. A lot of associates, as you can see. But the ones he was close to, he looked out for. That includes you."

Troy took his aunt's hands from his face and looked down.

"I know," she said, making her way to the door, "that y'all didn't get along. Don't think I don't know. But one thing you gotta remember about Bill is that he was hardheaded. He didn't always know any better."

Troy looked up. His aunt was looking right at him.

"All he wanted from you was to be better than him," she said. "You know that, right?"

"I don't know if how I want to be better is how he wanted me to be better."

"In my opinion, you're halfway there. You got time." She turned to Dominick. "Listen at me, spilling all this family tea. Dominick? Take care of this boy. He's all I got. The only good man I know these days, 'cause Lord knows I've dealt with some bad ones."

"Haven't we all?" Dominick said, helping her with her jacket. "You know, maybe we can go out and have some wine. And have a real conversation about how trash these men are."

"Honey, I've been dealing with dogs since God was a boy. Y'all ain't ready for what I got to say, OK?"

"Try me."

"You ever walk in on your man with somebody else?"

"As a matter of fact . . ." Dominick said, folding his arms and letting the words hang.

"Well, have you ever walked in on your man with a *white* somebody else?"

"Try *me*," a voice called.

The three turned around and saw Remy emerge from the office.

Troy and Dominick looked at each other, then back at Remy. Gwen eased out the front door.

"Troy, I'll text you when I get to the hotel," she said.

Bill Clements's dining room was back to being the quietest place in Detroit. The three boys sat around the Chippendale table, each of them waiting for someone else to break the silence. Remy finally did.

"Roderick didn't show up today. I did."

"You'll be happy to know that we broke up," Troy said.

"Oh. Well. Congratulations."

"Guys," Dominick said, attempting to diffuse the tension. "Can we . . . read the room a little bit here?"

"We're *catching up*," Troy said, sarcastically. "After all, I haven't seen Remy in weeks. Did you see them breaking ground on the new condos next to the school? It's hard to miss the excavators. Do you have it all now? And Dominick told me you had gone to Palm Springs? Was it everything you dreamed it would be?"

"You'll be *thrilled* to know that situation is over," Remy said.

"Guess Dominick's the only one getting laid around here."

"At a time like this . . . how can you be so . . . whatever this is?"

"Guys, please," Dominick pleaded.

"Remy, I will put you the fuck out if you don't stop," Troy said, "and once you're out, you are out."

In more than a decade of friendship, Troy had never spoken to Remy so sternly. It shook Remy so much he felt tears well in his eyes. Dominick could see Troy was crying too.

"Troy. Remy," he said.

"I'm done with Roderick," Troy said. "There's something else you both should know too."

Dominick and Remy looked at each other, unsure of what would come next.

"Dominick, right around the time you came back, Roderick pushed me and choked me one night. And just a few weeks ago, the real reason why we broke up? He threw me against the wall. Hard. He moved out just before my dad died. I haven't seen him since."

Dominick put his hand to his forehead and sighed deeply while Remy wiped away tears.

"That muhfucka put his hands on you?" Remy asked. "Why didn't you say anything?"

"Because! I was fucking humiliated! Embarrassed, demoralized!"

"I'm your friend, Troy, you're supposed to tell me these things."

"Now you wanna talk about how we're supposed to tell each other everything?"

"Why didn't you tell us?" Dominick asked.

"Because look at you two! Look at you, Remy! You can't relate with any of this! You're Mr. Detroit! And you, Dominick, with your perfect New York life, and then you come back home and get a new job without even skipping a beat. And then you and Remy are all buddy-buddy, and I'm just here starting to wonder where I fit into all of this."

Now Dominick was angry.

"All right," he said. "You right. Remy and I do get along great, but you were here first. I've known you longer. I told you things I never told anyone else. You were always here for me. And I was always here for you. That hasn't changed, no matter what you think my life *looks* like."

Troy felt his eyes well up.

"You just don't understand," he said.

"Can I try to understand? Can you give me that?"

"I can't right now."

"Troy, I did not have a perfect life in New York. I had a façade of one. And it wasn't until I left New York that I realized how hollow and empty the whole thing was. And I'm still not feeling like myself here in Detroit."

"It sure seems like you're having a blast."

"You know what I'm dealing with here? I live with my mother, and I hate my job. And don't even get me started on relationships, if that's what you'd call whatever it is I'm doing. I'm not happy."

"It's temporary for you. Eventually you'll move out and get back on your shit," Troy said. "You always do. You're going to be happy and fine. And I'll just be who knows where."

He sighed.

"Troy. You will be happy again, too," Remy said. "I'm going to make sure of that. Bet. I at least owe you that."

"You don't have to buy my friendship."

"I'm not trying to buy something that we've always had naturally," Remy said. "Don't you understand? *You* saved *me*, remember? And now it's really time for me to . . . do the same in return. I can't see you struggle like this. So here's what the deal is. Us—*all* of us—are going to get through this together. And none of us are going to keep any more secrets from each other like this ever again."

Remy got up, walked over to Troy, and draped his hands over his shoulders.

"I'm sorry, Troy," Remy said. "About Roderick. About your father. About this stupid development."

Troy, overcome by the sudden touch, sobbed into the crook of Remy's right arm.

"I'm sorry, too," Troy said.

Dominick sat in silence, remembering the first night they had become a trio and how they had never gotten around to finishing up making the rules for their boys' club. It didn't matter, though. It had taken time, but now, rule number one—no secrets—was finally solidified.

CHAPTER TWENTY-FIVE

Terrell wants to take me on a walk through North Rosedale Park, so that's where we go. I know the houses on Bretton Drive, sort of. They look straight out of *Pleasantville* or one of those other teen movies from back in the day. Hard to believe it's Detroit proper. They never go up for sale, though, so I don't usually come out here like this.

"I figured we could just walk and talk for a little bit," Terrell says. "Is that OK?"

I know I've got this funny look on my face—I can't help my cynicism sometimes—but I go along with it.

"OK. What do you got?"

"See that one?"

He points to this huge Tudor with brown trim and rose bushes in the front yard.

"That's the one I want," he says.

"Well, how are you going to get it?"

"I've been saving. One day," he says, looking at me, "I'mma get one on this street. But I really want that one."

"I never knew you wanted to buy a house. On the west side at that."

"Whatever. Detroit has beautiful houses all over. I know how much you like to talk about that."

My heart.

"Yeah, I do talk about it a lot."

"On your radio show. You know I listen, right? I catch the replay on the weekends."

"That radio station is so damn ghetto they just replay anybody on the weekends," I blush. I'm lying. I know they use my show as filler. I just don't want to puff it up too much.

"Well, you say good things, and I listen."

"Not just because of my voice?"

"What does your voice have to do with it?"

"Never mind," I say. "Let's keep walking, I don't know if there's white people on this side of Rosedale, but if there are, I don't want to look like we're up to something."

"You right," he says, and we keep walking. I didn't know he wanted to buy a house on Bretton Drive. I didn't know he was listening to my show. I didn't know we could just walk and talk like this.

Pretty soon, we walk and talk for about twenty blocks. Terrell asks if I want to get something to eat. We get in the car, and the next song on his shuffle catches me off guard. I hear the opening piano keys, then the saxophone, and then the vocals.

"Recognize this?" he asks.

"'My Favorite Thing.' My mother's song."

"I only hear it at your place, and I was stuck on it, so I downloaded it."

"You did?"

"Yeah. You're a bad influence."

We get on the Southfield Freeway. Terrell has one hand on the steering wheel and the other on the gearshift, but eventually, the hand on the gearshift moves toward my thigh. I'm scared. I hear Hari Paris singing, "Holding you, squeezing you, loving you," and then I feel Terrell's hand move to my hand. He doesn't take his eyes off the road. And before my mind can fix itself to ask what he's doing, what he's up to, if he's crazy or just playing games, I lean back in the seat, relax my spine, and clutch his hand just a little bit tighter.

It soothes the hurt a little but not completely.

"I was just thinking that if you bought a house like that, you can't live there by yourself," I finally say, looking at him.

"Oh, I know. I was thinking I might have kids or something."

"Or *something*? That's not a light decision."

"I'm not thinking about that right now, but you know. Shit, anything can happen. Maybe we can adopt."

"We?"

"I meant me."

I suck my teeth.

"Whatever, blasé-blasé," I say.

"Your phone's buzzing."

"What?"

"Your phone. It's going off."

I had been in so much in a daze, I hadn't even felt it. I look at my phone and see it's the McQuerry boy. Whatever it is, it can wait.

"Who is it?" Terrell asks.

"No one important." I say, and I mean it.

"Another one of your lil' friends?"

I roll my eyes.

"No. I'm done with all that," I say, "I'm doing me. From now on."

I hear Terrell sigh.

"What?" I ask.

"Nothing," he says. "I just thought . . . I thought maybe just now, I was, you know . . ."

"You were what?"

"I'm trying, Rem. OK. This is new for me. This thing I'm doing. I ain't never been with another dude like you. I mean, I've been with dudes, but I'm trying with you."

"You're trying what exactly? Say it."

Terrell is struggling to find the words, but I'm wondering if I'm giving him enough space to do so. We head further north on the freeway. We're all the way to the part where it turns into Southfield Road when he finally says something.

"I haven't had a boyfriend before. And I don't know how to be one to you, but I want to try. But you're so . . . you're so . . . experienced that I just feel stupid even telling you this right now. So yeah. There it is. I want to be a boyfriend."

That's not what I expected him to say.

It's what I wanted him to say, I just didn't expect it.

He's trying.

He's been trying all this time. He's been putting in the effort. The steak. My song. Holding my hands.

And damn it, if Roland hadn't hurt me so bad, I would be all in for this. But I don't know if I can trust Terrell right now. This soon after Palm Springs, I still ache. Terrell isn't able to give me everything I need right now, but he's trying. Oh, God. I can't tell him what I really feel. He doesn't even know about Roland. And if I tell him, he'll break. And one thing I know for sure—just because I'm broken, I can't just break someone else. I just have to take it slow.

Slow.

Right.

Because I wanted everything too fast with Roland. I had the job, the house, the car. And I was trying to force Roland into that. But Terrell, I can . . . go slow. We can be friends first and then lovers, taking the time to really find each other.

"So, uh . . . tell me what you were doing in Palm Springs," he says.

"What do you mean?"

"Don't play dumb. I saw your Instagram Story."

Fuck. I forgot Terrell is one of my close friends on Instagram. I didn't know he was paying this much attention, though.

"Don't worry about it. Some dumb shit," I say.

"That Roland nigga?"

"Excuse me?"

"Remember that night at MoCAD? When Troy called me Roland?"

Motherfucker.

"OK," I say. "So what do you already know?"

"A lot of blanks. Fill me in."

I suck my teeth again.

"OK, so what had been happening was," I say, "it started with me and Roland talking on Scruff. And we started this, I don't know, long-distance . . . situationship thing or whatever, and, long story short, I caught feelings. But it turns out while I was in Palm Springs, I found out this motherfucker was engaged, *and* I also found out he was the one fucking with Dominick's ex-boyfriend when he left New York."

"Daaaaamn. So you went to Palm Springs to confront him?"

"No, we were on some baecation-type shit, and here I was thinking I was going to move to London for good and we'd just be this happy little couple or whatever."

"You were in love with him?"

I know I have to rip this Band-Aid off and be real.

"Yeah. I was," I say. "Clown shit."

"It happens."

"Do you hate me?"

"Why would I?"

"Because, you know. I was . . . messing with both of y'all at the same time."

"You were messing with a lot of people."

"*Excuse me?*"

"You know what I mean. Like you said that one time, we're not exclusive, right?"

"Well, we can be exclusive if you want to."

The words fall out before I know for sure if they're the right thing to say. There was that *we* again. Only this time, I had said it, too.

And when I look up, I can see we're well past the Southfield border and damn near Birmingham.

CHAPTER TWENTY-SIX

At Motor City Wine, the three boys walked in, and Troy immediately recognized Natalie Oladapo seated at the bar. His first instinct was to take the glass of wine she was sipping from and throw it in her face, because even though Renaissance High, where they had gone to school together, produced Black excellence, it also produced Black pettiness. Troy had never forgotten how Natalie used to make fun of the rayon, Asian-print shirts he wore when he was going through his sophomore-year anime fashion phase, nor how she had used him to write an essay about Richard Wright for English class and never paid the $25 she had promised.

"Look what the cat dragged in," he said, loud enough for half the bar to hear.

Natalie turned to her left to follow the sound, and smiled.

"Troy, my love. Come give me a hug."

"It's good to see you Natalie," Troy said, extending his right hand, leaving her arms outstretched. "Dominick said you would be here, and I see you've been all over the place."

"Hi, Natalie!" Dominick said.

"Dominick! Hi! How are you love?"

She turned toward Remy and extended her hand.

"And just who might you be?" she asked.

"I'm someone that could handle your business. Are you in the market to buy a house?"

"Perhaps, love. You look familiar—are you . . . .?"

"Mr. Detroit, yes. The face on the billboards—Remy Patton."

"Yes! Nice to meet you. Should we sit at the table over there, love?"

"Yes, *love*," Troy responded, rolling his eyes.

The thing about alumni of Renaissance High School is that they never peak. They're always climbing. Folks that come from the suburbs into Detroit always say how the popular kids peaked in high school. Renaissance was so damn full of overachievers who moved mountains with ease. Natalie and Troy's classmates were judges now, mayor's appointees and restauranteurs and Grammy nominees and pilots and fashion designers.

"Well, I actually came to talk to Dominick," Natalie said, as they found a table and ordered a bottle of cabernet. "But I don't see why you all can't be in on this too. I finally finalized this partnership I've been working on to be a brand ambassador for Shinola, the watch brand. Have you heard of them?"

"I'm pretty sure we all have," Troy said. "They're 'made in Detroit!'"

"Right! It means I might be going back out into the world soon, I guess. Building the Oladapo brand."

"It's amazing how far a Detroiter can go if they've got a last name people can recognize."

"And you'd know better than anyone, wouldn't you, Mr. Clements?"

Remy couldn't help but snicker while Dominick tried to diffuse the tension.

"So, Natalie, I remember you said you wanted to stay here at home for a while before you get back out there traveling and whatnot."

"You're right," Natalie said, sipping her wine and tapping the glass. "Remember when we chatted at MoCAD? I went and looked up your stuff from before you were at GearWorks. You're good. Real good. I mean, all of you are good. Troy, I follow your Instagram, and the work you do with kids is amazing. And you," she said, turning toward Remy, "well, I don't know you too well, love, but if this is the company you keep, then you must be . . . good."

All three of the boys offered bewildered gratitude. Troy didn't realize Natalie had been following his Instagram.

"So if you're not going back to the travel thing, what are you gonna do?" Troy asked.

"Dominick, are you set at GearWorks?" Natalie asked. "I mean, have you ever thought about doing something different? Even starting your own agency?"

"I've . . . kinda been through that," Dominick said, suddenly flooded with memories of Atomic Ranch. "It's a risk I'm not sure I'm emotionally prepared for."

"Well, what's standing in your way?"

"Huh?"

"You heard me, love. What's standing in your way?"

"Well, if we're keeping it honest. I can't afford to fail. So maybe there's a fear of failure."

"I've had this calling here in Detroit, loves, this awakening, and Dominick, you are part of this. That's why I called you. After we talked last, I got thinking. And last week, I figured out that what I really want to do is start an agency right here in the city. A full-service branding, marketing, design, and advertising agency geared toward helping Detroit brands connect with diverse audiences."

"Multicultural," Dominick said. "Industry speak is multicultural, but anyway, keep going."

"Well, when I got this thing with Shinola, they had plans for me to visit some of the Asian markets. But I asked them if they had a strategy for connecting with audiences right here. I mean, it's a walk in the park for me to be an ambassador. I've done brand partnerships before, and I'm known all over the world in some demographics."

"Do tell," Troy said, dripping with disdain.

"But what about our people here at home? How are Shinola, and all the rest of these brands, connecting with regular, everyday Detroiters? You have so many companies starting up in Detroit now. I want to help them connect with the common man right here."

"And I'm supposed to help with this somehow?" Dominick asked.

Natalie set down her wine and looked directly at him.

"I want you to be my partner," she said.

Dominick and Troy laughed. Remy leaned in and started listening more closely.

"Natalie, honey, how much have you had to drink, girl?" Dominick said.

"I'm serious! Don't laugh at me! I want to start an agency with you."

"Natalie, you don't have an advertising background," Troy said.

"I've got marketing. I've got business. I've handled all of my family's business affairs for years and I still do. I'm not *just* on Instagram, love. It's not impossible. Don Coleman did it."

"Who?" Remy asked.

"Shit. Shit, shit, shit! You don't know who that is? *The* Don Coleman," Dominick said, slamming a hand on the table.

"I don't know either. Who is it?" Troy asked.

"He's a legend," Dominick said, while Natalie nodded. "He ran the largest Black-owned advertising firm in Detroit. They had every contract. Keyword: *had.* They overbilled some, there were lawsuits, there were layoffs, everything. But damn, Don Coleman was the fuckin' man for a minute. He's still one of my personal heroes. My personal Obama."

"Natalie," Troy said, "are you even sure you can do this? I mean, you just invoked the name of this Detroit legend, and right now, you just have a one-off with Shinola."

"I want to build off that. Maybe Dom, you can be creative director on this project, and then we could go from there?" Natalie said.

"What about funding?" Dominick asked. "Do you even have an office?"

"Not yet, but I'm in the door with Shinola. They liked the deck I presented to them."

"You gave them a deck?" Dominick asked.

"See, I know what I'm doing. I'm going to get this contract with them. But I need someone to carry this over the goal line."

"Now you really sound like you're in advertising," Dominick laughed.

"I'm telling you, I think we were all brought here for a reason," Natalie said. "When I came back to Detroit, I didn't have any of this planned or anything. I never even entertained the idea of a creative director until I saw you at GearWorks and Shinola got in touch with me. I might have manifested this now that I think about it."

"Well, isn't this all coincidence," Troy said.

"Or maybe not manifestation. Fate is what brings people together," Natalie said. "And look, Troy, I know you're not feeling me right now. It's because of high school, right?"

Troy, caught off-guard, didn't have words.

"I know," Natalie said. "I was a real bitch back in the day. You're not the first one to check me on it. Which is why I'm saying sorry to everyone. I had a lot of shit going on with me that I've been working out in therapy. Part of that process is apologizing."

"You're in therapy?" Remy asked.

"I have a standing Zoom appointment with a Black woman therapist in Ann Arbor. I connected with her on Twitter, and every other week, I can talk to her from anywhere in the world. I just Venmo the fee after we're done. Welcome to the digital age, love."

"That's powerful, Natalie. Good for you," Dominick said.

"I know, right? At first, I thought I was too good, too busy for it."

"Too busy?" Remy asked.

"You're never too busy to confront your issues," Natalie said. "Know that. And yes, loves. I have issues! Coming out of the issue closet like you boys did!"

She laughed, putting her hand on Troy's shoulder.

"Are you in therapy because you think you were a bitch in high school?" Troy asked.

"I'm in therapy because I'm learning how to overcome my own self-esteem issues by not putting other people down," Natalie said. She clutched his shoulder tighter. "And maybe a little anger management, too."

"First of all, thank you for your honesty," Dominick said. "And secondly, gentlemen, we have to remember that there's no judgment for people who choose to seek therapy."

"Well, since it's honesty hour," Troy said, "Natalie, you were one of many people who made my life a living hell back in high school. And I'm sorry if, for some strange, twisted reason, I haven't quite gotten over it, even though I'm too damn old to still be thinking about it."

"Tell me everything on your mind," Natalie said.

"That's all. And the fact that you still owe me $25 for that essay I wrote you in eleventh grade."

Natalie laughed.

"Do you use Cash App, Venmo, or Zelle?" she asked.

The following Sunday, Dominick stopped in at the Shinola store in Midtown. The watches might be a bit gauche and New Detroit, he thought, but the stationery was undeniably nice. Either way, this was a brand he could work with. So he bought one of their cheapest journals, took it to a coffeeshop nearby, wrote "IT'LL HAPPEN WHEN IT HAPPENS" at the top of the first page, and made a list of all the things he wanted to do: Live abroad for a year or two. Get back into videography. Read a novel every month by a Black author. Visit Africa, finally. Drive on the real Autobahn. Kiss a boy on New Year's Eve. Start a podcast called *Views from the Top*. Send Mom on a cruise. Talk to Dad more often. Run a marathon.

He scratched the final entry out, changing it to a half-marathon. Then he paused and added one last entry: A healthy, fulfilling relationship.

Because that, he thought, *will happen when it happens.*

He tore another page from the journal and titled it "AGENCY GOALS." Under the heading, he made a list: Recruit the best Black talent in Detroit; 1099 them at first before converting to full-time. Have ten clients on roster by end of year. In-house photographer. In-house videographer. Messaging through identity experience. Office space by 2022—Midtown. Continue to build roster of emerging POC talent. (He wrote Esmerelda's name in small print next to that and marked it with an asterisk.) Then he wrote two potential clients to immediately pitch for small-scale, local ad campaigns: Clements Printing and the 2501 Agency.

He folded the list and put it in the pocket of his bifold wallet, but not before kissing it and mumbling a quick prayer.

"God, give me the strength to take another chance," he whispered.

The following Monday morning, Dominick walked into Monique's office with his resignation letter. He simply said it was time to move on and thanked her for helping him out. She said she understood, and Dominick could tell she did. He swung by Esmerelda's desk, thanked her for her friendship, and said he hoped they could remain friends. They followed each other on Instagram.

This time, there were no personal effects for him to gather at his desk. He left the company-issued laptop there, as well as the binder full of signed paperwork and the company swag he had never touched. He'd walked into the office at 9:00 a.m. with just his Fjällräven backpack and ID, and he left the ID at the security desk on the way out an hour later. He was in the parking lot before Krystin and Kristen got the heads up from HR, and he was on the Lodge headed downtown to meet Natalie for coffee while he ignored three of their calls.

CHAPTER TWENTY-SEVEN

"Everybody say hi to my little cousin, y'all!" Remy said. "Turn this way, turn this way!"

The schoolyear had started again, and Paris had FaceTimed Remy to see if he would speak to his class on Career Day. For once, Remy didn't mind being the center of attention. He knew his cousin needed a role model, and he knew if the other kids saw that he had one, maybe Remy could be one to them, too. He could show kids on the east side what a kid from the east side could do.

But now he wanted to formally introduce Paris to two of his role models.

He, Dominick, and Troy were sitting on the back patio of the house on Burns, working on their third bottle of Lambrusco from a winery in Italy that no longer imported to the States. Bill had two cases of it in the wine cellar, and they had been gathering dust. Troy had put a few bottles in the fridge the night before in anticipation of this afternoon's boozy brunch. When he and Dominick saw a child's face in Remy's screen, they each pretended not to be as drunk as they were, waved into the camera, and went back to carrying on as soon as Remy said his final good-bye and hung up.

They were in a celebratory mood and wanted to make sure that from now on, they'd stay there.

Dominick found an apartment in Lafayette Park and became an east-sider. Living with Tonya rent-free had allowed him to put away all his earnings from GearWorks, so he had a nice financial cushion until checks started coming in from freelance copywriting work. Monique had been kind enough to quietly connect him to a few local firms that needed one-off assignments. Justin had also been right about Tandy and Simms, and after a quick Zoom conversation with his old firm, Dominick successfully pitched the idea of working remotely with some of T&S's lighter client work. He even made amends with his old boss, Tom, who had moved to another boutique agency and who asked Dominick to look at some projects they were working on. Dominick figured he'd cobble together just enough to stay afloat until he and Natalie could officially launch their own firm.

After hearing that the Mahaffey School was closing for sure, Troy had fully intended his summer vacation to be permanent, but a few weeks after his father's funeral, he decided to become interim CEO of Clements Printing, asking Bill's second-in-command to help him learn the company. When everything from Bill's estate was finally settled, Troy was surprised at just how much money his father had left behind. With the windfall and his new income, he could finally think about buying his own place. Bill's house was way too big for one person, but there were too many bad memories in the old apartment. Troy didn't need anything fancy, though. *Minimalism is the way forward*, he thought, realizing that though he and Roderick would never get back together, there were things from his previous relationship he'd continue to carry with him. Besides, he didn't need a huge house. He'd been spending quite a bit of time at Gogo's place and he really liked it there.

In late July, Troy also decided to use a large chunk of Bill's money to set up a new education foundation for students in Islandview. He was already in talks about endowing an after-school program and a number of college scholarships, and the board of Clements Printing was committed to setting aside a small percentage of its yearly proceeds to make sure the foundation could keep going. Troy was determined to see it through. He was going to try to be better in the way Bill would have wanted him to be. He was more than halfway there. And he had time.

Remy had approached the McQuerrys, asking them to consider at least making some of the microstudios on the Mahaffey site affordable. He knew the answer would be no, and when he got it, he asked to no longer be involved with the development. The project would go on, of course. Developers were going to keep swooping in across hot parts of the east side and doing what they were going to do. So Remy decided to take his own approach. He hosted an informal meeting at his townhouse with an architect, a contractor, and a loan officer, presenting them with a list of commercial comps across the east side he was interested in. He wanted to set up a strip of commercial-ready spaces in a year, and he wanted to know how much it would cost and how much he would need to borrow to make it happen. He already had at least one tenant in mind once Dominick and Natalie got their agency off the ground. Maybe the second tenant could be Terrell and his butcher shop. But Remy knew not to pressure him. If it was in the cards, Terrell would do that in his own time.

And speaking of time, Remy took a closer look at how he was using his. Maybe Natalie was right about making time to confront your issues, so he decided to go ahead and reach out to her therapist. But not before doing something he'd been inspired to do because of recent goings-on with his friends—he paid a visit to his father. It had been long enough. And while they didn't have long to talk, Remy promised he'd visit more often.

"I'm telling you, you should turn this motherfucker into an Airbnb," Remy said, taking a big sip of Lambrusco.

"Airbnbs in Indian Village. Then it really will be New Detroit," Troy laughed. "I'm going to go get a new bottle."

"Don't," Dominick said. "This is our fourth one, and we're not even done. I can barely see straight."

"There's no way I'm going to finish off that whole cellar by myself!"

"There's like two hundred bottles down there! Keep them!" Remy laughed.

"The way we drink, shit. We might be done by Thursday."

When Troy returned to the patio, he had a bottle in one hand and an accordion file in the other, the latter of which he plopped in front of Remy.

"This is all my dad's paperwork on this house. Deed, repairs, all of it," Troy said. "I need your help. I want to sell it."

"I know," Remy said. "This would be a lot to maintain."

"I want to sell it to you."

Remy took a long sip and then guffawed in disbelief.

Finally, my Indian Village house? he thought. *What I've always dreamed of?*

He paused, looking out at the backyard and then inside at the giant living room.

"I'm not ready for this yet," Remy said. "This is too much for me."

"You can afford it."

"It's not the money," Remy said. "I don't want to live in this big-ass house alone. I want to raise a family. Have a husband to wake up to every morning. Throw parties with people I actually like, help my kids with homework in the living room, let them have sleepovers. If it were just me here, I'd just . . . I'd just wake up alone."

"You," Dominick said, putting his hand on Remy's shoulder, "are more than enough. And you've always been more than enough. We *all* are."

"I appreciate this, all of this. But . . . Troy, *girl*, just let me sell this house for you! The commission on this bitch? *Sheeit.*"

The boys laughed.

"Never change, Remy," Troy said.

"I'm serious," Remy said. "After all my fuck ups, you all have just been so . . . just . . . hand me that bottle. I need a refill. I want to do a toast."

"I'll do the honors," Dominick said, taking some effort to stand upright and raising his arm. "Let it be known that we are done selling ourselves short. We are done with men that don't value us at our worth, we are done with jobs that don't value us at our worth, and we are done not knowing . . . not knowing . . . not knowing . . ."

"Our worth?" Troy asked.

"Yes. Our worth, but I was trying to think of something a little more sincere."

"I'd like to toast," Remy said, standing up, "to being done with no-good niggas who can't commit, to doing away with men who live secret lives. With just men period."

"A toast to men who cheat, and a toast to lazy, broke, shiftless men who waste all your energy because they have none of their own," Troy said, standing to his feet.

"A toast to dudes with shitty booties and stank balls!" Dominick said.

"Why are you toasting that?"

"Why not? Y'all are toasting everything else!"

"Wait, wait, OK, that's enough. A toast," Dominick said, "to us. Us boys. The *clique*."

They clinked their glasses and drank their wine in one gulp. They crashed on the patio chaise lounges, and Remy reached for the bottle.

"This one's empty," he said. "Should we even open that new one?"

"I have an idea," Dominick said, pulling out his phone. "Get up. Let's go somewhere. I don't want to sit here and waste all this good sun, especially with fall getting closer and closer. Remy, let's stop by your house first so you can put on something more casual. And then we're going to the Isle."

"I do not want to go to that fucking Yacht Club," Remy laughed.

"We're not. Just walk with me here."

Turns out, with some creative finagling, passengers can take a rideshare to the Giant Slide on Belle Isle, which does not have an address, by putting in just the right coordinates. Dominick had summoned a rideshare for the three of them, and when the driver dropped them off on Loiter Way, Remy and Troy immediately deduced Dom's tipsy plan.

"You're crazy. I haven't done this in years," Remy said, as they stood outside the gates of the slide.

"Neither have I. Come on. We're all doing it," Dominick said.

"We're too old for this," Troy said. "We're over thirty! My knees hurt just looking at the stairs."

"Listen here. I'm officially, unequivocally, undoubtedly *tired* of this over-thirty bullshit that we put up with. All of us. Me, you, and especially you," Dominick said, pointing a stiff index finger at Troy, "are still fucking young with so many years ahead of us. OK? High school wasn't that long ago! You all act like we've got one foot in the grave."

"We don't?"

"We're going up those stairs and down that slide."

Remy and Troy looked at each other then looked back at Dominick.

"Fine," Remy said. He grabbed a burlap sack and began stomping up the metal stairs. "So are you bitches coming or not?"

Dominick grabbed a burlap sack and followed Remy.

The climb was a little longer than they remembered. It also seemed a bit higher.

"Shit, I'm feeling seasick," Remy said at the top. "I might go back down. I'm too old for this."

"Move, and watch me," Dominick said. He laid the burlap flat at the top of the slide and sat down on it, steadying himself on the edge and imitating Rasputia from *Norbit*: "I'mma show you how a bitch goes down a slide."

"You go backwards?"

"It's the only way I know how! Backwards, with my eyes closed."

"You'll break your neck!"

"Have you ever heard of anybody breaking their neck on the Giant Slide? I rode this muhfucka for years. Only shit that changed is the color."

Dominick crossed his hands against his chest. "Wait! Where's Troy? He didn't come up?" He pulled himself back up on the platform and looked down at the bottom of the stairs. "Bring your ass up here, Troy!"

Troy looked up at his friends from the bottom of the slide.

"I don't think I'm ready for this," he yelled.

"Troy, let's *go!* If the two of us can do it, you can!" Remy said.

All I have to do is climb up, close my eyes, and let it all go, Troy thought.

An adrenaline rush kicked in that cocaine never could match, and Troy met his friends at the top with burlap in hand and without even losing his breath.

"OK, are y'all ready? I'll see you at the bottom," Dominick said.

"Wait!" Remy said. He shimmied his arms and legs, did a quick jumping jack, and laid his mat on the edge of the slide, sitting on it backward, parallel to Dominick. "I ain't no punk."

"Have you ever done it like this before?"

"Nope, but if anything happens, I'm gonna beat your ass."

"Your turn, Troy."

Troy took a deep breath and looked out across the island park in front of him. He looked up at the sun. It was blinding. He took off his glasses and put them in his front pocket so they wouldn't fly off his face. He unfurled his mat and carefully sat himself parallel to his friends. Steadying himself on the edge, he extended his legs.

"OK, on the count of three," he said.

ACKNOWLEDGMENTS

This book could not have happened without Belt Publishing taking a chance on it. Thank you to Anne Trubek and the team at Belt—Michael Jauchen for editing, Meredith Pangrace and David Wilson for design, Phoebe Mogharei for publicity—for giving all us Midwest writers a megaphone for our voices to be heard. Thank you to all the booksellers, libraries, vendors, and small businesses in Metro Detroit (and everywhere) who supported *How to Live in Detroit Without Being a Jackass* and *The Detroit Neighborhood Guidebook*; to all the readers who gave those books a home on their shelves; and to anyone who's ever tweeted, texted, or emailed just to say, "Hey, thanks for writing this"—thank you all.

To all my "boys," but especially Brandon (it was all our boys' trips, and the lush, necessary conversations within them, that laid the groundwork for this book) and Lee (who made the crucial suggestion to change the main characters from three women to three men and write from the heart). To early readers of *Boys Come First*: Marsalis, Esther, *and* Nick (see! I promised), and Steve, and thanks to Peter Senftleben for the first edit. My parents, grandparents, siblings, aunties, uncles, cousins, family everywhere (I *will* miss someone if I do name by name, so everybody. All of y'all.). Andy, Drew, and Valerie—thanks for your pep talks when I was down, and a special thanks to Drew for being the first to publish my fiction. Rohin, just for listening sometimes about trying to do this whole queer POC writer thing—we need you up next. Keith, just for listening. My dear friends at JSK at Stanford. And much gratitude to the many bars and coffee shops in Metro Detroit (especially Motor City Wine and Java Hutt), the Bay Area, and Brooklyn for accommodating me while I banged out this story.

I'd be remiss if I didn't personally shout-out day-ones who have supported my grand writing ambitions from the beginning. At various points in our K–12 education, I promised—and never forgot—dedications to Nicole Wells, Christian Rollins, and *probably* David Porter, and I have to also name-check Michael Lawson (who probably doesn't remember me outlining this story while stoned on a Harlem rooftop . . .), Ryan Henyard, Matthew Williams, Veronica Loper, Edwin Andrews, Henry Conerway III, Will McCray, Katie Dover-Taylor, Lhea Copeland, and too many others who've been on the journey.

The one and only Ms. Kyra Stephens—because many years ago, as we were laying out our BlackPlanet pages in Mr. Fadden's graphic design class, you wrote on yours to make sure to dedicate my first book to you. I'm holding up my end of the bargain and desperately wishing you were here to toast.

For Shirley Allison Day, who in 1992 took her eight-year-old grandson to Kinko's to make photocopies of the first story he ever wrote on his mother's Canon typewriter and bound them nicely in plastic report covers.

If I missed anyone, you know what we used to say back in the day: Blame it on my head, and not my heart.

ABOUT THE AUTHOR

Aaron Foley's reporting and writing on Detroit, blackness, and queerness has appeared on *This American Life*, *Jalopnik*, the *Atlantic*, CNN, several anthologies, and the PBS NewsHour, where he is currently a senior digital editor. A Detroit native, the city's first appointed chief storyteller, and a former magazine editor, he is the author of *How to Live in Detroit Without Being a Jackass* and editor of *The Detroit Neighborhood Guidebook*. He currently lives in Brooklyn's Bedford-Stuyvesant neighborhood.

ABOUT THE AUTHOR